Beneath The Kintai Moon

Other previous works by the author and preceding books to this fictional series:

"My Brother's Keeper, Secrets of Tarnished Shields"
Copyright by Olivia F. Counts Willis July 2010

"Hong Kong by Moonlight, Exiled to the Orient"
Copyright by O.F. Willisomhouse October 2011

"The Diaspora Returns, a Healing for the Soul"
Copyright by O.F. Willisomhouse March 2013

"The Diaspora Returns, the Healing Continues"
Copyright by O.F. Willisomhouse August 2013

Ms. Valerie Summers

Beneath The Kintai Moon

The Journey of Life

O.F. Willisomhouse

O.F. Willisomhouse 1 Oct 2016

Copyright © 2015 by O.F. Willisomhouse.

Library of Congress Control Number: 2015911691
ISBN: Hardcover 978-1-5035-8777-9
Softcover 978-1-5035-8776-2
eBook 978-1-5035-8775-5

All rights reserved. No part of this book may be reproduced or transmitted in any form or by any means, electronic or mechanical, including photocopying, recording, or by any information storage and retrieval system, without permission in writing from the copyright owner.

This is a work of fiction. Names, characters, places and incidents either are the product of the author's imagination or are used fictitiously, and any resemblance to any actual persons, living or dead, events, or locales is entirely coincidental.

Any people depicted in stock imagery provided by Thinkstock are models, and such images are being used for illustrative purposes only. Certain stock imagery © Thinkstock.

Print information available on the last page.

Rev. date: 09/26/2015

To order additional copies of this book, contact:
Xlibris
1-888-795-4274
www.Xlibris.com
Orders@Xlibris.com
714281

Contents

Dedication vii
Prayer Pledge ix
"When Monique Came Out To Play" Song xi
"My Brother's Keeper" Oath xiii
(Child's Prayer) Max and Milani's Prayer xv
"A Prayer for the Ages" xvi
Daily Prayer xvii
I am a Navy Sailor xviii
I Am an Army Warrior xx
Preface xxiii

Chapter One: Keeping Our Promises 1
Chapter Two: Second Round of Pleasure 23
Chapter Three: Kate's Secret and Confession 39
Chapter Four: Our Saturday Morning Excursions 68
Chapter Five: Weekend Wends Down 75
Chapter Six: A Social Call Back into Exile 86
Chapter Seven: Great Grandmother's Demise 93
Chapter Eight: Back For The Future 119
Chapter Nine: The Daily Classified 165
Chapter Ten: Last Mission for My Brother 195
Chapter Eleven: Border Crossings 224
Chapter Twelve: Milani's Healing Begins 256

Chapter Thirteen: Life's Adjustments............................ 258
Chapter Fourteen: Naughty Girl's Talk.......................... 288
Chapter Fifteen: My Brother's Keeper Reunion............. 342
Chapter Sixteen: Dead Men Walking 362
Chapter Seventeen: Beneath the Kintai Moon 376

For All the Test of Time (Old Lang Syne Tune)............. 383
About The Book 385

Dedication

This final book, in this five-volume manuscript, is dedicated to all my readers and all who supports my creative hobby. I hope that each reader can identify with or discover something that evokes an unexpected response, due to traits of at lease one of the characters that I have created or expound upon, in this semi-fictional narrative.

"I believe that power not used for good is not true power, but merely the product of a series of selfish acts motivated by arrogance, greed, lust, and the misunderstood need to control."

O.F. Willisomhouse

Prayer Pledge

"Christian Sisters Of Faith"

We are Christian Sisters of Faith with the belief that we can improve our lives and the life of others through prayer. We acknowledge and embrace God's Grace over our existence. We will meditate and study His word often so we will recognize his voice whenever He speaks. We realize and appreciate that our lives are divided into individual and single journeys with a collective goal and a sole purpose destination. Yet we understand and believe that it is unwise to travel life's road alone and without the guidance of The Word. Therefore, we wholeheartedly welcome the anointed Spirit that God has sent to guide us. We are not perfect, nor do be believe that this is a requirement to receive His transforming gifts. Nevertheless, we have made a pledge to strive to become more like His Son in every way. We pledge to keep our minds, hands, and hearts open so we can freely share our gifts and His bountiful blessings. We Christians of faith display this portion of cloth as a united pledge of our mission to spread the Good News of Grace and Mercy.

I drape this sash around me and wear it proudly as a reminder that Grace and Mercy is a portion of my life's compass. For I am not alone; as my sisters and brothers in faith share my struggles and pray for my weaknesses, while I pray for theirs. I will strive to become a more persuasive influence towards the brighter beacon of hope and to the One and only True Light. For Christ alone searches and knows the heart of every man

The twin beads displayed at the ends of this cloth is a reminder that I'm paired with a prayer partner that I can call day or night. The red bead represents Christ's blood and confirms that I'm a consummated heir of the Holy Family. The silkiness of the cloth is symbolic of the peace-of-mind I am awarded when I obey the protective and guiding-Spirit messenger. The visual texture of the sash is a confirmation that our path may not always be a smooth one to travel; yet it is possible to stay the course with His gift of Mercy and His Divine Intervention. Today with limited understanding, I take this pledge. Tomorrow, with Christ's help, I pray to take a more obligated stance, Amen.

"When Monique Came Out To Play" Song

It was a warm April day when Monique came out to play
Her cheeks were red as fire and so filled with life that day, But her mother never heard her cries
And her daddy never wiped a single tear from her eyes
And that is how this story all began

Chorus

*You have to find a friend you like and love them-don't quit. And when the two of you fight, just learn how to grin and bear it. Keep all your heartfelt secrets for a very rain day
And that's how it was when Monique came out to play*

Well months turned into years, as the days just rolled away. Monique grew up and found a new role she had to play
Somehow she found a friend and loved them to the end
And that's how her story all began

Chorus

Well her father just grew old and the story was never told.
And everyone just prayed that that day would stay away,
But old hearts can't take much pain
When there are lies between friends it leaves a stain
And this is how the story always ends

Chorus

Now their hearts have all been broken and the friendship is just a token. Of an oath taken on that warm April day Now the truth has to be spoken, to mend hearts that have been broken
About that day that Monique came out to play

"My Brother's Keeper" Oath

The Lord God is my Shepherd; Therefore, I am my brother's keeper

I will do everything in my power, with God's help, not to become a slave to sin

I will meditate often, so I will recognize the Shepherd's voice when he speaks

I will attempt to restore all the lives I have disrupted
I will reward all whom I have inconvenienced

I will not judge my brother, for his journey is not my own. I will embrace and appreciate our differences, and allow God to chastise his (our) faults

I will pray to overcome my fears of death, for physical death is only another phase of eternal life. I will respect my body, as I respect the Temple, for it is not mine to abuse

I will shield my spirit from greed, lust, arrogance and unjustifiable acts of survival
For each and every life is precious

I will focus on my purpose and not my past, for it is over and I can never go back
I believe great self-sacrifice will reap great spiritual rewards

Therefore I shall forever be, "My Brother's Keeper"

(Child's Prayer)
Max and Milani's Prayer

Thank you God for this day,
again tomorrow I will pray
And just in case I forget so later on,
I won't regret
Focus my eyes to stay on you and
teach my lips to tell the truth
Tame my tongue so I may speak words
of wisdom and not defeat
Instruct my mind, sins to confess
and train my hands to do their best
Guide my feet on righteous path;
protect my spirit from evil wrath

Heavenly Father high up above
teach my heart how to love, Amen

"A Prayer for the Ages"

Lord I pray to grow old with grace
While not fearing the death I face
Keeping my eyes forever on you
For man is flawed, but you are true

To do your work is my noble goal
Guide my steps and guard my soul
Protect the hearts of the ones I hold so dear
Focus theirs eyes to see their paths clear

And when my sight begins to dim
and this old frame becomes too weak
Release the ghost, except my soul;
allow me rest at your feet, Amen

Daily Prayer

Sovereign God who reign from above
Teach our wounded hearts how to love
Relax thou mind and grant it peace
With a lion's heart and gentleness of a dove

Give us the will to pray each day
and study your word and your way
Grant us hope and faith too increase
So in your grace we will stay

Guide our footsteps on the righteous path
So we may avoid the deceivers wrath
We count our blessing so evil will flee
Be our ship's guide, not at our aft

At days end as we take our rest
Instill in us to do our best
Open our eyes so we may see
We are your family and not a guest

I am a Navy Sailor

I guard the ocean waters that are
so deep and true blue
'Cause I am a Navy Sailor, this is
who I am, this is what I do.
I stand on the ship's deck at parade rest,
as family on shore slowly fades away.
My chest burns with hope and painful
regrets, but I dare not look away
For this will be my final glimpse of
them, until my mission is through
Because I'm a Navy Sailor, this is
who I am; this is what I do
Each night I pray to God, for he
alone controls the waves
I try to protect each son or daughter,
yet none alone can I save
Return with a full crew intact, is
forever our plan and prayer
My voice shout stern orders and demands,
while my heart is filled with tender care
I sometimes answer to 'Skipper', with sir
placed carefully at the end of my name
Yet my soul is no different than my shipmates,
as I share in their desperate pain
At night I may stand a watch, so my
fellow man comes to no harm
Forbidding a flood or fire, I must always
be there to sound the alarm

While deep below her decks I tread,
listening to her purring sounds,
and sometimes a lonely tear escapes the
eye, when no one else is around
Excitement brews for any port-of-call, 'cause
I'm a family man through and through
First sounds of home slows a rhythmic heart,
while checking on my homeport crew
The warm sun sets with such beauty,
now it's back to the cold ocean blue
Because I'm a Navy Sailor, this is
who I am, and this is what I do

I Am an Army Warrior

I stand strong and proudly serve,
while my cause remains true,
'Cause I'm an Army warrior; this is
who I am; this is what I do.
I took an oath; we're on a mission
to keep our homelands free,
Our fellow comrades took the same,
to protect our sky and sea.
I leave my family in the distance, to
travel to unknown barren lands,
From jungles with danger lurking, to
beaches covered with hot desert sands
Day in and out I carry heavy gear and
a heart that is fearless and true
'Cause I'm an Army Warrior, this is
who I am, and this is what I do.
At night my weapons becomes my bunkmate,
but I dare not close my eyes to sleep
A slower rhythmic heart, eyelid lightly shut
is all, until the watchman taps my feet.
I'm up, I'm up I reply, give me a
moment to check my field gear
For I know it may be a week or more
before sleep is enjoyed again I fear.
I tighten bootstraps, and reach for a cover
that served as pillow for my head,
I listen to whispered list of the recovered
wounded and the unfortunate mournful dead.

On watch when it's quiet and still, for
this is the worst time for me
I pray and wonder if there is another
sunrise waiting there to see.
When I return to my love one's arms, I
dare not share this moment in time
For they are the warrior's burdens alone
to bear, painful to the soul and mind
I've learned to pray often, because
God alone knows my true heart
Of the pain that I endure daily when
my family and I are apart.
Yet make no mistake about our dedication, for
we are Army Green through and through
'Cause we are Army Warriors, this is
who we are, and this is what we do.

Preface

A wise person once stated 'Home is where the heart is'; well with this group, the idiom serves as truth. For some members of the group have now returned, perhaps to shift into a more quiet and latter stage of life, while embracing Grace and Mercy as their Divine Compass. While others may have come back out of merely necessity for survival or to live out their lives with people who understand them and love them, with no reservation.

Yet the phrase **'the journey of life'** can be awarded an array of meanings for each individual of this diverse alliance. For Alex; it meant a long voyage home to the truth and the fact that everyone he adored in his life, appeared to die or leave him before he had spent, what he believed, was sufficient time with them, or for him to embrace their departure with acceptance.

For Helen it was a voyage of discovery of whom she really was and the facts about her true biological lineage, that had been kept a secret from her all of her life, up until this point.

She was awarded a third companion, which was somewhat conceivable to be the man that she was initially to have.

All and all for Slapp, it was a mission of learning to trust and forgive, while carrying the burden of such a wounded and tender heart. However, for Fred it was an expedition to humbleness as he came to understand that his power over his life was very limited, and at times his decisions were very unsure.

Tate's comeback, after facing his greatest demons of privacy and shame to the point where he had taken the wrong fork in the road, was when he returned to the path of Divine calling for his life.

Gayle's homecoming was similar to that of a prodigal son, as she tried to escape her past by nursing her heart injuries in a foreign land.

While Miss Beasley's return journey was one from an unexpected reprieve from exile, after she testified against those men earlier in her life, for the reward. The desire to use a shortcut was what had tripped her up and derailed her original future plans.

Mr. Oscar's loved his gift of music more than he did the giver of the gift. This priority disorder had caused him to live a lie and a life of deception for fifty years. Now he had returned to the church to use his gift only for God's Glory.

Then there was Uncle Burney who had taken part in a façade early on for the right reason; yet had allowed many opportunities to correct that earlier pretense to escape. He realized that he should have informed Slapp, decades earlier, of his true identity. The fear taunted Burney and Miss Beasley constantly that perhaps Slapp wouldn't be able to handle the truth from either of them, his parents.

Father Caleb who had been given the greatest comeback of all when he had been allowed to spend his latter years by his son Tate's side, whom had been born during the priest's previous misguided and misunderstood years of his youth.

Nevertheless, not one portion of their lives had been wasted, by no means. For this is one of the beautiful unexplainable mysteries of Grace and Mercy, for those who believe and trust in the Master's plan. The sub-agency 'My Brother's Keeper' had in fact helped hundreds of young people to obtain a higher education and better opportunities, whom would never have obtained one without the online scholarship website. If the group wouldn't have been forced into exile, perhaps three and half year old Milani would have never been found and brought back to her father's homeland, by her Uncle Alex and stepmother Helen. With no parents, grandparents or siblings to protect her, Milani would have surely ended up as part of the sex slave trade, after her great-grandmother suspiciously passed on.

Gayle and Tate's path perchance would have never crossed and she wouldn't have experience the love of a husband, which had been Divinely designed for her. Slapp discovering and reuniting with his parents and his true heritage allowed his wounded heart to heal to a degree, which without a doubt prepared him to be a better father and husband to his trouble minded wife, Kate.

Of course, there are the children to consider in this amalgamated family, who has survived quite a few serious and devastating events, during the early portion of their lives. Who can say how this will change the course of their journey. For William, Max and Milani who can predict, well let's just say, for the sake of argument, that God hasn't, in no way, forgotten them, amen

Chapter One

Keeping Our Promises

Assuredly some promises are designed to be kept and then there are other vows, which are premeditatedly crafted with no substance of a true commitment that are frequently invented to be used as a manipulation tool. Yet there is a third category of inferred possibilities that are merely dreams from an imaginary corner of ones distorted mind. However, **I believe that we should live our lives so the latter two instances are never accepted as the norm nor should their influence be tolerated.**

Alex and I gave our word to Milani's great-grandmother that she would be given an opportunity to travel back to her homeland at least once a year, or permanently if she so desired. We both agreed this was a promise that we needed to keep at all cost, and that was what had taken place.

One weekend while Tate was residing at the old warehouse slash soup kitchen slash My Brother's Keeper's headquarters, the same one that Ole Father Caleb had setup with his portion of the take from the illegal bounty hunting business and the very same one that the bureau had pledged to shut down; Tate had a sudden impulse. The urge Tate had was to go home and spend a quality three-day-holiday weekend with his, somewhat, new wife Gayle. Gayle was now living in the apartment that Tate had lived in before he had departed for Hong Kong, while on the run and acting as my personal bodyguard. As a matter of fact, Tate had lived in this apartment since his previous wife had died. His doctor and therapist suggested, and both had agreed respectively, that this might help shorten Tate's recovery time from the tragedy of loosing his wife; if he moved into a new place that didn't remind him of her and all the time that they had spent together.

Of course back then the first order of business, for all the renegade agents, had been to update the new apartment's security system from the basic requirements that was mandated by the department, for an agent to live alone without a bodyguard. To Gayle, Tate's apartment seemed more like living in a small fortress or an over-sized prison cell, if you weren't familiar with the complicated structure of the security unit. Tate had briefed Gayle well about all the dangers and if that wasn't sufficient, she could always call Slapp or Bruce the finance guy if she wasn't sure or had forgotten a portion of the procedures. Now that Tate was back at one of the local university as a student in their theological program, completing a degree that he had began almost twenty three years before; while living temporarily at the warehouse with his biological dad Father Caleb, Tate decided that it would be safer for Gayle if he disconnected all the life or death features of the house security component. At this point, the most damage Gayle could do was to send a false alarm to the local police department, when and if she forgot to proceed to the second bedroom to deactivate the backup signal. There were several guns throughout the apartment and Gayle was well versed on hand weapons and exhibited no reluctance in using them, if and when the need arose.

It was 6:00pm one Thursday evening when Tate decided to skip his last theology lecture and had asked his father, Father Caleb to sit-in for him, during the first few minutes to take notes or pickup the homework assignment. Gayle was curled up on the long sofa as she waited for her daily after-class phone call from her husband Tate. It was now late summer, but she still had a couple hours of daylight before closing the drapes and turning on the lights. Sometimes she and Tate's conversations would linger late into the night or into the early morning, depending on how you viewed time. Some of their cessions were pretty sexually heated, after all there were weeks when all they had in the way of intimacy was a steamy late-night chats. Tate had mentally and physically determined that he had spent enough time away from his sexy wife. He was aware of her daily routine after work each day and he knew that she would be on the couch waiting.

Tate rang the doorbell and waited with his dirty laundry bag in hand. He also had flowers and a bottle of wine. Gayle viewed the front entrance with the aid of television screen through the camera security system. She was surprise to see that it was in fact Thaddeus (Tate). She quickly sprang to her feet and sprinted to the door to greet him. She had been lounging in a long silk spaghetti strap nightgown with a matching cover and thongs. She had taken a long bath, shaved and waxed all the appropriate areas. This was her routine to free-up her Friday nights in case someone invited her to dinner or if Alex and I perhaps ask her to watch the kids to give Milani's great grandmother a well needed break.

Gayle quickly opened the door to receive Tate, as he stood motionless. He was wearing soiled clothes because he had been up on the roof of the warehouse slash soup kitchen trying to patch a leak. It had been three weeks since Gayle had seen Tate and during that time he had chosen to grow a beard. He wasn't sure what Gayle's reaction would be to the extra hair on his face. So he stood quietly to observe her response first hand.

"Hello Thaddeus", said Gayle in a real sexy tone, while holding the door only partially open. "I didn't expect you to come home tonight. Is there something wrong? I was lying on the sofa awaiting your call." Tate smiled deeply and answered quickly to put Gayle's mind at ease.

"No, no baby, nothing is wrong. I asked my father to cover for me in class because I couldn't wait another day to see you." Gayle opened the door wider now and leaped forward to hug Tate with open arms as Tate lunged backwards and attempted to explain his rejecting action. "Please Gayle, don't hug me. I'm filthy. Give me a few minutes to clean up and then after that I'm all yours." Tate stepped inside the door and dropped his laundry bags and leaned over to untie his dirt-covered shoes. Gayle looked on while smiling and trying to decide if she approved of his facial hair. He laughed to himself as he noticed her taking a closer stare at it. "So tell me Sweetie, how do you like my new look?"

Gayle stepped back a little more as she playfully stroked her chin, while pretending to be in deep thought about the question that Tate had just placed before her. "I'm not sure yet, Thaddeus. You'll have to give me more time to decide. What inspired you to grow more facial hair at this time?"

"Oh no special reason. The only time that I've grown a beard before was for work; for an undercover assignment." He continued to undress right in front of the closed entrance as they made small talk. "Gayle, please bring me a trash bag for these clothes. There is no way of knowing what's on these garments after going up on that warehouse roof, which is at least a hundred years old. I cut my hand a few times. I probably require a tetanus shot, or at the very least I should scrub my body scraps and punctures with a antibacterial soap, before getting into the tub." Tate walked towards the bathroom to take a quick decontamination shower before slipping into the tub that Gayle was now preparing for him. She was cheerfully smiling to herself as she wondered how much time Tate would spend with her before returning back to the warehouse and school. She was afraid to ask and Tate wanted to reveal that information to her, about that detail, a little later as a surprise. He slowly slid into the hot bath water as he continued to ask questions.

"So tell me, Paper Doll, what have you been doing with yourself besides talking sexy on the phone every night to a holy man? You know that I told you that you could go anywhere you like. You don't have to wait around for me to call. I will find you or I will call you back later. Do you still talk with Sam every week?" Samantha was Gayle's daughter and the closest Tate would ever come to having a child of his own. "How is work coming alone?" Tate began to lather himself as he waited for Gayle to answer at a minimum, one of his probing questions. Gayle sat on the edge of the tub and watched him bathe, while daydreaming about the intimacy that they were sure to share. Tate knew Gayle well enough to know what was on her mind and he also realized that three weeks plus, without any physical contact, was much too long for a new wife to have to endure. He had given his word to make it up to her and this weekend he would, to some degree, plus partially try to keep other promises as well.

"Oh I'm sorry Thaddeus, I guess I wasn't paying attention. What did you say again?" Tate laughed and looked downward before he repeated the questions, as he added more shower gel to his washcloth. She answered slowly as if Tate repeating the questions had only moderately broken her fixation on his sexiness. "Oh, nothing different baby. Sam calls me each week and last weekend I watched Milani and Max for two nights. I met Kate for lunch on Monday and Bruce stopped by to check on me yesterday after work. I guess I stay busy enough. What about you?" Tate responded quickly before Gayle could finish her sentence.

"Oh, I'm very busy. Between the soup kitchen, playing Bob Villa the fix-it guy and school I only get about four hours of sleep." Then they made eye contact because they both realized that the lack of sleep had been caused by the two of them staying on the phone so late at night trying to heal the loneliness with extended sexually heated phone calls. They each agreed that this was a young couple's game, still they played it and pretended each night that the following evening would be different. Tate rinsed his thick wavy hair and gripped the sides of the tub to stand up and stepped out to dry off. Gayle walked over to the sink to brush her teeth as they continued the relaxed dialogue. Gayle suddenly remembered something.

"Oh Thaddeus, did you eat already? I put the food away just before you arrived. I can heat you something up."

"Yes Gayle, I ate at the soup kitchen. That new guy that came in about a month ago is a great cook. Father is thinking about hiring him, just to keep him around. He is between jobs and had to put everything he owns into storage. He's a very nice man that is a little short on blessings. He came to the soup kitchen to save money and have a place to stay while he looks for another job. The storage unit takes all his unemployment benefits. He's too proud to take a handout, so I promised to help him find a job."

"Oh that's so kind of you Sweetie. I knew that there was some reason I fell in love with you." Tate walked up behind Gayle and made physical contact for the first time since he had arrived. She continued to brush her teeth as he slid his hands around her at the waist and forcefully pulled her away from the sink and closer to him as he responded to her last remark.

"Oh, is that so? I though you fell in love with me for my handsome looks and my big-_____?" Gayle swiftly turned to face him as she chastised him and prevented him from saying that last word of his response.

"Thaddeus! is that anyway for a man of the cloth to be talking?" He laughed out loudly as he grabbed a handful of her butt cheeks and forced her even closer to the front of him, while wearing only his damp towel.

"That is the key word right there, 'Man-of-the-cloth.' I'm a man and a human first; born into a sinful nature. And for the record, I do have earthly manly needs. Lately, if I may add, during my more depth studies, I have also come to believe that if God has physically created anything better for man than a fine beautiful and sexy woman, then He has secretly kept it all for himself."

"Ooh! Thaddeus, I don't know what to do with you. God is going to strike you down. That statement has to fall somewhere near blasphemy or at the very least disrespectfulness."

"What are you saying Baby, responded Tate? The way I see it, that was a compliment from me to all women kind and to God himself. Perhaps it's just my sick way of thanking God for you and all the pleasure and happiness you and this gorgeous body has brought to me in the past couple of years, give or take." Tate then began to rub his bearded face against Gayle's cheek and neck, as he inhaled the scent of her as a reminder of what he had been missing. Tate then lowered his voice volume to a whisper in that sexy disarming level that Gayle continued to have no defense against, before he spoke his next sentence. "Plus, I was sort of hoping that you would rip this wet towel from my naked body and take me right here on the bathroom rug." Gayle smiled warmly as she slid her arms up around his neck as he tilted his head downward and titled it to the side to softly and gently kiss her fresh toothpaste clean lips. The caress was long and forecasting as she waited for him to release her from a portion of the pressure that he was now applying to her body as the sexual moaning sounds escaped Tate through his nostrils. Gayle slowly broke off the kiss and then spoke, with a change in subject.

"That will have to wait until I hear all about school and how long I will have to continue to have phone-sex with my new husband." Tate reluctantly released his grip as he began his explanation that Gayle had heard at least twenty times before. He slipped into a robe from behind the bathroom door and followed her into the living-room slash den area of their large spacious two-bedroom two-bathroom condo that Gayle now occupied alone. There was a third bedroom that Tate had transformed into a walk-in closet and a weight room. The whole condo was the size of a medium-sized house and no comfort amenities had been spared.

"Come on Gayle, baby we've talked about this before. I know that I promised you that it was only for a few months and two semesters, but my father is getting on in age and he needed me to help with the soup kitchen. I know that it has almost been fifteen months." He trailed behind Gayle to the long wide sofa that Gayle had turned into her primary sleeping area whenever she didn't want to sleep in their king-size bed alone. There she had laid out a set of bed sheets for the top and bottom and a light blanket, plus two pillows from their bed, just incase she wanted to prop herself up to read. A near by tray held an ice bucket filled with ice and her favorite can soda and a tall crystal Waterford ice-tea glass. The tray also included a small bowl of fruit, unpeeled and a small and large towel for her hands or to catch the crumbs that might escape her mouth, as she had prepared for yet another lonely sexless night on the phone with her husband Tate. However, tonight would be unexpected and welcomingly different.

There they sat on the sofa facing each other as Tate lobbied for more and well-needed time apart, to complete his studies.

"Gayle, I'm almost finished with my training and education. Tell me Paper Doll, what I can do to make this up to you?" She hesitated before she answered.

"Thaddeus, I can't believe that I've been placed on the backburner behind everyone else in your life." Tate found Gayle's analogy amusing and laughed out before he could prevent himself from expressing it in hardy chuckle. His response annoyed Gayle as she pulled away.

"Baby, I'm sorry for laughing, but who are these other people that you speak of? It's not like I'm having an affair with another woman. Surely you can't be jealous of God and an old priest. I know I lied to you about the time frame, but I didn't plan to lie. Some of the classes that I had taken before were too longstanding for me to receive credit for them, in this new program. Plus there are more people depending on the soup kitchen than ever before. My father has been a great help to me. I believe I will be able to finish ahead of schedule and get an assignment that I really want. Can't you just be happy for me? I feel like this is my last chance to do something that I should have done years ago. Besides Gayle, you owe God as well for allowing us to meet in Hong Kong. Surely me giving Him a little of my time to study His word more deeply was worth that blessing."

Gayle didn't answer as she stared downward at her hands, while Tate held them inside of his own. He stood up and pulled her to her feet. "Gayle, take the wine and two glasses into the bedroom and wait for me. I want to start my laundry. I will be right in." Tate kissed her on the nose and turned to retrieve his dirty clothes from by the front door.

Gayle smiled timidly and did as she had been instructed. In the bedroom, she pulled back the covers halfway the length of the bed, removed her silk gown cover and moved to the center of the bed to wait for Tate. She could hear him start the laundry on the other side of the condo and then she traced his footpath by the noise his slippers made as he stepped quickly back towards the bedroom. He picked up the bowl of fruit and the two towels from the tray as he passed by Gayle's nightly snack setup.

Tate arrived in the doorway of the master bedroom and stood for a moment to stare in Gayle's direction as she lay seductively in the center of the bed with one breast only inches from completely escaping her spaghetti strap nightgown. He took in an excited deep breath and let it out quickly as he slowly moved closer to the side of the bed, while he enjoyed the view of his wife's body. In that split second Tate realized that he had made the right decision when he opted to move into the warehouse with his father while completing the remainder few semesters of seminary training. A woman with a erotic body like that would have been too much of a distraction for a man of his maturity; while going back to school full-time.

Tate placed the towels on the pillow near his side of the bed and the bowl of fruit next to bottle of wine and the two glasses. He smiled again before he spoke his next group of words.

"I'm glad that I decided to come home this weekend earlier than usual. I think I heard it in your voice last night that you were really missing me."

"Oh, is that a fact, Thaddeus? Or did you come home tonight Thaddeus because you were missing me more?" Tate let out a confessing chuckle.

"I think the latter statement is closer to the truth." He smile again with those wonderful green eyes of his and then looked away to pour each of then a shot of wine in the glasses that had been staged by the bed. "Gayle do you remember when we first met?"

Gayle answered without any hesitation, "Indeed I do Thaddeus and I also remember how crass you were on our first date in that nice restaurant. The couple at the next table were listening to us and I became so embarrassed until I had to get up and just walk out."

"Okay, you have me there, but I meant after that Gayle. Our second date at the apartment and the first night we spent together." Gayle laughed out loudly as she recalled how she wondered if she had gotten herself involved with a weirdo. Back then Tate was a very private person with painful secrets and fears that he didn't share with anyone. In addition, he appeared to have no sense of humor and very quick tempered to put it mildly. Yet now he was almost like a totally new person. Gayle waited patiently to observe where this stroll-down-memory-lane was headed, as his eyes continued to sweep her entire partially covered body. The long gown was practically around her waist and the front patch of her matching thongs was almost visible. The crotch portion of Gayle's thongs were now marinating in her female juices with anticipation, as the light foreplay conversation continued its course.

"What I do remember Thaddeus, and quite clearly if I made add, is that there was no sex between us that first night and I only received a partial and weak explanation the next morning of why that undeniably had been the case. For a while I thought you had something outlandish to tell me like you were bisexual or something worst." Tate took a quick sip from his glass of wine and dropped his head to smile deeply as he remembered how his actions and the wording of his explanation could have led Gayle to this unlikely conclusion that she was now humorously expressing, almost two and a half years later. He turned his head slightly to face her more, as he sat sidesaddle on the side of their bed. His green eyes pierced her stare as he waited for the answer to his next question.

"Is that really what you thought of me when we first met, Gayle? Wow! I had no idea. I'm just glad that we cleared all those misconceptions up when we did finally make love that first time." He placed his glass on the table, stood up and removed his robe to reveal a sculpture body of a much younger man. Gayle knew that he had continued his gym training and that some of the work around the old warehouse was quite physically demanding, but she had no knowledge of how much work Tate and Slapp were doing to save money and influence the city to save this safe-heaven for the poor and forsaken homeless. Besides noticing his muscles she also noticed his tan-lines. He eased into the bed with her and waited for her answer to his last inquiry.

"Yes Thaddeus, I was a little puzzled at first about you, until Helen assured me that you were worth it." Then Gayle leaned in to kiss him, as she remained propped up on one hand, arm and bent elbow on her side while facing him. "Of course now I'm simply elated that I listened to her." Tate received her welcoming kiss as he mimicked her posture in bed. Then he slowly reached over to stroke her naked exposed hip and caress one of her smooth fleshy butt cheeks as he checked to reveal if she was wearing any panties. She smiled and watched him move closer as they continued their sexually stimulating word game.

"And what do you think of me now; now that we have been together for a while? Am I a good mate for you or are you just toying with me, while waiting for something or someone else better to come along?"

"I guess I will keep you around a little longer, but only if you promise to come home a little more regularly and stay longer. Oh! By the way, are you home for one night, a few hours for a piece of ass or do I have you for the entire weekend?" Tate laughed out loudly and pulled away and put up the single digit, excuse-me please church-finger as he answered.

"Wait Gayle, I think my laundry has just finished. Hold that question I will be right back; and is that any way to talk to a man of the cloth? I'm going to have to light a few candles in our next Mass for you little girl. A fervent man of God should get more respect than that." Gayle let out a sigh of annoyance as Tate spring from the bed naked and ran from the bedroom as he giddily laughed. He knew Gayle had remained a little upset with him because of his last short visit and this had been another reason that he decided to come home early and stay as long as his tight schedule would allow.

Gayle had now rolled over and laying on her opposite side with her back to the entrance of the bedroom when Tate returned a few minutes later. He took another quick sip of wine before he crawled back into their bed and pressed his warm naked body right up against the back portion of hers. Tate then rolled Gayle to her back towards him and brushed her soft flyaway hair back from her face to the pillow beneath her head.

"Hey lady," he whispered. "Ask me your question again. I think you will like the answer." He then slid his wide thick soft hands underneath the hem of her gown and forced it up even further as she responded to his words and touch. She spoke quietly and slow in fear of his response.

"So how long will you be home for this time Thaddeus? Are you doing the laundry tonight because you have to leave first thing in the morning?" He smiled as he leaned over her as he continued to caress her butt and stroke her bare upper thigh and stomach.

"I wanted my length of time here with you this weekend to be a surprise, but I guess I should tell you now, since you asked so nicely," he said sarcastically while staring down into her eyes. "Sweetie, we have three whole days together. I don't have to be back until Monday morning. Whatever you want to do; I am all yours. If you want to stay in bed, lay around on the couch for the next three days, it's fine by me." Gayle sprang up off the bed a little and through her arms around Tate's neck forcefully and pulled him down on top of her as she giggled.

"Do you mean it Thaddeus? Please tell me it's true." Tate returned her aggressive embrace as he stroked her body tenderly.

"Hey, slow it down lady, I'm a middle-age man with energy limitations in more areas than one, if you get my meaning.

Yessss Lady, it's true. I have to relieve my father early Monday morning for breakfast down at the soup kitchen. If I can't make it early enough, Slapp said he would cover for me a few hours before he goes in for his first lecture at 10:00am or Kate will go in if something happens to that plan. Now will you please stop talking and show me how appreciative you are about all the arrangements I had to make, so our extended interlude could be made possible."

Their lips met just as Gayle closed her joyful tear filled eyes and Tate removed her gown straps from off her shoulders. He shifted to the superior position and began to smother her face and neck in light controlled kisses. He cupped her left breast in his right hand as he fingered the nipple with his thumb and index finger. Gayle released a quiet moaning sound as she whispered in his ear. "That feels so good." Tate moved his lips from her neck to the right breast nipple and pulled it forcefully into his mouth as he continued to finger the tip of the other breast. His lips and mouth made loud sucking sounds as he added more pressure just shy of pure pain. Gayle held him gently around Tate's neck and the back of his head with one hand as she slid the other one between the two of them to stroke his over-sized manhood a few times before massaging her own moistened clitoris.

Gayle opened her legs as wide as possible so Tate's body could rest partially on the bed between them. Now he was holding a breast in each firm hand as he moved back and forth to give each mound equal stimulation time. His tongue moved swiftly back and forth over each nipple before he took one in and gave it a nibbling pull with his powerful lips. This sent Gayle into a controlled frenzy as she enjoyed every kiss and caress. Tate continued to move downward on Gayle's starved body with his mouth as she pinched her slippery clitoris between her fingertips. Her coupling nectar was now oozing from her juice box as it slowly rolled down the separating crease of her butt cheeks, while trickling towards an area on the fresh tight sheets beneath them. Tate's wet mouth descended downward even further, until he reached her belly button area. He inserted his long firm stiff tongue into its shallow crater as a forecast of what was to come. He then released one of Gayle's breasts and inserted his longest two fingers inside her mouth to satisfy her need for her oral cavity to be nurtured with stimulation during foreplay and intercourse.

He had noticed and came to the conclusion that her mouth was a sexual stimulation area of her body. A caressing kiss that involved massaging her tongue lit her fuse like a matchstick to a rod of dynamite. Tate wasn't sure exactly which spot in her mouth was an erotic zone or if it was the pressure on her tongue or the sucking motion that she craved doing intercourse, but he was sure that over time he would learn more about her and her sensual cravings.

The stimulation to her clitoris and breast had now caused her to pant and her body to squirm around on the bed. Tate attempted to calm her by kissing her stomach softly and releasing her other breast nipple. He wanted to prolong the foreplay a little longer and enjoy his wife's loveliness more, before engaging in the traditional coupling. For him the best part of the intimacy was the foreplay. Tate wanted Gayle's orgasmic experience to be felt so deeply until remembering the encounter would cause her to become moist, even when he wasn't there, days later. He believed the only way to accomplish this was to extend the foreplay time for as long as Gayle would allow him, during the first session and then follow-up with a more aggressive round of sex than the previous one. Tate moved downward and rubbed his soft prickly facial beard between Gayle warm smooth hairless thighs and slowly pulled her hand away from her cavern. Gayle couldn't believe how much pleasure she was receiving from the facial hair of Tate's beard, longer than usual mustache, and hot breath on the inside of her upper thighs, just below the center of her personal. The texture of the hair sent an electric charge through her body and she couldn't wait to feel the roughness of the beard on her naked exposed protruding clitoris.

Tate then pulled her legs up to a bend knee position and opened her thighs as far apart as possible. Her private area was totally hairless and supple as if it had never grown any hair before. He noticed the wetness of the area as he stared down at her nakedness. He continued to talk to her to calm her as he pulled her vagina lips far apart. She waited, with her eyes shut tightly and breathing heavily, while anticipating his next move. She could feel the coolness of the room and the hot breath from his nostrils as it bathed her moist eager well. She continued to stimulate herself by caressing both breast nipples between her fingers. Then Tate pushed back the foreskin around the clitoris so it would protrude even more into view. He stared at its firm standing erectness and a deep desire to taste her femaleness washed over him like never before. He suddenly remembered how easily a person could become injured while in the clutches of passion. That was the moment in which Tate decided that slow-and-easy was the best way in a situation like this one.

He gradually leaned in towards her smooth steamy inviting crotch to kiss her pelvic area just above her exposed clitoris. His hair-covered chin brushed against the very tip of the extended female organ as he moved in closer.

Gayle let out a deep demanding groan as if she was in pain. She then reached down to guide Tate's lips to her hunger femaleness as the desire for him to taste her consumed her.

Tate held her thighs apart with one shoulder and arm from the other side as he attacked her entire bouquet area with his mouth. First he licked and drank all the available juices from the area and then sucked as much of the clitoris between his lips as humanly possible as his tongue darted deeply inside her warm crater walls and nectar filled cavern. She was now grinding her crotch up against his oral orifice in hope that the contact would become even more intense and possibly create a moment for a long needed satisfying release. Gayle begged Tate not to stop and he kept the pressure as intense as he knew how. Tate continued to moisten the area with his mouth and pierce the inside of her juice box with his tongue and then nibble on the female protrusion with all the pressure he believed it could tolerate. Then he entered her vagina with his two middle fingers and stroked her deeply as he kept his teeth and lips locked around her clitoris tip.

Gayle soon let out a loud scream of released pleasure as the explosion happened. Her entire body jerked up off the bed as if she was having a seizure. Tate released her thighs and her legs slid back down to a straight position as they made full contact with the bed beneath her. Tate continued to calm her by slowly massaging the entire area with his tongue and mouth as he stroked her stomach and between her full breasts with one open palm hand. Tate slowly crawled back up to Gayle's breast and mouth to kiss her. He was breathing heavily. His manhood was still erect, but he was content that he had so deeply pleasured his lady. He pulled the cover over them as Gayle trembled with satisfaction and from the excitement that Tate had created within of her. She was off-balance as she tried to stop shaking and allow the afterglow to bathe her sexual senses. She took deep long breaths as she tried to contain his tongue inside her mouth. Instead, Tate pulled away to talk.

"Gayle baby, are you cold? The air conditioner is set pretty low. Come here, I'll warm you up." He rolled to his side and pulled the covers up higher around the both of them as he propped himself up just a little on two pillows. He pulled her deeper into his warm arms as he massaged her breast and shoulder. She hugged him lightly as she slid her hands down to his rock firm over-sized penis. She stroked it strongly and he let out an approving moaning groan.

"Tate are you ready for round two?" He kissed her forehead as he answered.

"No big hurray baby, we have all night."

Chapter Two

Second Round of Pleasure

"Isn't that a little uncomfortable having an erection that strong?"

"It is Gayle, but to tell the truth I'm so excited about being here with you right now, until I don't want to lose control by coupling with you with this mind-set. You remember what happened the last time I wasn't paying attention to what I was doing. You were sore for a few days."

"I do recall that time and the fact that it was a long time ago. Do you still have that fear of hurting me during our lovemaking Tate?"

"No, not at all, well not as much as before. I just want to take it slow. I came home to please you. I can wait; trust me. I don't want you to feel like this is a booty call. After that last short visit, I can understand why you would feel that way. At the time I though it was good idea to come by for a few minutes and make love to you, or should I say 'Sex you up'. I though it would be a little better than the phone sex we had been having, almost every night. To be honest with you, that same night when I heard your voice on the phone, I began to realize that this was probably the worst thing I could have done. I guess we haven't been married long enough to just have an intimate moment and leave it at that. The cuddling afterward means more to us than I understood at first. So this weekend I promise to hold you for as long as you need me to, is that a deal?"

"Oh that's so sweet Thaddeus, but I do have a confession to make. The quick stop you made that evening was just what I needed. I'm only upset that you haven't dropped by more frequently before, with the same plan. Twenty minutes of some quick d—k is better than none at all. I was upset because you couldn't stay long enough for me to show you my personal appreciation tactics." They both laughed out as he turned his head to look down at her.

"I was right about you all the time Gayle, you are a closet sex fanatic in denial. You never cease to surprise me, Paper Doll. And by the way, I am quite aware of the tactics you use to show your appreciation. If I would have stayed for that, I wouldn't have been able to concentrate long enough to complete my homework assignment. Wait right here, I need to check on the clothes again."

Tate jumped up again and disappeared down the hall. Gayle went in the bathroom to freshen up a bit. She realized that she was still a little unsatisfied. Gayle required some hard long male organ inside her, perhaps a lot of it. After all the time she had spent with Tate, she continued to find it difficult to ask for what she sexually needed from him. She got back into bed and waited for Tate to return. After a few moments of waiting and daydreaming about his firm over-sized manhood, she pulled down the covers and opened her legs wide and began to massage her vagina again and pinch her nipple with the free hand. Suddenly she noticed a moaning sound in the room and realized that it was familiar.

Gayle closed her eyes and drew her legs up as she lay on her back and opened her thighs wide like before. Tate arrived a few moments later and stood in the bedroom's doorway to watch. It excited him to observe his woman pleasuring herself alone. He didn't want to startle or possibly embarrass Gayle, so he backed away and made more noise with his slippers as he made his second approach to the doorway of their bedroom. Gayle heard his arrival and continued to masturbate in hope that he would help her release the second time. Tate moved onto the bed slowly and stroked her pelvic area a couple of times, placed two fingers back inside of her and then took his previous position between her thighs as he repeated the oral nurturing procedure over her entire female organ area.

This time Tate added more force and intensity; this appeared to please Gayle even more. Then she let out a loud breath panting sound. He slowly entered her with his manhood and began a slow powerfully stroking motion deeply inside her begging hot juicy cavern. The heavy moisture caused smacking sounds each time he drove his d—k into Gayle's wet c—t. Gayle held Tate firmly as he took his fill of her. Gayle moved on top and clamped her vagina walls tightly around his penis so strongly until she noticed the surprise on Tate's face. She kissed his mouth and sucked his tongue with all the strength she could muster. The pace picked up and Tate grabbed Gayle by the hips and released in three bursts. They rolled to their sides and he continued to stroke Gayle deep and long. A few moments later they fell asleep. They woke up near midnight and took a shower and brush their teeth and she put on her night cream. She rubbed a little onto Tate's face as well as he stood motionless. They finished off the fruit and turned off the lights. They fell asleep with her back to him and two of his fingers placed deep within her mouth as she sucked them to pacify herself. He slid only a couple of inches of his manhood into her from the rear, but reframed from any movement. Gayle body twitched sporadically as it remembered the pleasure, until she fell into a deep sleep. Tate continued to whisper to her to calm her as he kissed the back of her neck, shoulder and back. He knew he had only partially appeased her hunger.

The next morning Tate slipped out of bed and allowed Gayle to sleep-in. He took a shower in the bathroom down the hall. Tate was an early riser because the breakfast shift at the warehouse's soup kitchen was his shift before going off to class. It was amazing how demanding homeless people presented themselves. If you advertised breakfast at eight, that meant that you had to be up and preparing the food by five. The number of people had increased in the last few months and this had caused an increase in the equipment that was required to serve everyone at once. Accommodating everyone in two shifts had failed and a couple of physical altercations had ensued when some of the special-needs short-yellow-bus homeless people had been asked to wait.

Tate prepared himself one slice of toast, juice and coffee. He then moved to the extra long sofa in the den to read the morning paper. There he lay with his robe on lying completely open, with a pair of boxers that provided only partial coverage for his well-endowed manhood. Gayle woke up in a drowsy-like state, as she first believed that the night before had all been a dream. Then she noticed her relaxed body and the soreness that radiate from between her vagina walls. Her breast nipples were tender to the touch as well and slightly bruised; yet satisfied by all the attention that they had received the night before. Gayle realized all her sex-box needs had not been met sexually and wondered how hard it would be to get Tate back into bed without him knowing that she was sore, but was willing to endure the discomfort to be pleasured a little more.

Gayle got out of bed and took another quick shower and changed the sheets on the bed. She sprayed the pillow with one shot of her favorite perfume that she knew he loved to smell on her. Then she walked through the den with one of his starched white shirts on and a red lace pair of thongs. She spoke quietly to him as she passed through the room.

"Good morning Thaddeus, did you sleep well?" He hesitated a little before he answered because of the concentration that he was applying to an article in the newspaper.

"Morning babe, yes I slept very well. What do you have plan for us today?"

"Hold on baby, I will be right back as soon as I start this load of sheets." Tate couldn't remember if he had taken out the second load of clothes from the night before, so he sprang up quickly to give Gayle a hand and possibly remove his laundry out of her way.

"Oh, Gayle let me help. I may still have clothes in the washer." She opened the washer and Tate arrived just as she was bending far over to place the clothes and a dryer sheet into the drum. He noticed how her thongs separated her thick tight butt cheeks and split her hairless vagina lips of her slightly puffy zone. Tate instantly became aroused and needy. He stopped in the doorway and reached down with one hand to stroke his firm manhood as he stared at her partially exposed moistened vagina. He could see that the moisture had caused a variation in the fabric's hue that was sandwiched between the inflated and inflamed vagina lips, and he wondered if she had pleasure herself before leaving the bedroom or if it was mere remnants of water from her shower. He knew that she was probably a little sore, but she had promised to inform him if the sex was too aggressive.

While remaining completely bend over, she looked over her shoulder to see if he had received her sexual signals. She was sure he had when she noticed Tate stroking his penis and staring in the center crotch seat of her string thongs panties. She stood up slowly and pressed the start knob on the dryer without looking in his direction. He slowly moved up behind her and reached around to unbutton the two buttons on his shirt that she was now wearing. She leaned back against his wide hairy chest as he rubbed his bearded face against the side of her face while standing behind her. He whispered.

"You want to finish up those clothes a little later and go back to bed with me?" He continued to squeeze her exposed breast in his massive hands, while he massaged his penis with the other. Tate stuck out his tongue-tip and licked the side of her face near her lips knowing that she wouldn't be able to resist reaching for it with her wet lips and forcing it inside her mouth. Gayle took the bait like he had planned. She turned quickly to grab ahold of his tongue and began to suck it with a hungry driving force. Tate stood quietly and allowed her to take as much from the deep kiss, as she needed to satisfy that part of her appetite. As she kissed him, she massaged his testicles in her hand while pulling and tugging very gently. Gayle had learned that this was something that Tate enjoyed a lot and she had performed this pleasure many times to stimulate him or put him to sleep.

He began to breath heavily as they stood there in the laundry room at the beginning of their foreplay. She pulled away from the kiss and smiled up at him as she continued his stimulating massage.

"Does that feel good, Thaddeus, baby? I think we should move to the sofa and discus this more thoroughly like two sexually healthy adults, don't you think?" Tate had completely zoned out and the only thing he could hear or feel was the pain in his groin area from the full erection that Gayle had now created. She removed her hand from inside his boxers and he turned and took her by the hand to lead her to the sofa. It was still covered with sheets plus a single pillow and the light blanket was thrown over the backrest of the couch. They arrived at the sofa and Tate took off his robe and threw it on a nearby chair. He positioned himself on the sofa onto his back with one leg stretched out on the sofa and the other bend at the knee and foot resting on the floor. He expected Gayle to crawl on top facing him to continue the foreplay. Instead she placed her hand back inside of his briefs and stroked his penis as she made small talk.

Tate thoughts were way beyond idle conversation at this point. He was hornier than he had been the night before. Gayle hadn't noticed. It was all an adult sex game to her. She pulled his manhood out through the opening in the front panel of his shorts and continued to massage it with one hand as her other hand was placed up one short's leg to caress his testicles with the other. She leaned forward and over him a little so he could reach her breasts as she talked.

"Isn't this a nice way to spend a Friday morning baby?" Tate was now clasping both of Gayle breast and adding stimulating pressure to the nipples as she leaned forward while sitting sidesaddle between his thick hairy thighs. She then moved and began to rub his penis up and down between the cleavages of her soft full-size tits. He closed his eyes while caressing each nipple. Then Gayle released his testicles, unsnapped the two closures on his boxers and placed that hand midway his shaft and slowly guided his penis to her oral cavity. First she licked the tip to see if he would object. He groaned a little, but didn't pull away like she expected him to.

This was something that the two of them had never explored much because of his sensitivity about his penis size. Gayle rubbed his stomach firmly with one hand to calm him as she took more of the head of his penis inside her warm slippery lips. Tate released one of her breast and grabbed the back of her head as if he was in fear that she would stop pleasuring him in this manner. This was Gayle's signal to proceed with more aggression and stimulating force.

Gayle quickly moved more of her body onto the sofa without releasing any pressure from the tight grip that her lips had around his pleasure. She was now positioned between his legs on the sofa as she moved into a comfortable position to please him as long as he needed her to. He lightly held the back of her head as she held his penis in a firm half-closed fist to control the strokes. Gayle became very excited as her lover's organ rubbed against her tongue, the inside cheeks of her mouth and beyond.

She retreated from his penis and decided to apply some pleasure to his testicle without removing one hand from his shaft. She ripped his boxer shorts open for more access. She made loud sucking sounds that drove Tate even closer to his sexual climatic exploding moment. Then she returned her mouth back to his jewels, as she lay flat on her stomach and placed two fingers inside her own cavern, to satisfy herself. She was moaning so loudly, as she forcefully slid her whole mouth up and down on Tate's fully erected penis, until Tate became concern.

He tried to pull away, but Gayle wouldn't allow him to. Then she released her oral grasp from is manhood and began to lollipop stroked the lengthy sides with her strong wet tongue, as his passion was liberated into a few uncontrollable jerking motions. Gayle then crawled upward as she place his penis at the edge of her counterpart opening. It slid inside of her and she began to express her desire and longing for him in deep forceful grinding motions. He held her at the waist and watched her throw her body down onto his penis until he climax with a loud deep scream. She was unsure if the noise that escaped him was caused by pain, pleasure or deep un-nerving satisfaction. Gayle had never experienced these sounds of passion that were now being released by Tate before.

They were both sweating a little and exhibited fatigue from the long coupling session. Gayle lay down completely on top of Tate as he covered them with the top sheet and finally a portion of the thin blanket. They both were out of breath, breathing hard and almost sexually satisfied. His penis was still inside so he continued to stroke her easily with passive penetration. She fell asleep for about thirty minutes or a little longer and then she woke up.

"Thaddeus, did I fall asleep? I'm so sorry." Tate laughed with pride in his voice as he kissed her forehead before responding.

"No problem baby, that's what happens when a woman get some good d—k like she has never had before. She just falls asleep without any warning." They both laughed out as Gayle turned her head to bite Tate in the chest just for displaying such arrogance. "Are you sore Gayle, because your body was stroking me fairly hard? I don't think my man can take much more of that trauma. Oh by the way, when did you decide to move oral sex to the top of your page and our arena?"

"Well Thaddeus, I just thought you might enjoy it for a change. You always please me that way if you think I want it. What's wrong, did I perform it poorly?"

"No baby, it clearly appeared to me that you knew what you were doing and yes, that pleased me a lot. I'm just not sure I wanted you, to routinely please me in that way."

"Thaddeus that doesn't make any sense to me. I hope I'm the only woman that you are sleeping with." Tate answered quickly.

"It's just that we never really talked about it much and I do feel a little guilty about enjoying it so much."

"Oh I understand now, it's more about the embarrassment you feel about the pleasure than the fact that I'm the one providing the enjoyment."

"No, no little girl, those are your words. I never said anything about being uneasy. I said I felt guilty about enjoying it." The room was quiet for a few moments.

"Okay Tate, if it makes you feel that uncomfortable, I can abstain." Tate let out a nervous laugh before he answered.

"Now I didn't say that I wanted you to stop either, if you enjoy doing it, I mean. I'm just saying that I have some mental adjusting to do in that area. That's all I'm saying."

"Okay Thaddeus, that's fair enough. Perhaps I was too aggressive and that frightened you. I can ease-up the next time, if you prefer.

"Gayle, can you explain to me why it seems that your pleasure is intensified when you have something inside your mouth, during foreplay and sex? I do realize that people have different erotic zones of stimulation. I initially noticed this the first time with you when I allowed my fingers to touch your lips once when I was feeding you something. I think we were on the sofa, back in Hong Kong, and I was feeding you some popcorn, or was it those brownies I made that night? I remembered how you licked all the crumbs from my fingertips; and then you let out a pleasure type exhale sound. I also remember once when I was making love to you from behind, you placed my finger to your lips where you sucked on it really strongly and that appeared to excite you towards a climax sooner." Gayle thought for a moment before answering.

"I'm not sure Thaddeus, I've never really thought about it or paid any attention to the pattern. I have experienced things with you that I've never shared with any other man before. I feel a lot more comfortable with you in bed than with my previous companions. Perhaps its because I never was sure if the others were cheatings on me or not. I never really explored my sexuality or thought about what I like and didn't like. When I was by myself, which was a lot of the time for various reasons, I privately pleasured myself, but I was always shy about it. I never had anyone to discuss it with until now. I must confess that I have had some experiences with you that I never dreamed of having. So I guess that's a fair question. I don't know, Thaddeus I never thought about it. Let's get up and throw these sheets in the next load and take a shower. We can explore this a little later."

They stood up from the sofa and Gayle took the sheets, blanket and pillowcase to the laundry room. He waited for Gayle in the master bathroom next to the sink. Gayle walked up to the sink removed his shirt that she was wearing and picked up the toothpaste and her toothbrush. Tate shifted behind her and reached around to slowly ease one of his fingers between the lips of her vagina. She opened her legs a little to give him more access and he slid the fingers in deeper. Gayle started to brush her teeth and basically ignored Tate's actions, yet to her it felt so relaxing and arousing simultaneously as Tate's thick smooth fingers pierced the inner walls of her wet warm tender-to-the-touch personal and as they brushed up against her protruding raw clitoris during the exit withdrawal stroke.

She could hear his breathing pattern change to a heavier exhale. Gayle thought initially that Tate was just amusing himself. He began to massage one of her breast with the other hand and she watched him from the reflection of the mirror. She began to feel the excitement build inside of her, but she tried to suppress it. He was now kissing and licking her neck and shoulders as he squeezed her breast nipple, while applying more movement intensity to the fingers that was now deep inside her wet sticky juice box. Just before Gayle leaned over to rinse out the toothpaste, Tate spoke in a seductive voice.

"Gayle, I need a little more pleasure from you. I'm aware that you might be slightly sore, but I assure you I know how to be gentle and please you again as well; and when we get out of the shower, I promise to massage your sweet moist cavern back to health with my tongue and lips." Gayle looked at Tate's reflection in the bathroom mirror and then reached back to grab his neck and head as a signal that she was willing to endure the discomfort to drain the last ounce of mating fluid from his loins. After all, who could pass up an offer like that from a man that was able to give her body so much pleasure? Usually that portion of foreplay is never long enough, she thought. Now to be able to fall asleep with someone making love to you in that manner was like a dream come true. She could almost feel his beard in the enter part of her thighs as he spoke the words of promise.

Gayle slowly leaned over onto the sink's countertop with her upper arms resting comfortably on a folded thick bath towel and opened up her legs and placed one knee up on top of the counter. He released her breast and placed two fingers near to her mouth. Gayle began to move her tongue around against his fingers and then she started to suck on Tate's fingers as if they had just been extracted from the sugar bowl. Tate slowly guided his throbbing penis to the bottom of her pleasure well and waited for a response from Gayle. Tate had mounted her from behind and once he was inside her, Tate's strokes became long, deep and controlled just like he had promised. A few moments later Tate reached his goal of climactic pleasure with a strong release. They both stepped into the shower. No words were spoken as he lathered both of them clean from neck to toes. He tenderly kissed the side of her face and very lightly kissed her lips with gratitude for her submissiveness to his sexual desire. He slowly slid down to his knees in the shower as the water continued to spray them. He then pressed Gayle against the side shower wall and opened her thighs as he licked her vagina lips and drank some of the water as it rushed down the front of her body. The texture of his tongue on the inside the lips of her swollen vagina was very nurturing and satisfying. She closed her eyes and waited for Tate to take his fill of her.

Tate dried Gayle off and carried her back to bed. She fell asleep nude with her legs opened widely and covered by a sheet, as

Tate took his oral lustful fill of her as he had vowed to do. He nurtured her nakedness near recovery and then he fell into a blissful asleep as well. Gayle woke-up late in the afternoon. Tate had remained in position, for an encore performance as he continued to drink all the available nectar from her female cavern. He stroked deep inside of her c—t with his tongue until she screamed out loudly with satisfaction. Gayle begged for more of his manhood to enter her, but he refused as he held her firmly in his arms. "No Gayle, your body has had enough trauma. I'm not going anywhere. Perhaps later." Tate slowly masturbated Gayle with his hand until she calmed herself. Tate knew that he had awakened a desire within her that she was unaware had existed. The body had to be satisfied in small increments of controlled pleasure and with care. He understood that most of this was new to Gayle and her desires were attempting to play catch-up, due to its late start.

Chapter Three

Kate's Secret and Confession

Breakfast at the warehouse slash homeless shelter ran smoothly that Friday morning and Slapp was able to return home after the morning rush, because classes had been cancelled at Quantico. Slapp and Kate were now the proud parents of a handsome son named Cameron. The baby was seven months old. He was happy, healthy and easy to care for; yet there was trouble in the Madison's household. Kate didn't need to work, but she wanted to continue her practice and provide assistance to the state's clients pro bono. Granted, this was late in life for Kate to be having her first child, and there was the fact that she had lived her adult life doing just as she pleased. Yet there was more going on than just post partum depression, like most of the inner-circle speculated at first. Furthermore, if that was all it really was, surely Kate was smart enough to figure it out and get some professional help. After all, this was her trained field of practice. She was a full-fledged shingle-over-the-door top-of-her-class psychotherapist.

Today Slapp decided that he had taken enough of Kate's rejection without a solid truthful explanation. She had severed all intimacy contact between them three months before the baby was born and now Cameron was seven months old. The two of them had made a few trips to the doctor and he had given them the thumbs-up to resume regular sexual activity months before. Kate had used breast-feeding as an excuse, yet this had been completed weeks before. She had told Slapp that she didn't want to take any birth control while she was breast-feeding the baby. Slapp thought that the way Kate was behaving was more like a response resulting from the nightmares that she was having, which had initially began a few months before Cameron was born.

Slapp wasn't sure if Kate had been molested as a young woman and now all the memories had returned in the form of bad dreams or something worst. She hadn't had a full-nights sleep in months, yet she insisted on going to work instead of staying home and bonding with their son. Whenever Cameron cried, it seemed to make her more nervous than Slapp thought was normal. When he had pointed this out to her, she would always say that the baby appeared more comfortable with him than her. It was true that kids did seem to naturally gravitate towards Slapp; perhaps it was because he was child-like himself in so many ways. The group of us had all experienced Slapp's child-magnetism through the relationships between him and Max and Millani, but we had all come to believe that it was something more than just Slapp being a great dad to any child that he came in contact with.

That morning when Slapp finished helping in the soup kitchen at the warehouse and was later informed that his classes had been canceled; Slapp called Kate and told her to meet him at their brownstone. Cameron was in daycare and he wasn't required to be picked up until around six in the evening. It was now ten in the morning, so this would give them plenty of time to have an uninterrupted discussion without the baby being a witness to some loud angry voices like previously.

When Kate arrived, Slapp was in bed with only a pair of boxer shorts on. He had planned to appeal to her one last time for an intimate interlude. Kate arrived through the front door.

"Alvin", she called. "Where are you? Is there something wrong? Why did you want me to meet you back here?"

"Kate, I'm in the bedroom. Come on back. I've been waiting for you." Kate became nervous as she removed her shoes and jacket at the front entrance. She knew if the baby wasn't home with him, he wanted to talk about something she had been avoiding. Kate headed down the short hallway to their bedroom. She looked into the baby's room as she passed by.

"Alvin, did they cancel your classes today?" Slapp sat up in bed more as he stared in Kate's direction as she continued her query. If you are out of class, why didn't you pick up the baby?" Slapp slowly slid out of bed and stuck his feet into his slippers and slowly walked over to caress Kate before he answered.

"Kate I didn't pick up the baby, because I wanted to spend some quality intimate time with my wife and perhaps understand better what is going on with her." Kate became panicky and distant as she tried to pretend that she had no idea of what Slapp was referring to.

"Oh Alvin, don't be ridiculous. We are together all the time. Slapp slowly moved closer to her and pressed his body up against hers, while lowering his tone to a deep sexy whisper, as Kate attempted to move away without Slapp noticing. Slapp's anger overpowered him and he aggressively grabbed her arm firmly and verbally pressed her for a more appropriate answer. He then whispered quietly, as he regained strength in his will to remain calm.

"Kate, I have no idea what has happened to our marriage, but I plan to find out today. We can talk about this or I can move out until you decide to tell me." Kate started to accusingly scream at Slapp and cry, as she defended her pretend-to-be-ignorant persona.

"What is it Alvin? Is it sex you want and is now pressuring me for? You are my husband so I'll just take my clothes off and lay on my back and you can take whatever you believe you are entitled to." Kate began snatching off her clothes very angrily and throwing them all over their bedroom. Slapp released her arm and walked over and sat in a nearby chair and waited for her to calm down a little. Then he slowly responded as he sat with his fingers laced together, while leaning forward with his forearms resting on his thighs just above his knees as he stared in her direction. Slapp appeared totally unaffected by her drama, because this was a replay performance that he had seen several times before.

"I'm sorry Kate, but your dog and pony show isn't going to work this time. I plan to get to the bottom of this today." There Kate stood naked, with her arms folded over her exposed nakedness, while trembling with fear and pretending to be angry, but in reality scared senseless, because she experience Slapp being a man of his word. Slapp slowly stood to his feet, walked over and picked up Kate's robe from the foot of their bed and gently placed it around her shoulders. Kate was still crying quietly now, but with a little more intensity. Slapp tied her robe affectionately around her and gently pulled her into his arms as he wiped the tears from her flushed cheeks with his thumbs and palm of his huge thick hands. Slapp stroked her back as she cried and while she listened to his spiel. It was more like a soapbox editorial as Slapp explained what he had figured out that was possibly the problem. He moved backwards to the chair and tugged her along by one arm. He sat in the large chair and guided her into his lap, while Kate sat sidesaddle across his thick naked thighs.

"Listen Kate, something has been wrong with you for more than a few months now. I didn't want to push you, but I don't think the baby and I can go on with you beating yourself up like you have. I talked to a doctor about you and he sent me to a psychiatrist. The analyst told me that he needed to see the two of us together, before he can give a definitive diagnosis. I also talked to Helen about what she had observed and she informed Alex. Everyone seems to be very concerned about you and the fact that you are trying to work, while you are not getting the proper rest. These nightmares that you are battling, two or three times a week, isn't helping either. The shrink thinks that something from your past, perhaps a secret, has come back to haunt you. Your pregnancy and childbirth has probably acted as a trigger and brought these things to the forefront of your consciousness. Do you have any idea what that could be? Come on Kate, this is your field of expertise. I'm only an over-paid profiler for the secret service bureau."

Kate listened quietly as she buried her face in Slapp's chest and underneath his chin. Slapp waited patiently for Kate to stop crying and to begin her soul retching confession. Slapp knew a lot more than he was revealing to Kate. Due to the bureau allowing Slapp to access Kate's complete file when the two of them first announced their engagement, to be married. In addition, Slapp partially reviewed Gayle's personal file portion that the **'My Brother's Keeper'** illegal bounty hunting sub-agency had discovered and so meticulously gathered as well. Between the two files, Slapp knew more about Kate than she knew about herself or than her mother had discovered about Kate before she had passed away. The analyst insisted that it would be more therapeutic for Kate if she buildup enough courage to tell Slapp about her past and also to hear the words come for her own mouth, in her own chosen time. Gayle's volunteered confession would be very advantageous to her healing process. The doctor presented a compelling route to take, so Slapp agreed. It is a known fact that we respond more strongly and believe more deeply when we hear something spoken in our own voice.

Slapp promised to listen to the specialist, so he waited and a few weeks more, which had now turned into several months. Their son Cameron was growing well, but sometimes Kate seemed to be short tempered with him and that had greatly concerned Slapp. At three months they had decided to place him in a daycare during the day, so Kate was free to do whatever she wanted. On some short workdays Cameron had spent a few hours with Milani, Max and Milani's great grandmother next door. Max was now ten years old and had proved to have a handle on the babysitting situation. Whereas Milani treated Cameron like one of her baby dolls, yet showed signs of jealousy because of her love for Slapp, whom was now obviously showing the new baby more attention than her. After all, Milani was only seven and was still learning the inner workings and emotions of relationships and family member's pecking order, as the old folks like to say.

All Milani understood was that the new baby seemed to be stealing some of her limelight and absorbing a large portion of Slapp's affection, which had been was entirely hers before Cameron was born. Slapp had reassured Milani on several occasions that Cameron was receiving so much of everyone's devotion because he was too young to do anything for himself and needed all of us to help take care of him, until he was older and bigger. The lecture appeared to work, but Milani still demanded that Slapp hold her on one knee, even if he was holding the baby. This meant that she had to hold the bottle in Cameron's mouth. Cameron didn't seem to mind the arrangement; after all this was all he knew from the time he came home from the hospital.

Ten minutes or more passed as Kate sniffled quietly while sitting in Slapp's arms, in the large chair that had been carefully placed in one corner of their bedroom. She was mentally exhausted from concealing the secret that she had been suppressing, and now felt some relief that Slapp was now forcing her to talk. Slapp softly kissed her forehead a few times as he waited. "Kate you can tell me anything. We can get through this Babe, if you just tell me what I can do to help."

The moment Slapp spoke those words; Kate realized that Slapp was hiding some unspoken knowledge as well. She slowly cleared her thoughts and decided to start with the part that she had never told her husband Slapp or anyone else for that matter. She had never spoke the words aloud, not even in school when it was mandatory for each student to clear their mental plate by telling a fellow classmate something private or secret, as a class project. Kate pulled away slowly and stared into Slapp eyes for a few moments. She was hoping that he would let her off the hook like he had done time and time again, whenever she had cried and snuggled up to him. His facial expression reflected 'no-escape-this-time.' She stood up and moved away from Slapp to sit on the side of their bed to face him as she began her story, while apprehensively gripping the overlapping closure of her robe.

"You see Alvin, after my parents died, I lived with my mother's sister. My two brothers weren't dependable enough to take care of me full time. I was twelve and they were already grown young adults. They maintained the brownstone that we lived in, but just barely. I moved back in the house with the two of them when I was eighteen. I had finished school early so this was my second year of college. My brothers were still pretty wild back then, but at least they weren't living crazy enough to go to jail regularly like they had in the past. Between the three of us we were able to hold on to the brownstone and pay the taxes. During my third year of school I met this older gentleman at school and I became pregnant. I couldn't afford a baby and he turned out to be someone I didn't want to spend my future with, so I had an abortion. I was okay for about three or four months and then I started to regret my decision.

This was when the nightmares began. I started to have dreams about a baby that continuously cried. The visions started to consume me and finally I had to take some time off from college and see a counselor. The doctor informed me that I was showing all the classic signs and symptoms. He said I was suffering from postpartum depression even though I hadn't given birth. The following year I returned to school and changed my major. I buried myself in school and within three semesters I was back on track to where I was before I took that year off. I was able place all the trauma in the back of my mind, but I was told that a related stress might bring back the nightmares. I was given a written prescription to take; a mild sedative daily before bed. When I became pregnant with Cameron it forced me to remember the child that I never gave a chance to live and this was after I stopped taking the medicine for a few weeks. Shortly after, the nightmares returned. I didn't know what side-affects the medication would have on our unborn child and there was the fact of my age.

During my first pregnancy, while in college, I thought to myself; my parents where gone, my aunt was too old to deal with a newborn while I went to school. My brothers could barely take care of themselves. I was so fearful of the mistake I had made that I didn't even contemplate having the baby and giving it up for adoption. My aunt would have never forgiven me. I just couldn't take a chance of losing my scholarship, if I had to decrease my class load, or drop-out for a while."

Kate took a long pause and gazed over to see how Slapp was taking all of this in. He showed very little facial expression, yet his eyes had been slightly redden by the tears that he fought to keep secret. Slapp continued to wait to hear something that the bureau hadn't discovered and released to him in her file. Kate took a deep restoring cleansing inhaled breath, before she moved forward with the enlightenment and confession.

"Later, after I became pregnant with Cameron and after he was born, the nightmares reoccurred. I started to hear baby noises, who I thought was Cameron, crying at night when in fact it was the baby from my nightmares. The reason that the counseling didn't help as much as before was because I had to deal with the secret that I was keeping from you and the pressure of believing that perhaps I wasn't a good mother. Plus I had stop taking the medicine, which was something that I had depended on for a very long time. Before I met you Alvin, I never thought about getting married or having any children of my own. I was happy just dedicating all my free time to the children at the orphanages and the troubled city youth. As a licensed social worker, counselor with a doctor's degree in psychology, plus being on record as a city and state contract employee, I could go to visit any of the children even after they were adopted. After all, who would say 'no' to a free counselor's visit that was familiar with their child before they had decided to make them a member of their family? So as you can see, I had it all worked out, or so I thought at the time.

When I met you, I didn't feel that it was necessary to drudge all this up again. Then when the dreams started, I became afraid to tell you. I thought you would look at me differently or be angry that I didn't tell you before we were married. That added even more stress onto me. I also take medicine for a bipolar condition. I continue to not take my medicine while I was breast-feeding Cameron. The doctor said that all I needed to do for him to remain unaffected was to lower the dosage. With my age as a factor, I couldn't take that chance, so I stopped all together. I'm sorry Alvin that I put you and our son through all of this. Will you forgive me?"

Slapp sat back deeper into the large chair across from Kate and stared with a very angry or disappointed gaze. He was hurt and outraged that Kate had disrupted their lives with something that appeared to be so petty to him. Slapp didn't want to ask several probing questions that he was sure would cause more emotional discomfort to Kate, yet he wanted her to understand how he had suffered and to make sure that she never made a decision not to inform him of something so important again. He distraughtly stroked his chin and gazed at Kate as she sat waiting for him to say that he forgave her. That didn't happen. Instead, Slapp stood up and walked over and pulled Kate to her feet to lightly hug her again. Slapp gave Kate one of those weak hugs that you give someone in church when the minister ask you to stand and greet your neighbor and you just so happened to be sitting next to someone that you know don't or don't particularly care for you. The hug had no emotion of acceptance, regret, and absolutely no healing or understanding pressure attached to it. It was just bland and unmemorable, to say the least.

"Thanks for finally telling me Babe. I'm going to put on some work clothes and go over to the warehouse to see if Father Caleb needs any help with the evening meal. I understand Tate took the weekend off. I will pick our son up from daycare on my way back. Do you want to go out for dinner or do you want me to pick something up on my way back?"

Kate was in shock that Slapp refused to say anything more or respond to what she had just shared with him. Kate knew that she had put Slapp through hell, by rejecting his affectionate advances without giving him a definitive reasons and keeping a secret that was so crucial to their relationship bonding. She realized at that moment, with Slapp abandonment and trust issues, that keeping her past a secret wasn't the best way for her to have gone. Her past and her medication history had answered most of Slapp's burning questions. Over the last few months, Kate had mastered elusiveness during their heated discussions of what was wrong with her behavior, so now Slapp had decided to give her a little taste of her own medicine, so to speak.

Kate had never experienced the cold-heartedness of Slapp's personality, but she was about to witness her first sample of his dark side, in which wasn't really that convincing if you had a profiler's instinct. Slapp's anger was more like bottled up disappointment and pain towards whomever he was involved with in the disagreement. He was only dangerous to criminals; people who hurt others without a justifiable cause.

Slapp kissed Kate cheek again before pulling completely away to go in the closet to find some worn-out clothes. Slapp remembered that the roof had sprung a leak in the kitchen area of the old warehouse. Tate had temporarily patched it, but he remembered that a truck had delivered the supplies to complete the repairs. Kate stared for a moment before she attacked his seemingly unconcern actions.

"So Alvin, is that all you have to say," shouted Kate? He snapped his head around quickly to face Kate's position with a choke-you-out scowl on his face. It frightened her a little as she returned his glare. Slapp spoke calmly in an I-couldn't-care-less tone, at first and then he had a slight meltdown.

"What the hell you want me to say Kate, after all these months. You could have told me that months ago and then we wouldn't have been so worry about you. Instead you played the

I-can-handle-this-alone card and not once did you consider how this would affect our family, me or our friends." Then Slapp took his editorial soapbox stance again as he firmly grabbed Kate's upper right arm and snatched her closer to himself and upward as she now stood on the ball portion of her feet. He stared down at her for a moment as his eyes instantly became red and swollen with increased anger and tears. "Listen to me Kate, when you came into my life you improved my relationship with God, because every day that I wake up I thank him for you and our son Cameron. I pray to be a better husband, father and friend; in that order if I may add. Kate your understanding and the love you have shown me was able to repair things within me that I didn't even realize were broken. Now I see that the deep love that I have for you; your silly ass can't even imagine. Perhaps that's my fault for not making this clearer before now. Everything and everybody that I have ever loved, I've lost. I pray more now because I couldn't bear loosing you or Cameron. The passion I have for you right now, that God has granted me, is so good and pure until the intimacy that we share between us, I feel, is an added bonus of pleasure that I didn't earn, deserve or had a right to ask for. Now can you understand why this little insignificant secret has upset me so and could have ruined our lives if I would have chose to do something stupid, like seek affection from another woman?"

Then Slapp's tone became elevated just a little more, yet very cold and nasty. "So perhaps now you can understand, Doctor, why I'm so disappointed and angry that you waited and took me through this nightmare with you about some trivial shit as taking a pill every day. All the other crap happened years before we met and has nothing to do with me nor the feelings I have for you."

Slapp then shoved her forcefully away while releasing the death grip that he had on Kate's arm and she landed on the bed. She was terrified to say the least with him being so much larger than her. Kate had no idea that Slapp was capable of expressing such anger towards her. Then he continued.

"You were very selfish and wrong in your actions Kate and I'm going to need a little time to work this all out in my head, surely all your advance education and training will help you understand this, even if it didn't help you make a good decision earlier about us." Slapp begin to wave his hand around as he formed his next sentence, while turning his back to Kate, for an enhanced rude effect. "Of course you realize that everything that you have just revealed to me, I already knew from the investigation report we preformed on you and your entire damn family. I thought you were about to tell me something that would explain why you shut me out. I thought perhaps you had been attacked as a young lady or something worst. I know getting married and having a child so quickly was a big adjustment for you, but I know you had to have been taught in college how secrets can become so damaging to a relationship and how a person with trust issues might over-react to any type of rejection. Everyone has baggage and I thought I laid all mine on the table when we first met or soon thereafter I returned from Hong Kong."

The tears began to flow heavier from Kate's eyes as she clutched her robe close and stare up at Slapp, from a partial supine position, where Slap had shoved her and she had landed on the bed. He continued to call her out on the decision, which she had made by not telling him about her past earlier. All of this was hard for Kate to hear, but she had to admit that it was a correct analogy, from Slapp's perspective. Now she had to wait for him to forgive her. She didn't want Slapp to move out like he had threatened to do.

That night Slapp slept in the twin bed in the baby's room. This was the same twin bed that Kate had slept in; to be near Cameron when she was breast-feeding and had also used it to get away from Slapp's sexual advances. This arrangement continued for a couple of weeks before either of them decided to talk about it. The routine with the baby and the household ran as usual. Slapp even allowed Cameron to sleep on his chest some nights, whenever he appeared a little fussy, while teething. Other nights Cameron slept in bed with Kate, in the master bedroom. They were both sure that Cameron could feel the tension between them, yet the destructive-games of non-forgiveness continued between them.

One night when Slapp had failed to lock the master bedroom's bathroom door, which was a new practice to isolate himself from Kate, she followed him in. He pretended not to notice her as he lathered his body, with his back towards the shower door. Kate removed her clothes, tied up her hair in a towel and opened the shower door to step inside the shower stall. Slapp heard her, but refused to turn to face her as he began to rinse off. Slapp towered over Gayle at least a foot or more and was more than twice her size. Kate reached up to stroke his wide smooth soapy back in hope he would turn around to acknowledge her and her advances. Instead he spoke as his back remained facing her.

"I'm almost finished here, Kate. I just have to rinse my hair. Watch-out for the soap, you might get a little in your eyes." She carefully reached around his waist and pressed her face up against his freshly showered muscular-bulging back to inhale the essence of him and the body gel that he had selected. Slapp became totally motionless as he looked up at the ceiling of the shower stall in hope that something from heaven would give him the strength to resist her advances, as he remembered how many nights he had approached his wife and she had rejected him out of pure meanness, or so he thought and his feelings believed. He stood still as Kate's hands moved gently over his body until they reached his manhood that had already begun to respond to her presence and touch and the warm soothing spray of the shower.

Slapp thought to himself, how many times had the two of them shared this bath stall prior to the derailment of the relationship by Kate's secrets? Which in turn had caused the nightmares, which had sequentially caused Kate's guilt that provoked her to reject Slapp's sexual advances. The two of them had shared a shower more times than either of them were prepared to remember without experiencing a moment of sadness.

Slapp was now trying to decide if it was worth it to him to standing his ground of anger or allow his marriage to move back to a happier and healthier state. The massage that Kate was now applying to Slapp's penis weighted in heavily on his decision-making ability. Perhaps he had allowed them to sexually suffer enough, by sleeping a part. His manhood continued to respond to her caressing massage as he waited for something to change. He lifted his arms up above his shoulders and laced his fingers together behind his head and neck, as all the pleasure memories of them together flooded his mind. The sensation that his body was now feeling had begun to weaken his reserve.

Kate smiled deeply inside because she knew that Slapp was still very attracted to her and the enjoyment that she could deliver to every fiber of his being, which was now flooding his thoughts and body sensations. Slapp turned slowly to face Kate as he noticed the smirk on her face, which could have easily been mistaken for gloating. About that time he heard Cameron waking up in the baby's room. Slapp looked down at Kate and then abruptly excused himself from the shower stall. He forcefully pushed the shower door open, by reaching above Kate's head, as his face revealed a discussed glance.

"Excuse me Kate, I think I hear our son trying to get my attention. I believe that he may want his bottle." Slapp stepped out of the shower stall and place a large bath towel around his naked wet body, slipped on a pair of house shoes and rushed to the next bedroom to comfort his son. Slapp used that same tone of voice that he used with Milani; slow calm and easy, yet firm. "Hey little man. What's wrong, did you think we just left you home alone? We would never do that to you. Come here, let daddy pick you up and get your bottle." Slapp took Cameron from the crib, cradled him in his nurturing arms and headed towards the kitchen to get Cameron a bottle. Slapp warmed the formula just a little and walked back to Cameron's room and sat in the big rocking chair as he rocked him and kissed his forehead as the baby nursed his bottle. Cameron moved his hand back and forth across his father's chest as he noticed that something was different about the feeling, it was wet.

"Hey big guy, you do realize that this is your night-cap bottle from the milk bar, so after this it is lights out, okay? Are you wet?" Cameron only stared up at his father as they continued to rock back and forth in the soundless gliding swing chair.

Slapp stuck his fingers in the front section of the Cameron,s pamper, while Cameron giggled because he thought his father was trying to tickle his belly. "Wow! Little fella, you have wet your drawers again? Hey! I thought we talked about this. Okay, I will change you this time, but next time you will need to call me before you have to go to the bathroom. I realize that you are only eight and half months old, but the sooner we get a handle on this 'pissing-in-your-pants thing' the better it will be for everyone concern, mainly me, alright?"

Slapp took Cameron over to the changing table and freshened him up and put on his pajamas for the night. Cameron was now holding his bottle and staring up at Slapp as they went on with their nightly one-sided word game. Slapp placed Cameron in his crib and the baby's eyes became heavy as his father rubbed his head gently. Kate walked into the baby's room wearing only a towel as well and pressed the front of her body up against the back of Slapp's back as he stared down at Cameron. She maneuvered her hand inside Slapp's damp towel and began to stroke his manhood for the second time.

At first he ignored her, but this didn't prevent his body from responding to her arousing touch. He turned slowly to face her as she maintained a firm massaging grip on his semi-erect penis. She gave his testicles a few rolling and tugging strokes and then moved her hand back to his private joystick.

Slapp leaned up against the baby's bed with his hands placed on each side of him on the top rail of the crib. He watched her and her hands as they pleasured him to the point of no return. Kate's towel dropped off of her freshly showered body to the floor around her feet. She then reached up to pinch her own nipple and then moved her hand down to locate her own pleasure center and the tip of her moist clitoris. First she stuck two fingers deep inside of her love-nest to wet her fingertips and then she began to stroke her firm clitoris with sensual pressure. She was now leaning up against Slapp with her face on his broad chest as she ran her hand slowly over parts of his chest and ribcage.

Slapp quickly looked over his shoulder to observe if Cameron was completely asleep. As Slapp stared at Kate's naked body, he watched Kate massaging herself and felt her hand stroking his penis; it sent sensual electric shock- waves through him, but he refused to weaken and give in. Kate then cautiously and slowly moved in closer stood on the ball of her feet to kiss Slapp, while sucking his lower lip in between her own. He was now strongly gripping the top of the baby's bed rail as he refused to take part in what Kate was doing. Suddenly Slapp pulled away and grabbed Kate by the arm and led her to their bed. It frightened Kate for a moment, because she thought that Slapp was only taking her away from Cameron's room, so he could yell at her again without out disturbing Cameron. Slapp sat on the side of the bed with his damp towel still in place. He pulled Kate's naked body between his thick massive hairy thighs as he spoke.

"Kate baby, you know how I feel about make-up sex. So what are you up to now? I don't think that it's ever a good idea. If we don't talk this out first, then after sex we will still have the same disagreement to deal with." Kate moved in closer, as she remain standing between his thighs, and took a hold of his penis again and then rubbed her breast nipples across his lips as he tried to speak. His smaller dominating head urged him to capture one of her hardened breast nipples into his mouth and enjoy it like he would never stop, but then she would win the discussion; and he couldn't allow that to happen so easily.

"Alvin, can we make-up first and talk afterwards?" He stared up into her eyes for a long time and almost smiled. He knew she wanted him as much as he desired her, yet his thoughts was that this called for a cooler play, if he wanted to make his point.

Slapp leaned back on the bed onto his elbows and upper forearm. She smiled and wondered exactly what was Slapp suggesting she do to get him back into their bed at night.

Kate stared into his eyes for a moment and then she eased onto the bed on her knees between Slapp's widely opened thick well-developed thighs. He returned her smile as he waited to see just what she would do to win him over or seduce him. She lowered her naked body down slowly onto the top of his as he received her with only one hand as he placed it easily around her mid-back and then stroked her shoulders. Kate then moved upward to kiss Slapp's lips and apologize again for her portion of the marriage derailment. She spoke to him with her mouth only centimeters shy of his. Slapp could feel her warm erotic breath on his mouth and face as he listened carefully for the key words that he needed to hear Kate say.

"Alvin, I'm really sorry about not telling you about my past earlier and the fact that I take medication daily. I though that I could handle this alone. Perhaps, the whole thing embarrassed me, at first. I never considered the fact that all this was revealed during your agency's background check or was it more like an investigation?" replied Kate in a somewhat aggressive tone. "At any rate, I'm sorry and I promise to never make a decision that will affect our family without talking it over first, with you."

Slapp opened his eyes wider and locked onto her eyes focus and face. "Wait a minute Kate, I think you can do a little better than that with your apology, in which I would like to point out almost landed us in a divorce."

She pulled away a little. "What do you mean Alvin?" He hesitated before answering as he probed her face for sincerity in her regrets or if the words that she had strategically selected were merely an oversight of what he preferred and had expecting to hear coming from her.

"I think what you meant to say was that you promise to never make a decision that is so important as that again without the two of us talking it over, regardless if it affect our family or not." Kate quickly looked away as if she had been caught in the act. Slapp noticed her demeanor shift just a tad and then decided that she was attempting to trick him. He swiftly pushed her from on top of him to the side of the bed next to him as the anger slowly returned. "I see Kate. You think you can just lay a little piece of sweet ass on me and I will forget everything. Well it's not that easy with me. You treated me like a second-draft-pick roommate for months and now that you are back on you medication and lobbying for some d—k, you expect me to just give it up, because you are my wife. Well it's true that this marriage thing is new to me, but I've been a profiler a little longer than you've been a shrink. So don't try to feed me your bullshit with cool-whip sprayed on top. Because I want tolerated it now or later."

Slapp quickly stood to his feet as Kate laid there in shock that Slapp had read so much into her apology. Slapp rushed into the bathroom and grabbed his robe, put it on and headed down the hall to the sofa in the living room. Kate followed him while wearing a thin see-though cover. Slapp slumped down deeply into the sofa and through his head backwards against the backrest edge of the couch. Kate came in and sat close to him and began to stroke the inside of his thighs until she found his starved manhood. His eyes remained closed as he attempted to ignore her.

"I'm sorry Alvin, I guess if I want to be forgiven I have to lay it all out on the table first, huh?" She opened his robe and stood up to straddle his lap on her knees, as she faced him. She was now braced up on her knees and leaning forward over his lap with both hands resting on either side of his head, as Slapp's head continued to relax back against the edge of the sofa's backrest. She continued to stroke his penis with one hand as she placed her breast nipples to his lips. While his eyes remained closed he spoke, but most of the anger was gone. He almost laughed as he spoke. He was remembering how he loved their word games with no boundaries.

"It's not going to work this time Kate. She went on stroking him and rubbing her feminine mound-tips back and forth over his lips. His penis was now firm in her hand and pulsating as she added a little more pressure and speed to her hand fondling. He was weakening and a playful smile washed over both of their faces. "You know I don't approve of make-up sex Kate. We need to talk this out first." Kate added more intensity as she held one of her breast while forcing the nipple into his mouth whenever he spoke.

"Just this once baby, can we have intercourse first and talk afterwards. I really need to feel you inside me and feel the pressure of your body on top of me. It has been a long time. Slapp snapped his head up forward, opened his eyes wide to give Kate a swift hard stare as he retaliated to her last comment. She jumped with surprise and was a little startled by Slapp's response.

"And whose damn fault was that Kate? It was yours, all yours Kate." Then Slapp's voice lowered a little in fear that he would awaken Cameron. He then screamed in a whisper. "How many times did I approach you and begged you to sleep with me. But nooooo, you always had a prepared excuse. All you had to do was tell me about your past and I would have backed off and given you all the time you needed. So now you want to have sex on your terms." Kate moved from straddling his lap to the sofa next to him as he quietly yelled.

Kate was yelling right back as she gave her analogy. "So is that what this is all about Alvin? You couldn't get a piece of ass when you wanted it, so now we have to wait until you are good and damn ready? Well that's just great. I tried to make this up to you, but if you don't want to, then that's fine by me. When are you going to let it go? I made a big mistake, Alvin and I will probably make a lot more."

Slapp realized that Kate was absolutely correct and then there was the fact that he was very horny as hell, as well. Kate jumped up from the couch to leave when Slapp grabbed her arm gently and pulled Kate back into his arms across his lap. She didn't resist him and waited to receive his deep passionate kiss. Her lips were trembling with diminishing anger and excitement as she placed her tongue deeply inside Slapp's hungry mouth.

Slapp nibbled on Kate's tongue and lips with almost painful force, as the deep need to penetrate her with his throbbing male organ washed over him. She slowly shifted back to the straddle-lap position without releasing him from the kiss. Then she slid her body down onto his hungry pride. Slapp let out a loud sigh of relief and hungry sound, while he wasted no time finding a rhythmic stroke in which they each received enjoyment. Kate glided up and down as her husband moved in and out of her dripping wet cavern. Slapp's intruder penetrated deeper within her, during the first few strokes. Her vagina was tighter than Slapp remembered. Perhaps the doctor had added an extra suture after Cameron's birth. This was the first time that they had engaged in intercourse since their baby had been born, plus a few months before. Slapp was afraid that his deep hungry desire would over power him and he would hurt Kate by accident, because of the body-size difference between the two of them and the long sexual dry-spell.

Kate was now stroking Slapp so strongly until he was concerned that she would be bruised later. He held Kate lightly at the waist as he waited for her to take her fill of him. She slowed her strokes to grind herself down onto his groin and pressed her breast nipples into his mouth. She loved it when Slapp enjoyed her breast while his penis was deep within of her vagina. He knew this, so he grabbed the base of one of her breast and massaged the end and nipple just shy of discomfort. Slapp exploded after only a few minutes during a deep upward thrust of his organ into Kate's juice box. He knew that this was only the beginning of their reconciliation sex.

Kate sprang to her feet and pulled Slapp to his feet so they could move to their bedroom. They both stopped in the hall to peep in on Cameron as they hoped that he didn't wake up for at least a few more minutes. They both crawled into bed, as Kate wasted no time stroking Slapp's penis into a second very firm state. He caressed her breast nipples into between his full lips as she grind her wet juice box against his upper hipbone. Then Slapp rolled Kate to her stomach and entered her femaleness from the rear. She gripped the pillow and headboard and braced herself as Slapp stroked deeper and deeper into her neediness. They both screamed with unbridled passion as the disorientation of basic primal lustful coupling consumed them. They held this position for what seemed like a long time as Kate begged him not to stop or surrender to his climax.

He squeezed one of her breast and nipples between his massive fingers as the other hand massaged her clitoris back and forth as it perturbed to its maximum length and became swollen to one and a half its at-rest normal size. Kate released a couple of times as Slapp slid his male organ in and out of Kate's sperm-lubricated female craven from the rear. She was jerking and meeting his plunges with wild strokes of her own.

Slapp climaxed the second time as they slid down to a resting position to kiss and snuggle.

A few moments later they both went into the rest room to clean up a little and relieve themselves. Now back in bed they lay quiet, in the total dark room and massaged each other sexual parts. No words pass between them; only familiar long starved desire-filled caresses and passion filled groaning. Kate rubbed his limp penis as he orally massaged her breast. Slapp soon fell into a deep comma-like sleep. Kate performed an oral massage while Slapp was asleep. He awakened at the very end.

Later Kate slowly scooted off the bed without saying a word and went in the bathroom to take a quick shower. When she returned and got back in bed she quietly questioned Slapp. "How was your oral massage Baby," whispered Kate as she hid her face from his eye contact?"

Slapp slowly titled her head up by placing two curled fingers underneath her chin and lifted her eyes to his level before he responded. "I have never experienced anything like that before, and to be honest, the powerful force of it frightened me a little. I feel a weakness that I've never felt before. I enjoyed the sexual portion of the encounter, but the after-effects are a little un-nerving, if there is such a word. Perhaps it's because I haven't had sex in a while and the expectation caused me to become too excited. Maybe I'm getting older and losing some of my stamina. I don't ever remember releasing that my times in a short period of time. You are the doctor, Kate; you tell me what I'm experiencing right now. All I know is that I don't want to get out of bed for the next few hours. Come to think of it, I don't think I have the strength to get up even if I had the desire to." Kate smiled warmly and then Slapp kissed her on the lips, before he released his grasp on her chin. She buried her face again into his chest and moved even closer and hugged him with all the strength she could muster.

Slapp whispered, "Kate, we are going to have that talk."

They held each other in bed for a long time, yet they never had 'the talk' that had been pushed to the side, for the sake of a lengthy unrestrained lustful encounter.

Chapter Four

Our Saturday Morning Excursions

The next morning Slapp woke up early, he left Kate a note next to the bed and took Cameron to see visit his grandfather at the National Botanical Garden. Slapp knew that it was his father, Retired Agent Dexter Allen Burney's weekend to work as a group tour-guide. The entire city was filled with people and buzzing with the usual summer excitement. Although Cameron was still quite young, he loved people and had no problem meeting strangers. Slapp would take Cameron to his grandfather's workplace, at the National Gardens, and place Cameron in a baby's backpack on his grandfather's back. Mr. Burney just loved showing him off. After about two short tours, Cameron would begin to get sleepy.

Their next stop, for a quick lunch, was at one of Slapp's favorite cafés right beside the Navy Memorial Monument's outside amphitheater, which faced Pennsylvania Avenue and directly across the street from the renowned American National

Archives building. The well-established sandwich and coffee shop café included a nice upscale bakery. It was also only a few blocks from the F.B.I.'s main headquarters offices where Slapp and Cameron would make their third and final stop to have a very brief visit with Ole Mr. Joe, who was the building's first line of security and the same man that operated the walk-thru scanner unit and x-ray conveyer belt to check you the moment you walked into the front locked door of the building.

When Ole Joe was on duty, everyone was checked; even Cameron and his overpriced stylish diaper bag. Mr. Joe would repeat the same phrases each time he was required to search Cameron's bag.

"Damn Baby P.I, why would a man your age need so many compartments to carry a couple baby sandwiches, a few pairs of clean underwear, some fancy wipe-your-butt toilet paper and a bottle of that weak juice-milk called formula. Back in my day it was either Carnation or that Pet Brand and if you were born with an allergy to either or both of them, well we just hoped that you grew quickly enough to eat table food before the allergies or that irritating rash did you in. Yet, sometimes we would strike a deal with an old goat farmer on the edge of town you see. Because if we had to purchase it from the store and travel down that short exclusive kosher isle, which was out of the question and way out of our grocery budget; well you just could forget about it. In addition to that, cloth dippers were still in fashion too. Yeah they had special milks for babies, way back then, but it came with a particular high price. Just tell me Baby P.I, who in the hell could afford it with six other non-working mouths in the house that required feeding. There was no WIC program back them. Yeah, I tell you one thing Baby P.I, you are one lucky-ducky to be born now and to have both parents that work."

Ole Joe continued to search the Cameron's diaper bag as he pretended to fuss about working so hard, before allowing Slapp and Cameron into the building. "I declare Baby P.I, I've seen men go out in the field for a week carrying a bag with less secret compartments than you have in this darn diaper bag."

That was the nickname that Ole Man Joe had given Cameron, and after a few months the name had attached itself to Cameron. Ole Joe went on, "And just looking at this travel pouch with all these gadgets, I know your parents paid an arm and a leg for this contraption. Does it do anything else Baby P.I., except hold your drawers and look good?" Then he would lean way back while holding Cameron in his arms and laugh out loud as Cameron stared into his face and smile only briefly as if he understood every word the old man had said. Then he would put his fingers in ole Joe's mouth, as Joe pretended to chew his fingers, while making crunching sounds.

After the full shakedown, like one would give a black-sheep-of-the-family at a family reunion and if there was a second man at the door that was perhaps in training; Slapp, Cameron and Ole Joe would sneak off to a nearby break-room for a quick cup of coffee so Ole Joe could play with the baby. Once the coffee had cooled and almost gone; Ole Joe would hold Slapp's cup up to Cameron lips so he would have bragging rights later on for buying Cameron his first cup of coffee, before he was old enough to drink one. At each visit, Ole Joe would find something similar to do with Cameron so he would be able to tell him about it later. During one of their visits to see Ole Joe, he allowed Cameron to lick all the sugar coating from a stick of chewing gum. Another time he had saved Cameron a red strawberry lollipop and the time before that he gave him a single cheerio from his snack lunch. Then Ole Man Joe would laugh and say, 'Baby P.I you are just like your daddy, you will try to eat anything that comes near your mouth'.

Ole Joe appeared to be more excited about Cameron growing up than his parents. I believe it was because he was pretty old and he wondered if he would still be around long enough to have a real man-to-man talk with Cameron. His health had begun to fail him so the bureau allowed him to work part-time and come in whenever someone required training. Ole Joe's wife had died many years before and they only had one son. That son didn't live in the area and Ole Joe lived alone. So the only thing that he had to look forward to was that job and the people that worked there that depended on him. Financially Ole Joe didn't need to work and his son had asked him several times to come live with him. He told his son that he couldn't leave his deceased wife in a dangerous corrupted city like this alone, he had to stay to protect her; even in the grave.

Mr. Joe would go to visit his deceased wife's burial place at least once a month sometimes more and clean it off and take fresh flowers. He would stay for a while and tell her all what had happened since his last visit; all that he could remember that is. He would start to talk to his deceased wife the moment he pulled the first weed up. He would be carrying a small spade, heavy work gloves, a little fertilizer in a zip-lock bag and a fresh plant of some sort. He would say.

"Hello Lil' Lady. I know I'm getting here kinda' late today, but the traffic was heavier than I anticipated. So go on and tell your love how you're doing today. I got a letter and a phone call from our son last week. He seems to be doing fine. You know Baby; he still hasn't found a woman to marry. I don't know about you, but I'm tired of waiting for those grand kids to be born. Oh! That reminds me Cameron and his father Slapp stopped by last week to see me, while I was at work. I told you about him years ago when he first joined the bureau. He was the very handsome young one, with a very quick temper. If you recall, I had more than a few stories to tell you about all the trouble he would get himself into. Till this day, I can't figure out how he had lasted so long. Hum? Well he did have a special relationship with Agent Burney and we just recently discovered that in fact Retired Agent Burney is his true father. Oh! I'm sorry I guess I got off subject a bit. I was about to tell you about that fine baby boy that Agent Alvin and his wife has created. I'm not sure what they are feeding that boy, because he is growing like a ragweed on Miracle Grow fertilizer. Yes, he sure is a fine boy and I really enjoy him, whenever he and his father takes a notion to stop by.

"Honey, Junior and I talked about me coming to live with him again; well to tell the truth it was more of an argument than a discussion. I don't know why that boy can't just get it through his thick skull that I can't leave you here alone in this old corrupt city all by yourself. I know that he thinks that I'm crazy because I'm old and don't agree with what he is saying most of the time. If he would get married and settle down, maybe one of his children would come and live with me. You know I never thought about finding another woman after you left. There are a lot of them around for the pickings, but I don't think I have the gumption to adjust to another. Well, I better be getting on home to the house before dark, my eyes aren't seeing as clearly as they once have. I guest that is all for now. I'll bring you some roses next time, I sure remember how sweet you use to be to me whenever I brought you fresh roses home."

Ole Joe smiled deeply and clapped his hand together once as a single lonely tear escaped each eye. Then Ole Joe reached up to use the head stone to balance himself as he stood up from his kneeling position and gathered all his tools and leftover fertilizer. He would sling the rest of it on the nearby graves and there was no doubt that the grass was greener in those areas. The graveyard caretaker wasn't sure if Ole Mr. Joe had a better brand of compost or if it was the love in which Joe used as he threw it around. The grave keeper was inclined to believe that the latter was the case.

It was now about two o'clock in the afternoon when Cameron and Slapp headed back to the brownstone. Kate had gone out for a few moments, but had returned hours before. When Slapp and Baby P.I arrived home it was a few minutes after three that afternoon. Max and Milani was right next door and saw Cameron and Slapp coming up the street. They both ran out to meet them. Cameron was hot, wet and cranky from his long day and appeared to be in no mood to play with them. Slapp promised to bring Cameron over next door, later, after his nap.

Once Cameron was down for his snooze, Slapp and Kate decided to take advantage of the moment and catch forty winks as well, before dinner.

Chapter Five

Weekend Wends Down

Sunday morning of that same long weekend, Tate decided that he should go in very early to the warehouse to help serve the breakfast meal at the soup kitchen. They were always short of help on Sundays. Around ten o'clock that morning, Tate was already headed back to his condo apartment to spend the remainder of the weekend with Gayle as promised. He was hoping that she was still in bed; no such luck. Gayle was lying on that long sofa, while wearing yet another sexy matching collection right off the pages of the Victory Secret's catalog. Tate had replayed a portion of the previous two nights that he had spent with Gayle, in his head, during his long drive back to the condo. However, when he saw her lying there waiting for him to return for a few more hours of sexual pleasure, those memories were washed away by the expectations that were now flooding the sensation of his male organ.

He stood in the doorway for a moment to stare at Gayle on the sofa as she lay with one leg and foot propped scandalously on the back of the sofa's backrest. The top of her head was towards the door, so Tate couldn't see if she was wearing anything under the long flowing see-through gown and cover robe. Tate suddenly remembered the oral pleasure that Gayle had given his personal the day before, on that very same sofa. He wondered if she would be willing to repeat that oral performance, so to speak. He got a partial erection just thinking about it. Now he suspected that she had begun pleasuring herself before he had arrived. He spoke quickly as he entered the front entrance of the condo.

"Hello baby, I'm back. Don't get up. I have to take a quick shower and I will be right back. Tate rushed into the master bedroom's shower. When he turned off the shower and stepped out to dry off, Gayle was standing there staring at him and his private parts. He smiled and realized that Gayle had been sipping wine. He wrapped the towel around him and went to the sink to brush his teeth. Gayle slowly rubbed his hairy chest as she moved closer and stood behind him, while reaching around to the front of him.

"So did everything go well at the soup kitchen? I've been waiting for you to come back. To be honest I didn't expect you back so soon, considering the length of the drive." Tate looked into the mirror and smile at Gayle's reflection while she continued to stand behind him.

"Traffic wasn't too bad today Baby, plus I wanted to keep my promise to you about spending some quality time with my favorite church-member. Is there anything special you have planned for us?"

"No, not really. I just thought we could lie around and perhaps watch a couple of movies. He turned slightly to make eye contact and give her another once-over look.

"Is that a new outfit you're wearing? I like that color on you. It's too bad that you won't be wearing it much longer." Tate smiled as Gayle continued to drink the shower water from his smooth well-developed muscular ribcage that he had missed, while she listened to his sultry predicting words. Gayle began to pinch her breast nipples as she leaned up against the back of Tate, while he completed his oral maintenance with some well-needed flossing. Gayle eyes were now closed as she pulled up her long gown, opened her thighs a little and started to slowly rub upward on the inside of her thighs until she reached the narrow thin fabric of her matching thongs that covered her moist swollen clitoris. Tate was aware of what Gayle was doing without turning around and he didn't want to break her concentration until she was ready for him to intervene. Tate stood quietly facing the mirror as he spoke to her in a whisper, while reaching over his shoulder and behind him to stroke her head and her soft curly out-of-control hair.

"Does it feel good?" She didn't answer. Gayle was now kissing and nibbling on a small area of Tate's back as she increased the intensity of the strokes on her clitoris. Her breathing was shallow and loud as Tate waited for her to explode. Tate smiled because he found this amusing and was pretty sure that Gayle had learned to please herself sexually without him being there, but found it much easier and more pleasurable to do so if he was present and or talking to her. He suddenly remembered all those nights that they had shared those sexually engaging conversations over the phone. There wasn't enough privacy in the warehouse sleeping area for Tate to pleasure himself. The old warehouse walls were tissue paper thin and the room that he and his father, Father Caleb, shared upstairs, in which was located one room over from the makeshift chapel, in which didn't have a dividing wall. All the homeless slept in two large rooms on the first floor; one for the ladies and one side for the men. Even after all the begging they had done to the city, they were only able to accommodate twenty overnight homeless at a time. Tate never even thought about satisfying his needs and was sure that some nights his father the priest had heard him whispering dirty comments to his newly acquired wife. Now that Tate had learned about Gayle's little secret, this would give a whole new meaning to late-night 'erotic phone talk'.

Tate slowly reached behind to stroke Gayle's butt as she massaged herself into a climatic calm. Gayle let out a low moaning hungry scream as her body jerked from the orgasm. Tate knew that she would probably become a little embarrassed, now that she realized that he was aware of what she had been doing while they were on the phone all those nights. He wouldn't dare mention the phone sex. He continued to rub and massage her butt cheeks without turning to face her as she attempted to quiet her breathing.

"Baby, are you alright," he said in his quiet deep sexy voice? She answered quickly while breathing hard.

"I don't think so; I'll wait for you in the bedroom." Gayle pulled away slowly as her gown dropped to its full length again around her ankles. Gayle left the bathroom and went in the bedroom and turned down the freshly prepared sheets. She removed the robe portion of the set and slid into bed. She took a partial-doggy style position to wait on Tate. The long gown pooled around her knees onto the bed. She removed her arms out of the top part and pulled it down to expose her upper body to her waist. Her knees were far apart and she laid her head on a pillow as she tugged at her nipples to force her body to generate even more warm-sticky mating fluids. The lights were low and the blackout curtain shades over the bedroom windows created the illusion of nighttime.

Tate emerged from the bathroom and there he saw Gayle with her buttocks titled high in the air as she waited. He noticed that she was fingering her breast nipples. He moved onto the bed with her as he positioned himself behind her on the bed, while on his knees. He stroked both of her lower calves of her legs that were visible from underneath the gown that was pooled around her knees on the bed. Then he slowly moved one hand blindly under her gown to rub the inside of her widely positioned thighs. He then slowly pulled the seat of her wet thongs to one side and placed two of his large thick fingers inside her dripping juice box. He moved closer so he could reach one of her breasts with the other hand to enhance her foreplay enjoyment. He was now kneeling on his knees to the side of her on the bed.

"How does that feel Baby? Can you feel what you need?"

Gayle offered no verbal response, as she thrust her body backwards to increase the depth of his fingers inside her femaleness. She was now panting and releasing loud moaning screams and forcing her body back and forth in a self-satisfying rhythm. Tate held his same position until he was sure it was okay with Gayle for him to take another. Then he withdrew his substituting digits from deeply inside her, released her breast and turned to lay on his back as he slid his upper body underneath her gown and between her open knees and just below her steamy thighs as she remained on her knees with her butt in the air. The hem edge of her gown fell across Tate's broad chest and created a private tent-like area so he could take his oral fill of her. The light from the nightstand shinning through her thin gown provided an inviting mood as it bounced off Gayle's body. Tate slowly inhaled the essences of the soap, mixed with the mating juice aroma of her vagina. He closed his eyes for a brief moment to enjoy the scent of the mixture. Tate became consumed with the idea of tasting her nectar and fantasized about later feeling it all around his penis as he slid in and out of her famished p—y.

Gayle was now experiencing Tate's hot moist breath on the inside of her thighs and her entire private area and could hardly wait for him to attack the area with his mouth, lips and teeth. Tate didn't want to rush the moment of pleasure for him or her so he slowly reached up with both hands and pulled the lips of her vagina apart and watched her clitoris swell and protrude even more. He began to kiss the inside of each of her smooth warm thighs as he moved each kiss closer to the target of her crotch, by pulling her entire body nearer to the bed beneath them. He noticed the juices escaping her juice box as he brushed a single fingertip over the very tip of her clitoris. Gayle jerked as if a sting from a high-powered battery had pierced her. Her breathlessness sounds increased as she waited. Tate became aware that his male organ was becoming firmer and more demanding that he do something to appease it.

Tate began to rub Gayle's healthy hips with one hand and stroke himself with the other to soothe his manhood urges. He continued to stare into the middle of Gayle's steamy crotch above him, as he enjoyed the aroma and watched the juices accumulate in the center, near its opening. He kissed, nibbled and licked the inner sides of her thighs as he waited. Gayle's vagina was hairless and smoothly plump. Gayle began to lower her body closer to Tate's open hungry mouth and eager tongue as she slowly gyrated her hips around to make his view more arousing and pleasurable. He slapped her upper hip hard a few times to express his approval and excitement about what was about to take place between them.

A few moments later, Tate released his male organ and firmly gripped both of her buttock cheeks and forced her luscious vagina down onto his drooling ambitious mouth. He uncovered her swollen clitoris and sucked all the fluids from her female cavern. She screamed with pleasure as he struggled to hold her in position so he could continue to pleasure her into an exhausting and satisfying climax. Long after her sexual release, he smothered her genitalia with oral massaging, passionate kisses, and unfathomable penetrating insertions with his strong aggressive tongue.

Gayle slowly lay flat on the bed and turned over to her back, as her legs remained widely apart to allow Tate access to her personal. The long gown continued to aid as a cloaking device of privacy, as he nurtured her every sexual need to the surface of her awareness. She fell into a light sleep and he moved upward to enter her with his powerful over-sized male organ. She woke up calmly and held him lightly as he stroked her with a light sedative force that she had never experienced from him before. They fell asleep with their bodies joined together.

Later that evening they got up and shared a light dinner before going to bed for the evening. They positioned themselves with Tate's limp penis deep within her and her breast inside his mouth. Each time one of them woke up or moved to another position, they made the proper adjustment so she could feel him inside and his mouth gripped tightly around one of her breast sucking with a nurturing relaxing pressure. Twice during the night Tate regained an erection. Each time it happened he would whisper to Gayle.

"Don't wake up baby, I'm just going to appease my male organ a little more with the help of your deliciously ripe …... He and

I just need a little more of you sweet tight juice box, that's all. Relax; go back to sleep this is only a follow-up pleasuring, for my greedy manhood and me. I'm sucking your breasts because I enjoy them in my mouth. Ssshhh, go back to sleep." Then Tate would roll on top of Gayle, while supporting all his body weight on his forearms and knees and stroke her until his penis lost its firmness. Then Tate would whisper again, "Now you understand why I live at the warehouse, good tight c—t like this could kill a man of my age." Gayle was totally asleep and never responded to his actions or whispers in the dark.

Just before that next morning had arrived. The two of them had rolled apart. Gayle's back was towards Tate as he woke up to go to the restroom. When he returned to the bed, he crawled up to the back of Gayle. Suddenly she rolled over to face him and he felt her breasts near his face. He moved to take one of Gayle breast nipples into his mouth again. She rubbed his face and head while still asleep. This gesture excited Tate, so he whispered to her the second time.

"Hey Baby, it's only me. Go back to sleep. I'm going to massage your luscious mounds with my lips and then pleasure you a few more moments. I know how much you enjoy me stroking you early in the morning. Just stay calm and open up to me so I can get to that luscious warm craven of yours." Gayle opened her thighs wide while lying on her back. Tate rolled on top and began to stroke Gayle like an animal in coupling heat. She woke up quickly to pull her legs up around his waist and began to scream his name and talk out loudly.

"Oh Thaddeus, that feels so good. Oh, oh don't' stop. Why didn't you wake me up sooner? Oh, baby this is what I need, a good screwing. Oh, oh go deeper. That's it baby suck'um harder. Oh yeah, right there. Ooooo yes, right there, Thaddeus. Oh baby, I'm going to need this one more time before you leave. Just don't stop now."

A few moments later they were finished. They both fell back asleep as though nothing non-routine had happened. Tate woke her up a few hours before he had planned to leave in case Gayle required some more sexual servicing, before he left Monday Morning. He took a shower and came and sat on the side of the bed to wake Gayle up quietly and slowly. He was wearing a damp towel and he slowly reached beneath the sheets to rub Gayle's back as he talked to her.

"Hey baby, I'm getting ready to go. Do you have to go in early today? Gayle slowly woke up a little and reached for Tate and her hand found the side of his damp thigh as he sat sidesaddle on the bed. She didn't open her eyes or speak as she moved to lay her head in his lap. Tate shifted more to the side and now placed his knee on the bed to welcome her head into his lap. The towel slid up and opened more as he made the adjustment and Gayle positioned her head on the inside of his bent knee. Now her face was only inches away from his unsuspecting penis. He rubbed her breast affectionately and she found his penis with one of her hands as she continued to wake up slowly. "Wake up sleepy head, its early Monday morning and I have a long drive ahead of me into the city. Suddenly Gayle fed his manhood into her mouth and began to suck it hard. Tate grabbed the back of her head to assist her and waited for her to take her fill of him. Gayle quickly moved off the bed to the floor on her knees between Tate's thighs and forcefully drained his vigor from him through his loins. He didn't have enough strength to pleasure her. Tate soon fell backwards back across the bed and Gayle released her grasp from around his organ. She went into the bathroom and took a shower and passed through the bedroom and headed to the kitchen to prepare breakfast.

"Tate, baby I thought you said that you were leaving?" Soon Tate got up and dressed for the day. He said good-bye to Gayle in the kitchen as she smiled, while pretending not to know why Tate was moving so slowly.

Chapter Six

A Social Call Back into Exile

Two years after we arrived back home. We decided to keep our promise to Milani's great grandmother and give her an all-expense-paid trip back home to Hong Kong. We figured that two months would prove to be a nice long rewarding visit to see her family and friends. A family vacation for us would be a great idea as well. Mr. Bruce our financial guide made all the arrangements. We still had furniture in storage in Hong Kong, so we decided to rent a three-bedroom condo near Stanley's Market. That was the same area that we had lived before, while in exile. Milani's great grandmother would stay with her daughter and the remainder of us would vacation at the condo.

We called a meeting to see who was interested in going back. My father was all in and made a few calls to set-up a comeback tour for himself and his band. Slapp was excited and told Kate that this could be the honeymoon that they never had taken after they were married. Slapp was sure that he could get his old job back part-time, not that he needed one; and that way someone from the motor pool could take a vacation without stressing out the summer's working schedule.

Miss Beasley loved the idea because she wanted to go back to see her old friends. After all, this had been where Miss Beasley had spent most of her adult life, while in the witness protection program. Tate and Gayle took a pass on the trip. Tate had completed school, but they were waiting for their first missionary assignment placement to be decided. Besides that, Father Caleb required weekly help with the soup kitchen. With Slapp and Kate gone, there was no one else that the priest could call at a moments notice to fill-in.

It was settled; Slapp, Kate, Cameron (Baby P.I.), Miss Beasley, Max, Milani and her great grandmother, my father Uncle Oscar, and I were all headed back to Hong Kong for the summer. Alex was unable to get away, but agreed to look in on Father Caleb and spend some nights at the warehouse with him. Alex agreed to try to come near the end of the trip. Bruce and Uncle Burney promised to be on-call in case the staff became too sparse at the soup kitchen. A few people from the church had agreed to fill-in also while we were gone.

We made our reservations for the second week after the kids had gotten out of school for the summer. My father left early to get the band back together and begin rehearsals before their first limited-time-only comeback performances. The contracting company arranged for Mr. Wiley to get his old room back at the hotel and resort. Slapp took his old position back at the embassy as a driver slash bodyguard for the ambassador. Even though it was only for two months, the motor pool staff was glad for the help.

The remainder of us all arrived around the middle of June that summer and it was as though time had stood still since our departure. The city was filled with the summer-rush of tourist. It was warm and the night markets were in full swing. The harbor seemed a little more crowded than we remembered, yet at first glance; this was the only thing that appeared to have changed. The ambassador sent two limos to pick us up and take us wherever we needed to go. Our first stop was to the condo to drop off the luggage and the second destination was to reunite Milani's great grandmother with her family in this small at-the-edge of the city village. They were all out in front of the small dwellings, patiently waiting. Most of the neighbors seemed to be there as well. There were tears of joy on almost everyone's face. It was truly a Kodak moment to save for a future reference.

Milani was a little withdrawn and we realized that two years and a half plus a couple of months is a long time to a small child and some of the memories takes time to process and bring back to the forefront of the brain. Milani was now seven. She left when she was four and a half. We spent six months or a little more in Iwakuni Japan, before moving back to the states. Milani's English had improved greatly and her great grandmother understood more than she was able to relay back in words.

We left Milani and her great grandmother there, but Milani had a slight problem with Slapp and Max leaving her behind. So Max agreed to spend the first night with Milani and we promised him that his Uncle Slapp would drop off him some fresh clothes later that evening. We made a quick stop to rent a SUV and release the second limo to return back to the embassy. We made a quick stop at the embassy to show our appreciation.

The staff appeared to be the same except there had been a replacement for Miss Beasley and Gayle's position. No one had been hired to replace old Mr. Charlie, the inside night roving patrolman. One of the guards from the security booth had taken Mr. Pauling's place on the watch bill at night and a new local guy had been acquired to fill that vacant position in the security booth. When we arrived through the side motor pool entrance the ambassador stood there smiling from ear-to-ear to greet us.

"Wow," he said as he welcomed us with out stretched arms. "I never thought that I would ever see any of you again and I never hoped or dreamed of laying eyes on you in a group. I am without words to express," said the ambassador as he held out his wide spread arms to embrace us. Miss Beasley moved closer first to offer a deep Asian style bow and then reached to shake the emissary's hand just as he completed his return-acknowledging bow. "My dear Mrs. Carrington, tell me, how have you been? You look absolutely radiant and I am so delighted to see that you are well and thriving." Next he turned to face Kate, whom he had met only briefly at the

Christmas party that we had enjoyed, before we had departed. "I remember this pretty lady, she was your girlfriend Mr. Alvin that came for a visit, if I'm not mistaken. I recently learn that you had gotten married so that means that this handsome young man must be your son. Well Miss Kate, it is truly an honor to see you again and your son and his family." He turned quickly to Slapp. "You have done very well for yourself Mr. Alvin and I'm quite pleased to see that you have matured a bit more."

"Yes Sir, and thank you." Then the ambassador leaned forward to take my hand as he inquired about Alex.

"Miss Helen, it's nice to see you again and tell me, how is Mr. Alex and your very entertaining father?"

"Oh, Alex is well sir and my father is here in the city and has set-up a comeback tour here during the summer, you must go to see him one night. He will be more than happy and surprised to see you one night in the audience." He bowed again before releasing my hand.

"I promise you Miss Helen that I will be sure to do that. Please give your father's scheduled appearances to my secretary. Now tell me, where will all of you be living? I do have a few vacancies here. If you require more privacy, Miss Gayle's apartment next door is still available, just as she left it, if I may add." I spoke up quickly.

"Oh no Sir, we have rented a condo out near Stanley's Marketplace, my father has his old room back at the resort. We have Max, Milani and her great grandmother with us and we plan to stay for the summer. We came back so Milani and her great grandmother could visit their family like we promised."

"Very well then, I will sign the orders so you all will have permanent visitor's badges while you are here in the city and if there is anything else I can do, please let me know."

We all departed the way that we came in, as Slapp decided to go down to the cafeteria to visit the old Asian lady that he harassed, almost daily, before. We all waited in the SUV.

Back at the condo, we unpacked our things. We gave Slapp the master suite, since he was a party of three. I took the smaller room with the twin beds and gave Miss Beasley the next largest room in case Mr. Dexter came for a visit. I packed a bag for Max and Slapp and I took the SUV to shop for food and drop off Max's pajamas and fresh clothes.

Two weeks after we arrived back in Hong Kong, Slapp, Kate and Cameron their son took a weeklong trip to Thailand. Miss Beasley and I took the kids to the Hong Kong Disney theme park. Milani was to young to remember her first trip there before we left previously. One month into the trip Alex informed us that he would join us a week before our return date. I didn't get to see much of my father. The comeback summer tour was a great success and the contracting company had booked most of the gigs on the road. We had a chance to spend a few dinners with Officer Su Ki Chang Jr. He was planning to relocate to the states and Alex promised to help him. His grandparents had passed on the winter before when the SARS virus had swept through the region. They were too elderly to resist the strain, even after taking the vaccine.

Our plans for the summer worked out great. Officer SuKi Jr. was able to travel back with us. He moved in with Milani and her great grandmother, which in fact were his cousins, by marriage. As I stated before, Milani and her great grandmother lived right next door to Slapp and Kate's brownstone apartment. My father was having such a good time until he agreed to stay another month or so and my foster-mother agreed to fly out the last two weeks of the tour. We closed our storage units down and brought all Gayle's personal items that she had left in her apartment, which was located next door to the American Embassy, Hong Kong branch. In fact, as I said before, it was apart of the embassy's compound. The ambassador threw us an unbelievable departure party, right there inside the consulate and arrange to have all our expenses taken care of to move our things back to the States. He used an employee's shipping contract clause that was attacked to Miss Beasley's long history of employment and shipped everything back as one order. There were happy and sad tears shed that night, yet none of us had a desire to look back to a place that had been the backdrop of so many mixed emotional memories.

Chapter Seven

Great Grandmother's Demise

The holidays arrived and were quickly over that year and now we had one more thing to celebrate. Tate and Gayle had accepted a missionary assignment back to Iwakuni Japan. We all felt that this was great, because we had been there before. It was a five-year mission obligation and we all promised to visit. Tate placed all their things in storage and gave up the condo where he had lived since his first wife had died. It was a bittersweet farewell, but we all knew that this was something that was coming.

Three years later, it was time for Milani and her great grandmother to travel back. Milani was almost eleven years old and Max was fourteen plus. We knew they were old enough to travel alone with Milani's great grandmother, so we booked their flight. A month after they arrived, the great grandmother mysteriously died. Alex and I flew over for the funeral. Tate and Gayle met us there from Japan. Afterwards, Alex and

I brought Max and Milani home with us. Milani became very sad and distant. She moved in with us full time, but spent a lot of time with her cousin Su Ki Chang Junior and with Slapp and Kate next door. At first we believed that she wanted to spend more time near Cameron. School called a few times about her slipping grades so we set up some counseling for her. Her grades improved, but her attitude continued to deteriorate.

We asked if she wanted to go back to Hong Kong for a while, but she declined our offer. When we had a meeting with the therapist, she said that Milani talked about a best friend that she had made, but it wasn't in Hong Kong. The only place we could think of was while we were all in Iwakuni Japan. We were there for about seven months and she met this little Japanese girl about her age, which was an only child as well and the two of them were inseparable from the time they met. Later, they had kept in touch briefly. The counselor informed us that this might help.

Alex and I were both retired at this point and we had enough income to place Max and Milani in private school, while in Japan. With Tate and Gayle there on their mission; it would be sort of like old times. We knew that Slapp and Kate wouldn't like the idea of us leaving them behind, but they were at a different place in their lives. Cameron was still young and Kate was still very interested in her charity work with the city.

Slapp's parents had settled in together, my foster-mother and father had decided to give it a go. Miles, Daniel and their mother were doing well. Miles had opened a second martial arts school. Officer Su Ki junior had transferred to New York to be near his father and further his career. Mr. Pauling's catering business was doing great. Old Mr. Charlie had moved back to his hometown down south and was living on the old homestead near his brother.

We talked it over with Max and Milani about moving to Japan for a while; perhaps until they finished school. Max gave a thumbs-up sign, but it didn't seem to matter one way or the other to Milani. We decided to just do it. At this point, we were willing to try anything to perk Milani up a bit. At this point we seemed to be losing a little more of her daily. She would spend hours looking at old photos of her father that she had never met and a few pictures of her mother. Sometimes late at night she would come into our bedroom and sleep at the foot of our bed, across our feet. She was like a sad puppy with a toothache; no happiness or pleasure to be found and no way to express her feelings.

We packed up our things and we arrived in Iwakuni around August 5th the following year. Alex had gone on ahead a few days before. When the children and I arrived Alex informed us that we had missed one of the largest annual firework exhibits that the town of Iwakuni displayed. The event was held each year near the Kintai Bridge, which appeared to be the center attraction for this small quant community. Way above this shallow basin and historical bridge perched on the top of a mountain was this old castle that hovered over the community like a ninja warrior that had been assigned to guard the people below since his birth. The mysterious castle created an amazing backdrop for this bridge and town and served as a deep embedded cultural reminder of an era that had long since passed away. It drew thousands of visitors each year. It was lit up each night as though someone lived there. The five wavy humped bridge and deserted castle perched high about it had now become a very busy and lucrative tourist attraction to visit for all who were unfamiliar with its story. A few of the local old-timers knew many of the stories that had been passed down through the centuries in the form of songs, poetry, theater performances and tall tales. These were repeated around the campfire or in this case at the village festivals, about the old castle and the five-humped bridge below and they understood the power in which they held over the people that knew and embraced their local history. Some newcomers would come to learn and fall in love with the mysteries as well. I became one of those people.

Our second arrival in the township of Iwakuni was completely different than the first while in exile, because this time we had returned with a more relaxed mindset and in search of yet another type of refuge. A place that would perhaps breath some life back into or little Milani.

We were received and embraced openheartedly by the residence; especially the ones that remembered us from before and others that were informed of our arrival by the local missionaries. There was a nearby military base that was shared by the Japanese Navy air wing identified as MCAS, Iwakuni, Japan. The first few weeks there, we were allowed to reside at the Munson lodging quarters, because of Alex's lengthy affiliation with the bureau. Alex quickly acquired a contract position at the medical clinic as a contract paper-pusher and I landed a job as a dental hygienist. We were able to enroll the children in school without any problem. We also signed them up for martial art classes.

Milani's interest in the ancient craft was a little disturbing. She began to read whatever she could find in the base library about the subject. The instructor even had us talk to her about how aggressive she had become in class with the other students. She earned a few belts very quickly. Milani had remained a small petite person like her mother, yet she was tough enough and carried more of the Jones features than Max, in many ways. At times this also bothered Milani.

After our arrival, I immediately joined the JAS (Japanese American Society) and we began to attend the chapel on base. I also joined a Wednesday morning tea group that was held in the base chapel's library. I met some very wonderful ladies there. The gathering was religious based to teach the locals about Christianity and give them an opportunity to learn more about American ways and to learn a little English as a bonus. Before I arrived, the tea had turned into more of an all you-can-eat weekly buffet. The ladies brought in so much food and would trade dishes. It usually lasted from around 11:30 until around 2:00 in the afternoon. Some local dishes were an acquired taste, yet I tried to blend in. Within a few days, I was totally taken in by the people, the culture and our breath taking surroundings. The bamboo covered mountains, the ocean filled with island rock formations, the lotus fields and fresh produce on almost every corner. While in Iwakuni, we had it all. Iwakuni is like a part of the world that is frozen in time that was created as a place of healing. Crime is so low until it's like living in a bubble. The pace is slow, easy and therapeutic.

Our first road trip was to another military base area. Sasebo Japan, which is about four and a half hours away. We had met the Medical Clinic's OIC secretary and she agreed to be or translator and travel guide. Her name was Missie-san and we took her along as well as one of her long-time friends that later became known as the broken-navigator or Broken-navie for short. We rented a car from the base car rental office and the four of us were on our way; Alex, Missie, Broken-Navie and myself. It was only a four and a half hour drive, but that all depends on how long you stayed at the rest-stop noodle shop, whether or not you missed the slit in the road and lastly if you followed the two Garmin GPS' that you had guiding you the entire way, in Japanese. We arrived a little after midnight totally exhausted from the trip and from laughing so hard that we had gotten lost with two resident Japanese ladies in the car and two the GPS devices. Hence the nice name was born for Masako as Broken-Navi.

If I remember correctly Lady Masako had a friend in the Sasebo area, in which she had met ten years before on a cruise, but had only kept in touch through letters, phone and the emails. On the trip, Masako's gracious lady friend agreed to show us around for a few hours, as they talked non-stop in an attempt to catch up. The lady was an extremely nice and informative hostess and took us on a famous tour in the area called the 99-island tour. The tour was given from a small pirates-replica tour boat. The weather was brisk while on the water, yet the sun was bright and warming. We took lots of pictures, hugged and posed while having the time of our lives without any prior inclination that this would take place. Once again friendship bonds were formed for life, even if we never saw each other again, plus some well needed healing was experienced as we all agreed that the day was a great one and would linger in our hearts long after we had parted.

A few miles away, is the town of Arita, in which is well known and documented for its china, porcelain and very important cultural history. We picked up a second tour guide that had agreed to spend a day with us. He was a doctor and was affiliated with the American based medical department. He was very polite, well dressed and proved to be a gracious host as well. We had lunch at a fabulous antique porcelain shop and restaurant. We decided that we would make this one of our regular stops, with each trip back to the area.

Even as I think back, Arita is unbelievable to me and almost impossible for me to describe with the passion that is required for one to understand how wonderful I felt as I walked her streets and took in the beauty and talent of her people, surroundings and the exquisite craftsmanship that the area has been known for, for centuries. The history and dedication that has been passed down from one generation to the next, as you view all the products; evoked a feeling deep inside that you may not have known existed until that moment. At that instance, one began to only slightly understand the place that God has allowed you to experience with your own senses. It was life altering for me like so many other places that I visited there, during my short stay in such a majestic land.

While in Arita and the adjoining towns, once again time seemed to stand still and some well needed healing took place while I embraced the neighboring sites that appeared to be more creative-inspired gifts from God. The first trip was only one of many that were taken with our tour guide Miss Missie-San and Masako-San better known to some as broken-navigator (broken navie).

After a few more short trips to the local flea markets, 100yen stores, farmer's markets that only opened up to the public every few years or so; that first summer was over. The cooler winds off the mountaintops swept in slowly each day as did the salty breezes from the ocean that encompassed us from two sides. The bamboo forest gradually changed into its fall-color attire as the underbrush and foliage, which lay quietly at its feet, shed their vast array of summer flowering hues as well. The beauty that my eyes experienced and soul embraced, for the sake of pleasant memory, has no words to express.

During this season, the tide continued to move further from the shore until all that was left in the isolated manmade lagoons and canals where lonely mud and barnacle covered fishing boats resting on their paint-stripped sides that bared a resemblance to a deserted graveyard of once sea- worthy vessels from years gone by. The pictures of them lying there, while seemingly uncared for, sadden me as I slowly drove through the narrow precise designed villages that were formed more than a hundred years before. Yet I knew that the spring rains would deliver fresh restoring tidewaters to these sleeping restful sea-travelers and all would be as before.

The lotus flowers and roots had all been harvested and the fields that had once displayed so much unexpected beauty, as far as the eye could see and ones heart could grasp, was now vast acreages of barren withered tanned hollow stocks reaching towards the sky out of the soggy wet-lands, which preserved their roots and prepared them for the next forthcoming season. Mother nature had mastered her craft of preservation by expressing her power in the next coming spring season with unexpected beauty.

The traditional American end-of-the-year holidays crept closer as the fall winds increased their strength, chilly briskness and speed. The tall bamboo forest trees only bowed briefly with grace to its force because of their numbers and their display of a tight-knit family-like unity, as they stood with the pride of the ages and strengthened by the determination of a culture to survive. The fall colors of the bamboo forest were nothing less than breath taking. Several times, as I attempted to absorb and catalog all the wonders around me to memory, I began to tear-up as I thanked God for allowing me to experience so much of his glory, while so far away from my birth homeland, amen.

***************Private Get-away*************

One night Alex and I decided to spend a romantic evening at the hotel that overlooked the Kintai Bridge. It was near the base and within view of the Kintai Castle as well, which was fully lit each evening so it could be seem for miles away and was somewhat of a beacon to the local folk. Our hotel room faced the castle and the bridge. There was a full moon that evening and lots of people enjoying the huge park on both sides of each end of the bridge.

The five-humped wooden structure was a walk-only pedestrian-crossing type bridge that linked two very important tourist portions of the park. Travelers came from all over, because of its history and this town had discovered a way to preserve the old ways of Japan while stepping into the future. The brook that ran underneath the Kintai Bridge was shallow, yet at various times displayed a very strong current. Portions of its basin served as a parking lot when the tide was out and a vast meeting area for several festivals that were held throughout the year. There were local venders selling memorabilia items and a variety of food choices. This was also a gathering area for the local youth and the natives that were still young enough at heart to know and remembered the old bridge and castle's long and historical heritage. The bridge and the castle were many things to many of the local people and tourist that came to see them. For some of the residence that had lived at their base for more than a hundred years, it was a reminder of remnants of a past distant life and a shrine to that era.

Yet to others it was a place to come and bathe in the beauty of the area while watching the melting pot of people meandering around with cameras, attempting to capture or lock a moment in time to photographic sheets of paper. Then there was Alex and I who knew and understood too little of the history of the castle and the bridge, yet enjoyed their awesomeness from our hotel window.

We opened our curtains so we could take in the full view from our hotel bed, as we sipped wine. Tate and Gayle had agreed to watch Max and Milani, in which required very little supervision. Iwakuni Japan was unbelievably safe and family orientated, until getting a sitter was merely a comfort task for piece of mind.

The night became chilly as it aged and the two of us snuggled and remembered pass romantic evenings together. The dim lighting from outside our window was the only thing that illuminated our room as we continued small talk prior to the much-enjoyed sexual foreplay.

"Alex, do you remember the last time we were together romantically and not interrupted by something or someone, one of the kids, or a phone call or even a change in your schedule?"

"It had been a long time Helen, or are you Monique tonight." We both laughed out loudly as we moved closer to each other."

"Oh, I don't know Alex, which one do you like the best?"

"I'm not sure Babe, let me think about it for a moment." Alex slowly reached over and gave one of my nipples a long tugging pressure pinch through my silky gown. Alex knew that this was one of my hotspots and he was aware of just what it took for me to become aroused. "I fell in love with you as Helen; a shy sweet innocent lady with very little sexual experience, even though she had been married twice before. Yet, I sort of became very fond of that woman that Tate created, while you two were in Hong Kong alone together. I still have a few questions about how he accomplished that." Then Alex moved leisurely and pulled my chin up to kiss me lightly on the lips, as we lie on our sides facing each other. He then moved his fingers back down to my breast as he continued the solo debate with himself. "It was easier to satisfy you in bed as Helen, but Monique brought more fire and aggressiveness to our love nest that I have learned to appreciate, and very quickly if I may add. Now I expect and enjoy that heat from Monique. Then there are other times that I miss the ole Helen."

I moved one of my hands to Alex's penis and started to rub it very lightly as he spoke with his lips almost in contact with my own. "So tell me Helen or should I say 'Monique', which person do you want to be tonight? I will be more than happy to make love to either of the two."

Alex pulled down the top of my gown to expose my breasts as he rubbed the back of his hand across the entire area. I added more pressure to my grasp around his penis and slowly stroked it. He kissed my lips as he sucked then into his mouth; first the bottom lip then the top one. I knew he wanted my tongue, so I gave it to him. He nibbled on it for a few seconds before moving his kisses to the side of my neck, then to my throat and then to one of my breast as he sucked it with a starved force that I didn't expect. I rolled on top as Alex continued to caress my breast deep inside his mouth. I made sure that each breast got equal time of pleasure, as I rubbed my tits back and forth over Alex's open and eager-to-please mouth and lips.

Alex shifted me to my back and moved his warm wet kiss downward on my sexually aroused body. His mouth finally arrived at my stomach where he slowed down his approach to my pelvic area directly below my belly button. I could feel my vagina secreting juices. My clitoris was now swelling and had become more exposed. I reached down between my thighs and opened my femaleness more in hope that Alex would somehow brush up against the enter walls of my personal organ. My body was producing heat and Alex pulled my gown off towards my feet. He then repositioned my legs at the knees and spread my thighs widely apart. I begin to pant with anticipation of Alex's hard powerful tongue extracting the accumulated moisture from my private juice box.

He gently moved my hand out of the way and spread me apart and massaged the area with his thumbs to tease my clitoris out even more into view. He placed one thumb inside my dripping wet juice box while the other hand reached around and over my bent thigh to pull back my clitoris' foreskin from the top. Alex forced his thick forceful thumb in deeper and deeper as I panted and begged for more. I grabbed the headboard and moaned out loudly. Alex then attacked my clitoris with his teeth very lightly, which drove me crazy as I squirmed around all over the bed. He then removed his thumb from inside and then moistened the entire hairless area with an open oral massage. I held the back of his head firmly for more pressure and in fear that he might stop before I reached my desired climax. Then his tongue stabbed deep inside my juice box as I held his head even tighter. A few moments later I came with a deep tone groan as Alex kept the pressure on. I closed my thighs around his head and pumped my body up off the bed against his mouth and intruding tongue. I released again and then relaxed back onto the bed and opened my thighs widely again.

Alex moved back up my body delivering sucking kisses as he ascended. He flipped me to my stomach, pulled my buttocks high into the air and slowly entered my cavern from the rear. We held that position for a long time as Alex took his time sliding his penis in and out from deep inside my female counterpart. It felt so good until I wanted to scream each time he advanced himself into me. He fingered and pinched my clitoris until I released the third time. Then he increased the speed of the inward thrusts until he reached an exhausting climax. We slid down onto the bed, while remaining coupled together and waited for a few moments before escaping to the lavished bathroom to freshen up.

Later that night, Alex and I placed ourselves in the sixty-nine position to pleasure each other in a way that we hadn't in a long time; slow and easy until we fell asleep. The next morning I woke up with Alex deep between my thighs taking his fill of me again. Then he moved up to enter me to stroke until he released. We made love in the shower and once more after breakfast. Check out was at eleven o'clock. Just before we got dressed while Alex sat on the side of the bed. I knelt between his thighs as I orally massaged all the remaining strength from him through his male pride. This caused me to become highly sexually stimulated again. We decided that we both needed a little more time, so we called the front desk to request a late checkout time.

We eased back into our hotel resting accommodations, as Alex reached for my substitute pleaser that I had packed. He turned it on and slowly inserted it inside of me as he kissed my mouth, neck and sucked my breast. I bucked around on the bed like a wild pony as I screamed with need. I took the toy from Alex's hand and slid down so I could take his limpness into my mouth, while the firm well-lubricated substitute satisfied my agitated vagina. I held that position for a very long time. Alex slowly rubbed my back and massaged my nipples with light pain and waited for me to complete my task.

When we got home, he went directly to bed, even though it was only three in the afternoon. Max and Milani thought that their father Alex was getting sick.

*********The Miller's Iwakuni Blues****************

After a few more weeks, we were introduced to the Millers. They were another couple that had been sponsored to be missionaries in the Iwakuni prefecture. They were traveling with one daughter, but we were informed later that they also had two other sons. The wife was second-generation missionary. I met her parents once and we all had lunch, along with Miss Missie-San. If my memory serves me correctly, there was Mr. and Mrs. Miller and their daughter Charity who was as cutie as a button. Plus there were Mrs. Miller's parents, Missie-san and I. We met at a little quant place at the base of the Kintai Castle and across from the Iwakuni Museum and large Public Park.

Mrs. Miller's Father and I sat across from each other that day, during lunch. He quietly relayed a very sad heart- retching story to me about how him and his wife had lost their entire first set of children, during a missionary relocation boat trip. Unfortunately his wife was sitting right next to him as he explained in detail about what had happened almost forty plus years before. There she sat very quietly as the tears, slowly and inconspicuously to some of the others, began to streamed down her face, as if this had only happened a few months before. I'm not sure why the elderly stranger felt that I needed to know something so personal about their family's history and something that appeared to have had such a painful memory for them. Perhaps he saw something in my eyes that I was unaware was visible. Or it could have been a spirit in me that he didn't want to waste anytime getting to know and felt that this was a way to break the ice, by sharing with me his most personal pain.

Perhaps it had nothing to do with me at all, and was simply a moment for him to enjoy more healing as he related the story out loudly, just once more. I'm sure that no one at the lunch table that day had any idea of the impact that the story had upon me or even gave it a second thought, after the re-account had been completed.

At any rate, there was an instant connection, which formed between the two of us as he repeated this emotional moment in time to me, from his long-ago past. Mrs. Miller father's story stayed in the front of my memory for a lengthy period of time and was reiterated each time I had the pleasure of seeing her. Even though God had shown his favoritism by blessing the couple with another family of children; each time I hugged Mrs. Miller; all the pain returned in my throat and chest just like it had done that first time I witnessed the story, relayed to me by her father. Even now as I pen it to paper, my eyes fill up with tears and my nostrils leak just a little. I had the chance to hear the highlights of that sad tale again. This time it was related to a group of us by Mrs. Miller husband Pastor Miller. He repeated the account with a tender heart and yet with a gladness that his wife, who was born in the second group of children to this couple, was now by his side.

It seemed that a boat was constructed and crew hired to take the missionaries and their family across the short distance to Okinawa. The weather was cold and the boat began to take on water. Soon all of them were in the water and the four children and two crewmembers were lost. The cold temperature of the water and the long period of time before the rescue arrived were too much to bear. I have learned some moments in life attach themselves to your emotional memory for an unexpected period. Occasionally they are transforming in some way and other times they just hurt each time you remember the details, during a quiet stolen moment.

***************Ambassador to Japan**************

The local people in Iwakuni appeared to embrace us with very little, if any noticeable, reservations. They contacted Alex through Missie-san and proposed to make him an Iwakuni Honorary Rotary Club Member. The Young Entrepreneur's club had been started decades before and had maintained quite a few of its original members that appeared to be well into their nineties in age. As a matter of fact, the night that we were asked to join them at an annual dinner, where they really put on the Ritz to celebrate the winter holidays, we sat with an elderly gentleman that was celebrating his 90th birthday. We sat at the first table with him and a few others. It was a great honor and an unforgettable experience. Missie-san served as our translator, and I'm sure she added a few improvised words of her own. Any spotlight was a dream-come-true for her. We later referred to her as busy Missy because she got very little sleep. She had more connections in the community than AT&T and she could get anything done in a moment's notice. She was free hearted with her wealth to a fault and everyone that came in contact with her benefited in some way or another. She made it a habit to help whomever she saw in need. It was nothing for her to stop her car and talk to a stranger or bring them to her restaurant for a meal. Then near closing she would take the food on base to the American men and women at the squadrons, so there wouldn't be any leftover food to through away. There was no doubt in our minds or hearts that Miss Missie-San knew, believed and trusted in our God. The missionaries in the area love her deeply and that certainly included Bishop Thaddeus Romano and his First Lady Gayle.

We were also invited to a couple of the annual Holiday Christmas parties, given by the associated doctors from the Japanese community that the local medical clinic on the military base had established a working, consulting and treatment relationship with. The sit-down dinner was held in the famous hotel, right across from the Kintai's Castle and Bridge. It was cool that night and rainy if my memory serves me correctly. Everyone was well dress and our party took lots of pictures with each other and the others that had been invited. A few strangers, whom we had never met before that evening, leaned in to take pictures with us, the Americans as we exited the elevators in the lobby. We thought that it was so quaint. They had had a few shots of Saki, no doubt however all in all it was very nice.

The quest at the dinner that night included the main doctors and nurses from the hospital, immediate members of his family, his staff and members of their families as well. In spite of the language barriers, which we found out later wasn't as much of a barrier as we thought; the holiday event was even better than Missie-san's prior briefing had prepared us. It seemed that the more spirits that the locals consumed, the clearer and better their English became. This was something that one had to experience to believe. I was informed later that the culture understands more English than they are willing to relay to you at first, afraid of being embarrassed if it is spoken incorrectly, but after a few drinks, this almost always goes away and they take on a entirely and more confident persona. I cherished these experiences and now later looking back, I find them tearfully heartwarming and amusing at the same instance.

Another portion of the event that I thought was wonderful at this annual social was that everyone in the room was given a gift. There was this very large table set up at the front of the room and just beneath the entertainment stage that is filled with fully wrapped gifts of all sizes. Upon entry, you check in at a desk at the door, and you are given a ticket with a number on it. Near the end of the night, different groups go up on stage and present their special presents. Then a team goes up and starts to call out the ticket numbers. When your number is called, you proceed to the table and chose any gift you want from the table.

You were allowed to stand there as long as you like to make your selection. The guest are so appreciative of their gifts and I can't tell you how much fun this was for all. Songs are sung, short speeches are made, and the night wouldn't be complete without live entertainment. This alone would force you to plan to attend the following year. In this culture, an event is never complete without live entertainment of some type, which they take very seriously. It seems as if everyone has a camera of some kind, and taking pictures to capture the moment is as important to him or her as greeting a person with a customary bow.

Dr. Shoji's holiday party was staged for after the Christmas holiday and was set with the same organized refinement that I had come to expect and appreciate. This

Culture of people had great respect for accomplishing things in a timely manner. No doubt, this precise attitude worked well for everyone concerned.

On some Saturday afternoons, Alex would meet one of the doctors from out in town and others at Missie-san's place, better known as Sako's restaurant. They were well known for their B.L.T.'s. It's a small quaint place and the food is very good. Most of her weekend success was in deliveries and locally held events, previously at the old location. There a few of them would sit, Dr. Tamada, Alex and a few other Saturday afternoon regulars as they drink tea, beer, or coffee. Music from old-school Motown would be playing in the background or classical, it all depended on the guest and the mood of the famous cook. I was informed later, to my surprise, the cook was a huge Whitney Huston's fan.

At any rate, Alex always seemed to return a couple hours later rejuvenated by the kind words and soft spirit of the local people that gathered their to share yet another stimulating moment. The male owner of the place wasn't a man of many words. He would come out the small kitchen to greet you and then hastily return to his large frying pan where he was preparing the bacon for their famous B.L.T's. The moment I met him, I fell in love with the calm gentle spirit within him and was drawn to hug him each time we met. I knew this wasn't a cultural practice for adults to embrace in public, but I felt that I had to take a chance my warm gesture wouldn't be misconstrued. After a few encounters, he seemed to warm-up to the hug greeting with a little more ease than initially. At a few events he walked up to me from behind and tapped me on the shoulder and waited for me to turn and give him my usual warm embrace. This is when I believed that he understood and appreciated my gesture.

The restaurant is located only a couple of blocks outside of the main gate of the American Military Base (MCAS), which is shared with the Japanese Navy Air Station and is backed up to the newly opened commercial Iwakuni Airport that so happened to celebrate its grand opening on 13 December, the year we were there. I understood that the area had a commercial airport, years before but it failed to draw enough travelers to maintain the need to stay open. This time it appeared to be different. The following year, Missie-san moved her restaurant to a larger location across the street and a few yards closer to the front gate of the military base.

We all settled into a winter's routine. The season was mild that first winter and we only received a few snowflakes even as the bright sun maintained its summery glow. The children in Iwakuni weren't rewarded with any snow-days that year, although we heard of some of the surrounding area that had. Milani and her best friend continued to find things to entertain themselves, like movie night at the base theater, sleepovers back and forth at each other's house and the list goes on. Milani appeared to be feeling a lot better and the pain of losing her great grandmother seemed to be subsiding. We continued her in therapy, back in the states via telecom. It was hard because of the thirteen-hour time difference. Max had his own circle of friends, as he and Milani seemed to spend less time together. We arranged for Milani to have her thirteenth birthday party on base at one of the housing community centers, building 1200. Needless to say, it was great. Of course the party theme was all done in Hello Kitty. The amount of photos we took was unbelievable. We later sent then off to a company to have them sorted and hard bound into a book with under-photo excerpts.

We were able to take a short trip to Tokyo to see the new Sky-tree that had newly opened March 2013. It was almost three times the height of the famous fifty-year-old Tokyo Tower. At the base of the new Sky-Tree was a shopping mall that was unforgettable. It was well designed and included shops and restaurant that insured that each shopper would desire to stay for hour, even if no purchases were made. The new Sky-Tree had its own separate gift shop and there was a fee to ride up inside and view the city, perhaps like very few people had ever seen it before.

Even while arriving to the city by airplane you could see the Sky-Tree for miles before you reached the city or land at the airports. The kids and I spent hours in the gift shop while trying to decide what we wanted to purchase for our closest friend and ourselves. In Japan its customary to bring back something from your trip to the family members, friends or co-workers that was unable to go with you. This custom and a few others can be very expensive if you are a popular person or if you have a large family or co-worker's pool. Any whew; when in Roman.

Max and Milani were doing very well in school. Milani was now learning a third language by spending so much time with her Japanese friend. I decided to pay for her to receive some tutoring so she could learn to write the new acquired language as well. As I said before, the winter was mild and we took long rides out into the countryside to observe how beautiful it was when all the foliage changed. Each countryside drive held an exciting experience as we discovered something that we hadn't noticed before.

A place called the Chicken-Shack was always one of our favorite stops for lunch or dinner. It was set up in a little old Japanese village type tourist area with gift shops, restaurants and places set-up for unbelievable photographic backdrops for pictures. The village is set in the side of a mountain. It has a waterfall, ponds, temple ruins, and old walking paths that included coy fishponds and gardens. The food is great and the service is fantastic. Removing your shoes is required tradition that we all quickly embraced.

The chilly spring arrived as it announced the Cherry Blossoms buds. The base chapel held Easter Sunrise Service on the

Kintai Bridge that year as we all stood shivering with our Sunday best on, which was unfortunately completely covered by our heavy overcoats. We took a few pictures and then raced back to the car. Later that Easter Sunday Morning I attended Pastor Miller's church at the 10:30 service. Missie-San was there, however I didn't stay for the brunch upstairs after the service. I dropped off the cupcakes for the kids and excused myself.

The 100yen stores and recycle marts continued to be my regular weekly stops as I was determined to return home with all the memorabilia and trinkets I could afford to collect to share with my friends and family, and to use as visual aids to express how much I loved and enjoyed Iwakuni Japan and its people. The people of Iwakuni had somehow manage to preserve the old ways and customs while allowing the new traditions to slowly weave its way into their culture. One good example of this was when I went into an old recycle shop near the Kintai Bridge.

There sat an old man in the very rear on the huge unorganized dusty shop, facing the front. At first and before your eyes adjusted from the bright sun outside, you didn't notice him at all as your focus was immediately drawn to all the artifacts. My first thought was that he must have collected all these items from two generations before. Then you realized that there was someone else there in the back. He was sitting on a low modest stool with a round pillow cushion, yet without a backrest. Behind him there was a large double sliding doors and just on the other side of those glass doors was a typical

Japanese garden that I'm sure that he had created. The scenic path, no doubt, lead to the living quarter of this vase unit compound. Everything was old and ancient looking, but well kept. And right when you believed that you couldn't be surprise or astonished by this unplanned stop, you noticed that this very old man had a laptop computer open and running right next to his abacus-calculator. That was my first confirmation of how this sleepy little village had integrated the new, while preserving the old. I hadn't seen an abacus being used since first grade when Mrs. Gary was teaching the class how to count and keep track. Soon we discovered other ways that the people had preserved their culture and way of life.

Being able to have our close circle of friends around had made this unplanned transition a lot easier. Tate and Gayle missionary work was coming along well and they made a few trips out of the area.

The next few years flew by and before we knew it Max was about to graduate from high school. We planned to send Max back to the U.S to attend college. Tate and Gayle had one more year before this assigned placement was complete and they would move back to the Maryland, D.C. area as well.

Milani was now 14 and Max was would be 18 on his next birthday. We gave Max a huge send off with all the bells and whistles, as they say. He had a choice of colleges and he decided to go to California State University. That was great because Gayle's daughter Samantha had remained out there and promised to look in on him from time to time.

Chapter Eight

Back For The Future

Two years later, when Milani was sixteen and after Gayle and Tate had moved back home, we decided that we should go home as well. Milani was able to graduate early. We promised Milani that her friend could come for a long visit and that we would sponsor her to attend college in the states if her parents agreed. Everything went as planned.

Two years into Milani's college major, she decided to change it to criminal justice with a backup in criminal psychology. We all thought that this was a very heavy load to carry in school, yet she was able to pull it off. Now at the age of twenty-six she had two masters degrees and one doctorate and spoke three languages. We all assumed that she wanted to teach, but when Milani locked herself in her room and filled out the application to the F.B.I academy, we knew that we had been dead wrong. At this time we had no idea that revenge had been her motive and driving factor for years. We never noticed or heard her angry silent screams.

There was nothing we could do to talk her out of it. The priest Father Caleb was an old man now and weak in health. We had even asked him to give it a try and he became momentarily ill stressed, during one of their in-depth talks. The priest attempted to explain to her how he had prayed for Alex and the others to find another line of work early on. Of course Milani listened patiently out of respect, yet nothing in her persona changed as Alex and I looked on. When she left the room, the priest asked if he could speak to us in private. He asked us how long had it been since she had seen the therapist. We informed him that it had been a few years. The therapist told us that she had done all she could do. Milani had closed off a part of herself that she wasn't going to let anyone inside.

Alex and I were now grateful that Milani and Slapp's relationship had remained strong over the years. Milani would talk to him about almost everything, but none of us had any idea what was up ahead of us as it pertained to Milani. We quickly realized that she had kept things from her Uncle Slapp as well. Over the next several months she became more and more withdrawn. One afternoon we heard her talking on the phone with her very best friend from Japan. She raised her voice and it sounded like she was cutting all tides. We thought that perhaps the depression had returned and she was thinking of hurting herself. It was like living with a stranger. All through the years Milani had continued her martial arts studies at Miles and or Daniel's marital arts dojo and gym. She had earned several more belts, with additional levels at this point and had expanded her training to other types of martial disciples that was a lot more vicious and deadly. Daniel told us once how she seemed mean spirited and he had to dismiss her from class on several occasions for being too rough with other students. Some of the others students were afraid of her and accused Daniel and Miles of spending extra time with her after class, because her technique was so advanced and because she was sort of like family.

We found out later that Milani had been spending a lot of time out at Uncle Burney's place, looking and studying his old case files. She told us that it was for her classes, but now we realized and begun to believe that her research had more of a sinister element.

When Milani turned in her application to the bureau's academy, it probably seemed as though she was asking to take part in the next graduating class. Twenty more weeks of intense training was the last thing that she needed. Alex and I invited Slapp and Kate over one afternoon to pick Slapp's brain (find out how much he knew about the decision Milani had made). They arrived around seven in the evening. Alex answered the doorbell.

"Come on in my brother." Slapp and Alex shook hands and gave a shoulder-to-shoulder tap hug. Kate brought up the rear as Alex guided her inside the door and into his arms as he gave Kate a kiss on the lips and then hugged her with both arms. Slapp laughed enviously as he commented.

"Hey Alex, be careful man. That's the mother of my child."

Alex waved his hand in a humorous manner as he replied, "You are kidding right? This night isn't long enough for me to tell Kate all the inappropriate things you've done to my women over the years; now your ass want to be sensitive about a little kiss." Alex pulled Kate in closer to drive his point home. Come on Kate sit next to me, perhaps I can cop a feel when no one is looking." Kate smiled as if she had been in on the joke with Alex to upset Slapp. The four of us took a seat.

"Well Alex, what is this all about? You sound really serious when you called me on the phone." Alex stroked the side of his face with an opened-hand as if he hadn't figured out just how to ask Slapp the question. Kate and I made eye contact briefly because I had already told her about Milani's plans. I could tell by the look of Slapp's face that this would be Slapp's first time hearing anything about this. The room fell into an uncomfortable mode as Kate and I held our breath until Alex spilled the beams, as some like to proclaim.

"Slapp, do you know anything about Milani applying to the Bureau's academy?" Slapp's mouth flew open as his entire face wrinkled up into an ugly frown of disbelief. It was almost as if he had forgotten to breath as he sprang to his feet and began pacing in a small circular area. Becoming upset didn't begin to explain Slapp's response to the news. Slapp felt the pain of betrayal instantly wash over him because he thought that no one was as close or as open as he and Milani had been over the years. They shared secrets with each other like no one else in the extended family circle. Milani had even become like a big sister to Slapp and Kate's only child Cameron. Why had she chosen this important move in life to keep it secret from Slapp? No one had a clue. Of course Milani knew that her Uncle Slapp wouldn't approve and she was sure that he would try to talk her out of it. She expected all of those reactions from him, so why the secret? Slapp snapped with the pain on the edge of his voice and in his mannerism.

"What the hell are you telling me Alex," replied Slapp after a few moments of shock? "Has anyone talked to her and told her how much shit we had to go through to come-in out the field and get a portion of our lives back? Did anyone sit her little ass down and tell her how I almost had to go to jail? Does she have any idea how much the bureau has changed over the years; so much until we don't know who are the good guys and who are the bad ones? Has she lost her damn mind?"

Then Slapp stopped for a moment to calm himself down enough to answer Alex's initial question. "No Alex, I had no idea what Milani was planning. I remember back when she changed her major, she asked me a lot of questions about what the secret service look for in a candidate. She also asked me what I had in my package when I applied years ago. I thought that this was all for a class and that she was merely using me as show-and-tell project, you know; to impress her instructor at school. I was flattered; to say the least and I assumed that she was asking me those questions because I was an instructor at Quanico. I had no idea that she was pumping me for inside information. I'm sure that all that time she spent out in the country with my father, going through his old unsolved files; that she had the same gratifying effect on him as well. As you know, it's always a good feeling when someone takes an interest in something that you are passionate about. I don't believe anyone enjoyed issuing a little street-justice more than the group of us, back in the day. There was no lack of passion in us in that regard."

Slapp then sank down hard onto his seat as he stared at the floor, while shaking his head negatively. After a moment he brought his eyes up to Alex's level. "So Alex, what's your plan? How can I help? I feel partly responsible for not giving you guys a heads up. As a trained profiler, I should have seen this coming." Then Alex let Slapp off the hook.

"Don't worry about it now, my brother. There was no way of knowing what she had been planning all this time. I just want to know why she decided this, while knowing what all of us went through to get out. Why would she do this to hurt us, why; knowing how we felt and how much we would worry?

"Has anyone else tried to talk her out of it, Alex?

"Yes, everyone has tried; even Father Caleb. As a matter of fact he became ill when he found out. He feels like he should have been praying that none of our children would decide to follow into our previous footsteps all that time he was praying for us to get out."

"Listen Alex, I will talk to her."

"Okay Slapp, I have to warn you that she can turn on you without a moments notice. For a while we thought she was on drugs when she threaten us. I backed off, because I didn't want to have to shoot her ass in a non-threatening location to get her attention. With her taking all those martial art disciplines and given my age, I felt that this might be my only option. The therapist said that she thinks that this is that dark corner that she was never able to get her to open up about, during their sessions."

"What exactly are you saying, Alex? Did Milani threatened to harm you two? Oh that's it; I'm going to whip that ass like I did that time she lied to me about where she had gone after school."

"No Slapp, she never threatened to hurt us physically, she promised us that she would leave and we would never see her again, if we pushed too hard."

"Oh, let me make sure I understand you. Are you saying I should be afraid of her? I will spank her little tender ass if she tries to give me any lip while I'm talking to her. I don't give ah shit how many belts she has earned in the martial arts. You all know that we spoiled Milani and now we have to deal with the little trifling monster that we have created." Kate looked over at Slapp as if her daily free-counseling sessions had somehow failed. Slapp noticed her glance. "What Kate, do you think I'm going to allow a little ninja-want-a-be to hurt me and just walk away? I don't think so." Alex went on as Slapp turned his focus back towards him.

"Slapp, look, we are asking you to talk to her as a last resort. There is nothing we can do, because she is of legal age. Besides, we don't want to lose her forever by crowding her. At any rate, can you just talk to our baby and try not to hurt her in the process." Slapp answered up quickly with a distancing tone at the edge of his voice, as though Milani had broken a blood oath.

"I'll see what I can do Alex, but all bets are off about me not spanking that ass. We spoiled her because we all loved her so much and now we have to deal with this shit. I'm ole-school and I believe that you are never too old or mature to get a serious ole-fashion ass whipping. I also believe that it cures a lot of short-term mental illnesses. I'm sorry Helen, but we have to go. I'm a little upset. I need to clear my head before I talk to Milani. What really bothers me is that she used me and treated me like yesterday's newspaper. And then there is the fact that I never saw it coming. What can I say, perhaps it's time to completely get out of the game when someone that you once gave a bath to, can take advantage of you and you don't notice any warning signs."

We could all see that this was hurting Slapp more than any of us ever imagine that it would. We realized at that moment that we should have asked him months before, about Milani and kept Slapp and Kate in the loop about her progress with the therapist. All of us knew how fragile Slapp could be mentally, or perhaps we had forgotten. Since he had made a commitment to Kate, he seemed much stronger. Now all we could do was hope that Slapp could get through to Milani before the bureau mailed her an acceptance- notice package.

A few days after that night, Milani moved out and got her own place. She asked me for some of the money that her father had left me. I didn't have a problem with that. Austin didn't know anything about her or that he had even fathered a child before he died, but I was sure that he would have wanted me to give her a share. Milani asked me for the money as if she was entitled to it. Now I understood what Slapp had felt a few nights before. I wanted to slap the diarrhea-shit out of her myself for her nasty smug attitude. I didn't care about her asking for the money, it was the way that she had approached me. Slapp did talk to her, but she showed no remorse for all the people that she had hurt with her decision and deceptions.

When the new class started at the academy the following year, she was enrolled. Milani placed her household-affects in storage and moved to a larger apartment once she completed the training. We lost track of her for a few months except when she called Max and little Cameron. They were the only two of us that supported her choice, so she kept them in her life.

Milani's Christmas Blues

The following Christmas celebration was held at our house and Milani arrived fashionably late, just before we sat down to eat. Well to be honest, it was more of a buffet free-style where you could eat whenever you decided that you wanted. Alex and I had purchased a home-lot site in the same area as Slapp's parents. The people that lived there before had decided to scale-down and move into something smaller.

When Milani arrived, she appeared a little more approachable than before, but remained focused to her cause while holding firmly to her ground, whatever the hell that was. She had gifts for everyone. The moment that she walked in and spoke, Slapp and I both became teary-eyed.

"Hello everyone," greeted Milani with a huge suspicious smile. Alex ran over to hug her and kiss her face. I tried to push the tears back into my tear-ducts as Slapp turned quickly and headed towards the bar to freshen up his drink. Slowly everyone else moved towards the door to welcome her with hugs and kisses. There we all stood, not knowing what to say or how to act in fear that she might become angry and leave. She definitely had her Uncle Alex's short temperament; who had now become her father through adoption.

There was Fred and his second wife, who had driven up from Florida, Tate, his mother and Gayle Tate's wife, Slapp and his wife Kate and son Cameron, Slapp's parents Uncle Burney and Miss Beasley, Gayle's daughter Samantha, our sons William and Max, my parents Uncle Oscar and foster mother, and to top it off just by chance was ole Mr. Charlie and his wife who had come for the holidays to see his half brother Deacon Sylvester Cunningham Sir Senior.

Mr. Charlie pushed his way through the gathering and paraded his drunken blind ass right up in front of Milani. The last time that he had seen Milani was when she was four and a half. Mr. Charlie was now sipping on his fourth drink of the evening, in which if I may add, didn't exactly mix well with his disposition or his impatient advance-in-years age. He was no doubt at the stage in life where he felt like he could say whatever he damn well please to whomever he wanted and then just walk away. After all, what the hell he had to lose? The least of Mr. Charlie's concerns were embarrassing himself and plus humiliating others had even taken a backseat to the previous non-worry I just mentioned.

He leaned forward and down a little as he addressed Milani who only stood about 5 feet 6 inches tall. Milani's back was still against the door as she waited to see if she was welcome to stay.

"Hey there Little Lady, do you remember me? You know sweetie, Ole Mr. Charlie from the embassy in Hong Kong," said Mr. Charlie as he waited while weaving back and forth ever so slightly. "I remember you well." Then Mr. Charlie stood up straight and paused for Milani to answer him. Milani just stared directly into Mr. Charlie's face as if he was a circus clown offering her candy that she had been trained to refuse and she then smiled briefly. Mr. Charlie became very irritated by her cold gesture and had no problem letting her know it. "Yelp! She's a damn Jones all right. None of them, that I have had the non-pleasure of meeting, has any respect for their elders or for people who are trying to be nice to their silly ass. I'm pretty sure if her biological parents were here, they would be whipping that ass around about now for not showing me the proper respect I deserve, even though I'm drunk. But these substitute stand-in parents has spoiled her little half-breed ass because she is so cute. But it's not going to work out for you, just mark my words. I've been around long enough to know that if you take the wrong fork in the road, sooner or later you are going to have to pay a serious toll for the path you've taken. These are the rules of nature, whether you chose believe it or not."

Mr. Charlie then quickly turned towards Alex to check Alex's reaction to his too-familiar out-of-line statements. "Well Mr. Alex, I guess you will be throwing my old drunk ass out your home right about now?" He then attempted to take another sip from his empty glass, while weaving back and forth, and speaking in a sadden tone, "And it's such a nice party too. You think I can stay if I apologize real nicely?" Some of us in the room smiled, while the young people laughed out loudly and still others totally ignored Mr. Charlie's behavior as they all kept their eyes focused on Milani.

Of course Slapp was quietly laughing out of control as the remainder of us stood firm, while waiting for Milani's full reaction. After a few more moments, Slapp quickly move to the front of the gathering and affectionately grabbed Ole Mr. Charlie around the shoulders and ushered him to the kitchen for a well-needed cup of black coffee or perhaps two. Slapp was using that easy voice, as he continued to only smirk a little.

"Com'mon Mr. Charlie with me. We need to freshen up your drink with some coffee, what do you think? The night is still young, and you need to slow it down a little." Mr. Charlie physically obeyed as he verbally objected.

"Coffee, coffee," he repeat as he held the glass closer to Slapp's face and eyes while yelling? "Are you blind like me Son, even I can see well enough to know that this is a glass, not a cup? I am required to pour good expensive liquor in such a fine led crystal glass like this one, not coffee, boy." Mr. Charlie's speech was slurred and every other word was now mixed with saliva spray, as he went on. "For the life of me I can't believe that your parents, as intelligent as they both are, produced such soft-headed son." Then Ole Mr. Charlie's voice sank to a loud whisper as he changed the subject in the middle of his insulting train of thought, which was a sure indication to Slapp that Mr. Charlie had had way too much to drink. "I wonder if the hostess will let me keep just this one glass as a memento of tonight's event."

Mr. Charlie held the glass up and closer to his eyes for inspection. "You would think, for a party this grand they would have a few engraved or something. We don't have anything like this at home. The way I have it calculated, Alex married a woman that already had money. Now that was a smart move. Alvin, did you marry a woman with money too? You young bucks could have taught me a thing or two after all, hum. My wife and I started out below ground zero, but we did alright for ourselves, don't you think?"

Slapp never answered as he remembered that in fact he had marry a woman of means, because Kate had caught the lottery before they had met. Then Mr. Charlie forcefully grabbed Slapp by his shirt collar, near his throat and pulled him in nearer as he spoke these words in a real whisper, as the subject changed yet again. "You know Mr. Madison," then he paused. "Don't look so shocked that I remembered your name. You know I have always been a little concerned about you and how bright you may or may not be, even when we were all back at the embassy. You do know that this is a party, and at a shindig this grand everyone is expected to drink plenty of good ole-fashion liquor. I've noticed that you are kinda' slow sometimes, so I'm gon'na help you out just this once." Then his voice escalated again as he released his grip on the front of Slapp's shirt and patted Slapp's chest a few times in an apologetic fashion. "But you have to promise me that you will never ever offer a man a cup of coffee at a get-together like this; can you do that for me, son? Go on and say 'yes' and make an old man happy." Then ole Mr. Charlie laughed out loud and slapped the empty glass to Slapp's chest as they continued to walk towards the kitchen.

Slapp finally answered yes as he continued to wrestle Mr. Charlie through the gathering and into the kitchen to a nearby chair at the kitchen table. Slapp turned on the coffee pot as he repeatedly tried to control his laughter in fear that his amusement would agitate Mr. Charlie further.

In the front entrance portion of the house, Milani removed her coat and continued to pass out the gifts that she had brought. Uncle Burney was the last person to give her a hug and you could tell that Slapp had relayed all the details to him about her decision and that he was disappointed and hurt. Milani's love for Slapp had made Uncle Burney feel like she was the little sister that Slapp never had or would ever have at this point. So that kind of made him her father as well. Anyone could observe that Milani's decision to join the bureau was more painful to her Uncle Burney than a disappointment. Uncle Burney left the room to go to the kitchen to check on Slapp and Ole Mr. Charlie. Slapp was now pouring the warm coffee into the glass that Mr. Charlie refused to give up. Just as Uncle Burney sat at the table to join them, Mr. Charlie cut Slapp to the quick.

"Oh, so you think I'm damn fool? You think I can't tell the difference between coffee and booze?" Uncle Burney chimed in as Slapp did everything he could do not to laugh out loudly. Burney took over with a scolding tone.

"Damn it Mr. Charlie, drink the coffee before both of us get thrown out. I know I'm too drunk to drive home and I only live right up the road. As a matter of fact, if it wasn't so cold and I had worn my other jacket, I could walk. I've already made my reservations to spend the night. What about you, Mr. Charlie", said Burney as his voice returned to a more pleasant and understanding tone? It's snowing outside right now. Another hour or so and that narrow road that leads up here won't be passable. You might have to visit your brother tomorrow. Now go on and drink the damn coffee, the bar isn't about to close yet. Sober up a bit and then you can start all over again. You still have a couple of hours before 'Last Call'." Then Uncle Burney turned to Slapp with Milani's pain still in his eyes. "Pour me a cup too Son, I think I've had enough hard stuff for tonight. Seeing that sweet child get all caught up in with the bureau's mess has just drained the holiday spirit right the hell out of me. I guess that it is all our fault."

Slapp left his father Mr. Burney and ole Mr. Charlie in the kitchen and rejoined us in the living room. The music was playing softly in the background, yet there was an irrefutable dreariness about the room. Cameron was now a teenager and had just completed his first year of college and stood taller than Milani. She walked over to him to give him a long compassionate hug and kissed his cheek, as he stood frozen while not knowing what to expect, then returning the syllabling-like affection. Milani spoke warmly to Cameron as all the others began to move around the room, and rejoin the conversations that were taking place, prior to Milani's disturbing arrival. Milani and Cameron were engaged in their own private conversation in the corner of the room. Max was standing close enough to hear them, but made no move to join the two of them.

"I know you don't remember this Cameron, but I was very jealous of you when you were born. Until you came along, your father, my Uncle Slapp was the closest thing that I felt I had to a real dad."

"What about Uncle Alex, didn't he adopt you and bring you here to live with us?

"Yes he did, and I love him too. But the first person that made me feel safe and still does to this day is your father, my Uncle Slapp. I can't explain it. Maybe it's because he never expected anything from me and he was hard on me right from the start. I don't know, maybe it was because he never treated me different. Now that I think about it, perhaps it was because we never knew our real parents when we were growing up and he understood that empty space in me. Even today Cameron, I still trust him with all my secrets, well perhaps not all of them. I never told Uncle Slapp that I was going to join the secret service. How is he now as a father?"

Cameron perked up quickly as the two of them continued their private talk in the corner, while some of us looked on.

"Oh, he's a great dad and I can't think of anyone else that I would rather have for a father, except maybe your father Uncle Alex. He has saved my ass more than once or twice when my father wanted to ground me. Uncle Alex always threatened him with some stuff from their past and my dad would come around pretty quickly and lighten up on me, just a little." They both laughed and moved closer to the table of holiday snacks, which included everything that you could dream of for a Christmas diner. I called it free-styling. The kids enjoyed it more when we weren't so formal and you never knew when a neighbor would 'come-ah-calling' as the old cliché goes.

The Christmas music was now playing and neighbors continued to drop in and out to deliver and receive their annual seasonal gifts, as the night continued to slowly age. Around eleven Milani asked if she could speak to her father and me, in private. The three of us excused ourselves and moved into the kitchen. Mr. Charlie was still sulking at the kitchen table, about Slapp pouring him a cup of coffee in an alcohol glass, when the three of us walked in. I spoke to Mr. Charlie as he unintentionally ignored my polite gesture.

"Mr. Charlie, would you excuse us for a moment?" Alex smiled deeply as we waited for Mr. Charlie to leave the room, but he never moved. He was leaning over with both arms and elbow bracing himself up off the table, as he spoke with a slight slur and pity in his voice, as he gave a forward wave with one hand, for us to continue whatever we had planned.

"Oh don't mind me, ya'll go right ahead. I'm just an ole man and his liquor glass filled with pissy-warm coffee. Do you think the hostess would mind if I took this one home?" No one responded, so he answered his own question as Alex and I smiled. "Oh I guess they come in a set hum, I wouldn't want to break up a set. I believe that you should never break up a set of anything. It's never right, after you break up a set of something." I spoke to Mr. Charlie calmly in an attempt to stop his drunken babbling.

"Sure Mr. Charlie, you can take that glass when you leave. We have plenty of them. And if anyone asks what happened to it, I will just tell them straight up that I gave it to our ole friend Mr. Charlie." Charlie sat up taller now as if this small act of kindness had add a little more marrow to the bone in his spine.

"You would do that for me Miss Helen? You know I have always liked you Miss Helen." Then he turned his gaze to Alex. Mr. Jones you are a lucky dog to have a wife like Miss Helen. I really mean it, in two ways. You are lucky that she is so nice and giving and lucky for you that you found someone to put up with your arrogant ass." Then he dropped his head and laughed out loudly as he slapped the table top once with his hand. "Okay, Mr. Alex, I take it back. This is really a nice party and please don't throw me out. I will apologize a little more sincerely tomorrow, I'm a sort of drunk right now, you understand." Then ole Mr. Charlie appeared to have a brief moment of clarity. "Oh, I'm sorry, go right a head and have your little talk. I won't say another word." He made that zip-your-lip gesture with his right hand and looked back down into his glass of warm coffee.

Alex, Milani and me formed a tighter circle as we stood near the refrigerator to listen to what Milani had to tell us.

"Ma, dad I have drawn an assignment, back in Hong Kong. I didn't want to tell you over the phone for obvious reasons. I'm going undercover and I have been assigned a partner." My eyes instantly filled up with tears, but Alex was able to hold it together to ask all the crucial questions."

"So Baby Girl, how long will you be gone? Who is your partner? Do you have a base handler that will track you two and update you on all the new information that becomes available by the minute? Has he ever been undercover before? What is your extraction signal if things get too hot and they have to send someone in to get you out?" Milani threw up both her hands to Alex's face and raised her voice as she tried to answer all his questions before he shot off another set.

"Stop dad and listen," yelled Milani. Mr. Charlie raised his head up a little more and leaped dead center into our conversation, which was about ten feet from where he was sitting.

"Yelp, she's a Jones alright. Now just look at her; I told ya'll that she needed a spanking before she left Hong Kong, but nnnooooo, no one listens to old man Mr. Charlie because he's crazy and don't know what the hell he's talking about. Well that maybe true, but I raised three kids of my own and two that belonged to someone else and I believe I know when a child needs an attitude adjustment in the form of a good ole-fashion spanking. Now it's to late and it's way to late when they break your heart or give your old ass a heart attack. Is it possible that she's on them their drugs? Because them their drugs will make you raise your voice to your parents and a whole lot of other shit too? I'm so sorry if she's on drugs. If that's the case, don't whip the baby just get her some help; she's young, it's not too late." Mr. Charles choice of word phrases proved that the coffee wasn't helping much, or perhaps Slapp's coffee brewing skills were too weak to accomplish the task of making Mr. Charlie more coherent.

The three of us all turned towards Mr. Charlie and waited until he had gotten it all out of his intoxicated system of what he wanted to interject into our private family conversation. Which turned out to be anything but a private household moment. It was as though he had a conscious blackout while he was talking towards us. He couldn't seem to stop himself, so we just waited until Ole Mr. Charlie finished. He finally realized what he had done or was doing and became a little unnerved, as he quickly changed the subject as he stood to his feet to exit the kitchen. He pushed the glass away that had remained half filled with coffee as he spoke out loud to himself.

"What the hell, I don't have to drink this coffee. I can have a drink. I'm a grown-ass old man and I can do what I please, or the host can throw me out." Alex covered for him.

"Go ahead Mr. Charlie and have another drink, we will find you accommodation for the night here or at Mr. Burney's. It's fine don't worry."

Mr. Charlie continued to stumble on out of the kitchen as he went on talking to himself. "Now just listen to that, 'We will fine you accommodation for the night'. I tell you, this is some kind of classy party. When you get too drunk, the hostess will arrange for you a room to sleep it off. You can't beat that. Wait until I tell the boys back home, they aren't going to believe this high-class shit here.

Old Mr. Charlie had broken the tension in the room with his outburst antics and we three found some way to smile. A few second later Slapp joined our huddle just as Milani took in a full breath to answer Alex and I questions.

"Dad, Auntie Ma and you too Uncle Slapp I don't have all the answers yet. I am scheduled for a mission brief in two weeks. I have put my things in storage; will you pay it for me if I'm gone for more than six months. My partner is a seasoned agent I'm told, but I don't have a name. I guess I will be given the extraction code word at the briefing. Please promise me that you won't worry about me."

The tears were running down my face and the knot in my throat and stomach was so big until I couldn't speak. Alex hugged me, while Slapp held tightly to Milani.

"Listen Milani," said Slapp. Do you remember the word you would leave on my phone whenever you wanted me to pick you up from school? Well, nothing has changed, I promise you I will track you."

Slapp left the kitchen with the persona that he had made peace with the decision that Milani had made for her life. To Alex and me, Milani was our baby, but it appeared that Slapp now viewed Milani as this tough kick-ass younger sibling that he always dreamed of having. Now that Slapp was out of the field for the remainder of his career, he was living a portion of his life vicariously through Milani. A few minutes later, Milani hugged us and exited the kitchen. When she left through the front door, the only people in the room that she stopped to hug good-bye were Cameron and Max as she blew a kiss to her Uncle Slapp, before closing the door behind her.

The party went on for a couple more hours after that, yet for Alex and me it ended the moment our baby girl closed that door behind her to leave.

We didn't hear anything from Milani New Year Day or a few days after. We all assumed that her assignment date had been moved up and she was on location. The first coded message we received was a blip in a local newspaper ad. She knew that the ole retired agent dogs read a particular portion of the local newspapers everyday, which had been their way of secretly communicating with each other and the loves ones that they would leave behind, during missions, years before. Mr. Burney was the first to notice it and recognize that it was a note from Milani hidden inside a classified ad. This made perfect sense, because he was the one that had created the code. Over the years the guys in the field had made a few changes to it. The first thing Milani did was to take out several classified ads in different sections and under various headings. Then she included a clue word that would get their attention. Milani's Uncle Slapp had taught her and Max all the code words that they used when Max and Milani were children, in the form of a game. The game had been created to keep Max safe in case he had been adducted from school. Milani was very young at the time, but she was always around so he included her in the game. Up until the first news posting, Slapp never knew that Milani was paying enough attention to the game to master the code.

Uncle Burney recognized the code immediately, as I said before, because he had created the code for Slapp when they first organized the My Brother's Keeper high-stakes bounty hunting sub-agency. Retired Agent Burney had designed the code so the twelve renegades could talk between themselves without the bureau being able to track them or their cases. He had no idea that Slapp had taught anyone else or that his creation had spilled outside the original group. It was a very simple code and Burney knew that the only people that would pick it up would be the secret service watchdog annalist group that had been commissioned to read, decipher, catalog, save and report all their findings. Their sole purpose was to scan, read everything and anything that was printed.

Back then, when Agent Burney had created the code, he was this group's immediate supervisor and reviewed everything first that they had to report. Burney knew, if or when, the highly trained annalists noticed some unusual activity in the local Capital's newspaper; hidden within the classified columns, he would have the initial chance to assure the annalist that he would have someone to look into it, from another department of the bureau, in which he had connection to as well. This would at least buy him enough time to alert Alex and the others and possibly readjust the code a tad. During the entire ten years of the life of 'My Brother's Keeper' sub-agency that situation only came up twice. Now almost twenty-five years after he had constructed the code, Retired Agent Burney was observing his encryption creation in the classifieds. To attempt to express how extremely proud Retired Agent Burney felt, at that precise moment, would be nothing less than an understatement.

Initially Retired Agent Burney thought that it was someone from the bureau trying to bait him, them he noticed the code word that he knew that Slapp had unknowingly added when he gave Milani her secret nickname; Kitty Ping Pong; Kitty Ping for short. The name had come about when we were all in Hong Kong hiding out. The iconic word Kitty was a very popular line that had been created in Japan in 1976 called Hello Kitty. Slapp said that Milani was sneaky and quiet like a cat. You never knew when she was going to pounce on you. Kitty was also a fitting selection for a code name because she was the youngest one of us in exile and kitty represents a baby cat. Little did Slapp know how correct he was at the time about the name and the label and it's representation, as it related to Milani. The second portion of the name was just something that rhymed with Hong Kong in which had been where we had discovered her. Plus at the time there was a Ping-Pong table set up in the Hong Kong American's Embassy motor pools' lounge area to give the men something to do, during their downtime. Whenever Milani came to the embassy, she would collected all the balls that she found on the floor and put them in Slapp's tool box, while believing that she was helping to clean up. After a while, all the other men in the motor pool knew exactly where to look if they couldn't find a Ping-Pong ball to play the table game; out in the repair bay; in Slapp's toolbox.

Once the scheduling supervisor spoke harshly to Milani about being in the garage bay with her uncles, Slapp and Tate. Later Slapp cornered him and threatened his life. The supervisor was afraid to report it to the ambassador and Slapp made sure that there were no witnesses when he intimidated the man. After that, every petite thing that Slapp did, the supervisor reported it, in writing, to the Ambassador.

Now twenty-five years later, Retired Agent Burney picks up the newspaper and sees his work in use again after all this time. The classified ad read: 'Small Kitty, who loves to play with Ping-Pong balls, needs good home. Young, six months old, doing fine without her family. Pass on ad to anyone that maybe interested in Kitty.' The phone number that she entered was Slapp's old cell phone number, which she knew didn't work any more. She used the old cell number as a code also because Milani knew that if anyone else from the group discovered the ad they would recognize Slapp's old number, take the newspaper to him and her Uncle Slapp would be able to completely decode the message that she had so craftily composed.

When Retired Agent Burney discovered the ad, he was on a break at the National Botanical Gardens where he had continued to give student group tours part time. He became so excited and hyper until he clocked out and drove to Quanico to show Slapp the ad in the paper. Slapp was in class at the time, when he noticed his father ease into the back row of the room and sit quietly to wait for his next break. This was highly irregular for him or anyone else to be allowed to come into his class without being announced or escorted in. After all, a portion of the curriculum was classified.

While Slapp was standing in front of the class lecturing, his father Agent Burney continued to tap the rolled up newspaper into his slightly curled palm of his opposite hand. He was smiling so Slapp realized that it had to be good news. Slapp's heart rate began to slowdown a bit. He gave his father a slight nod that he understood as he went on with the lecture. Unfortunately Slapp had already covered non-verbal communication 101 in his introduction lecture; however, a few of the twenty students picked up on the obscure head gesture and turned to looked back to observe Agent Burney, in an attempt to piece together whom he might possibly be. The students began to whisper among themselves and lose their focus. Slapp soon lost all control of the class as they all began to look back and smile and wave, while hoping that Slapp would introduce them to the legendary Agent Dexter Allen Burney extraordinaire.

Slapp soon came to grips with the reality that he was no longer in control of the class, so he dismissed the group. Two thirds of the students immediately rushed to the rear of the room to inquire who Burney indeed was. Agent Burney smiled with pride and was flattered that the new young-bucks were so interested in an old-timer like himself. At first Slapp was a little irritated that his students were so intrigued by his father, Agent Burney's presence in the classroom, before they knew for sure of who he was. Slapp continued to stuff his lecture notes inside his oversized briefcase. He looked up several times to observe the students as they flooded Agent Burney with questions.

"Wait, wait gentlemen;" Burney repeated with a wave of his hands, while displaying a little arrogance smile as his chest became swollen with pride. "I can only hear one question at a time future guardians. Please forgive me for interrupting your studies. I only came in to exchange a few words with your instructor, briefly for a moment." Yet one student continued to insist.

"Sir, will you tell us your full name. We all believe you would have to be an agent or previous agent for security to allow you walk in here without an escort of some type. As you know, currently we are not authorized to view any files with photos. Our clearance hasn't been upgraded to that level. Most of us believe that the bureau's photo album is a sham anyway. They only post the dead ones for training, and those never leave the confinement of the bureau." Burney delayed them again.

"Well as you can see, I'm pretty old. If your statement is correct, perhaps your wait to learn who I am is shorter than you now believe it to be."

They all laughed as Slapp looked on. Burney stalled and stuttered for a moment longer, because in that instance he realized that storming into his son's classroom was absolutely the wrong think to do, for so many reasons.

"I'm not sure if I should answer that or not, since I'm an uninvited guest who just popped in. I will give you a clue." The students all held their breaths as they leaned in towards Agent Burney ever so slightly with great interest and anticipation that the clue would be enough for them to reach the correct conclusion about Burney's identity. Burney cleared his throat to add even more drama to the moment, as he maintained his wide smile of approval that they were so persistent. "I'm Agent Alvin Madison's proud father and he was named after my deceased partner, as it were. Surely that should give you enough information to research for my full name, if you are ever allowed to look into the archives." This was all a crafty game to Slapp's father and one that he hadn't played in a long time with a group of green recruits. A smile revealing great pleasure washed over Agent Burney's face as he tried to smoother his inward laughter with an amusing chuckle.

Slapp decided to bail his father out of the jam by repeating his previous announcement. "Gentlemen, class is dismissed. Please cut my father some slack. You know the rules about 'need-to-know'. I will see all of you tomorrow in the lab." The students left the classroom. Slapp moved even closer to his father, in the rear of the room, to ask what was so important in the classifieds that he was now ecstatically holding in his hand.

"Hey dad, what was so urgent that would cause you to walk off the job and into my classroom in the middle of the afternoon? I had planned to stop by on my way home to see you. You really frightened me for a moment. I thought something had happened to mother, and you had come to take me to her." Agent Burney laughed and waved his hands as he spoke.

"No, no nothing like that Junior, but you know you should repair that wound between you to. It pains me sometimes to see you love her up one moment and then pull away the next." Burney quickly unrolled the newspaper, while shaking so strongly with excitement it made it impossible for Slapp to read the ad or even focus on any portion of the paper, for that matter. "Look Alvin, I think that it's a encrypted message from Milani. I recognized the code after all these years, then I saw the little pet name that I heard you called her once when all of you first came home. It just has to be her." Slapp snatched the ads from his father's trembling hands and gazed at the paper for a moment while Agent Burney repeated again and again. "Well, is it her, well is it? Say something for god's sake; I'm an old man. How long do you think I can hold my breath before passing out, Son?"

Slapp glanced over at his father quickly and then back to the page. "Wow Dad! Mother always said you were pushy; give me a minute dad, so I can be sure." Slapp read the ad the third time and then looked at his father. "Yes dad, I think this was sent to us from Milani. I had forgotten all about this. I remember teaching Max the code, while playing a game, but I never dreamed that Milani was picking up on any of this. I am sure she has honed her skills more, while she went through all your old files at the house. Knowing you the way I do, you probably just turned her loose in the basement with all that old moldy stuff and never gave it a second thought. She must have read all your footnotes and markings in the margins and figured it all out. She has always been smart beyond her years."

Agent Burney was so excited until he became too busy, while gloating in the moment that his code had surfaced in a new generation, until he didn't notice that Slapp was trying to lay some of the blame, of why Milani had joined the bureau, at his feet. Then Agent Burney snapped back.

"So what should we do," whispered Agent Burney? "Can you decode it and tell what she wants us to know?" Slapp had made a couple of changes to the code when he began to teach it to Max and Milani in a game form. Slapp stared out into space for a moment with a guilty gaze. He felt that Alex and I would now blame him even more for teaching Milani the code. "What's wrong son? Isn't this good news; no one has heard from her in over six months or more, isn't that correct?"

"Sure dad, you're right. I was just thinking. I will call Alex now and tell him that I will come by his house tonight. I will stay out in the country tonight at the barn and drive back in the morning."

At this point, Slapp and his family had maintained the brownstone in the city, because it was close to Cameron's school. Most of their things had been moved into the big red barn that Slapp's parents had renovated for him years before. As I said before, Alex and I had bought a house in the same development up the road a bit. Once Cameron had completed school and moved on the college campus, they would sell the brownstone and live in the country full time, but hey hadn't gotten around to it yet. Cameron was already in his second year at GWU.

That evening we all gathered around the dinning room table at Burney's as Slapp decoded the message for us. I called William and Max and told them very briefly what had happened. The coded message from Milani conveyed: I'm fine, have to go deeper undercover, I miss and love all of you, perhaps six more months before I can come home. I began to cry as Slapp read the coded massage out loud.

I decided that I should start planning a huge welcome-home party, just incase Milani was able to sneak home for a quick visit. It was now July and that meant that perhaps right after the major holidays. We decided to leave the Christmas Trees up at all our homes and not open our presents until she arrived.

Milani's First Mission

In Hong Kong, Milani had arrived and had been assigned only to collect some Intel about the human trafficking that appeared to have had a serious increased in the passed eighteen months. Of course Milani was the perfect person for this assignment. She was young, very beautiful, and innocent in appearance and everything that the traffickers were looking to sell on the black-market. Because she was of mixed ethnicity in which wasn't valued there, and was viewed as more of an embarrassment than a gift, they were counting on no one looking for her if she was caught up in the snatch. What the criminals didn't know or understand was that Milani was an undercover agent that had been planted to infiltrate the entire organization and bring the cloaked top inside-man to light. Not one of us, or anyone at the bureau had any idea that Milani had her own personal and private agenda for taking this assignment. Milani had planned this out in her mind for years. Now the time had finally arrived for her to take her revenge.

As soon as Milani arrived she checked in with the local Hong Kong authorities. No one here could be trusted, so she lied about why she was in the area, so she would be authorized to carry her concealed weapons. She signed in as a private contractor looking for someone who had skipped bail. There were other lies told as well. Her martial art training was her ace-in-the-hole, which she never discussed or revealed to anyone. Then Milani reported to the American Embassy and spoke directly to the ambassador and told him who she in fact she was. The newly assigned ambassador knew nothing of her past or who in fact she was as it related to her family. She asked if she could use the apartment next door, which had been Gayle's place when she worked as the embassy's security receptionist. The ambassador agreed because she had all the proper paperwork to prove that she was indeed an agent on assignment. The small dusty apartment, which was perched over a well known ma and pa noodle shop and bar, that was on the back portion of the embassy's compound had been empty for a while and was now being used as storage. The new emissary didn't have a problem with it's new use as long as Milani promised not to bring any of her work home with her, in the form of an informants, battered bystanders or wounded assistants; Milani agreed.

Milani slept and surfed the Internet during the day and walked the streets at night sometimes dressed as a prostitute and other time she strolled the lobbies of the finest hotels and resorts, dressed as a high-priced call girl. This went on for about two weeks. Her price was always too high and that was how she kept from being picked up. One night a pimp tried to muscle her into his corral because he told her that everyone had to have a handler to be in that particular area to work. First Milani tried to reason with him by telling him that she wouldn't be around long enough to cutting into his profit margin. He didn't like her response, so he grabbed her and she beat him to death right their. The next couple of weeks she moved to another section of the city to avoid the heat. One night she stumbled onto a night-market warehouse party and a sting sweep came through and she was caught up in the mix.

They held all the young pretty girl's in a back room and this man came in and told them that they could work this arrest off or go to jail for thirty days. It was five of them and they all agreed including Milani. The first couple of weeks, they just entertained crime bosses that came through with a little dancing, and touchy feely. They informed the selected girls that they could reduce their thirty-day time, if they agreed to have sex with the men for free. Three agreed and Milani and another girl refused. So Milani and the other girl continued to dance every night while serving drinks and wearing very little to nothing, in the way of clothing.

One particular night an older heavy local man came in and sat at one of the darkly lit booths. When Milani heard his voice, she knew instantly who he was. He was now retired, but he was the same chief of police that was there when she was a child and the same one that she had seen committing a crime that second summer when she and her great grandmother had traveled to Hong Kong for a visit with their family. That day the chief of police had seen her and ran to her to threaten her not to tell anyone what she had witnessed. She was eleven at the time and was very fearful that he would hurt other members of her family after she left that summer, in which she had no choice in leaving behind. Now fifteen years later, Milani came face to face with a man that had changed her life forever.

Milani was so shocked until she had to go in the restroom to regain her composure. She was shaking, but this time it wasn't with fear but with an almost uncontrollable anger. She realized that with her training that she could kill him at least ten different ways without leaving a trace. Yet she wanted him to know who she was before she killed him and possible take out a few members of his crime family as

well. Milani knew that she would start working her own case, while placing the bureau's assignment on the back burner, so to speak. They were expecting a report every ten days or less. There was also the consideration of her partner who always kept a safe distance, while watching her back. She didn't want to involve him or tip him off that she had a second agenda that was much more personal. In addition, there were young girls that were being traded like fresh scraps of meat at a slaughterhouse.

After the girls were locked up for the night, Milani lie on her single cot and devised a plan that she was sure would work. If she agreed to have sex with some of the men, she would get to go in deeper to the source of the organization. She didn't have away to tell her partner of her plan without blowing his cover. Her bodyguard and partner was none other than her second cousin, first removed on her mother's side Officer SuKi Chang Junior, who had joined the force after he moved back to the states. The last person Milani wanted the retired chief of police to discover was that former Officer SuKi was back in Hong Kong. The department had labeled him years ago as a traitor when they found out that Officer Suki had helped us locate Milani and had called his father all the way from New York, to come home to Hong Kong to mediate on our behalf. Although Officer SuKi had altered his appearance and was undercover as well; Milani couldn't take a chance that SuKi's old boss would recognize him.

Milani completed a portion of her thirty days as a party slave for the corrupted elements of the police department and she then was released back onto the streets of Hong Kong as an independent. Milani and her cousin devised a plan and Milani wrote out a second ad notice in case something happened to her and she couldn't get out. Milani's cousin Suki Junior began to question Milani's motives as she informed him of her new modified plans.

"Milani, I don't think this is a good strategy. All you were sent out here to do was gather Intel for the big guns to come in and take them all down. What is this all about? I don't understand why you want to hurt this man so badly? What has he done to you?"

"Listen SuKi, because I'm only going to say this once. I've trained and waited all my adult life for this chance to take this bastard down. The only reason I didn't kill him the first night I served him that drink in that snake pit, is because you are so close to retirement and I didn't want you hurt. Please don't make me regret my earlier decision. All I need from you now is to know that you have my back."

A disturbing hush fell over the room as Milani waited and held her poker face tight. Officer SuKi was now forty-four years old with a wife and two children. Between his time as a police officer and now added to his time with the bureau, he could retire in three years, and then easily transition into another line of work. After five minutes or a little more of contemplation, Officer SuKi finally answered.

"Okay, I'm in, but under one condition Milani and if you lie or leave anything out of the story; I promise you that I will shoot you myself and drag your dysfunctional ass back to D.C. with an oxygen mask and a morphine I.V. drip, am I clear? I have too much at stake for your plan to fail. You have already adjusted the mission three times to satisfy your own personal crap. I've had with you. Tell me what's going on with you, or I'm catching the next flight the hell out of here." Milani stared for a moment and then she began.

"I don't remember much about all the paperwork that it took me to be able to leave here with my great grandmother and travel back to America. Later I heard different parts of the story as I became older. Once Daddy Alex told me about the meetings that were held on my behalf, at the American consulate. He explained to me how you had flown your father in from New York to help out with all the red tape. Everyone seemed to want me to have a better life in America except my great aunt and the former chief of police, whom I think was your boss at the time. When my great grandmother and I came back the first summer, I was about seven. I overheard her and my great aunt arguing about me, and all the money that she could have gotten for me, if she would have held out and sold me to my father's American family." Milani took a break to look over to see how her cousin SuKi was taking all of this in. He was pretty close to tears, but he managed to hold it together as Milani went on.

"After that summer, my great grandmother wasn't interested in coming back here to Hong Kong. I think my aunt badgering her frightened her a little. We didn't return on the regularly scheduled times that my new parents had promised, but we did come back when I was eleven. My great grandmother and I stayed in the village with our family. My great grandmother became ill. To tell you the truth I think my great aunt put something in her tea that she wasn't supposed to have. I also learned that the chief of police and my great aunt had attended school together. Then I start to believe that my great aunt wanted to sell me to the chief of police. Anyway they rushed my great grandmother to the hospital, pumped her stomach. After a few hours or so, she started to come around. When I went to see her one afternoon, I found the chief of police standing over her with a pillow clutched in his hands. I was stunned. I couldn't move. He dropped the pillow and rushed over to me and snatched me up and started threatening me that I better never tell anyone about him being in her room holding that pillow. Policemen in parts of Asia represent a different sort of power and great portions of the population fear them, due to the corruption throughout the ranks. The medical staff informed us later that she had had a heart attack. Well that was possible, but why didn't he want anyone to know that he had been there that afternoon. And why was he standing over her bed holding a pillow and seemed so alarmed and nervous when I walked in? I was in shock and depressed for weeks and cried each time someone would try to talk to me and ask what was wrong. Ma Helen said I didn't speak for weeks after that. I don't remember that part. What I do recall is that one day I woke up and I was back in the states at my parents house with Max, my dad Alex, and Ma Helen. I was able to block it out for a while and then I started to have bad dreams. My parents placed me back into counseling and I started to withdraw. We all moved back to Japan so I could grow up with my best friend. During that time I was the happiest that I can ever remember being, that is, before my great grandmother died. When we all moved back to Maryland, so I could attend college in the States, something triggered the old memories in me again and that's when I decided to change my major and become an agent and come back over here to do my own investigation. So here we are. I promise you that I won't sleep until I shut that old fat bastard down. After seeing him in that illegal club the other night, I'm sure that he has something to do with this human-trafficking ring. I just have to wait and move around a few more weeks to tie it all together. So will you help me or not?"

Officer SuKi took in a slow deep breath, held it in for a second and then let it out slowly before he answered.

"I'll help you Cousin Milani, against my better judgment. Why haven't you told your parents after all this time? I'm sure they have enough connections to open an inquiry."

"No SuKi, this is something I have to do myself. My great grandmother was all I had, after my mother died and my grandparents refused to accept me because of my mixed heritage. Besides if something goes wrong I couldn't bare the thought of hurting my aunt and uncle, after all they have done for me. I think I have harmed them enough over the years, by keeping this from them."

"What the hell are you talking about? They are your family and they are only doing what families are expected to do for each other. They love you so much and you have put them through hell these last few years. Ole Mr. Charlie was right when he said that you are a Jones; stubborn to a fault. If your biological father was a live, this shit would have killed him for sure. You know he had a weak heart from birth." Milani retaliated in her next breath.

"What the hell you know about it Suki? If my real father would have lived longer, I wouldn't have to do this, because I wouldn't feel the way that I do." The room went silent again. "Oh by the way, once I go in undercover, give me three days before you try to contact me. If I don't contact you, take out a classified ad in the top three capital newspapers in D.C. This is the way I want it to read: 'Lost frightened Kitty, searching for owner or new rescue home, loves to play with Ping-Pong balls, call soon, planning a vacation in three days.' "SuKi please don't mess this up. This is a coded signal for the cavalry to fly in and save our sorry asses. Please don't break your cover to come in after me. You need to be available to give an update brief to whoever comes to save us. Besides, I pretty sure that your old boss is a part of this trafficking and I don't want him to recognize you and make a run for it."

Suki realized in that moment that he had agreed to something that he wasn't prepared for, yet there was no turning back.

"Who the hell is going to come in to save us," yelled Officer SuKi? "Who the hell are you taking about, Milani? The bureau doesn't know what we are planning."

"I don't know who will come SuKi, but if someone sees this ad, someone will come, I promise you. Better yet, just give me two days from the time we lose contact. I will call you or text you every night between midnight and one a.m. If I need to get you a long message, I will leave it at the sushi bar below my apartment next door to the American embassy. The owner there is a strange cookie at times, but he is okay. He has been there for a very long time and understands how important discretion is while operating a business this close to the backdoor of the American Embassy."

That night it was hard for Officer SuKi to sleep. Milani returned to her apartment to change clothes and take her position on the wet streets of the red-light district of Hong Kong. The alleys were darker tonight than usual because there was no moon. For a split second she remembered all the night-suns that she had witnessed when she was a teenager, as she and her best friend would sit on the Kintai Bridge in Iwakuni Japan. Her friend always referred to the moon as the night-sun because it was so bright and to add drama and romance to the moment. Remembering her old friend at that moment did provide a warm moment of comfort from a wet dreary night. That night there was a light drizzle of rain coming down. This had forced most of the ladies-of-the-evening to seek shelter in the doorways of the rundown buildings and closed business that all were covered with rolled down sheets of metal over the regular glass doors. This wasn't a safe area at night between the hours of midnight and four a.m.

Milani knew that it was just a matter of time before she would be caught up in another sweep or she would see that former police chief some place that she felt was inappropriate for a man of his status. Two more weeks went by and young girls continued to disappear from various locations of the city. Then one night it happened; another backroom illegal club-sweep. Milani had just arrived and went straight to the ladies room to take off her high heel shoes to rest her feet for a moment and relieve herself. She was at the sink refreshing her lip color when she heard gunfire resonating from the main populated area of the nightclub. There were people screaming, chairs and tables being turned over as people attempted to exit.

Milani quickly ran into an empty toilet stall, wiped her fingerprints from her backup weapon and duck taped her handgun under the water reservoir of the toilet, as she texted her partner Suki to tell him where to retrieve it, after all the smoke had cleared from the sweep. With all the confusion of the sweep, Officer SuKi would be able to come on the scene, quickly flash his old Hong Kong police badge and go directly to the stall. An hour passed, Agent Suki received the text and realized that Milani was now undercover with no badge, cell phone or sidearm. Everyone carried a cell phone or two, but if this were an illegal sweep the first thing the men would do was to take everyone's cell phone. Officer SuKi decided that if Milani didn't call him in three hours he was going to call the states and place that classified ad, which she had written up, in the newspapers like he had been instructed to do. Milani leaving her gun behind had caused Officer SuKi to panic. A couple of hours later, Milani did call from a borrowed phone and instructed him to give her twenty-four hours to work her mojo (charm).

This was a police department sweep and now they separated the girls, just like before. All the girls were held over- night and most were released the next morning after being interrogated about who their pimps (handler) were. Milani assumed that they were testing the waters to see how much competition they were up against from the small fish in the corrupt pond. The selected girls were searched the second time and the carted off out in the countryside to this large secluded resort sized house on a hill that overlooked a large portion of the harbor. The nine of them were locked into this large suite with a large bathroom attached and told that they were going to be hostesses at this exquisite party. Clothes had been brought in for the ladies to wear and everything that a woman needed to get dress for a formal evening was provided in that room. That night around eight, a man came in the room and asked if anyone have ever worked as a bartender. Milani immediately raised her hand. She was instructed to get dressed and report to the kitchen. She felt that this way she wouldn't have to be available to be fondled as much

In addition, Milani was hoping that this would give her more access to move around the place and possibly steal one of the guest's cell phones to call her partner. Well-dressed men from several age groups and ethnic backgrounds began to arrive around nine that evening and the orchestra began to play. This was a very classy affair and the girls that had been selected from the sweep appeared to know exactly what to do, if they wanted to stay alive. We were at least an hour drive outside the city limit and up this steep mountain with a winding narrow road. Cliffs that dropped off into rocky terrain surrounded three sides of this mountaintop resort size house. From the rear gardens you could see parts of the city and Hong Kong's harbor. The house and the grounds were like walking through a museum. However, Milani knew that instead it was a playground for the rich, powerful, and corrupt. She cataloged everything about the house that she could to memory and promised herself that she would return one day soon and burn it all to the ground.

Around eleven that first evening, the former retired chief of police arrived and walked directly to the bar to order a drink. Milani knew that he wouldn't recognize her, so she took a couple of breaths to suppress her anger and poured him his drink of choice. This confirmed what Milani was hoping; and that was that the old retired police chief was aware and possibly apart of this human trafficking ring. A few more girls were brought in around midnight. Most appeared to be drugged and they weren't well kept. They were auctioned off to the highest bidders. One of the young girls Milani recognized from the first sweep that both of them had been caught up in prior. Milani became so upset by what she was experiencing until she had to excuse herself and go in the bathroom to throw up and cry.

Now Milani was putting all the pieces together. During each sweep, a few girls are held. If no one comes looking for them or tries to bail them out, them they are labeled as independents and sold at the next gathering, after the next sweep. The younger the girls were, the higher the bidding appeared to go. Mixed ethnic young girls brought in the second highest amount, shadowed only by the ones with more European features.

There were many different languages being spoke and translated in the room. Milani was able to call Officer Suki each night, but the second night she called too late. SuKi had activated the classified ad. The party lasted two nights and after that, Milani and the others were released back on the streets after their lives and their families' lives had been verbally threatened.

Chapter Nine

The Daily Classified

Here at home, we all waited and read the classified ads every day in hope of getting another coded message from Milani. Another two months had now passed and we held on to our optimism and dreams that she would return before the day of the big planned party that we were setting up for her. Then early one morning Slapp called Alex to see if he had received his morning paper. The tone of the conversation was totally different as I listened from Alex's end. The two of them were speaking in secret-code mode and the tension was high.

"Hello this is Alex, go ahead."

"Alex, this is Mr. Madison. Have you received your morning newspaper?"

"I have and was just about to read it now. I will talk to you tonight." The phone call ended. Alex opened the newspaper quickly and turned to the classified to search them. He looked up at me as I sat frozen across the table from him, knowing that something was seriously wrong. I immediately became teary-eyed, as I held my hand over my mouth in shock.

"Helen, don't get upset. I think Milani is in trouble and we are going to get her."

"We who Alex? How do you even know where she is? I can't bear to lose any of you. Why can't the bureau send someone in? Where is her partner, doesn't she have a partner?"

"Just calm down Helen, Slapp is coming over here tonight and we will all decide then. In the mean time I have to pack my gear."

"What the hell are you saying, Alex? You haven't been to the firing range in years." He turned to look at me as if I was completely wrong about what skills he had continued to hone after his retirement. Alex walked over to me and forced me into his arms and hugged me tightly as he explained his position on the matter.

"Listen Helen, this is our baby girl that we are talking about. There is no way in hell I'm staying behind. If I don't make it back, there is nothing that I can do about that. It's all in God's hands, and up until now those hands have served me well. Stop crying, I can't think straight when you are crying." By now the front of Alex's shirt was wet with my tears and nose excretions. He pulled away slowly to go into the attic to retrieve his gear.

It was all secured in a locked heavy trunk. Weapons, vest, ammunition, old communication packs, camera, GPS devices, passports with former aliases from his past when he was with the bureau and cash from various parts of the globe. I had no idea that Alex had stored all of these items from before. Some of Alex's gear I had never seen before and wondered when he had moved most of it into our new home. He loaded up a huge camping backpack with most of the gear that he wanted and then pulled out some camouflaged camping clothes. He took out U.S. dollars, Asia dollars and money for at least four other countries, which included Thailand and Cambodia.

Alex was quickly moving into that mission mode that I though that I would never have to deal with again. I left him in the attic and went back to the kitchen to clear the morning breakfast dishes. I started to clean things, just to keep my mind busy. The day passed quickly and that evening Slapp, Kate and Cameron arrived for an unpleasant visit. Tate and Gayle showed up a few moments later and just as the men all sat down to the dinning room table the doorbell rang. Everyone look around at each other as if no one was expecting anyone else. Alex checked the security camera on the front door on the television monitor and to his surprise it was Slapp's father retired agent Burney. Alex swiftly opened the door and in walked Mr. Burney and behind him were Tye and our sons Max and William, and bringing up the rear was Fred; all the way from Florida. I assumed he had been getting the newspaper delivered all the way south by mail and had been tracking Milani movements like the remainder of us. I immediately broke down into a heart-retching cry. I moved towards the door as I fell into Max and William's arms, just as they cleared the threshold of the front door. Alex quickly closed the door behind the five of them and then opened it up again, as he gave a glance outside to see if anyone were watching. Everyone stood their ground as they waited for me to gather my composure. Uncle Burney spoke first.

"Hello everyone" bellowed Agent Burney. "Tye and I found these three sniffing around my barn. I'm just glad that I had disconnected all the alarms so Cameron could go out there to play his games on the big screen, otherwise all of us would be trying to get our black suits cleaned. Max and William spoke up quickly to defend themselves as all the men in the room began to laugh.

"Uncle Burney, we stopped there because we saw a light on in the loft. We though that perhaps Uncle Slapp had come out for the night. We noticed Uncle Slapp's car. We had no idea that everyone would be here. Besides, we got to his house first Uncle Burney. This was going to be our next stop." I released Max and William to huge Tye and thank him for coming. The years had been very kind to Tye and I was informed that this was his last six months with the bureau before retirement. As a matter of fact, he was on terminal leave and had completed all his paperwork for his transition.

"Thank you so much Tye for coming to help us find our baby girl." Tye smiled shyly before he commented directly to me.

"Nothing couldn't have kept me away, Miss Helen. I know I haven't spent much time with Milani, but her brothers tell me that she is quite the hellcat and a force to be reckoned with, if you have the misfortune of meeting her out in the field. I'm just glad that she is on our side. Don't worry Miss Helen; we'll bring her back safe. I'm more concerned with the safety of the people that are holding her. She has spent a lot of time with her Uncle Slapp over the years, probably too much time, if someone asked my opinion. So I'm pretty sure that she won't hesitate; if given a chance to escape."

Tye looked over at Slapp during his words of hope as Slapp signaled Tye to choose his words carefully in fear Tye would add more stress to my situation.

The men all moved to the dinning room table; Tate, Alex, Slapp, Mr. Burney, Tye, William, and Max. Of course Alex moved to the head of our table to run the extraction plans.

"I want to thank all of you again men, for coming to our rescue. Helen and I are forever in you'll debts. First I would like to say, Max you can not go with us." Max jumped to his feet while bumping the table so strongly until he caused three partially filled cups of coffee to spill. I had only witnessed Max challenging his father Alex a few times before, but never with the anger that I observer that evening. William sprang to his feet as well, to calm Max down and remind him whom he was speaking to, their father. William was sitting right next to Max and was startled by his outburst.

"What the hell, Dad," yelled Max? "I know you didn't just say that I can't go on this mission?" Alex stood up slowly to defend his position on the matter as Slapp smiled and placed his hand partially over his face to hide his amusement. Tye suddenly pushed away from the table with the indicative body stance that he was aware that this portion of the planning was a family-affair and he had no intentions of interfering with a bloodline discussion. Tate took his usual position in these matters and tilted his head downward and waited for the dust to settle. This was Mr. Burney's first time at the show, so to speak, because he had never been a direct part of the My Brother's Keeper sub-agency, but he had heard stories about these meetings from his son Slapp, and most of the recalls, which had been relayed to Burney, after they had been shut down, were almost always the heated ones. Now Uncle Burney was about to witness for himself how strong and quickly the tempers surfaced without any forewarning.

"Listen to me Max", objected Alex. "I need you to stay here with your mother."

"She doesn't need me here, Dad. Besides I'm a grown man and I can make my own decisions; isn't that what you taught us kids. To be men and women and only make decisions that we are willing to live with, possibly for the rest or our life. Those are your words Dad, and I won't allow you to modify them when it's convenient for you to do so."

Everyone in the room became motionless and quiet as William continued to stand with his hand and arm on and gently around Max's neck and shoulder as if he was ready to snatch him closer if Max appeared to become more worked-up and say something that he might regret later, to their father. The truth of the matter is that Alex was Williams' stepfather and was he almost an adult when we met. On the other hand, Max was Alex's biological son that looked almost identical like his deceased twin brother. Taking the bloodline into account and the fact that the two of them had formed a relationship much sooner had only intensified this disagreement. Now that Max was a youthful man, he looked even more like Alex's deceased brother Austin. Max just couldn't understand why his father held the reigns so tight, when it came to his children. Alex had acquired children late in life and coupled with the fact that he was very protective, this didn't allow much wiggle room for an offspring to voice their opinion, once Alex would state the rules. Alex searched for the words that would overpower Max's last statement and save face in front of some of his oldest and dearest friends. Alex raised his voice a little, which we all agreed didn't help him in that moment at all, as the tides turned on Alex in a flash, while he stood in his own home.

"Maximilian, son this is my mission and I say who goes and who stays behind." Once again Alex had failed to correctly choose his words and had insulted a couple of the other men in the room, all in the same breath. Tate knew the moment that Alex spoke the last word of this thoughtless statement that this would be a opportune time to excuse himself to go into the kitchen to get a snack or refresh his cup of coffee; the little coffee that had been left from Max's explosive spill.

Tate stood up slowly with his head and eyes still focused downward in that divine pose that he had acquired from his vocational training or his father, we weren't sure which had been the case. Alex looked over at Tate for support, just like he had done so many times before, but Tate didn't offer any this time. It took a few moments for what Alex had said to sink into Slapp's consciousness, as he appeared to continue to enjoy the disagreement between Max and his father, Alex. To be forthcoming, Slapp had spoken to Alex on several different occasions, over the years; about the way he treated his children. Slapp informed Alex that they would grow up in anger if he held them too tight. Then Slapp spoke quietly as he remembered Alex's anxiety condition. Initially Slapp slumped down into his thug like lean for a moment, stroked his chin briefly and then sat forward again, while placing both forearms and elbows on the dinning room table as he sat across from Alex and right next to the two non-biological brothers, Max and William.

"Hey, hey now Alex my brother that's not exactly true about you leading this mission," refuted Slapp with a slow speech and in an almost whispered volume. Slapp gave a dry one-corner-lip-lift smile as he brought his eyes up to Alex's level; as if that was going to help Alex's painful absorption of what Slapp was now stating as fact. "I think that I'm the best person to fill that position." Alex became very angry and excitable as Slapp did everything in his power not to upset Alex any further. Tate had now returned and was standing in the doorway between the kitchen and the dinning room while drinking a fresh cup of coffee. Gayle, Kate and I had all moved to the other double doorway space that connected the formal living room space to the dinning room. The voices being raised had gotten our attention, so we all moved closer to investigate the disturbance that was now radiating for the dinning room area. At this point, Slapp, Alex, Tye and Mr. Burney were the only three that had remained sitting as the meeting of the minds continued to turn into something more closely relayed to a three ring circus. Alex was now yelling, and four people were all speaking at once.

"Slapp, this is my damn family and these young men are my children. And if you take a closer look around, you may notice that this is my damn house." Alex was now standing as he tapped his chest with both open-palm hands. Slapp demeanor didn't change in the slightest bit as he responded with a restraint that none of us had ever experienced before in him. It was as if Slapp knew that this was an argument that he knew Alex wasn't going to win. Slapp answered with sarcasm by using a word to begin his next sentence that isn't usually used and to lighten the mode of the room a tad.

"Thus, this is true; therefore you have the power to ask me to leave your castle at anytime. However, please keep in mind that I believe the classified ad was written for me and I think I know her a little better than you, because we share a common bond." Slapp hesitated as he tried to get a read on Alex. "Oh I see what's happening here. Is that what's been bothering you all these years, Alex? You know, the fact that your children have always been drawn to me and on a few occasions, came to me first? Do you really want to do this here and now; you know what I mean, clear the air on that subject? We are all aware when you are not in charge you sometimes have a problem with that. Well this is a new day Brother and if you can't keep up with the changing times, then I'm sorry. These are not children; they are men in every sense of the word. Let me say for the record that I am proud to call them my nephews."

"No Slapp, I don't want to talk about your relationship with my children, but I won't forget how you threw this crap up in my face at a very sensitive time.

"Well, before you decide how far you want this discussion to spend out of control, I need to remind you that I know more about where Milani is and the mission she's on. I can go on my own, but you can't go without my intel. With that being sad, I don't think you have the right to eliminate anyone that I might be considering for my team. We are all men here. Granted that some of us are still wet behind the ears, while others are over-the-hill. The fact remains that we are all adults and have the power to make up our own minds." Alex anger caused his lips to tremble as he spoke his next phrase.

"Slapp, if you agree to take one of my son's on this dangerous mission, I will never forgive you." Slapp just smiled and stood up.

"Yes you will. I will just step out of the room so you and your family can decide, and then I will come back and layout the mission's plan, fair enough Alex?" Mr. Burney appeared to be in shock of how heated these meetings were and wondered how had they been able to maintain their relationship and side business without hurting one another. Tye sat very quietly and still with his arms folded across his chest and made no eye contact with anyone.

By this time Alex was hyperventilating. He excused himself from the table to go into the kitchen to take one of his pills. Max followed his father into the kitchen because he now felt guilty about being a contributor to his attack. William was out of the house when Alex was diagnosed and was totally unaware how badly it had gotten.

"Look Dad, I know you see me as a little boy and you don't want anything to happened to me because of your brother, but I know Hong Kong better than you because of all the field trips I went on while in school and all the runs I took with Uncle Slapp, Uncle Tate and Mr. Pauling when they drove limo for the American Embassy. In addition to that, no one will recognize me after all these years. I can move around without attracting suspicion to myself. Also Dad, I don't think that you are well enough to go in first and there is the chance that someone might recognize you when you worked on the police department those few months. What if someone on the Hong Kong police force is on the take? The moment you show up and someone remembers you, they will scatter."

Alex was listening to Max's every-word, maybe for the first time ever. Max's assessment was precise and his argument very compelling. Alex turned slowly to face Max from where he had been leaning slightly over the sink as he waited for his medicine to start to work. Tate was the only other person in the kitchen's doorway that was privileged to the conversation between Max and his father, Alex. Alex clutched Max's head and face between his huge hands and kissed him on the side of the head before forcefully pulling him into his arms as he whispered these words with tears in his eyes. Max held his father lightly and then tighter, once he realized that the feelings and words were coming from a painful place, from deep within his father's heart.

"Max, I don't know what I would do if something happened to you. You are the strongest reminder and connection, besides Milani, that I have to my deceased twin brother. When my brother Austin died I lost a piece of myself that I can't put into words. Then when I discovered you, I got a portion of him back. Don't ask me how; I'm not sure? Do you understand that my heart would just stop beating if something ever happened to either one of you three? You are more like my brother than you realize. You have more of his compassionate ways and qualities. You are smart, kind and a gentle soul; yet strong enough and fearless enough to march for a cause. I didn't even want you to go out of state for college. Your mother, Auntie Ma, convinced me that I shouldn't allow my personal fears to interfere with your life and it wouldn't be right for me to hold you too close." Max pulled away slowly as he tried to console his father and convince him that he should be a part of the team.

"I know Dad, and I love you too; but the team can really use my help. I know the neighborhoods and the dynamics of the villagers. I know all the back streets that my uncles and I would take to avoid the traffic during the busiest times of the day. Once or twice, Milani's great grandmother took us outside the city. No one would question me about coming back for a few weeks to visit." Then Max's mannerism changed to a more defiant one. "Dad, I would like to go with your blessing, but if that's not going to happen, I understand. I love you Dad, but I am going on this mission if the team will have me." Will you promise to look after Auntie Ma Helen?" Max released his grip on his father, turned and slowly walked back, directly pass his Uncle Tate, into the dinning room while waiting to see whom his Uncle Slapp would select to include on his team. Tate gave Max's head, neck and left shoulder one full stroke while Max walked pass, as Tate held his eyes closed. We were sure Tate was praying for Max now that he was certain that Max had made his decision.

Alex stood there for a few more moments before looking over his shoulder in Tate's direction; who had been standing in the doorway of the kitchen the entire time listening, yet never offered to take a side. Tate wanted to console Alex like he had been trained to do at seminary, but he had no words that he felt would fit the occasion. Alex was the last one to return to the table as Slapp had now begun to pass out the assignments. The doorbell rang and I rushed to the door. It was Miss Beasley all wired-up about the situation.

"Hello Miss Becky I meant to say Miss Sarah, come in. The group is all here."

"Thank you, Miss Helen. I sort of figured that they were. I saw the newspaper on the kitchen table. I noticed that an ad had been creased. I was surprise that I was able to decipher some of it. It's been a long time since Dexter Allen first taught me the code he constructed. You have no idea how shocked I was when I saw the old code being used again and the fact that the next generation was now using it." Miss Beasley sashayed in with the same smart, yet genteel persona as always and with one that we all had become accustomed to. Mr. Burney stood up from the table and moved towards the front door to greet her with a quick peck kiss on the cheek.

"Come on in Babe, I meant to leave you a note, but I became so excited about the ad until I'm not sure if I remembered to locked the front door behind me. You know all of us have been worried sick for months about our little Milani out there, somewhere all alone. Some of us even feel responsible for the occupation she has chosen."

Of course Slapp would never allow anyone to include him in a statement so broad, even if it was true. Then there was the fact that the room had been so tensed prior to Miss Beasley's arrival. Slapp yelled from the dinning room towards his father and to whoever was listening and had refused to defend themselves from the blanket comment his father, Mr. Burney had just made. At one time or another we had all done our part to make this cloak and dagger job seem glamorous, or perhaps necessary.

"Don't speak for me old man. If I remember correctly, you were the one who allowed her to go through all your old files while you cried about the ones that got away. She probably joined the bureau to appease an old man's heart of vicariously closing some cases, way after he had retired."

"Excuse me for a moment Sara Lynn (Miss Beasley) I have to get back to the table and see if there is anything I can contribute to the plan to find and bring Milani back." Mr. Burney rushed back across the room to the dinning room table huddle, which now included Max, William, Slapp, Alex, Mr. Burney, Tye, Fred and Tate who had remained standing in the doorway of the kitchen. At this point it was pretty much settled that Slapp was in charge and Max was on the team. All Slapp had to do now was find assignments for the others that refused to stay safely behind. Slapp turned his head quickly over his left shoulder to me, where I had been in the living room, still trying to bring Miss Beasley up to speed.

"Lady Thore! (Helen) Be a doll and give me a few sheets of paper and a pencil. I need to take notes as I talk."

"Sure Slapp, no problem." Alex stared over at Slapp with a disapproving glare. Slapp noticed Alex staring angrily in his direction, so he responded in a defensive, yet sarcastic, tone. Slapp then purposely miss-read Alex's glance as he emphasized his erroneous observation with a question.

"What's wrong now Alex, you don't want me talking affectionately to your wife." Tate chimed in as he stood just behind and to the right of Slapp. Tate was trying to smooth out the riff between Alex and Slapp.

"Mr. Madison, (Slapp)" said Tate. "Lets stay focus." Slapp acknowledged Tate's suggestion by addressing a question to him.

"Bishop Romano," Slapp proclaimed with serious sarcasm. "Are you in or out?" Tate answered-up swiftly with his conditions interweaved firmly into his response.

"I am absolutely all in; as long as I don't have to carry a gun or weapon of any sort." Slapp replied with deep gratitude in his voice laced with relief. Of course there was humor attached to it.

"Fair enough, ole holy one, but I may still require your expertise when we select our armaments for the mission. Can I count on you for that?" Tate responded instantly with his own taste of humor, as Slapp made a few notes on the first sheet of paper.

"But of course ole heathenish one, God's work is never done, and neither is his chosen." William and Max busted into laughter as Burney dropped his head while only smiling briefly.

Slapp continued. "Usually we have a strong computer person on our team. Linda has since moved on and Father Caleb is not here. Billy the Kid (William) can we count on you?" Before our son William could answer Alex sprang to his feet the second time, while still in a rage.

"Wait a minute, just hold the hell up. Slapp are you telling me that you want both of my sons to go out on this mission with you." Slapp took in a breath and moved very slowly before he spoke in a controlled retaliating sye as he pointed a single scolding finger in Alex's direction.

"See, see that. That's your damn problem Alex. These aren't boys these are grown ass men. Excuse me ladies. They have a right to go and help rescue their little sister." Slapp then quickly looked over his shoulder to Tate before he continued. "Excuse me Pastor, but Alex is about to force me to lay my religion down for a moment." Slapp returned back to face Alex, while each of them were now standing. "Look Alex, these are two young men that want to help us go and retrieve Milani, your only daughter and the only daughter that your old gray ass will ever have. Sorry Miss Helen, after all these years I still get caught-up in Alex's controlling shit." Slapp turned back to Alex and sat back down and leaned into the table as if the rest of us had left the room. Alex slowly sat back down as well.

Mr. Burney shifted his head back and forth from Slapp to Alex like one would do at a tennis match, while leaning forward as well so he could hear clearer. "Listen Alex," confessed Slapp with sorrow on the edge of his speech. "You know that I love these two young men as if they were my own sons. I know you don't' have any doubt that I will do whatever I need to do to protect them, even if it means taking a bullet if necessary, and I believe that you would do the same for my son Cameron. So what is your problem with me placing them on the team, now that they have already decided that they are going with or without your approval or blessings; for that matter? Who knows, perhaps my plan might be a better one than the crap their little tender asses cooked-up behind our backs. Or do you prefer then strolling the nightclubs at night, dragging people into allies and slapping them around while asking them, 'have you seen my sister' while smashing a photo in their faces too closely for the people to focus clearly?

The room was quiet except for a low sniffle from Kate. She just wasn't strong enough to take all the fighting between such tight-knit friends and family members. Plus the statement about her husband taking a bullet for someone else didn't help sooth her concerns neither. The mission sounded very dangerous to Kate and to all the remainder of us as well. To Kate it appeared as though they all knew that it was an even wager that some of the team might not make it back in one piece. That was the least of my concerns, because I was more familiar with their skill levels and what they were capable of if the situation push them to that point of no return. Although Tate had taken a vow of peace and less resistance, he had the greatest fear of being hurt or being killed. Pushing him into a corner was about the most dangerous position one could take. Slapp had lived a life feeling as if he was alone so hurting you to protect the few people that he loved was almost like second nature to him. Tye, on the other hand, was a man of reason like Alex, but had a family and staying alive to live out his days with his love ones was priority one. So if you wanted to go on breathing I suggest that you do as you are told and tell him what he wants to hear. After all these years in the bureau's service he still could fall asleep anytime and anywhere. Mr. Burney had mean streak in him and had never completely healed from his first partner being killed so young, even though the men that had killed him had been brought to justice or killed that very same night. Fred had always been a humanitarian at heart and the others wondered why he had joined the force in the beginning. Fred always told them that it was because the ladies always love a man with a gun and a badge. So my deepest worry was that my sons would get caught up in the crossfire, or Slapp would go on a killing spree from guilt. and all of them would end up in jail. Yet, I felt comfortable with Tye and Slapp protecting our sons.

Slapp gave Alex a moment or two to absorb his words while he moved on to Mr. Burney to give him his assignment.

"Dad, I need you and Ma to leave first thing tomorrow. I need Mother's translating skills and she knows Hong Kong and the surrounding areas better than any of us." Slapp then turned his head to yell in the next room where Miss Beasley his mother who had been sitting on the sofa trying to console his wife Kate who was the last member to join the menagerie, so to speak. Except for Kate, we all knew how they had pledged an oath in their hearts to protect one another and us; and do whatever it took to accomplish this task.

"Hey Ma," Slapp yelled into the next room.

"Yes Sweetie, what is it," replied Miss Beasley very calmly and lady-like?

"Can you get off for two weeks from volunteering and fly to Hong Kong for me?" Miss Beasley answered without taking in a fresh breath or hesitating, as she held Kate around the shoulders lightly.

"Sure Alvin, what time does my flight leave?" Slapp replied and gave a huge pride-filled smile as he leaned back in his chair and chuckled, as he answered her without making eye contact. Slapp shook his head up and down in an arrogant way as if that was exactly how he had expected his mother to respond. She was a tough ole bird and fearless in every sense of the word. Plus she had a big heart; these were the strongest characteristic bonds between her and her only child Slapp.

"Yelp that's my girl," announced Slapp and he then answered her question. "Mother I have you on a flight from Ragan National at 06:45 a.m. Showtime is at 5 o'clock. A limo will pick you up at 03:30; all you have to do is be ready. Your ticket and itinerary will be at the gate. Go directly to the front of the TSA security line and give them this memo. Someone will be waiting to take you to your seat on the plane in first class." Then Slapp turned quickly to his left where his father

Retired Agent Dexter Allen Burney had been sitting patiently awaiting his assignment.

"Dad listen," Mr. Burney leaned in as if getting closer to Slapp's face would somehow make his instructions clearer or easier to understand. This was very exciting to Burney, because it had been twenty years since he had done anything in the line of dangerous fieldwork. That bar tendering gig to gather Intel that Alex had asked him to do for the 'My Brother's Keeper' side business had been the last operation for him, and there was hardly any danger involved. Well not enough to get an ole die-hard like Burney excited or get fresh blood to the brain. In Burney's mind that assignment didn't count because he didn't have to leave the city or strap on an additional weapon. This new assignment was like a dream come true. Then Slapp lower his voice so only the people at the table could hear.

"Dad, I need you to leave tomorrow night from Baltimore Washington International (Thurgood Marshall Airport). I will need you to use an old alias from work. Don't worry, I already went by and updated your passport and your international drivers license to match. All I need you to do now is protect mother and shake the dust off some of that money that you have in the house safe. Draw some currency for China, Thailand, and Taiwan and of course carry some U.S dollars. I haven't figured this mission completely out yet. Once we leave the city, using a teller-machine isn't an option. We don't want anyone tracking us once we leave the states. Give mother half of the money so the TSA inspectors won't raise the red flag at the checkpoint for traveling with over the limit of cash without special paperwork."

Mr. Burney was slowly bobbing his head up and down continuously in an agreeable manner the entire time Slapp was relaying his assignment. "I will give the remainder of your assignment to you on location. Your main assignment now is to watch mother's back."

Miss Beasley and Mr. Burney both stood up to leave while reflecting. I didn't have the words to express to either of them how indebted I felt that they had agreed to perform a service that was so dangerous; to give our daughter slash niece a chance to return home safely and in a more timely manner than the bureau could arrange, without jeopardizing any memorandum-of-understanding with the Chinese government. I walked both of them to the door and hugged them firmly.

Slapp slowly turned back to the two brothers, Max and William. "Listen you two. I don't want to ask you two to do anything that will weaken or disrupted the relationship that you'll have with your parents. I am short on manpower, but I do have a few other options." Slapp laced his fingers together while he waited for the brother to answer. They both looked over at their father first and then at each other. Alex dropped his head, because he was sure of what their answers would be. The two brothers each slapped the tabletop simultaneously as they replied.

"Uncle Slapp, we're all in."

"Well alright then" replied Slapp as he gave each of them a high-five hand slap. "Let's hear it for the boys. Remember guys this is not a computer game. The bullets and interrogations are real, if you are caught. If you have a problem with those pretty faces being rearranged, you need to speak-up now. Max, William, you both should still have in your implanted tracking devices that we had placed sub-dermally when you first became a part of this shit-fitters outfit, for lack of a better term. We will use them to find you if you get snatched off the street for snooping. All we have to do is locate the old paperwork with the codes and reactivate the devices. We kept a few of our old outdated communication packs, but you two will be using burn phones. The moment you arrive on location, purchase three throwaway phones; each from different locations. It's not unusual for tourist to purchase temporary cell phones while they are out of their country. Use your personal phones to call home to your mother or girlfriends, like you would on a vacation, but only talk about the mission on the burn phone. I have already called your service carrier and had your phones upgraded to international status."

This fact excited Max as he quickly pulled out his I-phone to check. "Hey! Thanks Uncle Slapp, now I can talk to all the out of country babes too." Slapp snapped at Max without thinking or remembering that he had once been young and easily excitable.

"Damn it Maximilian, this isn't a game. Pay attention, because if your ass get hurt, because you deviated from these plans, you better hope you are killed, because if not I'm going to shoot you myself." At that moment everyone in the room looked in Slapp's direction. Slapp then realized what he had just said out louder than he had intended. "Okay, perhaps I didn't mean that, but I need your full focus, alright? Both of you do remember how to post an ad. If you are unable to post an ad in the classified section every two days, we will assume that someone has taken you. You can set up an account in advance so all you will have to do is dial in and push one button. Set up at least three different types. 1) I'm fine I need more time, 2) I think I'm on to something could use another set of eyes, 3) I'm inside need six hours. If we don't hear anything, we will assume that you are in serious trouble and we will track you down using the sub-dermal implant. Are we all clear? No guns okay. Each of you will be outfitted with a long-range panic button attached to your watches, which can also act as a GPS so we can find you. You will also have a back up in fatty portion of your butt cheek that I will inject tonight. All you have to do is press the spot down hard with your thumb and hold it for one whole minute. After 60 seconds, it will start to send a signal until we find you. The area will be sore for a day or more, but other than that, no problem."

Max spoke out of term again, "So Uncle Alvin, does that mean that our ass will pickup radio stations too, because I do have a favorite play menu." Slapp slowly turned to Max as the remainder of us held our breath. Slapp wasn't in a playful mood. He had a lot on his mind and was worry sick inside that something might happen to his best friend's sons. Then Slapp realized that Max didn't know the serious side of him and he was the uncle that was always telling jokes and playing tricks for fun.

"Max if you say one more stupid thing during this briefing, I'm going to kick you off the team so you can heal from a personal beat down." Slapp broke off the eye contact with Max after he gave a quick threatening smile. We all exhaled as Alex and Tate smirked just a little.

"Sorry Uncle Alvin", said Max. "I was just trying to lighten the mood in the room. I'm listening, I promise and I'm not going to mess this up.

I noticed that the excitement and joy of the two of them going on this mission, seemed to drain out of them the more Slapp talked and gave his restricting instructions. William spoke up first as Alex managed to smile now that Slapp's plan to keep his sons safe was so detailed and well thought out.

"Damn Uncle Slapp, it sounds like Max and I are only going to be bait for this mission."

Alex spoke with a slight smile, "Move that man to the front of the class and give him an A."

Slapp looked down and suppressed his laughter as Alex just let his ripped. "Yeah Guys", confirmed Slapp, "that's about the size of it. Now if you have any objections and are determined to go on your own, I will be forced to have both of you arrested and held until all of us come back. So gentlemen, what will it be; my way or the highway?" William let out a loud sigh and Max giggled because he was just glad to make the team and was shocked that his father Alex hadn't asked Uncle Slapp to arrest him in the beginning, just to be on the safe side. Max replied for the both of them.

"Okay Uncle Slapp, we can do it." Then Max smacked William with the back of his hand on his mid-arm, "Right big brother," said Max to William?

"Very well then, welcome aboard," said Slapp with an approving chuckle. "William, you listen to Max when it comes to the layout of the city because he knows the area and all the places that we traveled before. Max also has more recent experience with the secret code and how to construct the information for the ads. Max listen to William because we trained him in a camp setting years ago and he will be able to anticipate our next move by watching the news. Now go and have a good time and don't spend up all our damn money on the women. Once you run out of money, we have to locate you or you have to catch a plane home and bring your tender asses back here; understood? We don't know how long this will take, so you understand that you can't draw any money from the banks, your credit cards or the automatic teller. We want to get in and out without leaving a trace. We don't want anyone to follow us home. You will be living in a cheap hotel near the one that your grand father Oscar use to live in; that way you Max will be familiar with the area and all the metro train stations and stops. Your covers are two young handsome men looking for a good time with some professional ladies of the evening. Please don't sleep with any of these girls. We don't want either of you to come home with the gift that keeps on giving, right; like a baby or a V D that can't be cured. Then we will see if your Uncle Tate can summon a miracle to save you." A few of us smiled, yet Tate showed no emotion or change in his serous facial expression.

Slapp continued, "Get as much information as you can, pay them and leave. Go to the strip-tease bars and throw a few bucks around. Max you need to work the villages because you are so youthful looking until, I'm not sure they will let you into most of these night spots and we don't want you to have to continue to show your identification all over the place. If they don't let you in on your first attempt, don't push the issue. We don't want any extra attention. Your flights leave tomorrow night like dad's, but from Ragan National and it will be on an Asian airlines. Got it? Now go pack. Wait a minute; here are your new modified passports. I had them made up just in case your father didn't shoot me for considering allowing you two on the team."

Tye was asleep on one end of the sofa in the living room, by this time. When everyone began screaming at each other earlier, he had found this moment to move away from the table. Slapp turned to Alex as Tate moved from the doorway of the kitchen, while still dressed in his clergy garments.

"Tate, Alex, I want you two to fly into Thailand and then drive into Cambodia. Our old communication devices should be able to pickup on a satellite. I'm sorry I didn't have time to test that theory, I was just glad when the crap came on and made a sound. From there I want you to track Max and William via computer. My mother and father's hotel will be our home base or command center in Hong Kong. I'm sure if they haven't changed all the codes at the American Embassy. Ma will be able to pig-back on them and tap you two into the boys via satellite. Tye and I will go in and become whatever or whomever we have to become to get close to where Milani and her partner was last seen. Oh, one piece of information I forgot to share with the group. Her partner is her cousin, formally known as Officer SuKi Jr. Alex you've worked with him before, years back in Hong Kong, you're the best person to profile him. I know he can be trusted."

Alex yelled again, "How in the hell could you overlook making that information available to us, Slapp?"

"Calm down Alex, I just found out myself, before coming over here tonight. One of my friends that I recently made at headquarters gave me the information without knowing what he had done so. He wanted to know if I knew a Chang from the New York Office? Apparently that was where Suki was recruited from for this mission. I was as shocked as you are." I guess the bureau chose him because he is from that region and would be able to blend in. Com'on Alex, you know how this works.

"And what did you say, Mr. Mission Leader Madison?"

"I told him that my attorney's last name was Chang, and perhaps they were related." I moved closer to the table from the other room and placed my hand on Slapp's shoulder in case there was something he wanted me to do. He looked up at me as I stood quietly.

"Helen I need you to stay here and try to run interference for us. I know the bureau has continued to watch us, or at least me, anyway. When I call in and tell them that I need to be gone for two weeks, someone will want to question this. If they ask me, I will tell them that my mother went on vacation to Hong Kong and got sick and I went to bring her back, after the doctors said it was safe for her to travel."

The four of us gazed over where Tye appeared to be sleeping like a baby, on the sofa. He was now snoring and had changed positions. Kate was sitting at the other end of the couch looking as if she needed to move before he placed his feet into her lap. Slapp shook his head in disbelief to Tye's calmness.

"Helen, do me a favor and wake sleeping beauty Tye up, please. Does he think he's at home? I never understood how Tyrone was able to survived this long in the department." Tye answered in the next breath.

"Every closed eye isn't asleep nor is every still dog dead, Slapp. Haven't you heard your grandmother repeat that more than once? I heard everything that was said. By the way, I was able to stay in the department all these years because I have a photography memory, I can draw or rough draft anything I look at for 30 seconds or less, I speak three languages and then there is the fact that I'm so damn good looking. Now what assignment do you have for me to assist in this mission?"

"Tye, man do you have any of your gear with you," inquired Slapp with annoyance in his tone?

"Hell no, Agent Madison, since our moonlighting adventure, the department has added GPS to all the new equipment including the toilet paper. I'm afraid to wipe my ass too quickly in fear it might set off an alarm. Please excuse me ladies, but I have a few more months before retirement and they are wearing my ass out with all the 'new rules and precautions' quote unquote. All I have on me is three passports, two currencies, an ink pen, a hand-wipe and a breath mint that I'm afraid to use. You can put poison in anything now adays. Last year the department gave me a nice gold watch for all my years of service. I was so damn paranoid, until I left it in my desk drawer at work. I came straight here from work, because I knew that retired Agent Burney probably has some old field equipment I can borrow and use."

Everyone was now laughing at the one-man comedy act that Tye was putting on. I never remembered the sarcastic humor in him. I guess over the years all of us had changed in one way or another.

"Okay," replied Slapp, I will take you over to the house and get you geared up.

Chapter Ten

Last Mission for My Brother

Two days later everyone had departed for the unauthorized mission, accept for Gayle, Kate, and I. Of course we didn't have the heart to tell my foster mother everything that was was going on. I'm sure that my father was very brief and uninformative when he told my foster mother he had take make a quick trip out of town. She probably didn't notice that his passport was missing. The girls and I even considered skipping church. Now that our men were gone, we had to fill in more at the warehouse slash soup kitchen with Father Caleb. Gayle took a week off from work, I was fully retired and Kate set her own schedule to fit her needs. Kate and Cameron spent a lot more time now at the Barn, which was their place next to Slapp's parents and across the road and up the lane a bit from Alex and I. Of course Cameron was livid that he couldn't go with William and Max to act as decoys or perhaps bait, for a more accurate analogy of what they had been assigned to do for the team. Gayle spent more time out in the country with us that first week she took off.

In Asia, Milani didn't actually get caught up in the second illegal sweep until two days after Officer SuKi prematurely pushed the panic button, by placing that prewritten coded kitty ping pong classified ad in the local Washington D.C newspapers. This meant that Alex and the others were fortunately in place only hours after she had been taken. SO it really was a good move on Suki's part.

Alex and Tate were now in Cambodia, only a few thick jungle miles into the bush. They were very shocked that some of the villagers there remembered them and welcomed them back with open arms. When Tate arrived fully dressed in his clergy attire, they thought that this was a part of their cover. Of course Tate attended the local Christian meeting and spoke a few times a week, with the assistance of a translator. The people were totally taken in by Tate and soon the attention was going to be a problem for the two of them and this mission. We found out much later, because of their visit years before, that Tate and Alex had became a folklore in those parts; or perhaps and unproven legend might be a better description.

After Milani was taken, her partner slash cousin Agent SuKi took a part time position at the airport as a janitor so he could watch for whoever would arrive with a suspicious look. He had to wear a disguise to make sure that no one from his previous police department in Hong Kong would recognize him. Although Agent Suki had been gone about fifteen years, he didn't want to take a chance. He didn't even contact any of his old friends or family members.

The first person to arrive that Suki was sure was a part of the cavalry was Miss Sarah Lynn (Pocahontas) Beasley. Known in Hong Kong as Mrs. Becky Sue Carrington. Agent Suki took a cab and followed Miss Beasley to her hotel; yet made no contact. Then he headed back to the airport to observe who else was a part of the rescue entourage. Agent Burney showed up on the evening flight and the next day Slapp and Tyrone (Tye) unexpectedly appeared dressed like two old washed-out rich pimps attending a hooker's convention that had been canceled without prior notice. It was totally obvious that they hadn't received the cancellation memorandum, by the way they were dressed. It appeared that a few other forms of written vital information had eluded them as well. For an example: the fact that we were now living and dressing in the 2000's and not the 1970's.

Agent SuKi became so amused by their arrival appearance until he couldn't stop laughing long enough to approach them at the airport and give them the update. Slapp was a tall full-size man and now age had taken its toll on his beach like body's posture. In addition to that unsightly surprise, he was wearing a pair of slacks so tight, until if he had been a female, they would have caused a yeast infection, within twenty-four hours. When we were younger, we just call the tight fitting pants monostate7, like the medicine that was sometimes used for the yeast-infectious cure. Slapp was also wearing a hundred percent Thai-silk silk shirt, opened all the way to his belt, a large gold medallion chain around his neck with the long-life symbol in 23.99% gold. He wore a diamond pinky ring on his left hand and ruby on the right. He colored his hair to cover the gray. Slapp was a true dark auburn redhead from birth like his mother, so he had to color his hair with a comb-in tint, in which he had done a poor job with the color match and gray-hair coverage. Lets just say, for the sake of argument, that the selected hair color wasn't an appealing shade and just leave it at that. Slapp added a wide-brim off-white hat to that mess, while carrying a black walnut stained cane with a sword hidden inside with a genuine silver duckbill handle. We never did figure out how he got it on the plane. Tye outfit was a little more appealing, but not by much.

Slapp and Tye checked into the New World Renaissance Hotel, Kowloon city. Miss Beasley and Mr. Burney were three or four blocks away in another hotel. The four of them met that first day after they had all arrived, at the double-decker Baskin & Robins ice cream parlor, at the entrance of one of the stops on the redline metro rail. The meeting location was reasonably safe because they could observe anyone coming in the front door and if it became necessary, a person could exit down the back staircase that placed you in the lobby of a hotel that also shared an alley with the snack shop next door. Slapp, Tyrone, Miss Beasley and Mr. Burney shared the information that they had gathered and had gotten from Agent SuKi, and then came up with a plan.

After Miss Beasley assured her son Slapp that he would never get any red-light-district action from the Ladies of the evening, with that washed-out pimp look, Slapp begin to come around. Slapp finally agreed, after all the others completed their body-jerking laughter and decided that he should have included my father in their operation as well; if for no other reason than a fashion wardrobe consultant. We knew that my father would know what would be appealing to the ladies on that side of the world and what would draw them closer, so they could be pumped for information.

Slapp had an epiphany as he took in his next breath, "Wow, what the hell was I thinking? If Helen's father was here and we wanted to break into the inner circle of the prostitution ring, with Mr. Oscar being so well known in the entertainment business, they would offered him any girl he wanted because he was an old single Mac-Daddy all those years before; with the capitalized "M" "D". Why didn't I think of this sooner? He could move around from brothel to brothel playing his music and no one would even question him."

Mr. Burney smiled as he titled his head downward, as they all four continued to eat their ice cream of choice. Mr. Burney finally responded, "I think you might be on to something there Junior. You know it does my heart good to see that all my instructions in the classroom at the F.B.I academy hasn't gone to waste. Now the only problem with your new modified plan is getting Mr. Oscar here in time to help us. After one of these girls is snatched off the street, every hour counts. I'm sure Milani, with her beauty, will fetch a pretty penny. She's young, smart, healthy, and her elegance alone will start the bidding at least around ten thousand. The mix heritage and the fact that she is bilingual will surely raise the steaks if a transport to Europe is in the picture. Yeah no doubt, we could have use Mr. Oscar on this one, for sure."

Tyrone looked over and noticed that Miss Beasley had stopped eating her ice cream and was now silently weeping. Even though she had lived in Asia most of her adult life, she was sort of out of touch with all the human trafficking that appeared to be getting worst each year. She was capable of reading and writing the local language, yet she only read the local newspaper for entertainment and track all the local village celebration to get a preview of when a VIP might arrive without notice to the American.

Tyrone spoke quietly as he leaned in a little. "Hey fellows, do you have to be so graphic, a lady is present and I don't think she has the stomach for this kind of discussion. Any way, if Mr. Wiley isn't on the plane as we speak, then there is no way he will get here in time, before we have to make our next move." Slapp turned quickly to Tye as he apologized to his mother.

"You are right Tye, I wasn't thinking; I'm sorry mother. Today is Thursday; Agent SuKi told me that they always have an elaborate party two days after the illegal sweep. The second night is when all the buyers gather for the big auction at the top of this mountain, at this fancy secluded resort type house. It lasts two nights and after that, no one sees the girls again. If Agent Suki's Intel is accurate, this means that last night was the illegal sweep and we are out of time. This is the second time that Milani was picked up. The first time, no one came for her or attempted to bail her out, so she had to work it off at the parties as a serving hostess. Now that they see her as an independent, with no family or pimp looking for her, she will go on the selling block for sure. We don't have time to find the holding location and steal her back, so our only hope at this point in the process is to get invited to the auction party and bid for her."

Well as fate would have it, my father had called me the same morning Alex and the others left and grilled me until I told him what was going on. He caught the next direct flight out of New York to Hong Kong and arrived only hours after the others. My father knew that he would have no problem finding Max, because he knew all the places that Max would tell William that the two of them should stakeout first. Some of the places my father Oscar had provided entertainment in many years before would be their main targets. Even back then my father had noticed certain things weren't kosher, but he wanted to stay alive, so he settled for tending to his own business and turned a blind eye to the entire operation. The truth of the matter is that no one ever pays any attention to the live entertainer and they are usually the first ones to duck and run when the bullets start to fly. This time would be different. The first thing Mr. Oscar Wiley did was purchased a gun off the street. Then he called his previous entertainment-booking agent and informed him that he needed to play the old local red-light-district circuit.

"Hello Mr. Tamada, this is Oscar the 'Entertainer Man'."

"Well hello Mr. Oscar-San. How are you? I didn't expect to hear from you so soon. We continue to miss you here in Asia. The new groups are young, very talented; however, with no sense of professionalism and they are not dependable, plus they don't present themselves very well. Are you in our city now?"

"As a matter of fact, I am in your beautiful city. I need a personal favor Mr. Tamada-San." Mr. Tamada interrupted Mr. Oscar with a yes answer before my father could complete his request.

"Sure Mr. Oscar-San, whatever you want I will do it for you. The two of us made a lot of money before, so I still owe you, I think. Just tell me, if I can help you; I will do it, no problem."

"Well, one of my friends little girls have run away. We think she may be on the streets as a working girl, if you understand my meaning. We are trying to find her before she gets picked up in a human trafficking sweep." Silence; then a flood of broken English with a stronger accent on the edge of his voice; nervousness no doubt, spill out from Mr. Tamada-San.

"Oooohhh, Mr. Oscar, that is very dangerous business, not sure I can help. People get seriously hurt every night in this city, very big business, lots of people from other places moving around."

"Mr. Tamada-san, Please hear me clearly; all I need you to do is call and get me a few gigs at the old locations that I started out in. You know, Mr. Tamada-San, the red-light districts. Can you at least do that for me? One show only, money is not an issue. I'm trying to listen for some talk about the ladies-of-the-evening. I need to find out where they are taken after they disappear off the street."

"Humm, I'm sure I can get you in. I can book three shows at different locations. I know you will need a piano keyboard of some sort on location, correct? Please remember, old friend, that I warned you about the danger. Those places that you worked before is not safe any more. Please be careful Mr. Oscar-San old friend."

"Yes Mr. Tamada-San, I don't have time to gather a band. I brought a few demo tapes along, to fill in on breaks. If you can get me a portable keyboard, I will be able to play more locations."

"Very well Mr. Oscar-San, I will set it up and call you in two hours, at your usual hotel." Mr. Tamada quickly hung up on his end.

My father, Piano Man Oscar rushed down to the Fenwick Pier to get his tuxedo adjusted and pressed at Mr. Toni's shop. This was the same tailor that had designed those dresses for us, and the very same man that had made Gayle's surprise wedding dress. Mr. Oscar arrived back at the hotel around 4:00 that afternoon and whom did he find in the hotel's lobby, but Maximilian. Before Max knew what had happened to his self, he screamed out across the huge hotel reception area with desperation and defeated emotion in his tone.

"Grandpa Oscar!" Max then hurried across the room to embrace his grandfather as he conveyed hopelessness to him in a strong embrace. Mr. Oscar quickly swung his tuxedo over a nearby lobby chair as he waited for Max to arrive at his position across the open space. My father clutched Max by both of his upper arms and pushed him away sternly to question him and to give him a tongue-lashing. Max had already begun to tear up about the situation that had gotten out of hand and out of all of their control. Max knew that his little sister had already been caught up in the illegal human traffic sweep.

"Max, What the hell are you doing out here son?" Max was too chocked up to answer quickly enough for my father Oscar so he gave Max a forceful shake as he held him by both arms, just above his elbows. "Boy you better answer me and I mean quickly. There is no way in hell your parents gave you permission to come out here. Who came with you?"

Max had forgotten all about the fact that he was suppose to be undercover and the fact that he was indeed a grown-ass man, as he had so boldly informed his father, before leaving against Alex's will. Now Max was crying like a baby, about the fact that his little sister was missing and they didn't know where to start looking for her. The excitement from the adrenalin of playing the role of an agent had completely worn off and the reality that his sister may never be seen or heard from again had begun to soak in to his emotional consciousness and had shaken him to his core. Max finally gathered himself enough to respond to my father's demanding assortment of questions. Max took in a sober breath.

"Grandpa, I had to come and why are you so angry with me?"

"I'm upset about the whole damn situation Junior. You are too young and inexperienced to be out here. It's too dangerous for you son; plus you have your whole life ahead of you."

"I'm not alone Grandpa, William and I came together. I told him that I knew my way around. He joined the team as the computer expert; you know to take Miss Linda's position when the team first was formed. Everyone knows that you can't run a mission without a cyber geek surfing the Internet to feed you all the latest available information." Grandpa Oscar became angry all over again as he continued to whole Max by his upper arm.

"Listen Boy, I think you have been watching too much C.S.I. and N.C.I.S rerun episodes. This isn't a game and you aren't Gibbs, Abbey or Hattie." Max jerked away real nasty like from his grandpa Oscar's grasp as he elevated his voice and roughened it up a little before he spoke his next sentence.

"They couldn't stop me from coming. I am a man, Grandpa." By the time Max could get the 'pa' part out his mouth, Grandpa Oscar had slapped his face.

"Oh, oh you're a man now? Just a few seconds ago you were here in the lobby crying like a baby with a diaper filled with diarrhea shit, but all of a sudden you are a man now in the next breath? Listen to me carefully son, don't you ever raise your voice or sass me."

Mr. Oscar regretted slapping Max the moment he felt the sting on his hand, but it was done now and there was no going back. Mr. Oscar lips were trembling and facial muscles were twitching from pure rage. Max stood there in shock as he stroked his red stinging face cheek. Mr. Oscar spoke his finally words with a much calmer tone, before continuing to his suite.

"Maximilian, contact William and inform him that I have arrived, he will know what to do. You keep your head down; I will be taking your position on the streets tonight. I'll be in my room making a few calls and getting prepared until then." My father swiftly walked away, while carrying his freshly pressed tuxedo. Max did as he had been instructed. An hour or so later Mr. Oscar's talent scout, Mr. Tamada-san called to inform him that he had set up three, one-hour gigs for him, all in the red-light district. Two of the places were well known for illegal police sweeps and were on William and Max's browsing list as well.

Later on that evening, William was in the audience when, his grandfather arrived at the first designated stakeout nightspot. William and Grandpa Oscar kept their distance inside the first club to make sure that no one had any indication that they knew each other. At the second nightspot, of Mr. Oscar's one-man one-night and one-hour-only show, Miss Beasley and Mr. Burney were sitting at table number five in the back of this smoky joint, because Slapp was at table one in his best pimp-daddy outfit, while flashing money around. Slapp and Tye had attracted more ladies of the evening than usually and consequently the people in the rear couldn't see or enjoy the show that Mr. Oscar was trying so hard to perform solo. After Mr. Oscar's first warm-up song, the manager slash announcer came on the tiny worn out stage and gave a lengthier introduction and some background on how long it had been since my father had played the circuit in Hong Kong or in Asia for that matter. The placed looked a lot smaller and more rundown than Mr. Oscar remembered; yet he was a showman and had vowed to give his best whenever and wherever he was invited to perform. The manager assumed if he could get everyone's undivided attention and then turn it back over to Mr. Oscar, the ladies at Slapp and Tye's table would become more tolerable. The single ladies of the evening continued to drift in as Slapp and Tye continued to throw money around and talk crude and loud. Slapp and Tye left about ten minutes before the show was over; and so did most of the girls. Slapp and Tye knew where Mr. Oscar's next performance would be so they went on ahead so they wouldn't all arrive at the same time.

Mr. Oscar, Miss Beasley and Mr. Burney all entered through the alley into the dressing room hallway of the next club. The manager was waiting with a wide smile. Mr. Oscar didn't remember him, he was new, but had gotten all the information on Mr. Oscar Wiley. The three of them whispered as Mr. Oscar spruced-up his appearance and tightened his bowtie.

"So Mr. Oscar, how did you find out about this little mission," inquired Mr. Burney finally?

"I called my daughter and she started to cry the moment she heard my voice. I don't know how much time you have spent with my baby girl Monique (Helen), but she couldn't tell a convincing lie if her life depended on it. When she told me that the two of you were out here, I figured that another pair of ears and eyes tuned into the nightlife couldn't hurt. I ran into Max and decided to take his place as backup for William. He is much too tender and green to be out here. I'm not even sure he would know what to say if someone offered him a piece of ass." Then he remembered Miss Beasley who had became very still in the corner. "Oh, sorry Lady Carrington." She answered up like a trooper, yet with the same genteel lady-like persona. My father had met and knew Miss Beasley by her assigned witness protection name while she was living there in Hong Kong for all those years. My father reverted back to it without giving it any thought. He just assumed that she was using her old witness protection name for safety.

"No harm done, my old friend," replied Miss Beasley. Uncle Burney then turned to Mr. Oscar.

"Are you covered?" My father Mr. Oscar eyes enlarge for a second in surprise that Uncle Burney had made such a useless inquiry.

"You mean, am I packing," responded my father? "You damn sure better believe it. There is an entirely new sort of generation on these streets. Once upon a time the night's entertainment members were safe and only caught a bullet when they got caught between the crossfire, but now this new breed will try to use you as a shield instead of trying to cover you. Ain't that some crazy selfish shit?"

"What about you Mrs. Carrington," asked Mr. Oscar as he laughed as if he knew the answer? The two of them had history of being in the same part of the world for a long period. Mr. Oscar asked her only in jest. Miss Beasley (Mrs. Carrington) answered, as her femininity remained totally intact.

"You know me Oscar, the only place that I don't take my weapon is in the shower. Nothing can surprises me in this town except perhaps a man buying me a second drink without asking me which room am I in for the night. To answer your question, I'm covered. I think we should go out into the front Dexter Allen (Mr. Burney), before the manager thinks we are trying to come up with a reason why we should be paid as well."

This club was twice as large as the one before. Miss Beasley suddenly remembered that back-in-the day this place was on the top of the red-light district places to stop for a quiet drink with your date before an event, yet later on it became very dangerous; after management changed hands and the illegal sweeps were performed sometimes twice within a weekend. That was the reason that the first owner sold the place and moved back to Japan. The new management had let the place rundown; the bouncers were on the take and the bartenders were receiving kickbacks from the girls. It was too dark to see with whom you were talking, and watered-down drinks had become their trademark. The ladies of the evening were too brazen and some appeared to be high. The sophistication of this place had been totally lost.

Slapp, Tye and their entourage of groupies from the previous club had already chosen their seats right up front when Miss Beasley and Mr. Burney appeared from back stage. There were now at least fifteen girls looking in their direction, hoping that they would be the candy-flavor for the end of evening, whenever Slapp and Tye made their selection. Slapp was playing the drunken big-shot rich womanizer and Tye was just his sidekick slash bodyguard. Tye and Slapp had duck taped their weapons underneath the table where they were sitting, upon arrival. Neither of them had a gun permit for Hong Kong nor had they checked in with the local authorities to identify themselves as American Federal Agents. They were aware that if the manager found the guns after a raid, the very most would happen would they would have to double back and pay to retrieve them.

William was now at the bar watching everything. Immediately after Mr. Oscar's finally song, the manager turned the jukebox back on and it was loud. Everyone moved to the dance floor. There were topless naked girls dancing on the tables and bar counter-top. Slapp and Tye decided to make it rain, as the new generation of strip-club goers call it. (Throw rapid-fire dollar bills at the dancers) William moved closer to the door and Mr. Burney and Miss Beasley stood up to follow Mr. Oscar backstage to exit with him. In the dressing room, the manager had left food, fruit and a cheese tray, a bottle of nice wine, and of course a pot of hot tea. So the three of them sat in this tiny dusted dressing room, which appeared to double as a broom and mop closet, to have a bite to eat, before heading back to the hotel or onto the third and finally performance stop, with my father, Mr. Oscar.

A low volume conversation was struck as Mr. Oscar washed his hands over this tiny sink in the corner. His hands were no doubt cleaner before he touched the facet handles. Miss Beasley giggled briefly as she reached inside her purse and pulled out two wet-wipes for her and Mr. Burney her husband, while my father Mr. Oscar struggled with the wrapping paper that had been so carefully placed all around the food trays. Miss Beasley quickly stood to her feet and passed her purse to Mr. Burney and rush over to help Mr. Oscar as if she had a much better understanding of the wrapping, which had been used on the trays, and as if this was a de'javu moment that she and Mr. Oscar had share possible before.

"Please Oscar, let me do that for you. Mr. Burney looked on as Miss Beasley nudged Mr. Oscar out of the way. Mr. Oscar took Miss Beasley's original seat next to Mr. Burney, while they both waited to be served. Mr. Oscar continued with a brief story as he looked slowly around the room and them back in Mr. Burney's direction.

"You know Dexter, this room reminds me of the dressing rooms on the chitterling circuit. Oh don't misunderstand me, I'm not old enough to be a part of that time and I don't think that I'm no where near as talented as they all were. It's that when I first started my career, back in Los Angeles I performed in a few of the same spots. Most of the places had changed hands and been renovated, but a few kept the old dressing rooms as shrines to the pass performers. You could say that the people on the chitterling circuit sort of paved the way for us newcomers. When I first started in the business it was rough. The pay was shaky and you didn't get the same respect as some of the other performer got, if you understand my meaning. Light complexion men with questionable ethnicity were-in, back them and that proved to be an advantage for me more than a few times, I'm sad to say. I just didn't understand all the ramifications of flying beneath the wire or the struggles of my fellow brothers in the music business."

Miss Beasley then passed each of them a plate and took a seat on a nearby old rice wine keg that had been draped with a piece of clothe to be used for whatever. The two men looked over at Miss Beasley and laughed at her as she smiled back with her pinky finger lifted way up high as she sipped the tea with her legs crossed at the knee, while they both drank the wine. Then Mr. Burney spoke for the first time in a long while.

"Can you believe it, Oscar? My wife can find it in her to still be a lady in this dust-ass broom-closet dressing area. If I was a woman I would have refused to come in here and would have waited out front for us two old gas bags, but not my sweetie, she followed us backstage and didn't even complain." Then Mr. Oscar turned to look at Dexter as he took another swig of his wine.

"Brother Burney, did I ever tell you how Sarah Lynn (Miss Beasley) and I first met?" Uncle Burney looked over at Oscar, my father, with a puzzled look and answered.

"No Oscar, I'm afraid that I've never got the highlights of that story. I kinda' figured that you and Sarah Lynn had to run into each other at least once or twice. Sarah Lynn ever did enjoy the night life and with you being a piano man and all, I just assumed that you two knew each other." Miss Beasley looked down shyly and rendered a deep smile, as she appeared to remember the first time she met Oscar as well. Then my father checked his watch and realized that they didn't have time for such a lengthy and informative enlightenment. You could say that they were saved by time.

"Good Gracious a life, would you look at the time Burney, we have to go, because I have one more gig for tonight at another location." Miss Beasley sprang to her feet, adjusted her weapon that was inside of her dressy mid-calf designer boot and began to tidy-up the small closet-like room a bit.

A few minutes later, the three of them walked to the side door to exit, which opened into the alley. Suddenly a local Hong Kong policeman stopped them and said that this was a raid. One of the police officers immediately recognized Mr. Oscar from before and tried to talk the senior officer into letting Mr. Oscar and his party leave, but the man refused. Miss Beasley translated everything to my father and Uncle Burney in a whisper about what they were discussing about letting the three of them go. The man said no.

William never made his escape out the front door either. Now they all had gotten caught up in the sweep; Miss Beasley, Uncle Burney, Grandpa Oscar, our son William, Slapp and Tyrone the handler slash bodyguard. Max was back at the hotel surfing the Internet and noticed the breaking news on the television as he waited for William to return. The news cameras swept over a few of the people as they were ushered into the back of police bus and Max recognized the jacket that William was wearing, from behind; in spite of the poor lighting and the continuous movement of the cameraman.

The sweep was carried out in the identical manner as before and the way Agent SuKi had described when they initially arrived. Down at the police station, most everyone was searched and released. The pretty-working girls were separated from the drug addicted ones, then that group were held over night. Slapp put on the performance of his life as the high-baller "john" that threatened to own this town if he wasn't compensated for his troubles (being caught up in an illegal sweep. Miss Beasley acted as the translator for the police department and she, Mr. Burney and Mr. Oscar my father were the first ones to be released and to receive a sincere apology. The three of them stayed around, as Miss Beasley became an interpreter for the police department, while Slapp's amusing staged-rage continued on.

"Does anyone know who the hell I am", demanded Slapp? "Take a good look at this face. I was on the cover of Ebony magazine two years ago and before that, this face pierced the cover of Better Homes and Garden. Do any of you know how hard it is to get your face on that magazine? Well, I did have to screw the editor's youngest daughter, but besides that little insignificant fact, I still believe I was the perfect face for that unforgettable issue. Oh, oh I also won that survival show the first season it was on, did anyone see that season. Look at me from the side; I was that guy with the bandana tied around his head." Slapp was screaming and punching the cell-bars like a mad man who daily meds were wearing off. "You can't keep me in here. I just got a callback from the Oprah Winfrey's producers right before I got on the plane; that meeting for taping of the show is next Thursday. Ya'll have to let me out by then, it took me five years to set this up. Hey excuse me, don't walk away from me when I'm talking to you. You come back here I haven't finish introducing myself. Hey Sir, don't I get a phone call, email or text or twitter or Skype call or something? I'm going to call Attorney SuKi Chang all the way from New York City to fly in here and tighten-up all your assholes. Excuse me mother."

For the first time since Slapp started to rant, a few of the officer looked as if they recognized the words 'Attorney and or SuKi Chang's name. "I know that some of you guys know him. Do ya'll remember the last time he came home to see his family? Somebody please give me a phone; if I call now, he will be here by noon tomorrow I promise you. You don't know whom the hell you are messing with. I just came over here to Hong Kong for a few days to purchase me a little Asian moo-shoe (local temporary companionship) and you throw me in jail on an illegal sweep charge. It's not like you don't have plenty of it all over the streets. Besides, no one in the club was doing any thing illegal. I went in the club for the nightly entertainment and to have a few drinks, before I made my evening companion selection. Is this really how you treat your rich American guests? I was informed differently. Perhaps I will spend my money in Japan next time I take a long vacation, in search of a exotic piece; if you get my meaning."

Tye was now so tickled by Slapp's antics until he walked to the rear of the holding cell and turned his back to laugh so the other police officers wouldn't realize that this was a ruse to persuade the police to release all of them, before their cover was blown. Even Slapp's mother, Miss Beasley, found it hard to keep a professional face while she translated Slapp's blunders. Slapp was literally making it all up as he went along. It was like watching a dry run of the Saturday Night Live comedy show before they tweak it, for the first recording-take. Over the top is putting it mildly.

The senior local Asian policeman became very angry at this point and was considering holding Slapp, just because of all the name-calling and threats he had made. The younger officers thought it was funny and gathered closer, as Slapp performed for at least a half an hour or more. They finally decided to release Slapp after he threatened to sue and dropped a name that they knew and respected; Attorney Suki Chang senior.

The former Retired Police Chief entered the main office, just before they were released. He didn't recognize Slapp from before, but he spotted and acknowledged Miss Beasley and Mr. Oscar instantly as he walked in. He became a little shaken by their presents, and the fact that they had gotten caught up in the illegal sweep, but played it off rather well as everyone continued to attempt to find out exactly what Slapp was lobbing to gain. Finally, the formal retired police chief informed him that there was a huge party the following night that a man with his tastes or line of work might be interested in attending. Slapp snatched the card from his hand that displayed the address and the time of the event, while pretending that he was still entertaining thoughts of calling his attorney and possibly causing a national incident.

Slapp and Tye left first. Then William departed alone as he was so nervous until he had almost soiled himself. As a young teenager all this dangerous cloak and dagger stuff was cool and stimulating, but now as a maturing adult, it was just plain scary. Mr. Oscar was given a complementary ride back to hotel by the department, because they found out that indeed he was the night's booked entertainment. Miss Beasley and

Mr. Burney called a cab, but the department picked up the tab because Miss Beasley had stood-in for the translator that had gone home early for the evening.

Once back at the hotel, William called in his coded classified ad back to the newspapers that signal that they were in. Max used his first burn-phone call to let his mother know that they were all fine and grandpa had showed up and saved the day. The next morning my father and Miss Beasley caught a flight home into the Reagan National Airport. William and Max left the following afternoon for Thailand to join their father and their Uncle Tate.

The following night was the big party that Slapp had gotten himself and Tye invited to by the retired police chief. Up until this point everything seemed to be going as planned. Around 1:00a.m the night of the party, the auction for the knapped girls began. Slapp and Tye were inside while retired Dexter Allen Burney and Milani's partner; Cousin Agent SuKi Chang junior was outside waiting for a signal. When Milani was brought out all drugged up and beaten, Slapp almost threw-up. Tye eyes filled up with tears and he became so angry he wanted to spray them all down with bullets, including the hired help. She had lost weight, and she looked dirty and un-kept. The bidding started and Slapp had to disguise his voice so Milani wouldn't focus on him and blow their cover.

The first few girls that hit the chopping block, Slapp only bided enough to keep it interesting and to let them know that he was in the game and a serious contender for the best they had to offer. It's a known fact and world practice to save the best for last for several reasons. Well, this event was no exception to that unspoken rule. Once Milani was spotlighted for the bidding, Slapp was the top bidder, so he sent Tye to the car to retrieve the briefcase with the money. The headman and host sent another man with Tye to watch him. Of course Tye went into an uncontrollable rage, turned and broke the escorts neck the moment the butler closed the huge twenty-feet double carved-wooden front doors behind them. The bidding continued inside while Tye, Burney and Agent SuKi discussed how to get all the girls out safely outside in the parking area of this resort-sized privately owned house. The second hired bodyguard came out the front door to see what was taking the first guard so long to return with the currency and the money-man Tye. Mr. Burney threw a field knife that split his sternum and killed him instantly. There were only two visibly armed men left, but they didn't know how many guests might be carrying weapons as well. The dilemma was whether they would be able to take all the girls at once, because they knew that whoever was left behind would surely be killed and the criminals would scatter to the four winds, like roaches from a fresh can of Raid. At that moment, the agents noticed a helicopter start its engines in the rear of the huge resort looking structure. The team wasn't prepared for an air escape and they knew that this meant they would have to improvise. The team was too small to check the back and there was the fact that there maybe more arm men to deal with. Slapp heard the rotatory engine start up as well. He knew that this meant that the bidding and the party was coming to a close.

There were multiple translators inside and Burney and Tye couldn't come to an agreement of whether or not they should be considered guiltless bystanders. Finally they agreed that once the shooting commenced, that everyone that pulled a gun or weapon of any kind should be considered the enemy and ready to give up his or her life for this devious inhuman cause.

Slapp was waiting across the room as close as he could to Milani, so he could grab her the moment the shooting started. Slapp noticed the sudden vibration of his communication pack as a signal from Tye that they were coming in with guns blazing. The double twenty-feet tall doors flew open and everyone that moved suspiciously or pulled a weapon caught a bullet. The spray of ammunition flew around the large foyer and receiving den for about a minute. Mr. Burney and Agent SuKi were wearing ski masks and gloves. At first, most of the auction attenders believed that this was a robbery, because all transactions were performed in cash currency from whatever part of the globe you were willing to delivery it from, to cover your bidding. Almost half of the crowd simply chose to drop to the floor with their hands covering their heads. As soon as the gunfire begin, the helicopter took off from the back of the house. When all the shooting had ceased, at least four men were dead, not including the two outside and six others were seriously wounded. The injured included, a cook, two bartenders, two translators and a daily maid that had decided to work overtime for some extra cash. Agent Suki identified himself in three languages and ordered everyone to freeze.

Agent SuKi had arranged for a government plane to take Slapp, Tye and the girls to Thailand. They rescued eight girls including Milani. Burney and SuKi stayed behind and called the police to help clean up the mess. They took all of the guest's pictures and fingerprints of everyone there to update the bureau's data bank of the human trafficking players, before they released them into the custody of the Hong Kong local police. Even the dead and injured was catalog before being released. They weren't sure how high up the food chain the corruption had spread, so they made files of there own.

That had been Milani's and SuKi's mission; to update the data banks. However, Milani had modified the mission a little when she wanted to find out why the chief of police, almost twenty-two years earlier, was so against her great grandmother helping her American family to adopt her. Milani had other secrets that she hadn't shared with anyone.

Agent SuKi Junior and Retired Agent Burney kept on their ski masks and gloves the entire time. Of course the Hong Kong police department had a huge problem with that, so SuKi and Burney flashed their badges real quick and said that they were the highest ranking men onsite and they had to protect their cover in case they were asked to remain undercover a little longer. Another false reason that they gave was that they had staked out some Americans that had also been involved in the trafficking and they had led them to Hong Kong. They gave them some bogus phone numbers that they could callback to in Washington D.C, at the F.B.I. main office if they had any problem. Of course the language barriers helped them out a lot, even though Agent Suki was there and spoke at least three different dialects from that region. The translator that had arrived on the scene was young and extremely nervous. Agent Suki kept him confused by mixing the dialects, while pretending that it was all do to his poor training. Suki and Burney also used street sling and technical jargon to keep them puzzled.

One phone number that they gave them was Ole Joe's number in one of the coffee break rooms inside the FBI building. Ole Joe had played this game with various agents in the past and knew exactly what to say and do. The second number that they wrote down for them was to the soup kitchen to Father Caleb's office. He had been briefed as well.

Just as the sun was coming up, everyone finished their part of notes relating to the crime scene and all the guests that hadn't acquired a serious injury was taken to the police station by bus. Agent SuKi and Burney promised that their agency would share all the information they had gathered and would send a copy of the report after the headman in charge of the operation had approved what could be released and what would be considered classified and part of the United States National security.

Directly after the shootings and before the local police had arrived Slapp and Tye took the girls immediately to this private airstrip and flew them to Thailand. After the girls, who had been critical abused were care for in Thailand, they were then secretly moved across the boarder into Cambodia, where Alex and Tate had been waiting for their arrival. Max and William continued back to the states from Thailand; after they pretended to be tourist for a few more days, while spending more of the cash they had been allotted for the mission.

Chapter Eleven

Border Crossings

The local American Consulate in Thailand approved the paperwork, after Slapp paid him a visit and explained what they were up against. Once again only a portion of what Slapp and Tye divulged to the ambassador was the truth. Alex and Tate had already greased the skid, as they say for Slapp to show up and complete or authenticate the lies. The emissary received them cheerfully with wide-open arms of trust, while not knowing the full layout of the mission.

"Please gentlemen, come in." He was smiling as he clasped his hands in front of himself. Tell me, how can I help?"

Slapp had the sentences all formed in his head before he and Tye entered the office. "Sir I'm suspended Agent Madison. I teach now at one of the academies. My niece is a young agent just starting out and she was given an assignment in Hong Kong, to gather some Intel. It appears she was snatched off the street and became prey in the human trafficking war. Well, my friend here and I, Active Agent Tye, decided that we should go in and get her. The bureau would have to wait for Intel to come in and we knew that it would be too late to save my niece, once they realized that they had taken an Agent on an Intel gathering mission. So we went in to get her out. When we found her about to be sold like a piece of outdated meat, we took her by force, after we offered the highest bid for her, of course. There were other girls there and some of them require medical attention, in which we can't afford or wait for the states to authorize. We need you to activate the Memorandum of Understanding for U.S. citizens to receive care with the local hospital to help these poor girls without us causing a national incident. Since these girls obtained these injuries while being held in a knapping criminal situation, and was rescued by some Americans on mission; namely us, I'm sure that there is a clause in your rulebook somewhere that allows you to finance their immediate medical needs."

The American-to-Thailand representative listened very attentively and watched Slapp and Tye's every body-language movement to ascertain if their story had any truth attached to it. When Slapp finished his explanation monolog the room was mute as the emissary did a long pause before he responded. Slapp took this as a sign to give a few more vague details, in hope that this might persuade the middle aged man to move a little quicker towards his decision to help the girls. Slapp attempted to continue, but Tye interrupted him with definite annoyance at the edge of his tone, which Slapp believed had been caused by the ambassador's initial hesitation.

"Sir, we realize that this may put you in an awkward position, and we also understand that this could be considered second-hand kidnapping; since some of the girls are under the age of consent." Slapp jumped in again, but Tye cut him off just as Slapp took in a full breath.

"What the hell were we suppose to do, Sir" insisted Tye? "We went in to save our niece and found those other girls there all strung out on drugs, undernourished, and not knowing who or where they were. You see Sir, our niece is an agent, quite green if I may add, and we went in illegally to extract her. We believed that her cover had been blown and they were holding her to learn how much she knew about their operation. The human trafficking angle just happened to cross over the original mission lines. She was sent to gather Intel, that's all. We came here to Thailand because we figured that they would have all the departure flights watched that were traveling back to the United States. We came here on a private chartered plane to lay low until we could figure out how much damage we had done to the agreement between the U.S. and China by taking these girls out of the country with no passports, visa and no ID, in case they want to return. We didn't have time to sort that all out at the crime scene. We are not trying to jam you or the consulate up, we just need some medical help for these girls without too many questions being ask; and some money from your slush fund, of course."

The emissary raised his brow a bit right after Tye used the words 'slush fund'. Those words held a lot of power that could mean something positive or negative. It depended on who was using the words and whom they were spoken towards. The man became nervous about Tye and Slapp's predicament and decided that the less he knew the better it would be for him. He stopped Tye's aggressive verbal outline and agreed with a few conditions of his own. Then the ambassador's tone took on a hostile nuance as well.

"Very well, I will help you. However, I will not acknowledge any awareness of the girls, and their predicament. However, I will activate a need-to-know memo for their medical care needs and post a guard while they are in the hospital. They will be assigned aliases names and I will pick up the tab. If my boss or supporters ask any questions; I will do whatever I have to do to protect my ass and this office involvement; am I clear?" Then his voice returned to a more professional tone. "Now gentlemen, if there isn't anything else. Please forgive me for not inviting you to stay for lunch."

Then the ambassador made brief eye contact and then gave a shallow bow at the waist and dismissed Tye and Slapp from his Office. It was obvious to Tye and Slapp that the ambassador didn't give ah-shit what had happened to the girls. Slapp made a mental note to do a thorough systematic investigation of his half-breed ass the moment he got back to the States. Slapp decide if he found anything that wasn't kosher with him, Slapp would fly back to arrest the emissary personally.

The three girls that required professional medical attention stayed in the hospital for three days and them were driven to Cambodia, with false documentation that Slapp and Tye had purchased; where they joined the others. Tate being a member of the clergy was able to get the girls a lot of help from the local village church and priest. After Milani recovered well enough to travel and handle her own, she was determined to go back to Hong Kong to complete her assignment and take revenge on the Retired Formal Police Chief and whoever tried to cover for his old wrinkled fat ass.

One night while they all sat around in the basement of the dilapidated church, Milani decided that it was time to tell her father Alex, whom was really her uncle, and Tate, what had caused her so much torment and anguish when she was growing up. Plus what she believed had happened that second summer when she and her great-grandmother returned to Hong Kong for a visit.

The room that they were all huddled in was a semi-sub basement that had very narrow windows at the very top of the wall where it intersected with the ceiling. Most of the items in the room were old discarded tables and chairs that should have been thrown out, but in this part of the world everything has value. The floor consisted of clay dirt and it appeared to be damp and musty most of the time. Kerosene lanterns were used to light the room and sleeping accommodations were makeshift slabs with sack straw on top if you were lucky. If not your bed was a rag pallet on a piece of waterproof tarp. There were several shelves on the far back wall that held a few items of food and other survival necessities like dry wood to start a fire, old clothes, and dry foods. When Tate and Alex arrived a few days before, they had improved the storage shelves by ten-fold. They wasn't sure what condition Milani would be found in so they brought in a first-aid kit that was so extensive until one could almost open up an emergency room. The kit included a twelve by twelve size tent that could be used as a clean room for minor surgery.

During the monsoon season, this basement was the safest and only dry place in the village. It was a large room and one could tell that it was used frequently for just this purpose, to secretly conceal newcomers in the village and shield them from the drug cartel gorillas that seemed to be controlling everything within a fifty-mile radius. Almost twenty years later, Alex and Tate both agreed that very little had changed.

"Listen Milani", said Alex. "I know that you take your new career seriously, but I think that you and Agent SuKi should return with what you have gathered so far and perhaps allow the specialist to work on this situation, from another angle. You will also have all the photos and finger prints that your partner Suki and Uncle Burney gathered at the scene, when they rescued you. Just tell me, Baby-girl why it is so important that you go back to Hong Kong now, after all that has happened. You know that all of us risked a lot to get you out of there. Please tell me why it is so crucial for you to go back right now. You realize that this won't be the only assignment that you will have in this region because of your language abilities? I don't understand why you have to go back now."

Milani stared into Alex's face as he spoke the words of reason. She could see his lips moving, but she had zoned out because she had already made up her mind that she would return now, no matter what her father said.

"Dad, there is something that I need to tell you and Uncle Tate. It happened a long time ago. Sometimes, I think it's a bad dream or a nightmare that I keep reliving over and over when I sleep. I once heard Grandpa Oscar say that 'We all have our own demons; some we can share and others we can't'. At first I had no idea what that statement meant or why he had presented that quote at that particular instance. Later on when I was about thirteen the meaning became clear to me and I decided not to share my demons with anyone. At first I was afraid, and later on I just became angry and I didn't know why. That anger became a driving force for revenge in my life, but still I refused to share my torments. Not even with the counselor that you and Auntie Ma spent your hard earn money for. Soon after, simple joys began to leave my life. I was too young to understand what was happening to me and too innocent to explain, so I replaced it with learning and buried myself into school. When we moved back to Japan, in which made me the happiest I had been in a long time, I soon noticed the anxieties started to return with other unexplainable spirits of revenge. The only way I could get rid of them was to face them. So I became a agent in hope that one day the bureau would send we somewhere close to the area, so I could strike. I had no way of knowing that my career would send me back so soon."

Now by this time Alex had frowned up his face in a very confusing stare. Tate lowered his eyes and head as he placed one of his hands on Milani's shoulder and began to silently pray. She went on with her story very methodically; as if a burden was being lifted off of her very soul, while she revealed the long-lived tormenting secret. There were at least twenty others in the basement at the time, including the rescued girls and a few villagers that were caring for them, yet most were on the other side of the room and outside the earshot or language barrier of this conversation.

"What are you talking about Milani? What caused this anger to rise up in you? What have we ever done that made it so difficult that you couldn't tell us?" Her eyes swiftly filled with tears as she quickly corrected her father's train of thought."

"No, no dad this had nothing to do with you and Auntie Ma. This happened that summer when my great-grandmother and I came home to Hong Kong for a visit and my great grandmother died. I stayed in the village with my other family." Alex interrupted her once more.

"What happened to you that summer, were you upset because you weren't with us at the condo, during our trip before? Did someone molest you or something, because you were never the same after that trip? We thought that it was because your great-grandmother had died so suddenly." During this entire time Slapp had been on the other side of the basement talking to the local priest. Slapp glanced quickly over this shoulder towards the three of them when he noticed the pitch shift in Alex's tone as he aggressively questioned Milani. Milani attempted to explain to her father, without upsetting him any further.

"No Dad, I wasn't molested or anything like that, but I was pretty unhappy about my great-grandmother passing. What I remember was that the first night that we arrived, the old retire chief of police showed up and was speaking with my great aunt and great-grandmother. At first I had no idea that it was about me. It seems that he was inquiring to see if I had returned to Hong Kong permanently or just for a visit. He seemed to become very agitated when my great aunt informed him that it was only for a visit and that the entire family was in the city for the summer. I believe that over the years my great aunt had been taking money from him with the promise of turning me over to him whenever my great grandmother passed on. She lived longer than they thought she would and plus they didn't know that she had went to the American Consulate to see if she could locate my father. Their plans were totally destroyed when you and Auntie Ma just happened to show up and wanted to adopt me. It was just pure luck, or perhaps divine intervention, as Father Caleb like to say, that you all chose Hong Kong as a place to hideout and that Aunt Gayle had saved that picture of my biological father in her files.

A couple of days after we arrived that summer, my great-grandmother became sick and had to be put into the hospital. The day that I went to see her alone, I found the police chief standing over her with a pillow clinched in his hands as if he had just smothered her. When he saw me he put the pillow in the chair and ran over to me to threaten me. He said if I told anyone what I had seen that he would hurt my relatives that I had left behind in Hong Kong. I was so afraid and distraught until I went into shock. I ran to her bedside and pushed the call button to summon the nurse, but she was already dead. The police chief had left the room before the medical person came in and I never told anyone that he had been there or that I had been threatened." This story had a negative effect on Alex and it happened so quickly.

************* Man Down Odd Man Out

Alex quickly started to show early signs of an anxiety attack as he nervously reached into his upper shirt pocket to take one of his pills. The mixed emotions that he was now experiencing was overwhelming to Alex and with his compromised health condition, he had no way of slowing down the effects that the information about Milani's past had on his vital signs. Alex became so chocked up while his throat and tongue instantly started to become dry, until he couldn't speak. Alex slowly stood to his feet and walked to a nearby corner and turned his back to the remainder of the people in the room, in an attempt to calm himself. Alex clasped his hands together in a squeezing grip in the front of him as the tears streamed down his face. Tate and Milani followed him with their eyes, as they became deeply concerned about how the reconstructed chronological account had affected Alex's entire demeanor. Slapp had completely withdrawn from his conversation on the other side of the room with the local priest and was now slowly moving on a path that would take him pass where Tate and

Milani were now sitting and to the rear of Alex, in the corner. It appeared that Slapp was more aware of Alex's medical condition and symptoms than the others. Tate had placed his arm around Milani's neck and shoulders and pulled her even closer, while wondering if telling Alex the story, after all these years, was the best thing to do, at this moment. I guest Milani wanted to clear her conscious if anything happened to her when she returned to Hong Kong to complete her personal revengeful portion of the mission. The damage was done and now she had to live with the fallout. Alex's reactions were no doubt mixed with the confusing thoughts of not taking better care of Milani, during her formative years. Alex felt he had failed Milani as a father and as an uncle. The stress of being there in Cambodia and the details of Milani's story was too much for Alex's condition all at once.

Slapp finally reached the rear of Alex, as he continued to face one of the corners in the room, as he stood as though an elementary teacher had placed him in time-out. His head was hanging extremely low as he silently cried for his daughter that he had been unable to protect or share such a horrific incident. Alex could now feel his heart beat increase in speed as it pounded against the wall of his chest. Then a hot sensation washed over him. Just as Slapp reached Alex from the rear and place a firm grip on his shoulder, Alex lost the strength in his legs and collapsed to the clay-dirt floor. Tate and Milani rushed over to Alex, as Slapp eased him to the basement's foundation and partially tarp-covered floor. Tate immediately dropped to his knees and placed one open palm onto Alex chest and begin to whisper a prayer.

Milani was now leaning over Alex while screaming quietly and lightly slapping her father's face cheeks in an effort to revive him. "Daddy, are you alright? Please Daddy; don't let anything happen to you way out here. Auntie Ma will never forgive me." Slapp quickly pushed Milani to the side as he loosened Alex's clothes and applied an inhaler capsule under his nose. The priest and a few of the girls all sprang up to observe what was happening on the other side of the basement. The local priest quickly rushed over to see if he could be of any assistance. Alex responded in the next few inward breaths as Tate and Slapp pulled Alex to his feet and steered him to a nearby old worn-out picnic table that had been used earlier as their dinner table. Slapp placed one of Alex's pills in his mouth and yelled for someone to bring Alex some water and the portable oxygen tank, while Tate continued to summon Divine intercession in the form of a whispered prayer. Tate's lips were moving, but his words were for God's ears alone.

Slapp had never witness this part of Tate before and had always teased him or had cracked jokes about his vocation, in which Tate had only recently chosen to return to, after almost twenty plus years. It wasn't that Slapp was a non-believer or that he disapproved of Tate's decision, it was that he never realized how consumed Tate had become with the spiritual power, in which was now using him as a healing conduit. After about fifteen minutes or a little more, Alex sat up on the table and demanded to be moved to a nearby chair. Alex appeared to have completely recovered without a clear full memory of what had taken place, as it related to his episode.

Milani and Tate decided that perhaps they shouldn't repeat her story to Slapp, because of his temper. She was only trying to get her father to understand how important it was for her to go back, finish the mission and possibly provide proof of the connection between the former retired police chief and the human trafficking ring, which had now been running under the retired chief's watch for years. Afterwards, Slapp insisted that someone tell him something that had caused Alex to collapse; Milani and Tate finally gave Slapp the watered down version, while leaving out the personal emotional demonic portions.

"Uncle Slapp, I was only trying to explain to my father why I'm compelled to go back to Hong Kong now. I believe that the former police chief have been involved with the female sex trade for the pass twenty years or more. One of the reasons I believe this is because he was so apposed to me leaving the country years ago. I think that he and my great aunt had planned to sell me when I became older. The police chief and my great aunt went to school together and I recently became aware that at one time she worked in the local bars and such. I believe she and the chief of police had worked out a deal to sell me and split the money. What they didn't count on was my great grandmother living so long, after being so sick." Slapp stopped Milani abruptly as he sank down hard onto an old nearby wooden bottle-crate, which had been stood on its tall end.

"Wait Milani, just hold the hell up. You are giving me the damn facts of the story a little too fast for my taste. I hear every word you are saying, but I need you to speak slower so I can process it. Besides, you were barely four when we all moved back to the states. Now start again and if you leave something out, that I feel is important. I'm going to have to spank that ass of yours. I've been promising you that for a few years now." Tate, Alex and Milani laughed out as though they knew that Slapp would never keep that promise and now it was definitely too late and much too dangerous. Milani had earned several belts in the martial arts. Slapp was so in shock of what he was now hearing, until he didn't know what he was saying. In his eyes, Milani was twelve years old again when he had hit her on the behind once for lying to him. She remembered that smack, so she decided to explain a little better before moving on.

"Uncle Slapp, I know that I was only four and a half, but I figured some of this out when I heard the chief police and my great aunt arguing about me. The former chief of police asked my great aunt if I was there for a visit or had come home to stay. You remember that summer when we all went back; I was around seven? Well I was almost twelve when my great-grandmother and I went back the second time alone. I remember how upset the former police chief became when my great aunt informed him that all of us had come back together for a visit. I believe that the only thing that had been standing in his way of kidnapping me was my great grandmother, who died that summer."

Alex and Tate gave each other eye contact as they prayed that Milani wouldn't give her uncle Slapp any more details about that summer and what she believed had caused the death of her great-grandmother. Slapp grabbed Milani's arm as he tried to suppress his anger. Slapp's first few words of his next sentences were spoken quietly and slow, and then it increased in speed and volume into an out-of-control burst of bitterness.

"Milani baby, why didn't you tell us all this before? Now your Uncle Slapp is going to have to go back with you and kill the old fat bastard. Tate sprang to his feet and grabbed Slapp in a half bear hug which forced him to release Milani's arm." Tate spoke quietly as he backed Slapp even farther away from Alex and Milani.

"Slapp, what the hell are you saying? Alex and I are trying to talk Milani out of going back and now you tell her that you are going back with her to commit a serous crime. Please explain to me what the you were thinking?" Slapp broke away from Tate's now relaxed grip as he realized that Tate was correct in his reasoning." Slapp's eyes were red with pure rage as his lips begin to tremble. The other girls and the priest, due to the language barriers and whispers, had no idea what was happening. Tate continued. "Look around Slapp; you have gotten Milani all worked and frightened the rest of the girls. They probably are thinking that we rescued them so we could turn around and exploit them for a higher price. Listen Slapp, we just want everyone to be able to walk away from this in one piece and give the girls, that we just illegally liberated let me remind you, a second chance to make better choices with their lives. I'm not sure if you agree, but I'm too old for this game any more. Slapp calmed down quickly and briefly smiled as he agreed with Tate.

"Yes, you are correct my old friend, but this could be my last chance to make it right for at least one person that I love." Slapp and Tate stared each other in the eyes as Tate began to understand Slapp in a way that he had never considered exploring before, in that Slapp's heart was much larger than his brain. Embracing that thought explained a lot of Slapp's actions and attitude.

"Very well," Tate acknowledged finally. "Mr. Suspended Agent Madison; if you can sell it to Alex and talk him out of tagging along with us, I will support you anyway I can; now do we have a deal? You do realize that weapon handling is completely out of the question for me."

"Yeah yeah yeah, Holy Man Junior and you have just sealed a covenant with me", replied Slapp with a smirk on his face. "Shouldn't we cut our hands and slap them together or something. It seems that in the bible there is always some blood spilled or involved when a promise is made from God to the people. Slapp knew that the word **covenant** was used in the bible so he selected and misused it to get a rise out of Tate, but Tate had long put that demon to rest in respect to Slapp ribbing him by pretending to completely act confused about the bible and its various passages. The two of them walked back over to Alex and Milani, as all the others in the room resumed their conversation in various locations of the sublevel space. Tate took his divine pose before he stated his and Slapp's ploy. Alex stared in his direction with the look of serious concern and doubt.

"Alex, Slapp maybe correct in his thinking. Milani is an adult with a job. We have no power over stopping her if she wants to go back. Besides, her partner is waiting to hear from her. I'm pretty sure that Burney has left him there in Hong Kong and disappeared somewhere to make sure that no one will follow him home, in case the police department figured out whom we all were. If you promise to go home, I promise to go back with Slapp and Milani and with God's help, bring them home in one solid piece and alive."

Alex looked up at Tate from a sitting position. He studied his face carefully before he replied. "I know I'm sicker than I though; if I've lived long enough to witness you buying into Slapp's bullshit. Is that what the two of you were talking about over there?"

"Yes Alex," replied Tate solemnly. "And I believe that for once, Slapp has a good idea. And please understand me, I never thought that I would live long enough to agree with Slapp either. We can't ask Milani to leave her partner slash cousin behind; so our only option is to send someone back with her. The two of us have volunteered for the assignment." Then Slapp turned to Milani.

"Listen Little Girl, you need a couple more weeks to recover, gain your strength back and for us to continue to flush your system from the drugs. I think that we are safe here for the moment. In the mean time, your father and Tate will drive back to Thailand and after a week of pretending to be tourist, Tate will put your father back on a plane home." Milani shook her head yes just before she started to console her father, by hugging him tighter.

"Dad, I know you want to come along, but your health isn't the best and none of us could ever go back and face Auntie Ma if something happened to you. Just this once Daddy, please go along with the plan that someone else has taken the lead on." Alex gazed into Milani's face and eyes and for the first time ever Alex saw her as an adult, even though she appeared to be the size of a twelve year old. Alex knew that with the Jones' DNA pumping through her veins and the training that she had received, from the time they came in contact with her at the age of three, she was the most dangerous and capable one of them all. Now all he could do was pray for whomever attempted to block her path. The Hong Kong human trafficking ring and retired former chief police officer were going to be shut down. Alex's only concern now was worrying about whether Milani was more like her biological father, his deceased twin brother Austin or had she become a product of her environment and turn out to be more like her Uncle Slapp; who believe that you should never leave an enemy behind when killing him is a sure safe option to embrace, for peace of mind. All Alex could do was hope and pray that the latter wouldn't turn out to be the case.

The next day, Alex and Tate went about their daily business with helping the local missionary priest with his daily chores.

Slapp, Tye and the girls remained in the basement of the church and out of site. The first aid kit, which was more like a small emergency room slash pharmacy, came in handy to the locals. So every day there were plenty of people to visit and dispense medicine. The little clinic was more like a field-medical station. They issued vitamins, dressed wounds and passed out antibiotics. They pulled teeth on some of the older folks and issued pain medication after mild procedures. Took off infected toenails, burst and dressed blisters. The first aid kit even had an array of meds for the children. The locals loved the fact that Alex and the others took such an interest in their offspring. One of the big sellers that the guys didn't remember, from their previous trip to that area, was the super strength bud repellent, which was a luxury item to them. Each morning they would line all the little children up and give them shot or two of the bug repellent and a piece of sugarless candy, before they went in the fields with their parents. Most mornings that was Slapp and one of the girl's task, because Slapp usually was a day sleeper and this line was formed before daybreak and way before any breakfast was prepared. They customarily ate later in the morning, after a few critical chores had been accomplished. Still all and all they had to be carful and mindful of their every move.

The jungle dwelling rebels had random times for showing up unannounced in the camp and there was no way these girls would be able to blend in with the locals for several reasons. The first detail that would surely give them away, if anyone got close enough to see them clearly, was that they were a different race. And then there was the fact that they were from the city so their skin was too fair to pass as farm workers; and lastly it was their clothes that were very sexy and very revealing. The villagers had donated some clothes for them to change into, once we arrived, but we couldn't take a chance that this would be enough of a disguise to deter the rebels from taking a closer look. The priest always assigned them inside work to do or a task that allowed them to stay near the church's entrance. The church was like a safe haven because the rebels never wanted to go inside. They knew that this was holy ground and they believed that something bad would happen to them if they did anything to defile the church. The girls never complained about their assignments, because they all seemed to know that the men had saved their lives from a rough road to hell.

Having extra hands and all the new equipment and medicine that Alex and Tate had brought in by truck, would keep the village people busy and content for at least a few months. This far outside the city made it very hard for the local rural farmers to get regular medical care of any kind. Their biggest problem was obtaining enough water to drink and water for their crops. There were always rebels in the jungle that would muscle their way into the villages and take whatever they needed at the time. We noticed that there were a few broken-down trucks. The priest informed Alex and Tate that the rebels would take whatever parts that they needed and the village people had no money and no way to go to town and bring back another replacement part. Most of the wars now were about territory, guarding their poppy fields and hiding out from the law.

One evening, while they were all huddled-down together in the church's basement, Slapp decided to ask questions to pass the time. There were only a few candles lit around the room and the girls were getting ready to lie down for the night. It was still very early, but the city girls weren't accustomed to hard labor and they usually slept in until ten or later, whereas the country people, as I say before, got up just before there was any light outside and ate breakfast later in the morning. Some had distances to travel, just to get fresh water or bargain for milk for the small children.

Slapp slowly moved over to where Alex, Tate and Tye had been sitting as they continued to put Alex's mind at ease about their next move. Slapp thought this would be a great opportunity to change the subject so Alex could give it a rest. The local priest was sitting in a far corner of the dirt-covered basement, with his own single candle light while drawing out an irrigation system to use up all the equipment that Alex and Tate had brought to him as their cover, during their initial arrival.

"Alex," yelled Slapp from across the basement. "Do you remember that run we made to the airport for the revised flu vaccine, when we were back in Hong Kong. I recall you saying that you and Tate had been here in Cambodia years before; on another mission. Is that why you chose this location to meet and to hold up in? I would like to hear the details of that mission, since all we have is time," said Slapp. Alex looked over at Tate, then towards Tye and then back again towards where Slapp sat waiting. Milani snickered a little as though she had heard a portion of the story before, but from another prospective and possibly second-handedly from Uncle Burney, Slapp's father. Milani was sitting right next to her father Alex and took this moment to slightly lean up against him as they both sat on a large sheet of canvas, which was later going to become their bed, with their backs pressed up against the wall of the damp musty basement.

Tate and Tye had been resting up against the table while standing with their legs crossed at the ankles. This was the table that had several uses. Slapp strolled over to join them. Tate slowly dropped his head and smiled a little as a signal that he preferred that Alex tell the story. He wasn't sure which parts Alex would leave out and there was no telling how much English the others in the room understood. Slapp then pulled up a nearby old broken crate and waited patiently for one of the two to begin the tale. Alex peered over at Milani and stroked her face as though this wasn't a story that a lady or his daughter should hear. Slapp spoke again.

"So what is the problem, fellows? Is this one of those tales that shouldn't be told in mixed company or is this recount filled with personal mistakes that you two have tried to forget? I just thought this would be a good time, since we are all here and I know for a fact that there aren't any complete files about this mission at the bureau, or anywhere else for that matter.

"Go ahead dad, I want to hear too," insisted Milani. "I promise not to tell Auntie Ma if there is an old girlfriend of yours in the story," said Milani as she clutched her father's arm tighter and leaned her head on the side of his upper arm. Tate slowly raised his head and slid into his divine pose as he waited to witness if Alex would relay the historical account.

"What mission", inquire Tye? "I've been around for a while now and a few years back when I got hurt and had to sit out for a few weeks, I spent most of my time in the archives making data entries and I never once found a record on file about Tate or Alex in Cambodia. Just hearing the highlights of that mission, in this god forsaken place, would make this trip way out here worth it." Then Tye quickly turned to see if the local priest in the far corner had heard him use the name of the Master in vain. "Sorry Father, no disrespected intended." The priest responded swiftly by slowly waving his hand in a downward blessing motion and then returned his eyes to the drawing, as he repositioned the single candle to another location on the narrow and poorly lit makeshift tabletop.

"None taken my child," acknowledged the priest. Then Tate placed his hands together in a prayer-like pose, possibly out of nervous habit, as Slapp directed his next comment towards him.

"What the hell are you doing, holy man in training? Are you praying that Alex will leave portions of the story out or are you hoping that he doesn't have to lie to keep it interesting?" Tye instantly began to laugh, but the others weren't sure which part of the comment that Tye found amusing. Tye then turned quickly to Tate to clear things up.

"I'm sorry Tate, you do realize that I believe you returning into the priesthood was the greatest decision you have ever made, for all our welfare; it's just that Slapp is so funny to me after all these years. He never stops with the humor insertions and the inappropriate name calling." Slapp rudely interrupted Tye.

"Shut up Tye and let Alex get on with the story. I can't sit up all night; and Alex if you don't want to tell it, I understand. I just thought it would be something to do to kill some time." Two of the girl's heads popped up off the sleeping mats from across the room just as Slapp spoke the word 'kill'. Tate turned quickly and spoke a few words of their language to assure them that this didn't pertain to them. He then addressed Slapp.

"Mr. Alvin", continued Tate. "You need to keep your voice down and be very careful about the words you choose, while expressing yourself." Slapp through up his hands and his face took on a confused scowl.

"What, what did I say? And oh, I'm Mr. Alvin to you now." Alex jumped in as the priest from the other side of the room looked up and over in their direction, for the second or third time.

"Slapp, you need to stop being so sensitive. Didn't you tell the girls to call you Mr. Alvin? Besides, slap maybe another word that the girls associate with abuse. Do you really think that they will understand that it is just your nickname and spelled with two 'p's. Come on lighten up. We are too far from home to be fighting amongst ourselves, just turn it down a notch and be careful how you use the word like 'K-i-l-l'."

Tye was trying to hide his amusement. Now that all of them were retired except for Tye and Milani and the fact that Tye was even younger than Slapp and had never been in the field with him, except with their illegal business that they had formed more than twenty plus years before. Tye was only one of the bureau's newcomers that they wanted to eliminate from the program, due to cutbacks. Yet Tye found the constant legendary rift between Slapp and Tate extremely entertaining. Tye had heard about the bickering between the two of them from other members of the 'My Brother's Keeper' team members, yet had never witnessed any of it first-hand. Surely at this point the disagreements were a lot less dangerous than they had been back when everyone was packing at the very lease two guns and a back-up knife, that was so sharp it could split a human strand of hair. It wasn't a mystery how dangerous that sub-agency was back then. Oh, they got the job done and took a lot of bad people off the street, but occasionally the collateral fallout was questionable.

"Slapp", said Alex finally to appease him and keep the peace. "Perhaps I can just give you the summary and then fill-in all the rest later." Alex took a lengthy pause before he completed his train of thought. Alex then turned his head to kiss Milani on the forehead as she continued to clutch his upper arm with her head leaning up against the outside of his shoulder. "Perhaps at your place one night, while under the encouragement of a nightcap or two? Or should I say the influence?"

"Okay my brother, if you think that would be best for everyone concern. I can wait," replied Slapp after a moment to give it some thought.

Tate stood up tall first, from where he had been propped up against the table. "Well, I think I should call it a night. I have to spend a few moments in the main sanctuary before I turn in. I will see all of you tomorrow."

Tate moved to the doorway that led to the steps that took you through this very narrow hall and up to the main part of the church building. The slender hallway passage was more like a very tight secret entrance to an over-size closet. The local priest in the opposite corner found this moment in time to excuse himself as well. He brought the single candle over to the table where the remainder of the agents had been gathered and followed Tate up the stairs to the main sanctuary. The two of them usually slept just to right of the altar in the modest built mission church. Tye took his position on top of the table as Milani and her father Alex laid down on their shared tarp. Tye was the armed watch and got up several times during the night to make his rounds inside and outside the church. Slapp rested his head up against the corner beam that braced the doorway that lead to the stairs that ascended out of the basement. Slapp slept lighter than a cat when it was required, and took most of his restful sleep during the day after lunch.

A week later, everything went as plan. Alex came home without our baby girl Milani and I cried every day. Alex read the classified ads each morning searching for a coded clue of how they were doing and when they would be returning. Five of the girls came to the states and two returned, because they couldn't see themselves leaving their families behind. The proposition of asylum, offered by the bureau, was only made available to the victims and their immediate family members; that meant husband and children. Which meant that the girls would have to leave everyone else that they loved behind; for some, the numbers and danger was too great.

While in Hong Kong, Milani and Agent Suki Junior, with the help of the others, had gathered enough evidence to prove that the former, now retired, police chief was a part of the human trafficking ring in that sector. They identified at least fifty in-power people that were tied up with the city's operation. From the dirty policemen at the various stations, to the people that worked the kitchen, on the nights that the auction parties took place. After it was all said and done, more than two hundred people were arrested. Of course some had enough money and connections to be released, but now at least we had them all on record, by association and photographed. Lying about ones name in this part of the word was as common as rice or noodles as the main dish for a meal. Having an alias was an expected and respected practice in the criminal world and the not so legitimate business world as well.

Once Tate was sure that Agent Suki and Milani had gather all the information that they needed to prove the retired chief of police's guilt, he left for the states. Just before Milani and Suki Junior departed Hong Kong they unexpectedly decided that they should burn down the big resort on the hill, in which Milani and the others had been rescued from. The resort had stood on that hill like a monument to all the corruption that had been going on in that city for decades. The police was involved, so the local people where afraid to speak out against what had been happening. Due to the fact that Hong Kong was and is a melting pot for people from all over the globe, it behooved you to tend to your own affairs. That had been proven to be the safest thing for you and your family members. Now if the local people witness the tower of corruption being burnt down, this would give them hope that their children would no longer disappear into the night, at least for a while.

Agent Suki Junior called in a tip to the local news reporter team and went up to the resort and lit it on fire. It had remained a crime scene and everyone had been forced to move out until a complete investigation had been performed of the shootout. Agent Suki knew that only a few men would be around guarding the place. He arrived with a clipboard and a large camera hanging around his neck. He quickly flashed his old badge and went inside and lit a small fire in one of the bathrooms under the sink near some cleaning fluids. Then he placed a cigar in the pocket of a jacket in one of the bedroom closets. The third fire was set in the basement that was fully stocked with liquor from every corner of the planet. Agent SuKi actually became giddy with excitement to see what he was now calling expensive accelerants. The commercial professional gas kitchen would surely help with his revengeful plan, after Agent Suki blew out all the pilot-lite on the stove burners. He had left the scene before the flames were visible from outside, yet they were surprised how many people showed up with the news reporters to cheer on the burning tower that had housed a serious sickness that had plagued their city. Milani and Suki Junior watched the full out-of-control blaze live on the television broadcast from Gayle's old apartment above the sushi bar that was next door to the American Embassy and inside its compound. The word had spread quickly about what had happened to the owner and his goon squad. It was almost impossible for the fire trucks to get through the crowd that had gathered and blocked the narrow road leading up to huge house and the front wide driveway and parking area in front of its doors. Once the fire trucks had reached the location, the firemen appeared to take their sweet time in getting to the point where one actually spread water or foam onto the flames. The firemen sluggishly suited up, as they appeared to shift into a leisure-nonchalant huddle. The group was discussing the situation with a clipboard and several pens in hand, as the fire ragged increasingly behind them, only a couple of yards away.

The onlookers continued to watch as they chanted, in several dialects and languages, to let the whole damn thing burn down. Then a few firemen rolled out the hoses as though they were doing an inventory and checking for damaged portions of it, instead of rushing to connect them to the nearest fire hydrant. During this time, people continued to arrive on the scene, while screaming and yelling **'don't put it out'**. The firemen spent most of their time and energy making sure that the onlookers didn't get too close to the furious flames as they continued to pretend to strategize a plan to battle the fire that could now be viewed from a third of the island and smoke from the remainder of the island. More fire stations begin to answer the fire alarm, but due to the narrow road and all the people that had gathered, their trucks only caused a gridlock traffic jam. The first fire unit had now been on the scene for more than twenty minutes and had not sprayed one gallon of water on the flames. However, the rescue unit had treated three people with smoke inhalation, as they applauded the efforts that the firemen were making to avoid putting out the fire. It was like a comedy skit from late-night television or safety lecture being given by Fire Marshall Bill. A group of short little men running around all over the place and not doing anything productive to contain or arrest the fire, which now had gotten the attention of almost two-thirds of the island's administration.

Agents Suki Junior and Milani watched the last site of smoldering smoke from their airplane flight out of the city. They each took pictures from their seats in first class with their camera phones. The flight home was long and draining as Milani wondered how she would ever make up for all that she had put her family through. She thought to herself, Auntie Ma Helen would be an easy touch, but Slapp was a different matter. Milani felt that the pain that she had caused Slapp was dissimilar than the others. Their bond and long standing relationship was based on trust, honesty, and private matters of the heart. Milani had taken advantage of that unspoken pledge and now she would have to suffer the consequences.

The fifty people that Milani and Agent Suki Junior had cataloged were picked up within a two-year period and sent to prison for an extended period of time. Some of the others that Burney and Agent Suki had fingerprinted that night of the sting, was able to reduce their life prison term buy only a few years at best, by filling in the connective dots in the reports.

The only problem with the squealers believing that the life-sentence had now been taken off the table was that in other parts of the world, a life sentence could be as little as six months, depending on how healthy you were when you were sent to prison. That life could be extended a little more, if you were a man or woman of means. At any rate, Milani was sure that she would out-live everyone that she had helped put away and this small fact would surely speedup her healing and recovery time.

Once they all were safely home, a party was planned. The holidays were fast approaching, but they were all cancelled when Father Caleb died in Ireland at the airport, while on his way to visit all of us for the holidays. Tate, his mother, Gayle, Milani, Max, Alex and I all flew to Ireland for the funeral. Slapp and Kate couldn't make it because Cameron had a really bad flu and the doctor advised against him making the trip. Tye, Ron, Walter and Bruce the finance guy surprised us at the funeral. Our most emotional shock was the surprise to see the formal American Ambassador to Hong Kong standing there to greet us at the Ireland Airport. It seems that he and the priest had fostered a deep friendship like they had agreed to do from the first time they met. Over the years they had made a point to visit each other. Slapp knew of this friendship and called the ambassador and informed him of the priest passing. He feared that Tate, because of his grieving state, wouldn't remember to call. Once again Slapp was correct. There were only a few people at the funeral that remembered Father Caleb, outside of his family which consisted of a couple of very old cousins and an aunt that was legally blind. They didn't know what to make of us coming so far. We explained that we were his family in America and that only a few of us had been unable to make the trip. We promised that we would all return in the next few years to place a tombstone on his grave that was fitting and one that would honor him properly. They agreed with tear filled eyes, chocked-up throats and heavy hearts.

Once back home, we spent the New Years together and my father Uncle Oscar Wiley, added another verse to that song that he had written for us, years before while we were all in exile. After Father Caleb passing and then Fred's death soon after, the song and newly added stanza evoked an even deeper emotional response inside of us, each time we were encouraged to sing the song and remember the past.

**When love one's journey is no more and night mourning becomes a new day, memories will stand the test of time; In our hearts they will forever stay.

For all the test of time, our love
For all the test of time
We'll take a sip of wine and dine
For all the test of time

Chapter Twelve

Milani's Healing Begins

Milani agreed to take a desk job at the bureau and Slapp maintained his instructor's position at Quantico. Alex resigned from his position, even as a part time consultant and in-house investigator. Miss Beasley retired from up-on-the-hill and became a translator at the National Botanical Gardens so she could spend every day with Uncle Burney. Before Fred's death his health had begun to deteriorate from age, so we all agreed that we would meet in Florida every year for as long as Fred and his family would have us. The Christmas after Father Caleb had died was the last time that we all made that trip as a group.

Two years later, our son William finally found the woman in which he wanted to marry for life. Alex and I were elated, to say the least, because now we would hopefully have some grandchildren to chase.

Milani met a nice responsible young man at Miles' martial art's dojo. While at her desk job at the bureau, Milani continued her studies and increased her belt level in the martial arts. Slapp and Kate's son Cameron attended the same dojo location as Milani and he showed signs of jealousy when Milani finally expressed some serous interest in her new boyfriend. The tables had turned and life had completed a full circle in reference to Milani and Cameron's relationship. When Cameron was born, Milani was jealous of him because of her closeness with his father Slapp. Now that Milani had a boyfriend, Cameron felt that Milani was spending less time with him on her days off, while driving him and his friends around, which was totally unnecessary. Cameron was an only child and Milani had been the closest thing he had to a sister. Milani and Cameron had sort of grew-up together because of Slapp's attachment to Milani from the first time they met. Now Cameron, who was older and smart enough to understand relationships, yet he still had a problem sharing his big sister with her new boyfriend. Cameron just wasn't ready for the relationship to change.

Tate's missionary work was all locally based now and this meant that he had a little more time to spend with his family. The group all agreed that they should turn the soup kitchen over to another non-profit organization, once the city had followed through with all their promises to approve the site as an official food-bank, soup kitchen and short-term shelter. Alex and the others continued to monitor the online donations for the scholarships and Bruce tracked every dime. Bruce had retired as well, but had agreed to remain as our personal and business financial advisor.

Chapter Thirteen

Life's Adjustments

After Cameron finished college, Slapp and Kate moved out into the country in the big red barn completely. Kate only worked part time and Slapp only went in when he was asked to cover for someone who had taken extended leave, gotten sick or retired without proper notice; which was another way of saying 'gotten him or herself killed, abducted without a trace or beaten too severely to return to the field'.

Alex tried to stay home and he did for about six months. Then he decided to become a probation officer. His doctor advised against it, but Alex wouldn't listen. To take the pressure off of Alex and his newly found hobby, Slapp took the over flow cases only for the enter city youths. He agreed to take only ten cases at a time. This was the first time that the inner city community had experienced anything of this nature in the court system. Slapp was like a big brother, probation officer, and social worker all wrapped-up into one. Ten at a time was all Slapp and Kate could handle and that was with his father's help and Tate's involvement from time to time. This wasn't a leap-of-faith for Tate because he was already into counseling the youth at his parish. It just meant longer hours some days when one of Slapp's kids appeared to be leaning towards a relapse.

The kids in question were convicted of lightweight stuff like first time offences; snatch and grab, bad check writing, small bags of weed. Slapp also specified that he only wanted to take the youth cases; men and women under the age of fifteen. Slapp believed that he needed at least two full years to work with them, as he attempted to get them back on the correct path. If the youth met the age requirements, and he or she appeared to be remorseful for their transgressions, (the words that Tate insisted that everyone use in the kids presence) Slapp would then ask his wife Kate to interview them to see where their heads were. If Kate and Slapp believed that the two of them could help, then Slapp would sign them up for a few classes at Miles or Daniel's dojo and pick up the tab. For the ones that had anger management issues, this helped out a lot. One reason that this was so effective for the angry children was that Sensei Miles and Daniel insisted that you concentrate on something positive before each punch. Then to test the strength or the power of the contact blow, they allowed the kids to punch them and then put into words afterwards how they felt and why. For some of the troubled students this took a lot of effort to process mentally. Now the focus was more on answering or understanding the anger than the anger itself.

There at the dojo they would receive a little more indirect counseling, all for free. The counseling sections where given in the form of brief portions of all our life stories as the martial art students took a ten minute rest on their backs, eyes closed. Miles would walk slowly around the room in between the rows of students, as they lay motionless on the large bamboo wood-covered flooring, while practicing their meditative breathing techniques. The first story that Miles relayed to his students, which included a few of our law offending recounts as well, was about himself during his early years. Miles would meander around and between the neatly formed rows of frozen ninja warriors, with his hands clasped behind his back and fingers enter-laced. Slowly he strolled back and forth between each column of various size bodies as he checked the eyelids of each of his students. He lowered his voice a little and his speech took on a tone of a seasoned storyteller that always placed doubt in ones mind whether or not the story was in fact true or fiction. A few of his students found it so soothing until they would fall asleep. The students each found their perfect position as Sensei Miles patiently waited for them to stop twitching and adjusting their bodies around on the hardwood highly polished floor. The younger students were the greatest offenders and found it difficult to close their eyes without testing to see if the instructor was paying attention. Miles assured them each time that he was, as he smiled to himself. Then without any introduction Sensei Miles begin his tale that had a morality element deeply entwined and purposely placed inside.

"There once was a very young man, living in Guam on his home island with only his mother and younger brother, one afternoon two men approached him about a job. The suspicious gentlemen said that they needed him to be a long-distance bodyguard for a short period of time and that there would be almost no danger involved to him or his family. I guess that sounded better than an armed private sniper. The young man questioned the men about why he had been chosen and the one man replied without any hesitation. The young man was in the National Guards at the time, you understand and his rifle scores at the firing range were legendary and had come to their attention. When they asked around about the young man, everyone agreed that his scores were authentic and he was the best man for the job. The young man was handsomely paid and soon returned to Guam and continued to work hard for his family in hope that they would call upon him again and employ his services and they did. After a few times, the young man asked if he could allow is younger brother to tag along, since there wasn't any danger and they said yes. After each job, the young man was quoted a specified amount of pay and was instructed to go to a teller machine and make a withdrawal out of the account for his pay. There was lots of money in the account, and the young man felt that he should have been paid much more, but he only took what they instructed him to take out for his wages. He thought that perhaps this was a test to see if he was an honest young man and one that could be trusted.

This arrangement continued for years and the young man's pay slowly increased. Later, his brother was able to come and stay longer each time because, now they were paying his brother as well. The two brothers became like family to these men and their families; they trusted the two brothers with their lives and their families' lives as well. Just before they retired, and the two brother's services were no longer needed they informed the young man that the account that he was drawing his pay from was his personal account that they had set up for him when they initially hired him and in fact all the money that he saw, appearing on the teller's screen many times before, was in fact all his. The young man couldn't believe it. Then to top it off, they acquired and give him a building to set up his business right here in this city. So he and his brother moved to the states and later, their mother moved here in the city as well."

Miles' quickly dried his tears before he released the class and before they were instructed to open their eyes. He clapped his hand three times as if he was awakening them for a hypnotic spell. They all sprang to their feet like little tin soldiers and took their normal class dojo neutral stance.

Clap, clap, clap! "Well students, that's all for today. Next week we may have another guest who will share a portion of their life's story with us. More than likely the narrative will contain the elements of nature, grace and mercy. You just never know. Now remember what I have taught you, 'always do your best, never trouble do you borrow, be sure to pass the test keep an honest face, because no one has seen tomorrow'. Class is dismissed."

One student raised his hand up quickly to ask Sensei Miles a question. "Sensei Miles Sir, please tell us, whatever happened to the young man and his brother. Oh oh oh, and who is nature, grace and mercy?" Miles grinned openly and widely held up both arms in a presentational posture, before he answered with deep pride in his tone of voice.

"The young man in that story is me, and my brother has a dojo very much similar to this one, on the other side of the city. Where we are standing now is the building that the group of men purchased for me to start this martial art school. Nature, grace and mercy is my active faith in a single entity within the universe that I believe is greater and more powerful than all." Miles had to be careful about using the word God in class. Many different families, cultures and races with an array of beliefs where represented in his class and school.

The twenty-five or thirty students present at the time, between the ages of seven and eighteen, which I said before included our selected delinquents as well, were all paying close attention to the Sensei's words. The children we sponsored to the program and all the others faced the Sensei Miles and gave a deep respectful required bow, from the waist.

Slapp and the remainder of us felt that this was our group's way of continuing to give back. If they turned their life around or choose a new and better path, Slapp would write a letter for them to receive some scholarship funds from the "My Brother's Keeper" online college fund foundation. Each student who received the funds had to sign a note promising to help someone else, perhaps later in life and tell their story, how we had helped them, and then relay our stories about how we had gotten to a point where we wanted and was financially able to help them. There was no binding contract involved, yet this was our way of keeping hope alive; and for some, it worked like magic as the kids say. We believed that if the stories were repeated frequently enough that some would be inspired by this small act of kindness and this would radiate through to the next generations. Some students kept their promise to us, while others made us feel as if the promise had been conjured up in our minds.

A few weeks later, Miles' guest was none other than the infamous Stone Cold Carl Jackson who had been saved, practically single handily, by Retired Police Officer James. James had found out about the online foundation and mentioned it to Kate one afternoon in general conversation. James relayed the fact that the young man was smart enough for college, but was raised by a single parent and there wasn't any extra money for college. Kate informed James that her husband Alvin (Slapp) was very much apart of this program and would be more than happy to look over his academic history. Kate's word was golden and the following fall Stone Cold Carl was able to go to college. Now years later he was returning the favor by speaking to Sensei Miles' martial art class as a favor to us. Stone Cold Carl story was about how he had been a thief in a local neighborhood store and how Retired Officer James never lost faith in him and gave him his first job in that very same corner store. Jackson was also one of the students that kept their promise to help others and had almost finished paying back the money to the online-scholarship fund. He was now an attorney and took selected cases for Kate pro bono.

That same year the president introduced an **initiative** and labeled it **"My Brother's Keeper"**. Of course the twelve original renegades where elated that their slogan and a portion of their online-educational-scholarship idea had been used and now would go down in history, for February 2014. They weren't sure if the president and the first lady had gotten the idea from reading the initial book that I had autographed and sent to them by his cook, while I was employed at the Washington Navy Yard Dental Clinic, building 175. At any rate, we all wished that Father Caleb and Fred had lived to see it come to fruition.

This charity work kept Slapp satisfied and occupied for a while and then he decided to spend more time, closer to home. His parents were retired and elderly, so he agreed to become their watchful caretaker so they could stay in their home longer and with the independence they desired. Both of them had continued to enjoy good health, it was just that their energy levels had begun to drop and sometimes they would get so involved in one of their many hobbies that they would forget to eat or drink enough fluids to stay outside in the sun all day. Slapp made arrangements for all the fireplace wood, in the future, to be delivered precut to the size that would fit the fireplaces. He informed his father that he didn't want him chopping any more logs; perhaps a sap covered splinter to get the fire started was all Slapp would allow his father Uncle

Burney to do. He checked on them twice daily and made sure that they took their medicine and ate properly.

A few years later their short-term memories had begun to fail and both of them were encouraged to give up their driver's licenses. The faithful live-in caretaker was still there, while doing most of the cooking and cleaning. He had continued to live in a room right off the kitchen. One day Miss Beasley heard him talking to himself about not having enough space for all his things, so she knocked out the entire west side of the house, which so happened to face the big red barn and add twenty more feet to one complete side of the house. This meant that the butler's room turned into a suit with a larger bath and a sitting area. Miss Beasley also hired a maid to come in once a week for a full day to help him clean the spaces.

The kitchen became larger in every aspect and ten more feet was added to the eat-in portion, which was now able to accommodate a larger table and still have room to spare. It was now like having two formal dinning rooms. The space received all new undated and upgraded stainless steal appliances. Red granite countertops were installed and new ceramic flooring to the entire new space. The renovation, on that side of the house was nothing less than breathtaking. We all knew then that the caretaker had planned to live out the rest of his days, while living there with Slapp's parents. Soon after the reconstruction of Julius spaces were completed we all started to call him 'The Butler', after that guy in the movie, that worked all those years in the White House, no less. Oh we weren't arrogant enough to believe that working in our homes were anything like working at the White House, but no doubt just as busy with all the old secret servicemen in and out of the house, while each told their own private story about the case files that had taken hold of them and drained all the energy from their spirits, yet were never solved. It seemed as though discussing old cases was like an energy- tonic to their very souls. At first that bothered me, then I just prayed that it wouldn't get out of hand.

As I said before, the 'My Brother's Keeper' illegal sub-agency was a diverse hybrid group that were made up of men from various branches, now that they were all out of the business, yet found it relaxing to share old case-file details, they quickly became aware that they had all been chasing the same multifaceted criminals and occasionally for different reasons. Retired Agent Dexter Allen Burney was never a part of the twelve-man field-renegade team. Yet he could claim to have been the 'inside man' or 'a silent partner', if you will. He had been only one of the many men and women in the bureau who had looked out for them and tipped them off about any heat that was perhaps coming down the pike in their direction. They never went to Burney's place back then because if was too risky for them to be associated, while not on a legal assigned mission by the bureau. If the truth were told, no one knew the exact location of Burney's place back then. He always maintained a post-office mailbox and all their property was in an alias name of a person that his associates in the office had created, when he first joined the bureau. The copied files that Burney had stored at his rural home, which was totally illegal for him to do, were now all mere props for stimulating conversation in which they all agreed, needed to be burned for national safety security reasons, if for no other reason. Yet they continued to delay the incineration of the pilfered copied files.

I'm sure for some of them it would be like giving up on a job that they had given an oath to finish and for others it would mark the end of an era, in which they refused to put to rest in their minds and hearts. Still others were just plain-old stubborn and enjoyed reliving a part of their youth when they believed that they were making a difference; by taking down the bad guys, and bragging about it later to their fellow agents. Who could be sure why they refuse to perform the necessary cremation of all the old copied files. I was in no position to question them about the matter. Alex had his stash as well.

Kate continued to work part time, but most nights were spent at Slapp's parent's home next door and then the two of them would travel back across the field to their place, which was the big red barn, the following morning. For Kate, helping Slapp with his parents was sort of like having parents as an adult for the first time. Either of Kate's parents had lived to see her become an adult. She made a fuse over Dexter Allen Burney and Miss Sarah Lynn Pocahontas Beasley as if they were her parents and this gave Slapp an unbelievable sense of joy and comfort. Each night, especially in the cold winter months, the four of them would sit in the large basement in front of the huge fireplace. They each had staked a claim to their perfect spot. The room was pretty close to a twenty by thirty feet size space, plus there were other rooms and closets that covered the entire foundation level of the original blueprint surface of the house. As you came down the steep stairs that lead from the main middle floor, to your left was a long over-sided couch with extra large chest-like end table at each end. On top of each oversized end tables were tall brass Stiffel table lamps, each with a double three-way light-bulb socket. There was a medium oblong coffee table in the center front of the sofa and two large round leather ottomans that doubled as extra seating when company came ah-calling, if you will.

Directly across from the couch and in front of the huge fireplace was two large swivel rocker and fully recliner-able leather massage chairs. They were only a feature or two away from being classified as an alternative to a bed. Between the two min-beds like recliner chairs were another small low tray table to hold your snacks or your beverage of choice. For Slapp and his father, Uncle Burney, who occupied those two special seats every night, the drink selection had been a stiff nightcap, from Burney's famous and well-stocked spirits bar. Kate and Miss Beasley sat on opposite ends of the long sofa near the powerful lamplights so they could obtain proper illumination for whatever project that they decided to work on to pass the time. There was a large flat screen monitor just below the small window at the very ceiling top of the side full wall. After all, this was an in-ground basement and no sub-level space, in this day and age, would be complete without a flat-screen television, even if it were un-necessary and sparingly used.

The four of them hardly ever watched television down in the basement, once the evening news was complete. Kate would be looking over her pro-bono counseling case files that she had brought home with her and preparing a schedule for all the shelter visits she had to make. She would also have her tape-recorded sessions with her earpiece in, while making notes to various files from the sessions. Sometimes Miss Beasley would be putting together a puzzle, while using this large lapboard that Burney had made for her and had upholstered the sides and bottom so it would be comfortable in her lap. Slapp would have his vibrating mini-bed fully reclined, while sprawled out and with his arms using every available inch of the chair's oversized armrests.

Mr. Burney, on the other hand, would be sitting up only slightly titled back, with his legs crossed loosely at the ankles while rocking intermittently as he stared deeply into the soothing soul-warming fire. Frequently he would be attempting to tell Slapp about all the things that he and Slapp's mother Miss Beasley had done, while he was in the orphanage; but after one nightcap, Slapp would be sound asleep as Burney went on with his story-lesson, as if Slapp was fully awake.

If Burney believed that it was something that Slapp really should hear or know, or if it was something else he should be apologizing to Slapp for, he would reach over and hit Slapp in the chest with a hand towel that he kept on the arm of his chair to clean his hands after he placed another log on the fire. Slapp would jump suddenly and become startled and

Miss Beasley and Kate would burst into laughter each time this happened, which was several times a week.

Burney would then shout, "Junior, are you listening to me? This is some important stuff son, and tomorrow I might not be able to recall it as clearly." Slapp would spring up and become annoyed that his father had startled him and disturbed his peaceful raw-heat fireplace-induced catnap.

"I hear you Pop', Slapp would respond while lying through his teeth. "Why do you wait until late at night to tell me something that only you believe is so important?" Burney would answer instantly as he returned Slapp's frustration with his own.

"Hell! Son, I may not remember all of it some other time. You know you are just like your mother, can't hold your liquor worth a damn." Kate and Miss Beasley would be sitting directly behind them on the long sofa and completely out of their view. The two ladies would then quickly cover their mouths and try to hold in their laughter, as the amusing skit would play out between Slapp and his father Uncle Burney the same each time, night after night.

"I'm a little tired Pop, why don't you write it all down for me? You haven't forgotten how to write have you?" Now this was the proverbial last straw, and Burney would become quickly heated by his son's attitude and him addressing him as pop.

"Don't sass me Junior, you know I love you more than pancakes love sugarcane syrup, but you know I will take a belt to you if

I have to. My mother and your grandmother just let you have your way because you had a touch of asthma. Well, you don't have it now and I don't have a problem with trying to help you catch up on all those ass-whipping you should have gotten back then and didn't."

Slapp would then change into a twelve-year old boy right before our eyes, just to appease and calm his father back down. Slapp then would move his recliner to a more upright posture and pretend to listen more intensely.

"You are right Dad, I should be paying more attention to you, and what you're saying. I'm sorry, can you go on now with the history lesson, please sir?" Burney would then adjust his gaze back towards the fireplace, as his rage would pass as quickly as it had arrived.

"Let me see Junior, where was I," replied Burney as he stroked his cleanly-shaven face, as he shifted forward a little, while gazing deeper into the warm flickering flames? "Well, it must not have been that important Alvin, because I can't remember." Then Burney would throw his head back against the back of the recliner and laugh out loudly and Kate and Miss Beasley would join him, where they had already been holding it in from the beginning of the frequently two-of-a-kind drama-filled entertainment.

Soon after that the live-in caretaker, Mr. Julius, would come halfway down the stairs and make his nightly, nothing less than bodily-harm, threatening announcement.

"Hello down there main-house occupants and red barn residents," he would yell. "The kitchen will be promptly closing in ten minutes. Please make all your final selections. You'll know that I don't like leaving any dirty dishes in my sinks, so tell me now," he said with slight announce carefully placed at the tail end of his selected words.

Miss Beasley would be the only one to answer up to humor him, as the rest of them remained mute.

"Please don't worry yourself, Mr. Julius", She would reply. "I will check before I go to bed, if I don't forget." After Miss Beasley's response, Julius voice would then soften to a more calm and gentle tone, as his entire demeanor would change, before answering to Miss Beasley the second time.

"That will be fine, Miss Sarah. If you forget, I will catch them in the morning before breakfast." After a while, there was no doubt in Kate's mind that they were all living with Julius in the big house, instead of the other way a round. I was completely inclined to agree.

####**Breakfast Coffee with The Butler**###

Early one mid-winter's morning I went over to Burney and Miss Beasley's place for breakfast. Allow me to remind you that Alex and I was living right up the lane on our two and half acre lot. We were all snowed in with no serious plans on how we were going to pass the time until the snowplows arrived. I rang the doorbell and Julius opened the door to receive me. He smiled briefly and quickly returned to the kitchen, in a slightly bent over short stride trot, as he updated me on the household's whereabouts.

"I'm sorry Miss Helen, but Miss Sarah Lynn and Mr. Burney haven't come out of their sleeping quarters for breakfast as of yet, so it will be just the two of us, I'm afraid; at least for now."

At this point, I had never been awarded an opportunity to get the caretaker's life story. And to be totally honest; I had never mustered up enough courage to ask any probing question about his personal life. He was known to be a no-fuss-no-mess kind of a man and quiet. Consequently, your conversations with him were somewhat limited. He was a man of few words and appeared to be a very private serious sort. However, I had only had the pleasure of seeing him outside his work environment a few times. Even when Julius ventured out and agreed to help Alex and I with our small gatherings at our home, he had always remained very serious and allusive. It could have been that he was shy and or very professional about his job. He spoke first again as he quickly returned to the stove as I entered the kitchen, only a few steps behind him.

"Morning Miss Helen, please come right on in. I had to get back to the kitchen before I burn the bacon, in which my employers shouldn't be eating anyway, if I may be so bold. Put your coat down anywhere, I will move it later."

I walked into the kitchen area and stood in the center of the floor and took a slow overview of the reconstructed portion of the house.

"Good morning Julius, you certainly have it smelling good and inviting up in here." He looked smugly over his shoulder as I followed him to the kitchen that was now twice it's original size, after the renovation.

"Oh Miss Helen, I'm truly sadden and disappoint to hear that you are also a slave to the pig's addictive power. I've warned Miss Sarah on several occasions that I was going to relinquish my position, if she continues to force me to cook pork every morning." The butler then hesitated a moment as he turned the bacon over in the pan and to see if he had insulted me by giving his un-solicited opinion about pork. Then he went on, "You think she took me seriously, Miss Helen?"

He looked up at me for a moment and pause to get my honest answer. I answered with a question, as I continued to admire the results of the extension to the house.

"How long has it been since you put in your pork-related resignation to discontinue your services, Mr. Julius," I cunningly replied without giving him eye contact? He looked back down as he gave the bacon and sausages a final turn. He paused again and then looked up with a wide unexpected smile and brief chuckle.

"I guess I answered my own question, hum Miss Helen. You are a pretty smart lady, Miss Helen. I like that in a woman. Would you care for a strip of clogged-artery and a slice of buttered toast? I can whip you up an egg in no time, to complete the deadly-cholesterol trio," he smirked.

"No thank you Mr. Julius", I sniggered. "But a cup of coffee would be more than welcomed." He swiftly moved around the kitchen as though he was the short-order cook at a busy ma and pa's restaurant. He knew where everything was without even a glance. He was smiling now as if a gratuity would be attached to his service, while he maintained his usual practiced subservient posture.

"Coming right up, Miss Helen. All the condiments are there on the table in front of you. It's fresh too, Miss Helen. It just finished brewing as you rang the doorbell. You know that it states in the bible that the man should always make the coffee."

"I'm sorry Julius, but I have never read that in the Good Book."

Julius laughed just a little before he defended his position on the matter. "It's right the in Hebrew Miss Helen. Get it He-brew. I got you Miss Helen, it's a joke."

"You got me Julius, I will remember that one. Will you join me Julius? His facial expression took on a stoic appearance as he secretly decided to interject some more humor into our whimsical conversation." He turned very slowly to give me passive eye contact, then spoke with a submissive tone.

"Oh, I couldn't possibly do that Miss Helen. You are the Burney's guest and I'm just **'the help'**." After Julius observed that I was shocked by his response, he burst into humorous laughter as he began to move very quickly again. "I got you again, Miss Helen. I thought that you would find that amusing since all of you call me the Butler around here. To be honest with you I kind'a like the title. Of course with all I do around this place, it's fitting; don't you think, Miss Helen?"

"Okay, Julius you got me." I laughed briefly before I completed my thought. "You have me there. I agree, and your service around here is greatly appreciated more than you know."

Then, without clearing my throat or taking in a full breath or air, I flipped the script on Mr. Julius by changing the subject. "Mr. Julius, how did you end up in these parts and where is your family?" He poured himself a cup of coffee and sat in the chair directly across from me, while his face took on that lifeless stare again, but this time it was quite different and there was no follow-up outburst of laughter. We both sat in front of this large bay window that looked out across the field where Slapp's big red barn dwelling was located. The peculiar way Butler Julius was staring, first out the window and then back in my direction, I was relatively sure Mr. Julius was trying to decide just where to begin his life's story or whether or not he wanted to reveal that part of himself to me at all. I could tell, by Julius' hesitation, that he hadn't enlightened anyone with his past in a long time and that it was a good chance that he had never divulged his complete life's history aloud to anyone before.

I held nervously motionless and waited as he avoided my stare for a few moments more. Julius meticulously stirred in the creamer and sugar into his coffee, while looking down in deep contemplation. Julius paused, released all the air from his lungs as if I had caught him completely off guard and he then brought his eyes back up to my focus level. He then placed the spoon on the side of the saucer as the tingling sound that it made, pierced the silence in the room. He slowly took a tiny sip of the hot freshly brewed coffee, perhaps to buy himself a little more time before he spoke his next words to respond to my question. The room had been completely mute for almost a full thirty seconds or more by this time.

"Wow! Now that's some good tasting coffee, if I do say so myself," replied finally. "This is my own secret special blend, you know. Would you like for me to top your cup off, Miss Helen? I answered swiftly with a wide smile and with a very light heartiness in my voice.

"Oh no Julius, no need. I assure you, I'm fine. You are a gracious host as always. And I agree, the coffee is quite wonderful. You must tell me your secret, that is, if you trust me with it." The decision to tell me about his past appeared to provide a momentary sparkle in his eyes as he took in a breath and almost smiled. I wasn't sure if the fleeting memory was a happy or sad one. The truth is that I didn't know Mr. Julius well enough to read his body nuances. So I waited.

"Well to be honest Miss Helen, it has been a long time since anyone has asked me those personal questions. I guess the best place to start is at the beginning; don't you think? I was born in Shenzhen City, China. That's a small area across the canal from Hong Kong. To be correct it's not a small area, it's Mainland China. Hong Kong is the island across from us. During the Vietnam War; this part of China was predominantly all farmland back then. My father was an America and I know that it's obvious to you, from my eyes and hair texture, that my mother was Chinese. My father was a scout for his military unit and one day while out on patrol he was badly wounded by a booby trap. My mother was about sixteen at the time. Her mother had been killed and her father was off fighting in another kind of war; the war on poverty. You see Miss Helen, during the Vietnam War, Hong Kong was an R&R (rest and relaxation) stop for the military troops. My father had been wounded, so when he got out of the hospital he took some time off from his accumulated leave and waited around to see if he would be able to return to his unit or be shipped back home. That's when he met my mother. She was young, inexperience about life and became pregnant with me. My father learned that she was with child and promised her that he would come back for the both of us. My father did return for us years later, but for my mother it was just a little too late. My mother had died the year before from hard work and a broken heart, no doubt. I was sixteen years old when my father came back for me and the war was over. To be perfectly honest I was surprised that he was able to find me. We moved around a lot. Most of the forwarding address system was all word of mouth, you understand. Even now, everyone doesn't have a mailing address or an identifiable or locatable address. The paperwork was difficult, but after a long battle, I was able to return with him. He brought me back here to this area. My father's family was from Maryland, Eastern Shore to narrow it down a bit. My father's injuries never completely healed and the fact my mother passed on so young, while waiting for him to come for us, didn't help matters much either. My father was a heavy smoker and drinker and so he died at a young age as well. I was now around twenty-two years old and once again alone. I had received some schooling when I first came to the U.S., yet not enough to compete for a serious job you see and there was the fact that I was a half-breed. We weren't popular by then, here or over there. Oh Washington D.C and the surrounding areas were progressive enough in their thinking and acceptance, yet this was before Chinatown was built in the area and we were all sort of scattered about. We weren't able to network, as it was required to survive and thrive. I got a job as dishwasher at this small private supper club. One night after I had been there for a few months, the manager informed me that I had to serve on the floor because one of the waiters had called in sick. That's when I met the family that lived here before the Burney's. He recognized my mixed heritage, and he knew I spoke his language. He was a contracted businessman and his job required him to travel a lot. His wife would be out here entirely alone. They didn't have any children yet, but they were planning for the future. When I came out here, there were only three lots with houses on them. The city refused to help the developer pave the roads up here; so new home construction came to a halt for years. The developing company during that time went belly-up and the land went back to the banks. The road was a lot worst than it is now and we became snowed in almost every winter season. After the previous owners learned that they couldn't have any children, they lived out here another five years or so and then sold the place to Mr. Burney. By then I had settled in and really didn't have any reason to move on, nor did I want to.

By the time the Burney's bought this place, I had lived out here almost twenty years and thought of this location as my home. So when I caught a ride out here, to the bottom of hill and walked up the rest of the way, I knocked on the door to ask the new owners for a job. I was tired, hot, and hungry and I'm pretty sure that I frightened Mr. Burney that day when I came looking for a job. A lot of my things were still out back in the tool shed. Mr. Burney had only recently moved in himself and was waiting for Miss Sarah to come for one of her semiannual month-long visits so she could decide what she wanted to do with all the stuff that the previous owner had left behind. Miss Sarah wasn't here at the time, and as a matter of fact I didn't see her for months after I got my position back. I liked her the moment I saw her and for some reasons I felt as though we were kindred spirits, so to speak. You know what I mean, Miss Helen? It was just something about her; I couldn't put my finger on it at first. She was too much of a lady for me to ask her any personal questions; I felt that it wasn't my place, she being my employer and all. She smiled a lot, but I could always see the pain in her eyes. I could see that something or someone was missing from her life. Of course I had no way of telling if the person had left or had passed on to another life. So I watched Miss Sarah Lynn and believed that on one heavy-hearted day she would tell me and she did."

"All I initially knew for sure was that both of us had experienced a long hard journey and there was no reason for either of us to look back. Of course I was besides my self when I learned that she spoke my native language. Sometimes she and I would speak in Cantonese just to irritate Mr. Burney. Sometime when you live this for out and off the beaten path you have to make your own fun."

Julius then quickly looked down and only gave a partial smile before his next sentence.

"Mr. Dexter never could take a joke, especially when he was the butt-end of it. A few years after that, Mr. Burney began that long expensive barn project. I went out there a few times and helped him a little and Miss Sarah even sent me out there on a few other occasions to tell him that he had done enough for that day. It was as though he was consumed by the project; perhaps obsessed would be a better term to use. Let me remind you again that Mr. Burney never mixed words with Miss Sarah, mainly because she was usually right about things. One thing that I love about Miss Sarah was that she is consistent about seeing the big picture and she is always able to maintain a strong sense of hope for tomorrow. I tell you Miss Helen, that she is one special lady. She has always been very kind to me. Once when she came for a visit, she told Mr. Burney that I deserved more money, because now I had two people to look after. So I got a raise and she always gave me a bonus for my birthday and Christmas time. She would always say that one should always remember your own birthday and Jesus' birthday because sometimes when people are being so mean to one another, that is the only thing that they may appear to have in common with Christ; being born of a woman. Yeah, Miss Helen, Miss Sarah is a fine sweet lady and looking after her and Mr. Burney is a joy and a Godsend. They are all the family I've had for a long time, of course until I recently met all of you. Having all this traffic coming through the house and Mr. Alvin returning like the prodigal son and all has blown some life back into this place and I will be forever grateful to all of you for that."

Julius took another quiet sip of coffee and gazed sadly out the widow again as if telling the story had somehow brought back sadness and joy, all at the same time. I couldn't read him well enough to be sure which emotion was dominant, but I am sure that both emotions were being experienced.

"Well, thank you for that Mr. Julius. It's very kind of you to say."

Julius cleared his throat as if the story had caused him to emotionally choke-up a bit and then he took another big gulp of warm coffee. He stood up quickly again as he spoke to me while moving quickly towards the microwave.

"Please excuse me Miss Helen, I need to warm up my coffee." He returned to his original seat as he tried to read me and get my story without crossing any boundaries, in the form of questions to an employer's quest. "Now Miss Helen, if I'm not being to presumptuous, I felt a similar spirit in you when you first came to visit here. Is there a sad tale in your past?" Julius swiftly threw up his hands in a stop motion towards me, like a crossing guard at a school's crosswalk, to let me off the hook if need be. "Now listen Miss Helen, you don't have to answer any of my questions. You are the guest of the Burney's and as the butler I have no right to impose." Then he looked back down into his cup as if he wanted me to have a private facial expression or perhaps to wait, in hope I would decide to answer his question nevertheless.

"No, Julius, you read a portion of me correctly. My mother died in childbirth and I was reared by my foster-parents. I only recently discovered who my real father is, after I became a mature adult. Perhaps it's true what they say." The room was mute for a few seconds, as we seem to absorb the moment that we had share.

"And what is that Miss Helen," replied ole Julius finally?

"You can never hide the pain in your eyes from a person that has experienced a similar one." The butler then paused before he responded and took another sip of his coffee.

"I would have to agree with that saying Miss Helen, because I also noticed the shadow of loneliness when I observe baby

Milani, and Mr. Alvin. Some wounds takes a long time to heal, while others simply scab-over and lie dormant just beneath a thin layer of emotional skin, while waiting to be reopened by another unpleasant situation. That is why I believe that it is so important to know and understand God's grace and mercy in our lives and ask him to stay in our corner daily, Miss Helen."

"Amen! Brother Julius." We both laughed out loudly as we reared back in our chairs, for the first time. "How did you become so wise, Mr. Julius?" He quickly and shyly dropped his head and rendered a deep pleasing smile. Just before he took in a full breath to possibly answer, Miss Beasley entered the room and the butler returned to his duties. The butler's persona also reverted back to a servant mode with a very professional attitude mixed in for good measure.

"Good morning, Miss Sarah; what would you like for me to prepare for you. Looking outside, I believe we are all in for today."

"Good morning Sir, Whatever you would like for me to have will be fine Julius." Miss Beasley joined me at the table.

"Hello and good morning Miss Helen, I assume that Mr. Julius has taken great care of all your comfort requirements and kept you entertained as well. I apologize for not greeting you earlier, and thank you so much for agreeing to have breakfast with us. Where is that handsome husband of yours? Alvin and Kate should be back momentarily from next door. After all, we are all snowed in, where could they possibly go?"

"Good morning to you Mrs. Carrington, Alex should be arriving soon."

"Oh please Helen, call me Sarah Lynn. I know you became accustomed to me as Mrs. Becky Sue Carrington, but we are back home now and relatively safe I imagine. So please call me Sarah Lynn. After all, it is my birth name you know. Now what should we do after breakfast?" She then clapped her hands together in front of her face as her eyes lit-up with excitement. "I know Miss Helen. Let's plan a party. We haven't had a nice party in a while. We can rent a nice suite with a conference room adjoining. We can have it catered so it won't be so much work; like last time. Well, what do you think Helen? We can get all gussied-up, like my mother use to say. That was her word for dressing up and looking your absolutely best. Perhaps now the men will allow us to take some pictures, to leave behind for our poor abandoned children, after we are gone. The holidays come and go so quickly now days, and I do love and enjoy a good party; don't you Miss Helen? I answered her promptly, as I tried to mirror her enthusiasm.

"That sounds great Sarah Lynn, we have all day to make plans for it. After all, we are snowed in, where can we go?" The three of us laughed out loudly as if we had just created a joke, or coined a phrase for the first time that was sure to become a family classic. Soon after, the butler excused himself from the kitchen; once he made sure that everything was turned off except the coffee brewer.

"If you two lovely ladies will forgive me and promise to be fine in my absence, I will be in my suite until I'm needed." Mr. Julius turned to face us and bowed deeply at the waist as he held his hands clasped in front of him. For the first time I could see undeniably that he had been raised earlier in an Asia atmosphere. Miss Beasley and I both found him very amusing at times and held our hand to our lips as we snickered a little, as Miss Beasley responded.

"That will be fine, Julius. I will call you when Dexter Allen comes out of his room. I can fix his breakfast if you like." The butler never responded with words, only a nod and a grumbling noise, as if he was sure that Miss Beasley burned everything that she had ever attempted to cook. Then Miss Beasley turned her head back to face me and expressed a strange smile as though she had a secret that she wanted to share. I wouldn't be honest if I didn't say that the look made me a little uncomfortable nor did I realize how further uneasy I would become.

Chapter Fourteen

Naughty Girl's Talk

"I probably shouldn't tell you this Helen, but what the hell; it's all in the past. All you can do with history is look back and learn from your mistakes."

Miss Beasley then leaned in slightly and lowered her voice, as her face took on this playful sinister look that I had remembered seeing on another familiar face, a few times before, on Slapp's face, just before he would tease William or Max, when they were younger. For the first time I noticed a deep resemblance between Miss Beasley and her only child Slapp that had totally escaped me; prior to this moment. She reached across the table and very lightly tapped the back of my hand as though she required my full attention, as if none of this story was ever going to be repeated, so I had better be listening closely the first time. She gave a devilish smile as she sat up tall, shoulders back with a straight spine again and then took a quick sip of coffee, with both elbows resting unladylike on the kitchen's tabletop. Her eyes cautiously scanned the room and then listened to make sure that the butler was out of hearing range. Next, right before my eyes Miss Beasley, Sarah Lynn Pocahontas Beasley to be exact; transformed into a person that I hadn't had the pleasure of meeting before or non-pleasure would probably better describe my feelings, at first, when she begin her story.

"You see Miss Helen, some years back when I was traveling back and forth from Hong Kong to see Dexter Allen and to spy on Alvin at the orphanage, I decided to come home one year earlier than Dexter expected. Dexter wasn't prepared, with his schedule at the National Botanical Garden, for me to arrive beforehand. So for the first week of my annual month-long visit he had to go to work. The second morning, after I had arrived, Dexter Allen got up early and kissed me on the cheek as he sat sidesaddle on the side of the bed, fully dressed for work. He would then rubbed my buttock as I lay face down and then he would always give me a little hand massage stimulation, just before he left out the room, if you get my meaning. I was still partially asleep when he informed me that he would start a load of clothes, before he left that morning for work. I'm sure I murmured something, yet I didn't wake up. About twenty minutes later I realized what Dexter Allen had stated about the laundry and I spring to my feet to take a few more soiled pieces that I had taken from my luggage, but hadn't taken them to the laundry room, downstairs; plus add my gown that I was wearing. I wrapped a bath towel around me and headed for the laundry room in a sprint. Just as I bent way over to take some clothes from the front-loader washer,

Julius walked in behind me and was now gazing directly into my personal, from the rear.

He tried to recover from the shock of it, but the male nature in him took over. 'Oh, I'm sorry Miss Sarah;' he said. 'I had no idea that you were in here.' I stood up slowly and was embarrassed beyond belief. As I attempted to gather my composure, with my back still to Julius, I dropped some of the wet clothes and he rushed over to the rear of me to pick them up. Just as he stooped down on one knee to retrieve the wet clothes; while still in shock that he had caught me wearing only a towel, I nervously and quickly turned to face his direction, which now placed his face only inches away from the front of my slightly opened towel that I was holding onto for dear life. I was so stunned by what was now happening, until I couldn't move or speak. When he was kneeling down and facing my femininity, I felt his hot moistened breath wash over my hairless crotch, as he slowly spoke his next group of words.

'Miss Sarah, the scent of you is quite intoxicating and very arousing, if you don't mind me saying.' Then without any warning, as I remained pinned up against the open door of the washer, Julius opened my towel and pressed his face right up against me to inhale the essence of me. I remained frozen as I gripped the top of the washer with one hand and tightly shut my eyes. Suddenly he began to stroke and clench the insides of my thighs with his thick soft hands, as I attempted to move away, but there was no place for me to back up to. I can't tell you for the life of me, Miss Helen, what came over me to allow this to happen. I had no interest in Julius, nor had I ever looked at him in that manner; but when I felt his hot breath on the inside of my thighs and private parts, some twisted-need inside me took control. I kept my eyes closed and held my head far back as I leaned up against the washing machine. I opened my legs a little wider to give him more excess. He slowly moved his massaging hands upward, closer to my hairless target. I had begun to breath hard and became frightened and excited all at the same time, in fear of what would happen next. Suddenly I let go of the towel and now the butler could view all my nakedness. He pulled my legs further apart slowly and with force as I braced myself back even more against the washer.

Next he slowly placed two of his thick long fingers inside my vagina as he whispered. By this time, Miss Helen, I had zoned out and my libido had completely taken over.

He went on murmuring, 'Yes, Miss Sarah, you are a fine woman and I'm so glad that you have allowed me to service you in this manner. I have thought of this moment often and wondered if I would ever be given an opportunity like this to service some of your personal needs.' Julius continued to stroke my vagina with his two fingers as he continued to force my legs further apart. The entire time his face was only centimeters from my crotch, as he knelt down in front of me. I felt his hot breath on my pelvis with every word he whispered. The finger manipulation felt so good until all I could do was enjoy it. He moved so slowly in and out and then he would change the speed and the pressure and then start from the beginning of the cycle that he had created. Girrrllll that man hand some magical hands and fingers, Miss Helen. At any rate, we held those positions for what appeared to be a long time. Then I heard a moaning sound fill the laundry space, as I reached my climax. Can you believe it, Miss Helen; the sounds were coming from me? Julius then buried his face into my, well you know, as he forced my thighs a part and consumed all the moisture from my cavern that he had cause my body to secrete.

Miss Helen, I can't describe how soothing the experience felt. He then slowly peeled back the covering of my clitoris and began to tease it with his strong lengthy textured tongue. It caused an electric sensation to rush through my body and I became weak in the knees. I shifted into my sexual-frenzy mode and realized that I needed a little more personal servicing, before I let Mr. Julius return to the remainder of his household chores, as it were.

He quickly stood to his feet, as he appeared to be out of breath as well and took one of my breasts in each of his huge strong hands and began to stare and rub both of them around like ripened fruit. He spoke again in a whisper, 'Miss Sarah, I've dreamed of sucking your breast until I fall asleep, so many nights. Don't be nervous Miss Sarah; I will be gentle, but it may take some time for me to satisfy my hunger for these perfect tits of yours. Just hold still and try to enjoy the deep pleasure that I have planned for your breasts. That's it Miss Sarah, relax and let me do all the work.'

My eyes were still shut tightly, as he murmured and began to lick and suck each nipple, while firmly holding and squeezing them at the base. 'Miss Sarah you have some real sweet tits and your skin is so soft and smooth. I can hardly wait to feel your warm soft c—t wrapped around my pleaser. I would be happy to be of service, in this manner, anytime that you prefer. I hope you are enjoying this part, half as much as I am,' he said.

"Well at this point, Miss Helen, I finally got up enough courage to reach between us inside his boxers and stroke his enormous male pride. I guess I wanted to see what he was working with, so to speak. Please don't ask me why, I can't answer that Miss Helen. I'm only relaying to you what took place next. It was firm and fully extended as he continued to orally massage my breasts. He slowly backed away, while leading me with his hands still gripped around my breast, to a nearby discarded chair that Dexter Allen and I hadn't gotten around to throwing out. Julius sat down and pulled me onto his lapped, while facing him. He guided his pride into my juice box, as I sat straddling his lap. Julius continued his monolog. 'Oh yessss Miss Sarah, your body is so juicy, warm and tight. Please, lets take it slow and easy so I can enjoy this while I help you to relax. Lean forward Miss Sarah so I can massage those fine healthy tits of yours in my mouth. Mr. Dexter is a lucky man to be able to come home to all this beautiful juicy loveliness.' Julius continued to babble about nothing important, as I bounced up and down on his lap and rode his pride like a freshly broken stallion. We both reached our goal and I slowly stood up and retrieved my towel from near the washer and headed back to my room."

When Miss Beasley finally reached this part of the distorted story and took a brief pause, I was able to catch my breath and speak for the first time. I tried to tactfully prevent her from continuing with the account.

"Miss Sarah, I'm not sure if you should tell me any more or if I want to hear the remainder of something so personal in nature." She laughed out loudly and then took another sip of her warm coffee before she answered with a smirk. By this time my chest was aching with sorrow for Mr. Burney. I never saw a cheating spirit in Lady Beasley and I couldn't imagine one in her earlier in her life. I couldn't become rude and just get up and leave. After all I was a guest in her home, drinking her specially brewed coffee blend, at her table and we were neighbors. While ignoring my displeasure, Miss Sarah continued her spicy torrid story.

"Of course I should tell you the rest of the story, Miss Helen, I haven't gotten to best part yet. After all, this is nothing more than a little girl's talk. Who will it hurt? Besides, this all happened a lifetime ago. Now Miss Helen, do you really believe that I would relay to you a story and leave out the best part? That would almost be like lying to you, while maintaining a straight face." Miss Beasley giggled a little before going on.

Then she insisted that she should proceed. I wasn't sure for whom the story was going to have a happy ending for. I had already placed a question mark or an 'X' next to Mr. Burney's and my name. Still Miss Beasley continued on reliving the event aloud, against my weak cowardly protest.

"Around lunchtime, that same day, Julius found me in the living room reading a book, while propped up on the sofa. 'Miss Sarah, are you ready to take your lunch now', said Julius, in his professional servant tone, as he refused to look me in the eyes?

Sure, I replied, I will take it in here, if it's not too much trouble, Julius.

'Not at all, he responded. What would you like?'

"Oh, I'll just have cheese and crackers with a cup of tea; oh and Julius bring a spoonful of honey on the tray please. I read somewhere that honey is very good for the body, all parts. I winked at him, but he never noticed. I was wearing an A'-line dress with the wide pleated lower half that button all the way up the front, of course no panties. I shifted deeper into the sofa onto my back and placed one foot on the floor with a bent knee as I rested the other one scandalously high up on the backrest of the sofa. I pulled the skirt of the dress up slightly more than halfway my thighs to expose my crotch to anyone who so happened to enter the room. In this case, it was only Julius. I thought of what had taken place between Julius and I earlier and before I knew it, I was pleasuring myself right there in the living room. I unbuttoned a few buttons from the top, so my breasts were exposed as I continued to satisfy a sudden urge. About three to five minutes later, Julius walked in with my lunch tray and froze, and became dazed and nervous by my posture. I don't know how long he had been standing there, because my eyes had been closed and my face turned to the back portion of the sofa. Finally, like a gentleman, Julius cleared his throat, to announce his presence in the room.

'Miss Sarah I will just leave the tray on the coffee table here, it seems as though you will be needing a little more private time,' said Julius in a very professional tone as if nothing had taken place earlier between the two of us. He walked over quickly and sat on the edge of the long sofa at the other end, to place the tray on the table, without spilling the full cup of tea. Julius was now staring deep between my thighs to my tutu, while I slowly pulled up my dress slightly more so he could have a better view. I spoke up immediately to detain him after I noticed that he appeared mesmerized by what my hand and fingers were doing to my private lips and clitoris. As I said before, I was hairless down there at the time and my thighs were as widely apart as possible.

'Please wait Mr. Julius,' I said demandingly. 'I need you to dip two of your fingers into that spoonful of honey and rub it right here on my sore battered juice box. I'm a little raw and I think that the honey will help. At first Julius didn't move a muscle, while he continued to gaze into the depth of my pleasure zone.

He licked his lips a couple of times, but didn't respond. I repeated my request in a whisper, laced with a seductive tone. 'Julius, please place your two middle fingers into the honey and place them inside my bruised cavity. I will hold the outer layer apart for you. He began to stutter as he thought about it.

'I I I I don't don't don't know Miss Sarah. I don't think that Mr. Burney will, I mean Mr. Dexter would appreciate me doing that. Can't you wait until he gets home tonight.'

I answered with reasoning, 'Sure I could wait, but I am sore now and you are right here. It's not as if we haven't touched each other before. The room went quiet as I continued to hold my vagina lips apart as his stare became even more fixated. He was honestly acting as if we hadn't been together only hours before.

Finally Julius agreed, 'Well I guess I could help you out.' He slid down on the sofa closer to my bent knee and reached over on the tray with his two fingers from his right hand and immersed them into the honey. Then he took his left hand and picked up a cloth napkin from the tray and spread it out just below my buttock, on top of the back inside portion of the skirt of my dress, to protect the sofa. I could tell that he was nervous, yet sexually aroused by what I had asked him to do. And then there was the view of my brazen posture that displayed my nakedness. He slowly brought the honey over on his two fingers and placed them at the edge of my cavern. I elevated my head up off the pillow to observe the nervous care in which he applied the honey. No Mr. Julius, I said, place it deep inside. He slowly slid the two fingers in as I gave the next command. Now move them around and back and forth, and in and out. Oh Mr. Julius, that feels so nice. He then leaned in to get a better-angled position as I closed my eyes and relaxed while still holding my vagina lips apart.

He moved his head in closer to my crotch. Now I could feel his steamy breath over the entire area. Then I spoke quietly, 'it's okay if you want to taste me Mr. Julius; there are other methods you can use to spread the honey. The other way that you are considering might do a better job than your fingers. He didn't respond, just continued to move his fingers in and out and all around with more pressure and commitment to the task. I moved my finger tips to my breast nipples and began to pinch and pull them to add pleasure to the therapy.

'Miss Sarah, your juices and the honey does give off a pleasant provoking aroma, perhaps I will take you up on your gracious offer. I notice that your flower is in full bloom, I'm sure that my lips and tongue can cause it to relax a little; that's if you have no objections to me doing so.'

Julius spoke in a therapeutic tone as if he knew what was best. Before I could say anything, Mr. Julius withdrew his fingers and replaced them with his large thumb. He then tightened the skin around my vagina with his other hand, as he attacked my entire crotch area with his open mouth, tongue and starving lips. 'Oh Mr. Julius please enjoy all that honey; I'm sure we have more in the kitchen.' His main target appeared to be my clitoris that was now protruding in full sight. I lay there with his face buried deeply between my hot sticky thighs, as I twitched from experiencing something that I had never felt before. I felt his teeth nibbling at the very tip of my female protrusion. It felt like it was attached to my entire nervous system. I released a couple of times before Mr. Julius released my crotch from his oral masturbation.

He then disappeared to his room and into his bathroom, no doubt to freshen up and hide his guilt. When he came out, there I was lying across his bed on my back with my legs far apart while holding my knees in a bent posture. Julius immediately removed his pants and boxers and rushed over to enter me with his marble hard manhood. I felt pain and pleasure, all at the same time. We both arrived at our destination, near the exact moment. I quickly got up and went upstairs to my room to take another shower; he did the same. A couple of hours later I found Julius in the kitchen taking a very late lunch. I walked in fully dressed in a jogging suit. We both pretended that nothing had happened between us only a couple of hours before. I sat down at the table, as he was finishing up. 'Would you like for me to get you something, Miss Sarah. I don't think you finished your lunch.' No Julius, I just wanted to thank you for helping me with my little problem. I quickly stood up and move towards Julius and then knelt down next to him at the table. I unzipped his pants and reached inside and took a hold of his limp sore penis. I began to stroke it like before.

He spoke. 'Miss Sarah I really don't think you need to thank me any more, especially in the way I believe you are suggesting. I understand your situation totally.' I slid under the table and pulled his penis out into view and began to blow my hot breath on the very tip of it in forecast of what was about to take place. I heard him let out a loud sigh as if he had no control or desire to stop me. I was completely under the table on my knees. We couldn't see each other's face.

'Miss Sarah, I assure you that this is not necessary for you to thank me in this manner. It was a pleasure for me to apply the honey to your sore personal. We don't have to speak of it again.' At that instance I closed my hot succulent lips around the head of his thick limp manhood. Julius lunged backwards from the table, as he remained sitting in the chair, as if a bolt of lightening had struck him. I anticipated his excited reaction and was able to hold on to his prize. Now he could see the back of my head as I took more of him in. That little encounter lasted about twenty minutes or more as I attempted extracted every ounce of desire from his loins.

He gripped the seat of the chair with his hands and mourned like a trapped pet as I took my fill of him. Once he leaned forward and unzipped my top to massage both of my breasts in his massive hands, while begging me to stop. I knew that it was only the guilt talking, so I massaged more of him and with added pressure. When I finished my task, I stood up and inquired about what he had planned for dinner. He sat there in a trance as I walked out the kitchen.

"Well Miss Helen, as fate would have it, Dexter Allen had to report for work the next morning, as well. After I recovered from the shock and a weak level of guilt, I decided that I had to have that satisfying pleasure wand just one last time. I was already in too deep to ever be forgiven by Dexter Allen, you see. So the next morning, after Dexter Allen left for work, I went to the laundry room in hope that Julius would come in. I sat on top of the dryer with a thin see-through short gown on, with matching thongs. I didn't have to wait long before Julius arrived wearing just a pair of boxers and a white tee shirt. He spoke first.

'Oh I'm sorry Miss Sarah, I can come back later.' It appeared to me at that moment, Miss Helen, that his remorse had been a lot more haunting than my own, you understand. So I detained him once more.

'Oh no! Please come in Julius; I've been waiting for you. I thought that maybe I could get a little more servicing, as you so innovatively called it.' He dropped his head and his gaze as he backed away closer to the door to leave. I jumped off the dryer and rushed over to reach inside his boxers to find his joystick as I moved in closer to let him feel my breath on his lips and smell my sinful perfume. He froze and turned his head away and closed his eyes while I stroked his penis firmly inside my hand. I was now pressing my breasts up against him as I beg for sexual servicing. His manhood quickly responded to my soft, smooth, and slow rhythmic stroking. He seemed embarrassed, yet he was enjoying every motion of my hand. I was able to pull him away from the door as I forced Julius into that chair again. I stood between his thighs and pressed my tits up against his full and wet luscious lips. At first he was able to resist me, but then the stroking of his penis weighted in. He grabbed me at the waist and pulled me closer as he began to orally massage my breast as if he was possessed. I began to heat-up and the moisture started to accumulate as my desire became stronger. He pulled my thighs apart and pulled me straddle onto his lap and droved his penis deep inside me. Well, a few moments later, after we were finished, I stood up to leave.

An hour or more later, Julius knocked on my bedroom door and yelled through the door. 'Miss Sarah I have your laundry. I'll just leave it outside your door.' I answered quickly. 'Oh no Julius, please bring it in for me. Julius slowly opened the door only to observe me with my buttock positioned high in the air, towards the door while I knelt on the bed smoothing out the sheets. Dexter Allen had moved a large chair into our bedroom you see and a small table, where he sat each night, when I wasn't there, to go over old case files that were never solved. This furniture arrangement had caused a very tight area behind the bed and the far wall on my side, so I sort of crawled in the bed to straighten the linen from one side. I could feel Julius looking intently at my crotch. I held that position and pretended not to notice his gaze. He slowly placed the basket of laundry next to the bed and near to where my butt had remained high in the air.

'Let me give you a hand there, Miss Sarah,' said the butler in a quiet voice. Then he walked closer to the back of me and immediately maneuvered the moisture soaked seat of my thong to one side and entered me with two of his fingers and began to massage me deeply, while breathing heavily. I responded, 'Oh Mr. Julius that feels so wonderful, please don't stop. He moved closer so I could feel his firm penis on my left butt cheek. I soon lie partially flat, slowly onto the bed; face down as Julius mounted me from the rear. He thrust his penis deeper with force as I received delightful pleasure and satisfaction.

Miss Helen, I can't tell you what made me act this way or feel that I was entitled to receive sexual favors from the in-house residing help. The mating sounds and the concentrated aroma of our bodies filled the room. Later he withdrew his pride from me and left the room, but not before he flipped me to my back and sucked my breasts until they were red as fire and throbbing with pain. I lie there awhile longer to enjoy the afterglow, as some like to call it. Then there came a different kind of knock at my bedroom door. I quickly sat up in bed, as I woke up and realized that the entire affair with Julius had all been one-night's dream, Miss Helen. Whew! You can't imagine, Lady, how relieved I was when I became conscious and fully awake. There was no way I could have explained that to Dexter Allen. Getting choked-out surely would have been in my future, if it hadn't been all a dream. That night when Dexter Allen came home from work that evening, he had to pleasure me before dinner, I couldn't wait. I couldn't give Mr. Julius eye contact for over a week. Isn't that hilarious, Miss Helen."

Miss Beasley (Sarah) quickly covered her mouth to muffle her laughter as I let out a sigh of relief as well. "Wow! Miss Sarah, you really had me going for a moment there. Your relationship with Mr. Burney has survived the test of time and distance, I'm glad it was all a dream as well.

A few moments later, just before Miss Beasley and I completely recovered from her imaginary-affair dream story, the doorbell rang. My foster-mother was spending a few days with Alex and I while my father decided to spend some time in the recording studio in New York. He had also traveled out west on a trip to see family. Miss Beasley quickly raced towards the door as she yelled to Julius the butler.

"Don't bother Sir, I'll get it Julius!" Miss Beasley (Sarah) opened the door and I waited to hear whom she would address. "Please come in, your daughter and I are in the kitchen having a second cup of coffee."

The butler had arrived at the front entrance only a few steps behind Miss Beasley, even though she had informed him that she would get the door. She then continued the welcoming greeting.

"I had no idea you were visiting us; way out here in the country. How nice of you to have come for a visit, as well. Look Miss Helen, look who has come ah calling, as the old folks like to say."

My mother followed Miss Beasley into the kitchen as she removed her coat and gloves. Julius stood quietly near and offered to take her coverings.

"I'll take those Madam," replied Julius as he gave a shallow bow and brief smile. It's nice to see you again Miss Buddy," Julius continued. Miss Beasley took her previous seat back at the table and pulled out a vacant chair for my foster mother. I spoke as my mother pulled her chair closer to the table.

"Hello Mother, I didn't realize you were awake yet, when I left the house." She smiled deeply as she waved her hand dismissingly in my direction. My foster mother took a seat on the side of the table, which placed her between the two of us, as Miss Sarah and I occupied the two end sections.

"Oh no bother Helen, Alex informed me that you were here; so I used the brisk walk here as some well needed exercise. I hear we are snowed in, so what's the plan to entertain ourselves?" Mother looked in both directions at each of our faces as she waited for a response. Miss Beasley became tickled again as she took in a full breath to speak, as her face took on a shy blushing appearance.

"Well Miss Buddy", Miss Beasley said after a lengthy pause. "We could continue doing what we were doing before you arrived." My mother repeated the tennis-match head movement again as I dropped my focus deep into my cup of coffee.

"And what exactly was that, may I ask," said my foster mother in a cowardly, yet demanding tone?

"Oh, we were merely sitting around reliving shocking sexual encounters," whispered Miss Beasley as she burst into loud laughter. I quickly and graciously tried to recant Miss Beasley's response, with no luck.

"Mother, pay her no mind, she is only teasing you." My mother seemed disappointed and confirmed her disenchanting look, with her next statement.

"I'm so sad to hear that, because girl's talk should always be about things that we don't want the men in our lives to know that we have repeated. And since we are snowed in and none of them are around, this would be the perfect time to reminisce; don't you think?" I chastised my mother as Miss Beasley agreed with her and snickered more.

"Mother!! I'm not sure I want to take part in this form of discussion, for the sake of entertainment." My mother snapped as if there was something that she had wanted to tell me years before, but couldn't take a chance on hurting my feelings or causing any more riff between the two of us than she had already caused by not telling me that my Uncle Oscar was really my biological father.

"Oh please Helen, loosen up woman. You have always been a tight ass, stick in the mud. Should I go on?" She then rolled her eyes and pressed her lips tightly with annoyance to my protest before continuing, as she retained her soapbox façade. "Well, let me tell you Little Missy; you didn't get it from your father or your grandmother on your father's side of the family. I've heard both of them tell some stories that would make a drunken sailor forget to grab his hat before running out of the bar."

By this time my foster mother had been a companion to my biological father Oscar for a few years. At their mature age, I never even imagine them sexually active on a regular bases nor did I want to hear the details about their coupling in mixed company, as it were. Miss Beasley giggled more and leaned in towards the center of the table as she topped-off my mother's cup of coffee. Then Miss Beasley glanced at me from across the table, as her pupils widened with pure excitement, from the anticipation of what my foster mother was about to reveal to the both of us.

"I can just feel it Miss Helen, that this is going to be a wonderful story," prodded Miss Beasley. "I can see it in your mother's body-language and eyes. Come on Miss Buddy, tell us; is Mr. Wiley a wildcat like I've been led believed all these years. You know I saw him with lots of young women when we were both living in Hong Kong. We were friends you see, but I never was brave enough to ask him, why there were so many women around. Now that I look back and reflect on things, I think he used being my escort a few times; just to get a break from all the other women that took a shinning to him. The local women were pretty upset when you first came to Hong Kong for an extended stay, Miss Buddy. Mr. Wiley made plenty of money over the years and spent big. Because he was so well known, people was always buying and giving him whatever he needed. So that allowed him to have a lot of money to spread around, but when you showed up, Miss

Buddy, he put all of that behind him. That didn't sit very well with the local ladies in Hong Kong, and that is all I have to say about that, amen."

My mother was smiling the entire time as I became more uncomfortable about the unspoken pact we three, undoubtedly, were making at that moment. My mother began her prelude to the story that she was about to tell with unrelated flashbacks. Still Miss Beasley looked on and waited with excitement, in her straight-spine posture.

'I knew about some parts of Oscar's lifestyle," my mother went on to say 'and the fact that it is true he was familiar with a host of women,' agreed my foster mother. 'Because he would always brag about his escapades; whenever he came home to visit us here in the states, I mean to see Helen. My late husband and I would sit and listen to Oscar, late into the night, as he gave us only brief cleaned-up details. At the time, I thought he was crass to kiss and tell, but he assured us that the relationships were mere perks of the music industry and no harm had been done. He would say, 'everyone wants a piece of the music man, and I gave them as many pieces as I could breakoff' he would say.

My mother turned to me again as she reached over and patted me a few times on the back of my hand that was resting palm-down on the table. My other hand had remained grasped around my coffee cup.

"Oh hell, Helen, lighten up. This is just two middle age ladies and one old woman sharing erotic chronicles. I don't think we are hurting anyone. God already knows what really happened, so we can choose to stick to the story or embellish it a little to make it more interesting. With this type of storytelling its all up to the one that's reliving the historical event or at my age, remembering the moment." Still Miss Beasley refused to pull back with her encouragement to my foster mother.

"Now just listen to that, Miss Helen," replied Miss Beasley. Who can argue with that piece of scientific logic?" Then Miss Beasley pretended to change sides right in the middle of the debate and then back to the other side; all in a single breath. "Of course Miss Helen, I totally understand how this could be a little unsettling to listen to, with Mr. Oscar being your biological father and all. However, there is still the fact that he was a grown sexually healthy man before you were born."

The two of them continued to laugh and taunt me, until finally I dropped my head, unknowingly in agreement to allow my foster mother to continue. My mother picked up her coffee cup as she sat there smartly perched between Miss Beasley and I, while peeping over its edge, at each of us; probably to make sure the heated debate portion of our conversation was over. I am pretty sure she was trying to decide just which event she wanted to relay to us, as she would undoubtedly enjoy reliving the moment. Then a strange smirk washed over my foster mother's face as she took another sip of coffee and rolled her eyes in each of our direction over the top of the large rim cup that Miss Beasley had selected for her, from the hodgepodge set that she kept on the kitchen table. To be precise, it was more like a soup bowl with a cup handle on it that someone passed on to you at Christmas time, which originally came with a mate, but they had broken it and now rewrapped the odd ball item for a last minute gift for you.

At any rate, as I watched my foster mother hold this cup-bowl to her face and peer over its edge like a eight month old mastering a sippy-cup for the first time. I did find it humorous and without any warning, a brief smile must have appeared on my face. This fleeting facial expression must have appeared to give Miss Beasley and my foster mother the unintentionally or accidental confirmation to 'go ahead' to exploit my father by repeating some private particulars of a sexual encounter that he had shared with Miss Buddy, years before when that first became an item.

As the two of them began to giggle and snicker more, I quickly and nervously sprang from my seat to take my cup of cold coffee over to the microwave to be reheated. My foster mother slowly looked over her shoulder as if she wasn't sure if I had decided to excuse myself or was taking my cup to the sink before departing. Miss Beasley was now sitting with an extra straight spine with both elbows propped on the tabletop as she waited for the story to begin. My concerned foster mother immediately inquired.

"Where are going, Helen; or do you prefer Monique these days?"

"Go on mother, I can hear from over here, I just need to warm up my coffee a bit."

"Oh," she responded with relief and jesting on the edge of her tone. "Because I know you don't want to miss this juicy story." My foster mother winked an eye towards Miss Beasley and dropped her head a bit to privately laugh at my discomfort. Then Miss Beasley turned back into that person that I had met a few moments before my mother had arrived, while she had relayed her personal sexual-laced dream to me. It was almost like the two of them had transformed into two maritime travelers, sitting around in a poorly lit smoky bar, while talking about all the ass they had manage to acquire, while on liberty in some foreign port-of-call. For a moment I wondered if we were all drinking from the same brewed pot of coffee. In Addiction, I was now questioning our lady-like facade that the three of us had somehow managed to perfect in spite of the dangerous companions that we had ended up with. I didn't remember leaving the room, since my earlier arrival, which would have given the butler time enough to spike the coffee pot. I nervously took my seat back at the table as my mother began.

"Well, I'm sure that both of you remember me coming to visit you all in Hong Kong, after I buried my late husband, Lord rest his soul. He was a wonderful man and very sweet to me from the very first day we met." Then my mother turned her head quickly towards Miss Beasley and she softly placed her hand on top of Miss Beasley's hand that was resting on the table, palm down. The two of them made eye contact briefly as my mother went on with her explanation and to set the stage or mood. I'm not quite sure which was the case. She then went on.

"I'm not certain if you are aware of this Miss Sarah, but my late husband was almost fifteen years my senior. I met him not long after I left Los Angles with Helen here. Helen's father had left her in my care, until she became strong enough to travel. Helen's mother, bless her fragile tender heart; passed on during childbirth. She was such a delicate little thing and very pretty, just like my Helen here. Helen was born premature and couldn't travel back to Asia with her father Oscar, so he left her with me. I was the delivery nurse at the time. We wanted to hide her from her mother's family, because Helen's parents were never married and Oscar knew that he had no legal rights to her. The laws back then were very different from what they are today and Oscar couldn't take a chance on losing her. Now that I look back, I realize that we were selfish for doing what we did and I'm sure that the law probably considered what the two of us had done a serous criminal act, as well."

My foster mother then took a deep breath, released it abruptly and then looked over at me to observe my responds, before she went on.

"So we reported the baby as stillborn to her mother's family and tagged her as baby Jane Doe, which no one knew to claim at the hospital. The truth is that the night Helen was born the emergency room was a zoo and that's putting it mildly. A baby had been found outside the E.R. doors dead so we swapped out the paperwork. She then became my little Helen. One of the ward clerks and I falsified all the documentation. Helen's father sent money back for the hospital bills. I took the baby home one night after my shift, when she was stronger. After all this confusion and illegal acts, I had to transfer from my job, because I had no way of justifying having a child. I was young, unmarried, and fresh out of nursing school; plus no one there would remember me being pregnant. I sent all my free time at the hospital working, trying to get ahead and keeping a watchful eye on my Helen here, until she was strong enough and met the weight requirements to be released from the hospital. Anyway, I moved back to the D.C Maryland area and that is when I met Helen's step foster father. Helen's biological father, Oscar was flying back and forth to see Helen as she was growing up. Sometimes he was only able to stay a few days, other times he would stay a week or more. Even back then, I had feelings for Oscar, but of course I was married at the time and would never do anything to mess up the arrangement that we had. I had told my husband about Helen's father and what the two of us had done to keep her a secret. He never said much, but I could tell that he didn't approve.

Each time Oscar came to take Helen from us, I had a persuasive reason why she should stay with my husband and I. Soon after I was married; I was informed that I couldn't have any children of my own. Maybe it was Mother Nature's way of punishing me for taking a child that wasn't rightfully given to me. That's when I decided that there was no way in hell I was going to give Helen back. I changed her name from

Monique to Helen and mailed in for a new birth certificate. Oscar was mad as hell, one time when my husband called her Helen during one of his visit. She was still a small baby at the time, so it wasn't an issue for her. She mostly responded to our voices and tones. Yet even back then, she seemed to know her true biological father and would light up like a Christmas tree each time she would hear his voice, even in a whisper."

************Our Song

Suddenly my mother stopped in mid story. "Wait Miss Sarah, I'm getting all off track. What I want to tell you about is that first stimulating rubdown Helen's father, Oscar, laid on me. Well, you see, I was in his room at the Resort in Hong Kong and he always took a long break between entertaining sets for dinner. He was the resort's musical attraction in the lounge area and played there at least three or four nights a week. Most of the time he didn't eat a full meal, he just took the hour. Well, he had booked me an adjoining room to his suite. When he arrived to his room for his break, I was there on the short sofa watching television. I had removed my shoes, but I was dressed in case he wanted to take me to the lobby for dinner. I was wearing this low scoop neck tight royal blue dress with most of my cleavage showing. Oh hell, lets just call it what it was; I had my breast scandalously hanging out." My foster mother stopped and quickly laughed out and slapped her hand on the table like she was playing a winning card in a card game.

She then continued, "He walked in with his jive-turkey strut. He addressed me with his smooth confident-filled charm.

'Hello Lady, did you find everything that you need?' I took my feet off the sofa and he loosened his tie, removed his tuxedo jacket, unbuttoned his shirt cuff and turned his shirtsleeve up one turn. He rushed in the bathroom to wash his hands, as he called out to me. 'Hey Buddy, call down to the lobby please and order some fruit and a couple of salads and we will eat dinner after my next set.'

I placed the order for room service, like he had suggested. A few moments later, Mr. Smooth-talking Oscar came out of the bathroom and sat really close to me on the couch as he stared at my breasts, which I said before, were spilling over the top of my dress. He placed his arm around the back of the sofa, as he continued to gaze down into my cleavage, while leaning in towards the side of me.

'You sure smell real nice, Buddy,' complemented Oscar. He then pulled me closer, with the hand and arm that had been resting on the backrest of the couch, as his hand accidently rubbed over the nipple of my breast, over the top of my dress. I became a little uncomfortable, but we had kissed before, so I didn't think much of it. He pulled my chin up to kiss me as the other hand that was around the back of me, slowly unzipped my dress. He felt me flinch with surprise; so that was when he began to whisper in that seductive tone. 'Just relax Buddy, it will be a few more moments before the food arrives.' He kissed me deeply again and the hand from underneath my chin was now inside one of the cups of my push up bra rubbing my breast with an open palm. It felt so good, but I remained withdrawn. It had been sometime since I had any male companionship you see, if you want to call it that. My former husband had been sick for some time. Anyway Oscar continued to talk softly in that mellow musical voice of his. 'Don't' fight the feelings Miss Buddy; we both know that you need this rubdown. That's it, just a take a deep breath and let it out slowly and relax and let it happen,' he repeated.

His lips were so soft and smooth and then he fed me a little of his firm tongue and I sucked on it like junkie with a giant candy cane at Christmas time. By this time, the top of my dress was almost in my lap, one of my breasts was completely out into view and I felt his soft thick hands between my hot thighs. He persisted to talk and instruct me and I continued to follow his seductive demands. It was like I didn't have a will of my own. Nothing like this had ever happened to me before, at least not in this way. I had now slid down deeper into the sofa as he leaned over me. He continued to massage my inner thighs as he moved his hands closer to my moistened crotch. His hand that was around my neck and shoulders was now pinching my exposed breast nipple near pain level, yet strangely it felt arousing.

'Open up a little for me Buddy, so I can give you the massage that I have promised you,' he whispered. I spread my thighs as wide as I could because now the lower portion of that tight-ass dress was almost around my waist. I was wearing stocking with the old style guarder belt with the four clips attachments, to hold up your stockings. By the time Oscar reached my crotch, I was soaking wet with mating juice. I wanted him to take advantage of me right then and there, but time wasn't permitting, as fate would have it. He snatched the seat of my unmentionables to one side and slid his two fingers deep inside my hotspot and began to massage me to the end of my journey, as it's sometimes called. Ladies, I was squirming around on that sofa and panting like a cheetah cat in heat. Oooo weeeh, let me tell you, that rubdown felt so good; do you hear me? I'm not sure how long he massaged me before I exploded into an orgasm, but it was so deep and satisfying until I was trembling in the moment. I found my hand inside his pants wrapped around his manhood. I was so sure he was going to whip out his joystick and give me a sample of what was to come later that night. You know, something to hold me over until after he finished up for the evening; but then there came a knock at the door. I quickly sprang to my feet and exited to my connecting room next door.

Oscar answered the door and took the cart with our salads and fruit. Then I heard him go into the bathroom to wash his hands, as he got ready to leave to return to the lounge to perform his second and final entertaining set for the evening. He put on a fresh shirt and put back on his jacket. He then yelled through the door between our rooms. "Hey Buddy, I have to go back for my second set, I will see you after that. I was so embarrassed about what had happened until I was glad that he had to leave. Later that night, Oscar returned and I was in my room with the door open between the two suites. I had my back to the door, while only wearing a full-dress type under-slip. No bra or panties. The truth of the matter was I was about to take a shower. I was only taking a few more things out my luggage to put them away in the drawers. I heard Oscar enter his room from the hall. Oscar slowly walked up behind me and I continued to fold my clothes, while bent over a little. Before I knew anything, Oscar had walked up behind me and leaned over my shoulder to whisper in his romantic voice again. 'Has anyone told you lately Miss Buddy that you have a fine shaped ass?' I started to turn to face him and he grabbed me from behind so I wasn't able to turn to face him. I fell forward onto the bed on my forearms and knees and he pulled up my slip and inserted two of those long thick fingers into my juice box the second time. I looked over my shoulder and that's when I noticed that Oscar was only wearing a pair of boxers and some shower shoes. I turned back to look straight ahead at a bare spot on the wall across the bed and listened to his voice and enjoyed those fingers inside me, while massaging me towards another orgasm. The Smooth Oscar began to whisper to me again.

'I'm sorry I had to leave earlier Buddy, before I finished your massage, but I'm finished downstairs for tonight, so I have time to do it properly this time.' I tried to answer him, but nothing came out. I was too wrapped up in the pleasure I was receiving. Oscar was rubbing my buttock with one hand as the other hand eased his digits deeper and deeper into my hungry g-spot. Then he would move one hand to my full heavy breasts that had completely escaped out the top of my slip.

'Let me say for the record, Buddy that you have some fine health breasts as well. I can't wait to turn you over and suck them to a satisfying state, but first I have to finish up this massage.' At this point, Oscar was now on his knees to the side of me as I felt his penis on the side of my butt cheek and upper thigh. Then he quickly shifted to the rear and removed his stimulating digits and guided his thick firm pole into my moistened shed. It sort of alarmed me at first. It had been awhile since I had shared a moment with a man and I was kinda' nervous. Then Oscar began to chant as he glided his intruder deeper inside me. 'That's it Buddy, take it all in. I know you needed this. I know it's been a long time since anyone has massaged you like this. Everything will be fine, I'm here now and I'm going to massage you as much and as often as you will allow me to. That's it Baby, take the entire pole in. I want your very soul to feel me stroking you. You know you need it and I've been waiting to give you a taste of my joystick for years. Oooo weee! Buddy, this is some good p—y. This is the kind of hot ass that makes you loose your mind, if you aren't careful. Okay hold on; let me do all the work. That's it take it all.'

Oscar then shoved his penis deep into my soggy cavern and slapped me hard on one ass cheek and then released in a few jolts. We both were perspiring a little as we tried to catch our breath. At the time, I wasn't sure if it was medically safe for the two of us to become that excited without a physical examination prior; considering our age and everything. Well, after the moment was over, he quickly withdrew his manhood from me and disappeared to his room next door. I thought that was odd, but I didn't say anything. I thought that perhaps the feelings he had experienced had frightened him as well. I took my shower and put on a gown and Oscar began talking to me without us making eye contact, as he yelled through the open connecting room doors. 'Hey Buddy, do you want to come over for a nightcap or have a bottle of wine with me?'

I answered, 'Sure Oscar, I'll be over in a few minutes.' When I arrived wearing my sexy gown and matching robe. There he sat on the sofa with his long terry-cloth hotel embossed bathrobe. He stood up when I entered the room in a real gentlemen's fashion. He walked slowly towards me with a serious look and leaned in to kiss me on the neck, as he held the glass of wine in one hand. I owe you an apology for this afternoon earlier. That was no way to treat a lady and I do realize that you are a fine upstanding woman. I feel like I took advantage of you and I wanted to say that I'm sorry. I sort of let my sexual desires get away from me.'

'No harm done Oscar, I enjoyed you as well. We are both well-seasoned adults and have been knowing each other for quite a while.' After that comment, Oscar kissed me on the lips briefly without caressing me with his hands and we both moved to the sofa in his room. He had ordered wine, cheeses, fruit and crackers. We sat as he placed his arm around the back of my portion of the couch and began staring at my huge firm breast again. So I opened my robe so he could enjoy the view of my cleavage better. He continued to apologize as he made his move on me for more intimacy.

'I would like to try to make up for what happened earlier today.' He passed me a glass of wine and I took a sip as I turned my entire body a little more to face him.

'Oh please Oscar, forget about it. I needed a little male companionship, and you were here for me; enough said about that.'

'Agreed then, Buddy.' He pulled me back more onto the back of the sofa with the arm that was placed on the backrest and moved in closer. We made small talk as he steered the conversation back into our past. He kissed me and eased the tip of his tongue into my mouth and I received it like I had been waiting for it. I placed my wine glass on the end table and slid my hand inside his robe. Oscar smiled shyly, 'Would you like another massage Miss Buddy, I did promise to orally massage all the life out of those fine breasts of your? He placed his wine glass on the other end table and dimmed the lights just a little. He held the sides of my robe so I could remove my arms and then he pulled my shoulder straps down on both sides of my gown as my breasts fell out. I sat perfectly still and waited for him to take them all in and then keep his word, about his earlier promise. He rubbed both of them into both of his hands as I watched his hands move across my breasts and I became aroused. He then pinched both nipples between his fingers until I said ouch.

Then he said, 'let me suck away the pain Miss Buddy.' Then he turned quickly and laid his head in my lap and pulled me downward so his mouth could reach my teats with ease. I reached inside his robe as he place one leg on the back of the sofa and I massaged him to complete freedom. I don't know how long we held these positions, but my breast was sore and bruised for a week a more later. Oscar finally sat up and moved in to kiss me. He enjoyed each other lips for a long time and then he pulled away. He stood in front of me and pulled me deeper into the couch, by my knees then he pushed up my gown to expose my nakedness. He propped my heels on the edge of the sofa and knelt down between my thighs. He was staring into my crotch as he whispered. 'I enjoy gazing at a woman's private area, I hope you don't think I'm strange.' He was now maneuvering the covering apart with the fingers from both of hands as he continued to stare and talk in a slow low tone. Your femaleness appears so ripe and sweet. I noticed that you keep forest-free, I like that in a lady.' He was now moving his face closer to my crotch as he spoke slower. 'I'm not sure about asking you this, but if it's okay with you, Miss Buddy I would like to sample your cherry nectar.'

I instantly began to shake all over as I quickly closed my eyes. Then with me being a certified lady and all, whatever the hell that means, I convincingly pretended not to know what he meant. I had never participated in this form of lovemaking before. However, I had heard about it, but had never experienced it for myself, you understand. I froze up; my entire body became stiff and rigid. I didn't know what to say, or how to respond to such a question. The room went mute as he moved in a little closer, while he appeared to wait for me to answer. Then I felt his tongue pierce the inner walls of my tavern. I force out a quiet screamed. Well, fortunately for me that was when Oscar started to talk to me again and added more controlling pressure to our position, while he coached me through this new pleasure-filled experience. 'Stay calm Miss Buddy,' he suggested. 'You will be fine and this will start to be enjoyable in a few moments. Just take deep breaths in and out and let me do all the work. That's it lady, just relax and let the passion and desire wash over you slowly.'

Then he placed his entire oral cavity over the area and began to nurture me like a virgin. He had me in a stronghold that I couldn't get out of. I tried to squirm away, but he was too resilient for me to break free. Then I relaxed and he massaged me down there until I released twice. Oscar slowly released me and I placed my feet back onto the floor. I then simply balled myself up on the sofa to recover. I was tingling in places that I didn't realize could be sexually stimulated. He went into the bathroom and came out a few moments later. I was almost asleep when he began rubbing my back.

'Buddy, would you care to sleep over here with me or in your own accommodations' he asked, once again, with that proper gentlemen's tone?' Of course I answered up quickly, I didn't want him to think I was a loose woman of sorts. How crazy was that, after what had just taken place between the two of us and earlier as well?'

My foster mother laughed out loud again briefly as she covered her mouth, as if the embarrassing moment had briefly returned. She continued.

'I'll sleep next door, Oscar, but thank you so much for your generous and kind offer, Sir' I somehow managed to reply.

'Okay, I'll walk you over and tuck you in.' Oscar then walked me to my room and sat on the bed, while I went in to brush my teeth and put on my nightly face cream. I was so calm and relaxed until I was acting like a drunken person on pain medication. Oscar was smiling, because he knew what was wrong, or should I say, what was right. I crawled in bed and Oscar pulled the light covers up to my neck. He stood up to leave.

'Wait Oscar, talk to me for a few moments, just until I fall asleep.' He quickly dropped his head and smiled deeply before he answered, as he sat back down on the side of my bed. He was aware of something that I didn't realize at the time and this amused him.

'Now Miss Buddy', he said as he tried to regain his composure. 'Both of us are way too old for bedtime stories, and deceptive word games, Lady; but I think you might enjoy a little of this, as a nightcap.' Oscar then hurriedly took off his robe and pulled back the covers and climb into bed with me. He didn't waste any time shoving up my gown and forcing my thighs far apart as he grabbed his manhood mid-shaft and crawled on top of me and began to pump his male organ deep inside me. Of course I pretended to be surprised and a little shocked at first, but Oscar was smart enough to ignore my fake expressions. 'Okay now Miss Buddy, lay quiet and close your eyes. Concentrate on going to sleep, not having sex. Feel me deep inside of you, because the strokes will become lighter and the penetration will becomes shallow. He reached over and turned off the light, on my nightstand and now the only light was the dim glow of his lamp, from next door. I got this strong suspicious feeling that Playboy Oscar he had performed this nightcap service many times before. I placed my hands up on each side of my head as it lay softly on the pillow. The stroked were firm and forceful until I had an orgasm, and then they became light and shallow. Oscar whispered to me as he took his fill of me and I can't remember, even to this day, exactly when he left my room that night. I tell you Miss Sarah, that man of mine has magical hands and gifted plumbing, if you two ladies will allow me to brag a little.'

Miss Beasley laughed out loudly for the first time in a while as I just held my head down and pretended not to have heard the entire recount. I was hoping that my foster mother was finished with her despicable sex stories about my father, but I wasn't that fortunate. Miss Beasley poured her a second cup of coffee as I excused myself to the restroom. For a moment I wondered if Miss Beasley had spiked the coffee with some of that tea from China, labeled Hong Kong by Moonlight. I had already been a victim of that brew once before, at a massage parlor, plus Tate and Fred had also experienced its unannounced enchanting powers as well. I could still hear them talking and laughing as I closed the bathroom door.

The snow was coming down heavier now and had managed to add a full and complete new coating to everything, since just before that morning's light. I was sincerely hoping that my interruption to go to the bathroom would somehow encourage a subject change at the breakfast table, but no such luck. My foster mother was hell-bound on telling, yet another, explicit shared moment between her and my biological father Oscar, whom she had now begun to, occasionally, refer to as stud-muffin. Personally I found the whole 'Girl's Talk' thing distasteful and embarrassing, but unfortunately I had been out voted by these other two 'ladies', earlier on; if I'm allowed to misuse the word to describe them. I finally returned to the table and they both could read the disgust on my face as I sat down. My mother tried to justify her exploits of my father, but I stood my ground. Then she reached over to pat the back of my hand, as she debatably supported her actions.

'Oh com'on Sweetie, we are just a few mature women sitting around the table, while snowed in, drinking coffee. What is the harm in that?' I looked over at Miss Beasley and she was gleaming with anticipation of what my mother would disclose to us next. Miss Beasley held one hand over her mouth as she tried to restrain her excitement out of respect for my blatantly repeated protest. On the other hand, my shameless foster mother refused to let it go as she cleared her throat, took another sip of coffee and again redirected her gaze in Miss Beasley's direction.

'Well Miss Sarah, there is another time that sticks out in my memory that I think is fitting for this occasion and one in which I have often thought about and found amusing, or stimulatingly comforting might be a better choice of words.' My foster mother smiled deeply and then a short giggle escaped her as Miss Beasley and I looked on. 'After we were married and back in the states here, Oscar and I were up one night late; very much like a snowy day we are having now. The city was shutdown of course and I decided to turn in early. Well, as you know or may not realize, we always had a piano in the house. That was the first thing that Oscar purchased when he arrived back to the states. He selected the most expensive one he could find. To be truthful, the one he wanted had to be ordered. He explained to the store manager who he was and they agreed to lend him one, until his came in and was properly tuned, you see. So this cold winters night Oscar sat at the borrowed piano trying to finish a song that he had partially written years before. Oscar called it our song, and I'm about to tell you why.'

I had no idea where my foster mother was headed with this story, but I wanted to attempt to cut her off at the pass, so to speak.

'Mother, for the love of God and nature, would you please not embarrass me any further.' My mother turn quickly towards me with a annoyed look on her face as she properly straightened her spine and took on the straight-lace lady like persona that I had grown up with all my life and never dreamed of experiencing anything differently from her. She then pressed her lips together and tilted her head down forward slightly as she made sharp eye-piercing contact with me.

She said, 'Baby-girl have you heard this story before?' I slowly answered as I look across the table towards Miss Beasley, whom had completely lost all her composure and was now silently patting her fingertips together, while laughing out of control. 'No Mother, I don't believe I have.' My foster mother then snapped her response back to me as she tilted her head back up to its neutral position, as her tone of voice took on a scolding nature.

'Then hush-up child and listen quietly; as old as I am, you should be thanking God that I can remember the particulars so clearly after all this time. Besides, you are the only one here at the table that's on their third husband. Surely none of this is new to you or has any educational value. And let me say for the record that each of those husbands of yours was and is pretty damn fine and capable if anyone had a mind to ask me.'

I stared in shock with my mouth slightly open, as my foster mother struck a blow below the belt, so to speak. She then continued, 'I still remember your first husband; Williams' father and quite well too. He was so stunningly gorgeous until I had to wear a panty shield whenever I though you were coming home with him in-tow. After he passed, I just knew you wouldn't be fortunate enough to find another man that nice and fine. So where is that fool who says that lighting never strikes twice in the same place. I want to call him or her a lie to their faces, because when you met Austin, and he was even finer than Williams' father, I knew then for sure that you had been assigned your own personal angel, before birth. Now you have been given a third man, Austin's twin brother Alex. If this was anyone else's will except our Divine God's,

I would call him out and tell him that he has been unfair to the rest of us.'

Then I yelled at my foster mother, while Miss Beasley snickered even more.

'Mother please, that has to be some form of blasphemy.'

'Oh please yourself, Helen; God knows the heart of every man and if he didn't have a sense of humor in some form or other, half of the population would be wiped off the face of the planet.' Miss Beasley then slowly bobbed her head in agreement with my foster mother, as she raised one eyebrow as if she had an epiphany moment. I quickly remembered that those were Father Caleb words about God knowing the heart of every man and realized for the first time that he meant at every moment, otherwise we wouldn't have a chance.

My foster mother shook her head from side to side, with her lips pressed strangely together, as if these facts about my three husbands were still hard for her to believe, even after she had stated them out aloud. Miss Beasley sat up taller now and looked on as though some of this she was hearing for the first time. Then my foster mother gave me another quick look and reached over to stroke the back of my hand to see if she had gone to far by putting my business out on the table. I twitched my face a little and stared back down into my cup.

'Helen, the truth of the matter is that you should be giving the two of us the lecture on how 'variety is the spice of life'.

Instead, you are fussing about being embarrassed.' At that point my foster mother's voice moved to a more consoling tone before she went on. 'Baby Heart, the day after tomorrow or perhaps next week, neither of us will even remember the details of these stories nor possibly telling them. The only thing that will linger on in our memories is the deep-soul laughter that we shared while revealing the narratives, and perhaps the healing sensation that the recollections stirred up within us, while remembering the long-ago moments so vividly. Now you can't ask God for more than that and hold a straight face.'

Miss Beasley placed one open-palm hand over her chest as if she was trying to recover from the vapors, or catch her breath and perhaps to slowdown her heartbeat, from which had been caused by such tedious laughter, while she wholeheartedly agreed with my foster mother with a mere nod of her head. My foster mother calmly relaxed back in her chair and stretched both arm out in front of her, as her cup-bowl remained between her loosely curved fingers. Miss Beasley was now attempting to dry her tears of laughter, by fanning her face with both hands, before they spilled out and ruined her mascara. I did as my mother had suggested and realized that perhaps she was right.

'Let me see,' said my foster mother as she rolled her eyes up towards the ceiling and pressed her thin lips tightly together. 'Oh, I know ladies. I was about to tell you about our song. As you know, Mr. Oscar has a passion or maybe it's an obsession, for his music or any music for that matter.' She then turned her head quickly to look at each of us as she clasped her hands together and then stared back up towards the ceiling and smiled deeply. 'I'll leave it up to you to choose the word you want to use. However, I'm here to tell you that he has other passions as well. Um hum.' My foster mother quickly leaned in and changed her voice again the set the mood, as she tapped Miss Beasley on the back of the hand.

"Well this particular night a couple of his passions collided, or should I say became intertwined. You see I wanted Oscar to come to bed, for obvious reasons and he wanted to finish writing the song. Finishing this melody had haunted him for days by this time and I'm not sure why this particular one or why in fact this was the case. There were lots of other compositions that he had never completed, you understand. Anyway, I waltzed right into the den as he sat at the piano and positioned myself as closely as I could, while straddling the long piano stool. He noticed me and smiled and then leaned in to kiss me, then immediately turned all his attention back to his sheet of music. He would stop for a moment, make a few more notations on the page and then repeat the melody again. It's a beautiful song, by the way, and he plays it for us from time to time, and laugh as he remembers that evening. Well, I felt as though he wasn't giving me enough of his undivided attention, this particular night, so I began to kiss the side of his face and rub the inside of my thigh as I pulled up my nightgown to expose myself to him. He took one hand from the piano keys and pinched my nipple through my gown. I unbutton the front of it to my waist and exposed my breasts. He smiled again, but he still was trying to finish the song.

Then I stuck my hand inside his pajama bottoms and began to hand stroke his wand. I knew I had more of his attention then, because he started to strike improper keys.

Then he looked at me and said, 'Okay baby, just a few more minutes and I will come to bed. I can see that you are serious about having a piece of the music man, 'Oscar responded conceitedly if I remember accurately. By this time he had obtained a full erection and I was well lubed-up and ready for action. I closed my eyes and had placed one leg across his lap and was humping the side of him like an animal in heat. Where is a water-hose when you need one, hum? Oscar found my aggressive sexual behavior amusing at first, but continued to stop intermittently to make notes to his sheet of music. Well Oscar soon noticed that my breathing pattern had change to that point of no return, you could say; so he pushed back from the keyboard, grabbed me and pulled me into his lap with my back to the piano keyboard and whipped out his penis and I slid right down on his pulsating pole. He was now forcefully sucking my breast into his mouth as he held them at the base. I had my arms around his neck as I sprang up and down on his manhood. He held me and kissed me until I released and then I hugged him tightly. He looked over my shoulder and continued to play the piano with one hand as we caught our breath. I slowly moved to the side, back onto the stool next him as he looked over and warmly smiled again.'

Miss Beasley fanned herself with her hand a few times and blew her breath on the tip of her fingers in a sign that this story was really heating up. Whew! She commented. They both laughed briefly as mother continued.

'Hey Buddy, are you okay? Inquired Oscar to me. 'I will be finished in a moment.' I didn't answer him as I leaned in closer with the side of my head on his shoulder and waited. About a half an hour later, he closed the top down on the cover of the keyboard and we went to bed. He moved back on top of me and gave me a good hard thrashing, if you know what I mean. I must have fallen asleep for an hour or so, because when I woke up and he was back at the piano working on that song. Well, I wanted a little more of that spanking, as he always affectionately call it, so I went down there to get him. He gave me that charming, I've-been-busted smile as I walked into the den. Oscar held out his hand for me to sit in his lap facing the keyboard this time. I pulled up my gown so our warm naked flesh could make contact. He played a few notes and then began to massage my full breasts with his free hand, and kiss the back of neck and shoulders. I began to grind my butt down against his private parts. Oscar found it very humorous whenever I would act fresh or aggressive towards him. He whispered, 'Alright Lady, I have a little more spanking power left in me and you know that I'm always in the mood to give it to one of my musical groupies.'

He then stood up from the piano again and led us back to our cozy little love nest and he took full advantage of me from the rear. I was clawing at the sheets like a scared cat as Oscar kept the pressure on until I collapsed onto the bed, while he continued to sooth me with his smooth goodness. Every few minutes he would give my butt a hard slap on the butt cheek, I would jump with surprise and he then would plunge himself in deeper. I'm not sure what the sharp slaps on the backside was suppose to accomplish, but I can tell you that I didn't mind the sting of it or what came next.

Then there are other times, while we are sitting on the sofa, Oscar will instruct me to lie across his lap, faced upward, for a little spanking, that is what we call it, which in actuality is a deep cavern massage, as we watch the evening news. First I lie across his thighs with my knees bent; then he pulls up my gown and rub my buttocks and hips for a few minutes or longer. Oscar then will slap my butt cheeks firmly a few times and then he slowly caresses me between my inner legs until I open my thighs to receive a couple of his digits inside my cherry patch. He then speaks to me very quietly, as he massages the inside of my cavern and breast. I can't describe to you two how relaxing this is, when I final experience a homerun. One hand will be gently rubbing back and forth around over my breast and their nipples, with an open palm. Then stopping to massage them firmly between his palm and fingers; while the other hand is moving his fingers in and out of my juice box. Sometime he would lean forward, during a commercial and suck my breast for additional pleasure or spread my personal and massage the clitoris with just two fingers. Sometimes it takes me a few rounds to reach my full peak, if you get my meaning, but he never has a problem with how long it takes.

After the news is finished for the evening, Oscar takes me into our bedroom to complete the massage. Ladies, after experiencing this part of life, I have come to understand and believe that slow nurturing intimacy adds years to ones life and that traditional coupling isn't always the method that is required to give the body the sexual nourishment that it requires. Yes, ladies that man is nicely equipped to work with my needs and I thank Mother Nature every day for blessing him with his capabilities.'

My foster mother then appeared to reflect back to that moment in time; as she stared out into space before going on, 'Well needless to say, the next morning, Oscar finished that particular song: music, lyrics, and all. And that's how it became our song. Now when he plays our song on the piano and we are alone, I go to the piano and pleasure him, as he plays the song. Most of the time, he massages me right there on the seat of the piano stool. Sometimes I sit in his lap and he reaches around me to play the song while I glide up and down on his......; please excuse my crassness. I get a little weak in the knees just talking about. I have learned another aspect of intimacy; there is sex and there is lovemaking, however, I love and appreciate them both.'

At that moment I saw my foster mother revert back into the genteel and proper lady that was familiar to me, and I felt more comfortable with; especially in mixed company.

When my mother finished her final words, I decided to go back to our house to check on Alex and get a quick therapeutic massage of my own, while she was over there at Miss Beasley's. I stood up from the table.

"If you two ladies will excuse me, I will run home to see what is taking Alex so long to come over. I will be right back." My mother rolled her eyes suspiciously as she pressed her lips together in that doubtful shape, while raising her brow as Miss Beasley looked down and rendered a peculiar snicker.

"Ah hum, tell us whatever you like Baby Girl," replied my foster mother. "I bet all this talk about sexual encounters has made you horny and you are going home to see if Alex will break you off a little something, before he comes over and while I'm out of the house; just incase there are some sounds of passion escaping your bedroom. Oh, I know you play a good game about being so shy about sex, but I know your biological father, personally if I may add. And if I understand anything about science and DNA, I'm willing to wager that some of his sexual attitude no doubt was passed on through the gene pool. Do I have any takers?"

Miss Beasley held her mule, as the old folks like to say when a bystander refuses to get involved with whatever the discussion is at that moment.

I wouldn't dare allow my mother to know that she was right, so I didn't give any response. I rushed back to our house, just up the road. I met Alex at the door, about to put on his coat to come over to Burney's and Miss Beasley's. I quickly walked in and asked Alex if I could speak to him in our bedroom.

"Hey Baby," said Alex without a clue. "I was just about to come over. What's wrong? Did you need something; I could have brought it over? Why didn't you call me?"

"Alex, can I see you in the bedroom for a moment?" I grabbed him by the arm forcefully and lead him towards the master suite.

"Can't you tell me right here? There is no one else here except the two of us. What's wrong Helen?"

"Nothing is wrong baby, I just need a intimate moment with you that's all. We were at the kitchen table and Miss Sarah and my mother were telling naughty sex stories and I became a little horny, that's all. Alex slowly started to laugh as he began removing his clothes. I became annoyed by his response to my honesty and became embarrassed again. "If you aren't going to take this seriously Alex, then forgive me for asking." I turned to walk out our bedroom as he caught me by the arm and pulled me forcefully into his arms. He realized now that there were other feelings in play, as my eyes became moistened with silly moody tears.

"Stop Helen, come here and talk to me." We were both standing in the middle of our bedroom, half dressed. I buried my face in Alex's hairy chest because I was upset that my mother had went on with the stories and I felt stupid that they had aroused me and hurt that Alex had laughed at me. Alex slowly pulled my chin up towards his face to kiss me. "Helen you know you can have me anytime you want me. I love you and I'm sorry that I laughed at you. Besides, you should be accustomed to your foster mother embarrassing you. So come on; come to bed with me."

"No Alex, I don't want to now. I feel like this is trivial and stupid. I'm not a young child. I shouldn't have come......"

"Don't be silly Helen, sexual desires don't age. When the moment strikes, we feel twenty-five years old again. Then we realize, in the middle of the sexual act, that we are fifty-five and pray to live through the experience. Come on; come to bed with me. I promise you that you will feel better." Alex then pressed his body up against me more and inhaled the essence of me through his nostrils with a loud groaning sound. "I know what you like and need, Lady Thornton." Alex tightened his arms grip around me and became more serious about my situation. "It has been a while for us, Helen; since our last lovemaking. Perhaps we need to make more time for intimacy. Remember we talked about this when we first met. It doesn't change with age, the body desires what the body needs." Alex then increased the pressure of his caress and delivered a slow-motion forecasting kiss. Alex and I slid into our bed and he made love to me slowly and deeply until I screamed out loudly in pure satisfaction. I made a groaning noise at each inward thrust as my body absorbed as much of Alex's passion as possible.

***********My Quickie Exposed

An hour later, I went back over to Miss Beasley's and discovered she and my mother had remained in their original chairs, at the kitchen table. They instantly began to laugh the moment I walked in. Mother spoke first, 'so tell me Helen, is Alex coming over later?' I tried to cover, but she was too clever, for me. My disclosing answer just slipped out.

"I'm not sure mother, I left him in bed." My foster mother immediately slapped her open hand on the top of the table and Miss Beasley reached in her pocket and gave my mother a twenty-dollar bill. The two of them had obviously made a bet as to why I suddenly felt the need to rush home to check on Alex. I was too sexually satisfied to care what they thought or why they were laughing.

"Sure you are, you went back over to the house and drained all the pleasure out of Alex's wonder wand. You don't have to pretend with me, Little Girl; I've been around this ballpark a long time, and I think I know most of the plays in the playbook. You and Alex hadn't been getting busy in a while, and even though my naughty stories included your father and me, your body still became aroused. Well I guess I do owe you an apology for that, but it's your fault for not keeping up with your homework, in the bedroom. I was only sharing a little fun history, for our entertainment. I apologize if I embarrassed Helen. I didn't think revealing a few forgotten moments about your father would cause any harm. Surely you realize that he was a man before he became your father."

Then suddenly our attentions were deflected by a familiar sound. The doorbell rang; it was Slapp and Kate from the barn-house across the field. Alex did come over later, and no more was said about how we had filled that snowy morning.

The following winter we got a couple more snowed-in days and the phrase did become a traditional idiom. We are snowed in, where can we go?) Fred passed on the following winter after that, while he and his family were living in Florida. Miss Beasley and Burney took the news to heart and chose not to attend the funeral. That same year my grandmother Nana Wiley also died. My father, Oscar and foster mother sold their house and moved into a two-bedroom condo. Our old house was being rented out. The boarder that we had living there with my former foster parents was forced to move, due to his failing health and age, so an assistance living facility was selected. Now there was finally a family that was large enough to fill that big house that my foster parents had purchase when I was very young. My father, Oscar used the excess profit, from the sale of their house, to take my mother to some of the Asian cities that he had worked, while on the entertainer's circuit.

My Cousin Jerome was able to retire from the Los Angeles police department and that was a party that no one wanted to miss. I believe that it lasted for about three days and nights. The most important reason for the lengthy celebration was that Jerome had survived the streets of Los Angles. His parents, which I explained earlier to be extremely capable;

were ecstatic to say the least that their son had lived and accomplished so much in life, while never veering too far off the path that they had trained him and his siblings to travel, amen.

Chapter Fifteen

My Brother's Keeper Reunion

One weekend Slapp posted one of those secret-coded classified ads to announce a small party at his place in the barn. The invitation was for the twelve original 'My Brother's Keeper' unauthorized agents, whom had set up this high stakes bounty hunting sub-agency and as many of their family members as they wanted to bring in-tow. Of course Fred and Father Caleb had passed away and we were sure that a few of the others would be absent as well, and this made all of us very sad. Slapp purchased the ads to run in every major and minor paper in the Washington D.C, Maryland and Virginia area, two months before the selected date of the event. After the sub-agency had been disband, the agents scattered to the four winds, for personal reasons and for safety, yet continued to take the local newsprints, as a way to track each other's personal and professional moments.

It was a cool early fall evening and the leaves were everywhere, while displaying an array of beautiful autumn colors. The evenings were brisk, yet not cold enough to present any discomfort. This was the prefect weather for a party; just before everyone becomes too busy with holiday shopping and planning. We had no idea who or how many people would attend this secret reunion. We were pretty sure that the gathering would overflow from Slapp's place and travel from Slapp's parents house next door and to our house, up the road a bit. The reunion was a big success. We hired those ladies from the previous holiday events to help Julius the butler and we helped out as well. The men had a great time and alcohol was flowing like water from a fresh discovered underground spring.

After the party was about to windup and we had decided who had consumed too much libation and was going to be forced to spend the night, Slapp and a few of the guys meandered back over to his place, the big red barn, for just one more nightcap or perhaps two, if I had to be perfectly honest about it. They shared our feelings that the party was so enjoyable until none of us wanted it to end. The entourage from next door included Alex, Tate, my cousin Jerome, our son William, Tye my old escort from the backseat of the limousine, Slapp and his father Uncle Burney. When the men all arrived at the barn, which was what we called Slapp's place because his parents had transformed it, Tate's wife Gayle and I was cleaning up from the party, that had spilled over from the big house. We had left Slapp's wife Kate over at the main house to help Miss Beasley and Julius the butler. Everyone at this point had agreed to spend the night at one of the three locations, including our faithful bodyguards and extended family members; Miles and Daniel, the two brothers from Guam. Those were the most blow-up mattresses and sleeping bags that any of us had ever seen out side of a camping supply store. We used every set of bed sheets we could find. Miles and his brother Daniel, who was now permanently living in the immediate area as well, had been asked to come for security measures. Now that three locations required guarding, we asked the brothers to walk the lane that connected the three houses. They graciously agreed; no extra fees were required.

The seven men I named earlier climbed the few stairs that led to the living portion of the big red barn. This was Tye's first time seeing Slapp's place from inside and all he could say was 'wow' as he landed inside and on the top step landing. Gayle and I were both hard at work cleaning up the place, mainly the kitchen.

"Slapp!" exploded Tye, "Man this is a really nice place you have out here. Your father did all of this for you?" Then he turned quickly to Uncle Burney that just so happened to be bringing up the rear. This is great Mr. Burney, and just think; from the outside it looks just like an old barn. No one would ever guess that this was top-notch living quarters, just beyond those doors, including a hacker's dream setup. Even seeing it with my own eyes, it's hard to grasp it fully. It's like a small command center in here." Tye quickly turned to face Burney again before he spoke his next words of unbelief. "Mr. Burney,

I don't even want to know how you managed to pull this all off, without being tracked as a terrorist cell."

"Well thank you Tyrone, and thank you again for not asking for an explanation. I did a lot of the work myself," replied Uncle Burney as he reared back and looked around and smiled with great pride. They all moved quickly to the bar area to the right of the staircase and began to fix themselves a drink. Tate took his overnight bag into his assigned bedroom, because he and Gayle had agreed to spend the night. Mr. Burney took one of the swivel rocking chairs and Tye took the other one next to him. Slapp sat on one end of the long sofa sleeper, that was in the room and Jerome took a seat on the other end. William pulled up two bar stools from the bar for himself and Alex, while Tate brought in a kitchen chair as he returned to the room and was the last one to be seated in the spacious area. Uncle Burney offered the first toast to all the young bucks; as Ole Mr. Charlie enjoyed saying, even though some of the men in the group found it offensive. Uncle Burney held his glass up high.

"I would just like to surrender a tribute to our brothers that have gone on before. I sure do miss Ole Fred and your father also Tate, Father Caleb. They would have been here tonight; if they were alive I just know that they would have. Perhaps we waited too long before having this gathering. Well, there is no looking back at this point." They all took a small sip and slowly looked downward to reflect. Tye continued to look around and then asked Slapp's permission to wander.

"Would you mind if I took a closer look at your place, Slapp?"

"No Man, of course not; please, be my guest." Tye swiftly stood to his feet to take a quick tour. Tye immediately noticed all the literary art that Slapp had collected, enlarged and carefully framed. Agent Marshall had been a man of his word and had given Slapp a copy of two writings for his wall, titled: **Navy Sailor** and **Army Warrior**. Slapp had also framed a copy of a prayer that his mother Miss Beasley had written years before for Max and Milani to practice and memorize. Miss Beasley call it a prayer to improve Max's resume'. The assortment of written art also included a prayer pledge that someone had penned for a special group of ladies at church. The final two panels of framed words was a copy of the spiritual song that my father had written to commemorate our safe return back to the states, and the other which in reality was just a new rendition of a New Years Eve song, Auld Lang Syne. This song also included an added stanza that my father Oscar had written in honor of the passing of Father Caleb and Retired Agent Fred, which also reflected the highs and lows of our lives. Songs, prayers, pledges, poems and oaths they were all displayed there on Slapp's entrance walls. The list continued and Tye walked slowly around to read a few words from each inscription. Suddenly Slapp broke the solemn moment with an outburst, which included an epiphanous tone at the edge of his voice.

"Oh, I know what we can discuss and perhaps clear up a few things." Slapp quickly took an unspoken survey of the people in the room to make sure that we were all from the inner circle. Gayle was the only person in question, but was now married to Tate and had carried a clearance for years, due to her previous position at the American Embassy in Hong Kong. Jerome had surely been tried by fire when his position had been threatened when he had driven Slapp from Los Angles to San Diego in his squad car in time to witness our hired surveillance guy's house explode from a preset gas leak.

"Surely we are all sober enough to do this", claimed Slapp. I've been beside myself to know, since the first time I heard about that secret mission, while we were in Hong Kong and then again in Thailand, years ago. Will someone please tell me about Tate and Alex in Cambodia, hiding out."

Slapp quickly scanned the room again to possibly read a body-tell of all who knew something about this specific mission and time. Tyrone was the first to through up his hands and wave the stare away from himself. Jerome's body language reflected the same, but there was a chance that this was a false-positive, as the laboratory technician like to say. Slapp knew that Fred had taken a special liking to Jerome, even from their first meeting encounter, and would tell Jerome things about the organization that he didn't have a clearance to know. Fred was a cautious man by nature, but he had seen something in Jerome that made him feel that Jerome could keep a secret as well as the next man, and as one of the original profilers, Fred had been correct. Slapp remembered this fact about Jerome and Fred's relationship and decided that a second glance in Jerome's direction might prove to be prudent. Jerome's body reflection didn't change, so Slapp moved his gaze in another direction. This had taken place years ago and Tyrone was even younger than Slapp, whom was now aggressively enquiring with his body langue as well.

Mr. Burney, Slapp's father, smiled briefly and crossed his legs with a knee-ankle contact as he took another tiny sip from his glass and then looked over at Alex. Slapp quickly responded to the informative glance that his father Mr. Burney had given Alex. "I saw that Dad. Why is it that no one wants to talk about that mission?"

Mr. Burney snapped at Slapp and then stood up and walked back towards the bar for a single piece of ice for his drink. The ice could have been to cool down his drink, or dilute it or this could have just been an avoidance move that Uncle Burney attempted to use to change the subject, after Slapp had called him out about the glance he had rendered to Alex. Then Mr. Burney fired an answer towards Alvin (Slapp).

"Maybe it's because it is none of your damn business Junior, did you ever consider that? Besides, it might be because it holds some painful memories for some. At any rate Alvin, it was before your time son and if a man doesn't want to share his past with you, you shouldn't push the issue, especially in our line of work. Everything that is done in the field never quite reaches the file. They are always incomplete; for one reason or another. You should know that better than anyone Junior." Everyone in the room gave a sly brief smile.

Uncle Burney was referring to the house fire and gas explosion that had killed their formal computer cyber-space security guard. The room was quiet for a moment and then our son William, known to some as Billy the kid, chimed in with a persuasive argument that no one expected. Gayle and I became very still, as we appeared to fade into the small surroundings of the kitchen like cheat wallpaper at a high-level clearance sale. This was very rare for the boys to talk so openly about a previous case, with any of us ladies in the room or within earshot for that matter. Gayle and I were in fact right around a half wall that separated the eating zone and cooking area from the sitting area. William spoke up and, as usual, out of turn and further pressed the issue, 'as it were', to quote Father Caleb.

"I thought you told me about all your old missions, Dad. I would be a liar if I said that I wasn't a tad bit curious, myself." After a slight pause, William then confirmed what the remainder of us was already aware of, with a momentary slur in his words. "Oh what the hell; claimed William, "I'm down-right damn inquisitive or nosey."

Uncle Burney quickly spoke to William with an authoritarian tone, as Alex turned towards William as well. "The bar is now closed to you Master William. I believe that you and your aunt Sarah Lynn could possibly be blood related, when it comes to holding your liquor," Most of the guys let out a hearty laugh.

Alex took this moment to snap back as well, "More like meddlesome as hell, if you ask me, Son." Some laughed, but

Gayle and I only smiled to maintain our camouflaged posture as we hid behind a half-wall, while we pretended to be busy cleaning.

Everyone was looking in Alex's direction for the answer to the burning question, even though Tate had been on the same mission and knew the entire career-changing story as well. Tate broke the ice and silence in the room, as he placed his hands in that habit-forming prayerful pose.

"I'll tell you'll what I remember", said Tate with a reluctant tone at the edge of his voice. "I'll just leave out some of the personal stuff of my brother Alex here." Tate hesitated for another few moments and everyone in the room became quiet and still. Tate took a long analyzing stare in Alex's direction before he began. "You see, Alex and I were on a mission in Northern Thailand and the area became too dangerous for us, so we escaped to Cambodia. Initially we weren't together, because as you know, I'm from another branch plus we had different assignments of course, but the danger and the results were closely related. I spoke enough of the local language to get us by or perhaps killed, I can't remember which was the case at this moment." Everyone released a short-burst of laughter as Tate smiled only briefly and looked back down into his glass and gave it a swallow swirl, before taking in his next full breath to proceed with the verbal re-enactment, in which appeared to be a very private and painful matter.

"We flew into Bangkok Thailand and then crossed into Cambodia on land. Alex and I discovered much later that we had been on the same case for totally different reasons. There was only one big problem, when we first met up while fleeing for our lives, and that was that we had to pass through some of the most gorilla-infested parts of the Cambodia boarder to get to a safe area. Back then the big up-rise between the local villagers and cocoa growers was over area land control. The drug cartel was in charge and keeping their poppy fields and processing plants a secret was priority one. There wasn't much cleared jungle land back then and the dope growers didn't want to work to prepare the fields, so they would force the famers to move their crops fields further and further into the un-cleared forest. Alex and I decided that we would pose as two men that were commissioned to check in and assist the missionaries that they had assigned to that area. At that time it was more like the Wild West during the California Gold Rush. Of course what we discovered was just a single priest suffering from sleep deprivation, a couple of student rejects from the Peace Corps and an empty church that required a lot of repairs. The local priest did have a few greenhorns helping him also. You know; kids right out of missionary neighborhood church training. To be honest with you, Alex and I were surprise that they were still alive. They were afraid of everything, even their own shadows. Let's just say, for the sake of argument, they hadn't put on the full Armor of God and leave it at that. I myself have been in some tight spots in life and I know better than most that it's hard to pray and stay focus when you are urinating all over yourself with fear. First, you have to embrace the fact that God loves you and that you may die and then pray to God that you live; all while giving God a good reason why He should allow you to do so, also helps a little to settle your nerves." The guys snickered again as Slapp commented.

"Damn Tate," said Slapp. "Who would have guessed, you finishing seminary school would provided you with a sense of humor and higher tolerance. We serve a good God, don't we fellows" said Slapp jokingly. Most of the guys responded with 'Amen' Tate only smiled briefly as he took in another full breath to continue.

"The local criminals had just about taken everything from this group of villager and some had even started to move on into other communities for safety. Well, our plan was a solid one, except we didn't have any merchandise to pretend to be delivering to the mission. We had to find something that the renegades didn't want and couldn't use, at least not right away. We couldn't take in our weapons or our numerous passports. So we left all our gear at the Thailand's U.S. Embassy. The ambassador informed us that clean drinking water had been a big problem in that region, so we decided to rent a large truck and take in enough equipment to dig the missions their own fresh-water well. It took about a week to get all the equipment together. The trip was tedious because we were traveling with an extremely heavy truck and the roads had been washed out, from the spring rain. We got stuck three times. We finally made it after four days, from a trip that should have taken one day and only a portion of another. The priest there took us in and explained to us what was going on and how the local insurgents operated, who were mostly men hiding out from the authorities and hired hands that had been employed to guard and work the drug fields and production plants. Something happened to the local water supply up river from the village where we were staying and water really became an issue. It was probably caused by the toxic waste runoff from the illegal drug production plant. Alex and I began to drill for water, but we also had to use the truck to haul water from further up stream, back to the villagers. The rebels had plenty of transportation, but they were taxing everyone to use their roads. To be honest, out in the jungle, there wasn't much use for money; you had to have something that the next man needed or wanted. There was no way in hell Alex and I were going to survive out there for very long without our weapons. Yet I have to admit that this was one of the first times that having tanned skin and a mixed heritage paid off for the two of us."

Most everyone in the room chuckled briefly again as I covered my mouth and smartly looked over at Gayle, who had now found herself a seat on a nearby stepping stool that had been carefully placed, so one could reach the top cabinet shelving. Tate went on.

"On the back forty portion of the jungle," insisted Tate, "The man with the largest and strongest firepower was the law. Money wasn't a problem for us, compared to the locals, so when we found out that we could hitchhike a ride back into Thailand with some of the Cambodians that worked in Thailand as cab drivers, Tate and I knew that we had a way to get our weapons in without too much trouble. So we caught a ride back as close to the village, where we had been hiding out in, and hiked the rest of the way back. While we were gone, the renegades stole the truck, so we went one day, masquerading as some newly hired workers and stole it back including all the gas we could locate. They didn't expect the truck to be stolen in broad daylight. After we stole the vehicle back, we started taking vital parts off of it each night and hid them somewhere in the village. The water problem became worst before we could finish the villager's new well. Some people from a less rural area heard about the problem and got together to send some water trucks out to the mission. The drug cartel would commandeer the trucks if the driver couldn't pay the road tax. Tate and I started to walk out a few miles and meet the trucks at night. We set up traps so it appeared that the hijackers were killed by accident. As everyone knows, the jungle can be a very dangerous place. This went on for a few weeks and we finally completed the well. We rigged a gas generator to operate the pump. We traded clean water to the renegades for gas. We drew a line in the sand around the village, as you might say and told the drug dealers that we would kill anything that moved inside that perimeter after dark. It was near harvest and the cartel couldn't afford to loose any more men to night raids. After a few more trips to the city, we had enough ammunition to hold off a small army, plus we had taught the younger men, they were boys really, how to protect themselves. The neighboring villagers started to move around a little more and trade different items with each other. The villagers were made up of mostly old people and young children that their parents had left behind, while they went into the city to work and would come home about once every couple of months. The villagers didn't want any trouble from the drug cartel, they just wanted to live, work their land and watch their grand babies grow up.

Soon people from the neighboring villages began to bring gas to operate the generator to pump the water. We initially set it up to be operated manually and automatically when attached to the generator pump. After dark, we were afraid to leave the generator outside, in fear that the rebels might take it. The village that we were in began to prosper, because we had the most reliable water supply and power. Now the crops had water to grow as well."

Tate took a deep breath in and Alex took the story over on cue, as if the two of them had planned it. Alex stared straight ahead to a blank spot on the wall, as he took on a youthful cocky-pose tilt in his seat, while his face projected a smirk about something that he had, no doubt, long forgotten. Everyone in the room noticed it and this made me feel a little uncomfortable, for some strange reason. Pure forgotten pleasure washed over him like a spring rain after a season of drought. Alex spoke with a quiet soft tone as if that portion of the story required it. Later on, I was inclined to agree.

"Then one day it happened. The most beautiful woman that I had seen in a long time, walked right out of the jungle and into my heart. She was caring her water pot on one shoulder and collapsed only a few feet from the well. Tate saw her first and yelled to me because I was closer, but with my back turned towards her. Tate was patrolling the boarder of our tiny missionary compound and had just climbed down from our makeshift tree watchtower. Every night we placed a man up in one of the trees with a sniper rifle and night goggles. For me, it was love at first sight. The priest and one of the aids ran out to help me take her inside one of the grass covered sleds and then later into a hut. Someone said that she was suffering from heat exhaustion.

Well, Tate immediately climbed back into the tree tower, because we initially though that this was a set up; you know, a decoy to draw us out. All before, most of the hits we had taken were just before dark. Tate stood watch that night and I stayed in the hut all night watching the woman. A few hours after dark, she woke up and the priest came in to give her something to eat and explained to her what had happened. She wanted to leave, but we told her that it was too dark and that we couldn't allow anyone from the village to walk her back. The priest knew who she was. He told me that she had come to a few of his Christian meeting services. He didn't know how far away was her village, but was pretty sure that she had to travel a long distance. The first year that the new missionaries had arrived, she was one of the first to be baptized and convert to Christianity. Back then; this alone had put a price on her head. She was educated and spoke differently than the local villagers. The priest said that she appeared very shy, but he was convinced that it was more like she had a heavy burden secret that she feared would expose her. She almost always came alone or with a couple of young children. Tate here spoke her language, in broken form of course, but for me that didn't matter. The very next morning she got up early and we found a water container, to replace the one that she had broken. She left and promised to return the jar on her next visit.

Unfortunately, I was totally smitten by her, and that's putting it mildly. She appeared younger than I, but she carried herself very maturely. We offered to take her back, but she strongly refused as if she didn't want us to know where she lived. Tate and I didn't push the issue. For the next few days all I could do was think about her and wonder if I would ever lay eyes on her again. Tate and I made another trip to a nearby town to get more supplies and some things that the locals needed in the line of medicine. A few more weeks passed and the lady returned with the water jar as promised. This time she had two, what appeared to be, teenaged boys with her. She told me her name was Kiri which means mountain in Cambodian. After that visit, Kiri came to our village about once a week. I tried to subdue my feelings for her, but as you all know; passion confronted by reasoning takes no prisoners. My rational thoughts, as they pertained to Kiri, were skewed to say the least. The heart wants what it wants and sometimes the body desires what it shouldn't have. About eight months after we were there the priest informed us that the village was getting ready to host one of their annual festivals. People would come from other surrounding villages and some would even stay a couple of days. There were games of competition, which Tate and I though was some pretty dangerous stuff. People brought food and homemade goods to trade. It was unbelievable of some of the talent and skills that had been passed down through the generations. Anyway, I got to spend some time with Kiri and she brought alone a little girl that could speak English very well. We talked for hours, as the three of us sat up there in that watchtower tree. The little girl missed out on a lot of the fun that first day and evening, because we needed her to translate for the two of us. Finally we decided that words weren't as important as the feelings we had for each other. Soon the festival was over and everyone departed. One month passed before I saw Kiri again and when I did, she informed me that she couldn't come to see me again. Tate told me that one of the elders from the next village over said that she was the daughter of one of the drug-lords that had raped her mother and that she was the result of that rape."

Uncle Burney quickly finished off his drink as though Alex's last statement was new first-hand news to him and it appeared very disturbing, to say the least. Perhaps this had stirred-up some old demons in Uncle Burney's past as well. I couldn't tell for sure. The reflected pain remained on Uncle Burney's face as he quietly continued to listen to the recount, which Alex preceded.

"Kiri's father had sent her to school in the city, but she came back to become a teacher in the jungle for the impoverished village kids. Everyone was afraid of her father, so she had never been married and had no children. Everyone knew who she was and that's why she felt so comfortable traveling through the bush alone. So I came up with this bright idea, in which I thought was good at the time, that I could take a couple of the local children with me and ask if they could attend her school; that way I could see her again. Her village was a full-day walk north and we arrived in her village at sunset, which turned out to be the heart of the drug-processing central. The three of us were tired, hot and exhausted. I'm pretty sure that we had gotten lost a couple of times. We arrived and was treated very badly and tied up in a hut. Kiri came in and told us that we should not have come. She was very upset. The headman in charge was due to arrive the next day. The two children that I took with me were terrified and cried most of the night. The next day I got to meet the man and it was one of Kiri older brothers, by another mother. He spoke English very well and one could tell that he was well taken care of. He was dressed like a bank-teller that had just received the key to the executive's washroom. It was hard for me to believe that he had traveled so far out into the wilderness and had been able to maintain such a tidy appearance. A helicopter was the only mode of travel that could have provided this option.

After Kiri begged him for our lives; her brother threatened us and then let us go. I saw Kiri again after that in Thailand, about two months later. She was there in the city purchasing classroom supplies for her school children. This time I got a chance to spend two days and two nights with Kiri. These two days were the most blissful fifty hours of my life and even now when I think of her, the pain of losing her so brutally is staggering. I returned to the village where Tate and I had been hiding out for pretty close to a year. By this time, the villagers had begun to treat us like royalty. I don't think that I need to tell you that I had lost all prospective on why we were there and the fact that we were operating totally separate from the bureau and that we were on our own. Somehow, the headman found out about our little unplanned meeting in Bangkok

Thailand and took it upon himself to punish Kiri. Late one evening she arrived in our village all beaten up and bloody. I though at first she had been raped or worst. I became sick inside, because I knew that this was ultimately my fault. She stayed in our village for a week, while the priest and the aids patched her up and nursed her back to health. I told her that she didn't have to go back and that I would take her away with me. She told me that her brothers and father would never allow her to leave because she knew too much about their drug business. If she tried to leave, other members of her mother's family from their village would be killed.

As Tate can tell you, I was new to the bureau, back then and didn't understand the limitations of my badge and gun when one is operating outside the mission's parameters of the department. At anytime you could become a misplaced renegade nobody. I had to learn this the hard way. She returned to her village and I went to Phnom Penh, which is the capital of Cambodia, to the U.S. Embassy to ask for help to get Kiri out of the country. The paperwork was unbelievable and would take a while. First we had to find a clause in the law that allow asylum for someone helping a U.S. government agent during life threatening duress. There is such a clause, but it comes with so many stipulations that I was unaware of at the time, plus there was the fact that we were hiding out and not on a real case at the time. Still I tried to work on her case, each time I went into town. We had been in the village now for almost a year and a half. It was time for us to make a move. I just couldn't leave her behind. The gorilla army had found out who we really were, so we had to change our location. The next time I saw Kiri, she was on the street of Bangkok and we made plans to meet. One night when she left her village to travel to ours, she was attacked by some new men that had been hired by the drug cartel that didn't know who she was. She was able to make it to our village that night, but not before she was raped and beaten and left for dead. She died in my arms that same night. She was six months pregnant with my child. A part inside of me died with her that night. I had her body sent back to Washington, D.C. It seems that it's easier to get a person an asylum after they're dead, than it is while they are still breathing. Well fellas, that's my story."

I noticed a few nervous twitches in the men mannerism as they tried to hide their sadness about the story that Alex had just revealed, with Tate's assistance. The entire time Alex was relaying the Cambodia incident, no one moved a muscle not even Slapp; which we all agreed later was a miracle in itself. Slowly everyone began to move around and refresh their libation of choice.

Chapter Sixteen

Dead Men Walking

William moved closer to his stepfather Alex to console him.

"Wow, Dad that was some story. I'm sorry that you had to go through all of that. Now I understand why you are so protective of all us kids and ma." Alex smiled a little, hugged William around the neck as he attempted to lighten the mood with his confession of a flaw in his personality traits.

"I thank you for that Son, but some of it is just me being too controlling. My friends here frequently remind me of that shortcoming, every once in a while. That is what good friends do; they keep you straight and focused." Slapp took in a noticeable full breath before speaking.

"So tell me honestly big brother Alex, did you and holy man junior here inflict any revenge on the men that killed your woman and child?" Alex refused to reply to Slapp as everyone in the room stared in Alex's direction for the answer to Slapp's burning question, which was all of our queried concern. Tate was totally unaffected by Slapp's reference to him as holy man junior. As a matter of fact, Tate was standing close enough to place one of his hands on Slapp's shoulder, right after he completed the finally word of his sentence. To be frank, Tate had grown a lot since rejoining the higher-calling clan for his life, by going back to finish seminary school. Tate understood Slapp much better and discovered that it was amusing that Slapp found some comfort in always pointing out this fact, in Tate's life. Everyone else in the room didn't take notice to the intentional pun, except for my son. William laughed out loudly, because this was the first time that he had ever heard his Uncle Slapp refer to his Uncle Tate in that manner. William immediately apologized to his Uncle Tate, as Tate continued to rest his hand upon Slapp's shoulder as everyone in the room continued to wait for Alex to respond to Slapp's question pertaining to revenge.

"Oh, I'm sorry Uncle Tate, I've been gone for a while and I can't tell you how I have missed being around all you guys on a regular bases. I didn't mean any disrespect by laughing at my Uncle Slapp calling you that in jest. I can't believe that I still find him so entertaining after all this time, or the fact that he hasn't changed much."

Tate smiled and grabbed William around the neck and shoulders with his other free arm and pulled him close to hug him. At that moment, Alex answered with a very stern answer, as it appeared that he was refusing to give any details of what had happened after Kiri had died. Alex repeated a sentenced that Tate had used earlier, but with a little anger at the edge of his tone. "Let's just say, nether Tate or I had put on the Full Armor of God at this point in our lives, and leave it at that." Everyone picked up on Alex's suffering anger and pain and was content with the portion that we had been told. Tate responded to William's apology and once again became the latest narrator of the Alex and Tate's Thailand-Cambodia mission story.

"No harm done, William. I've made my peace with your Uncle Slapp's personality traits. The core of your Uncle Slapp will never change and at this point I'm not too sure that I want it to." Tate stroked the back of William's head, as if he was twelve and then moved back to his seat before he took over the story from Alex. Then Tate reluctantly filled in the gaps of Alex's account of the Cambodian 1980 triangle drug bust.

"I was new at the branch," reported Tate. "But I had a couple of years more of experience under my belt than Alex here. I was told that I had a partner who was already in the field and that I was supposed to meet up with him. My mission was in Chiang Mia, Thailand, but when I arrived I found out that my contact had been killed, of course I panicked. Alex and I paths had crossed a couple of times before that, but never on a professional level. We both were power hungry and arrogant back them. You see, agents have a few places in the Washington D.C. area that they feel safe to go for a drink and let their hair down. Just like policemen, except we have to be more careful about what we say to the bartender and whoever else that may be in the bar listening. Anyway, Alex and I had a few years of age on some of the guys, because we had joined a little later in life than most. We were more settle, and neither one of us drank enough to even be in the bar. We just went along because someone had invited us to hangout and besides; we wanted to be considered one of the boys. Let me recant on one of my earlier statements. I had forgotten all about this. The first time we joined forces was when we went under cover at GW University. When Alex arrived, my branch had already sent me out to answer the task request. Years ago, sharing information between departments or agencies was considered taboo and was usually only done to be used as a bargaining chip. There was plenty of money in everyone's division; so what the hell, why not spend it. The two of us had both been sent out as singles from different branches, so we teamed up and rode the gravy train, you might say. As I said before, we were real cocky back then. We were tall, tanned and tough, while wearing an unforgettable buff six-pack abs, with the promise of eight a pack, if you looked closely enough. We didn't want to go back and tell the office that someone else was already on the job; besides we were hanging out on campus with a lot of beautiful young women from every location on the globe. We had an expense account so we purchased a few new items of clothing to blend in to the college campus scene. I was Alex's partner at the time when he managed to get himself in a jam with those twins that night. You all know them, Linda and Lisa. Now they were as green as a weeping willow in springtime and young, but that's another story, for some other time."

Everyone laughed out loudly as a few took a sip from their glasses. Tate went on.

"We became friends during that field mission and when I saw Alex in Thailand that day, I thought I was safe. I thought that Alex had been sent in to extract me, even though he was from another branch. Little did I know; Alex had his own problems. I spoke a little of the language in the region and was studying ever chance I got. There was a lot of tourist in Bangkok, so most of the businessmen, cab drivers, hotel desk clerks, and cashiers spoke some English and was willing to teach me a few words. Anyway, after I figured out that Alex was a hot tamale'(a—hole deep in trouble) as well, we decided we should get out of the city, until someone came looking for us. That was how we ended up together in that little missionary village in the Cambodian jungle, with some of the most dangerous drug cartel on the continent, at the time. The only thing saved us was the village priest vouching for us; and the fact that we stayed pretty close to the church, while working hard to help the missionaries in any way that we could. Once Alex saw and met Kiri, he just lost his damn mind." William laughed out again.

"I tried to explain and warn Alex to not become too involved with the natives, but as all of us men know so well, that sometimes our little head has a mind of its own." Tate suddenly remembered that Gayle and I was behind the partition and was probably listening to the recount as well. Tate quickly corrected his words.

"Please forgive me ladies and young man for my crass language. Perhaps it was easier for me not to fall to temptation, because I had a wife waiting and praying for me. Alex on the other hand, didn't have any string attachments and he had told me about Helen and how he had gotten out of the service and went back and she had grown up, went to collage and met and married Williams father. I could tell how deeply this had bothered him, so I was sort of happy for him in away. I also knew that it would be hard for us to get out of the country with a local girl in tow. Even back then, human trafficking and sex slaving was big business. They would probably shoot us in the back at the airport for trying to take a woman out the country that gorgeous. I have to admit that she was one of the most beautiful women I had ever been that close to. I'm not sure what mixed nationality was her father, but she appeared to have taken the best features from each of her parents. She was taller than most of the local women and most of her height were in the lower portion of her body. So it goes without saying that she had long gorgeous shapely legs with a lean well developed body to match."

Every now and again, some of the guys would look over at Alex to view his response to the way Tate was describing a woman that he had been so emotionally involved with. There appeared to be no indication of jealousy in Alex's facial expression, as Tate so eloquently articulated that portion of the event. Yet a few of the men, that were present, did denote a tinge of remembered pain in Alex' demeanor, as Tate went on with the story. Tate even hesitated a few times as he decided if it was a good idea to proceed with the flashback.

"Kiri's hair was the darkest and richest black, that was well documented for that region, but hers had a unusual waviness to it, sort of like my mother's hair. Her lips had a deep rose-red color to them as though they had been permanently stained with some kind of wild growing fruit from the jungle. Around her eyes reflected a natural border shading enhanced appearance and she had the eyelashes that most women only dream about. She stood about five feet seven inches. I know this because when I stood next to her, her head level lined up on me about the same as my first wife. She had a real calm and loving spirit; similar to the wife Alex has now, Helen. Her present brought out the best in you, just by being around her. Now as I reflect back, she seemed to have on more of the Armor of God than either of us had acquired, at the time." Tate looked over quickly in Alex's direction and smiled warmly. "Wouldn't you agree Alex, that she was somewhat like Helen?" Alex answered slowly as if this small fact had never occurred to him before that moment.

"You know Tate, I would have to agree with you. That could have been part of my attraction to her."

Tate went on. "Once, Kiri came to our village alone during a time when Alex had taken a three-day trip to a nearby town. I never let her out my site, because I feared that Alex would shoot me if I allowed anything to happen to her while he was gone. She even spent the night in the tree watchtower with me, one night when I had surveillance duty." Tate then hesitated again to shift the mood to a lighter one. "Wow, Alex it seems like I'm always somewhere alone with one of your women, hum?" Alex shyly smiled and a few of the others laughed out loudly.

"Well at any rate, Alex loved Kiri the moment he saw her, but after a while I realized it had progressed way pass that at this point; it was more like, perhaps shifting towards an obsession. The first time Alex slept with her inside the village, everyone could hear then mating like two prison escapees and they didn't seem to mind. To this day I still don't believe that Alex knew how loud the two of them had been. It was as though both of them were engaged in sex for the very first time, and the orgasm had frightened them. I'm not sure if they realize what was happening to them. Water was too precious and scarce for me to turn the water-hose on the two of them, so I had to just let it go."

Everyone laughed out again as Tate attempted to lightened the mood with some inappropriate humor. Even Alex smiled deeply, as his face seemed to reflect on the moment as if it had all happened the day before. Alex then took another sip from his glass, as Tate apologized before continuing.

"Sorry about that Alex, it just slipped out. After that night, I knew that Alex would never leave Kiri behind and that frightened me more than anything I could remember up until that point. I knew the rules a little better than Alex did, regarding asylum. The bureau had no problem allotting funds to give an informant a chance to relocate and start over, but coming to America; well that was a whole other ball of wax.

After Kiri was killed, Alex became someone, not only that I didn't know; but someone that I had never met. He made a trip back to the city and brought enough firepower to take a portion of Cambodia off the map, or at the very least make it uninhabitable for a while. Alex told me that he was going to let the chemicals from the drug processing plants do the rest, like a chain reaction. We informed the missionary priest and all his staff that they needed to move closer to the Thailand border for a while, they agreed, but had no idea what they were agreeing to. So he and the others packed up their mules, wagons, sleds and whatever could roll or be dragged and headed from the boarder.

The villagers scattered to the four winds, because they knew better than anyone what would happen to them if the drug-lords suspected they had anything to do with their crops being burned or their labs being blown-up. Three weeks after Kiri's death we had a plan. Alex was getting very little sleep by this time and his temper was too short to measure. He was totally fixated and committed to revenge, even if it cost him his life. Alex made arrangements to send Kiri's body back to the U.S. Her father didn't spend any time with her, Kiri's mother died during childbirth and the brothers that she had were only her half-brothers, which were about to be sent to jail or killed by our brother Alex here. The boss admitting that he knew her or that she was his daughter would be like opening Pandora's box for him and his business associates. At any rate, the plan was set. A few of the men in the village knew exactly where to find four of the main underground labs in that sector. I prayed that this would be sufficient to satisfy Alex's rage. Alex figured that with a wide sweep like we had planned, he was bound to get the man or men that had done this evil thing to Kiri. We found cocaine in Kiri's hair, so we knew that the man had to be high when he assaulted her. The government came in after we had started the cleanup raid, because villages were complaining about being attacked at night and sustaining serious fires and property damages. The locals from nearby villages, who had been working in the drug fields and refining labs, began to run away and the men in charge were hunting them down and killing them in fear that the outside world may learn the locations of their most lucrative enterprise or that the men might talk to the authorities, in exchange for leniency.

In three weeks or a little more, Alex and I must have covered over a hundred square miles. Alex hardly slept at all, so he kept watch while I and the others got a couple of hours of rest. At this point I had totally given up on ever coming out of that jungle alive. During my life I have come to believe and understand that in each lifetime long relationship, which is forge between two people, usually has a bonding moment. You know, something that happens to both of them simultaneously or something that the two of them experience while together, like an 'ah ha moment or an epiphany that they each have experienced. Well for Alex and me it was that mission to Thailand. After I had made peace with death and God, in the reverse order of course,' A couple of the guys quickly tilted their heads downward and smiled profoundly, while a couple laughed briefly, 'the two of us became worst than anyone we have ever tried to bring to justice. Alex was completely blinded to reasoning with rage and pain and I had succumbed to a fear that I can't begin to put into words; even to this day. It wasn't the fear of dying so much as it was dying without having any closer to my life. I was so far away from home and the people I love. I thought if something happened to me, they would never know why and I felt that they deserved better than that. We took food, stole and hijacked trucks, we beat information out of people, and we threatened old people. Once we even kidnapped a young man to act as a guide through the forest. How many men we killed or how many lives we destroyed, who can say for sure? We certainly can't.

When the bureau's extraction team located us, we were both near death because we had contracted a fever. Most likely from a pest bite, bad water or from the multiple parasites that had attached themselves to our abused bodies. An old man had found the two of us and stashed us in his cave and had taken it upon himself to bury or hide all our leftover weaponry. He lied about how long we had been with him. He knew that if we were found with all that high-level firepower, they would speculate and kill us for sure and him also for helping us. We owe that old man our careers and our lives. They said that he was an old witch doctor. Everyone for miles around were afraid of him and no one knew for sure how old he was. Anyone who had a clue about his true birth was long dead and gone.

The undercover cleanup squad took us back to Thailand's capital, Bangkok and placed us in the hospital. They never learned that we were the two, along with a few others, that had caused so much destruction to the drug trade in the region. If they did learn about our involvement, they never said anything to me about it. It was a good thing, because that would have been the end of both of our careers. Alex was never quite the same happy-go-lucky person after that mission. He became very critical and demanding that every detail of the mission was planned out. I, on the other hand, never regained full control of my nervous system, you could say. I was always looking over my shoulder and had real bad dreams for a while. It was years later when we decided to set up this sub-agency. Alex had to talk me into it. I had my time in and I couldn't wait to give up my badge and gun. He promised me that it would only be for five years and then my father came aboard, and we all know the history from that point on. Well family and friends, that's all I have to share with you or perhaps all I care to remember."

A few of the men slowly stood to their feet to retire to their assigned sleeping area for the night. Alex was the last one to move. It was as though the story had somehow paralyzed him. Some of us could detect that after all this time; the recall had caused some of the pain and possibly the regret and guilt to resurface in Alex. What we couldn't decipher was if the pain was caused by losing the love of his life and his first and only biological child or how he had handled himself after their death, by going on a killing spree and dragging Tate along. That night more **'secrets of tarnished shields'** were revealed as the healing process continued to lighten the burdens in all of us, by speaking the truth. I never asked Alex about the Cambodia- Thailand mission and he never volunteered any more details. I guess you could say that I believe that some things should be taken to your grave, or at the very least never put into words or spoken aloud.

The room was silent for a few moments, after Tate's finale words; as the group of us allowed the tale to penetrate our souls and find a place to hide in our memories. Our son William broke the muted room with a summons to Slapp's father.

"Come on Pops", said William as he pulled Uncle Burney to his feet. Burney didn't like being referred to as 'Pops', but he only corrected Slapp, his son, about the endearing title. "Auntie Sarah will start to worry about you if she thinks you've been drinking all this time and haven't taken your nightly medication. Okay guys, we will see you all tomorrow, hopefully at Julius' breakfast extravaganza. Believe me, you don't want to miss that fellas."

William and Uncle Burney descended down the few steps that led to the floor of the barn and then across the field towards the big house. William held Uncle Burney affectionately around the shoulders and neck as he made brief comments about the recount that he had just witnessed. Uncle Burney only listened and gave no response. Tyrone and Jerome followed behind the two of them, as the highlights of the story appeared to wash over their facial expressions again, as well. They all briefly waved to Miles and Daniel, our roving patrol bodyguards, as they walked the lane that connected each of the three residents. The main house, the barn and then to our home; which, I indicated before, was up the road a bit.

I learned a lot about my husband Alex that night and I'm sure that the men became aware of other facets of each other's personalities traits, as well. I knew that the details of the story, which Alex and Tate had revealed to us about the Cambodia-Thailand mission, would remain with all of us for a long time, or perhaps to the end of the time we all had left. For a moment I wondered if Fred and Father Caleb were made aware of this story before they passed on. They each were the type of men that searched and saw the best in everyone. Plus, relentlessly embraced the hope that daily one would have the desire to repent and heal from their shortcomings. Well no matter, for they both had been blessed with the gift of almost perfect adoration or at least the closest to what I imagine it should be, or had ever observed in another; and was only shadowed, in my opinion, by the Master's perfect love, amen.

Chapter Seventeen

Beneath the Kintai Moon

One summer, Alex and I decided to take a trip back to Iwakuni Japan. This visit was brief, yet one that we truly enjoyed. We got a chance to see all our old friends and to thank then for their friendship and accepting us into their families without any reservations and hopefully with no regrets. Alex and I spent as much time as we could just ridding around the countryside and taking pictures that would, with any luck, help the next generation to understand how passionately we had become about the people there and all the families we met and how our encounters with them had positive affects and altered our lives and hearts forever.

Our daily afternoon trips were to the Kintai Bridge as the Kintai Castle kept watch over us from high above on a hilltop in this well-planned and designed park. This created an unbelievable pictures' scene. Just like so many others who had traveled from near and far, we would meander around at the base of the mountain and near the bridge for hours. We must have walked across that five mound wooden bridge fifty times throughout our stay there that summer and each time it stirred an emotion in us that was so peaceful, yet imposed a disturbing desire to learn more of its historically value to the local people and all the others that had traveled there to explore the area. We could not explain its enchanting power, which it appeared to have on all who came to visit; us included. During our last few trips to the bridge, we decided that we should take a moment to pray and thank God for all the beauty that he had allowed us to experience there in that park. We also gave Him praise for all the love that we received from the people there and promised that we would relay the spiritual and life-altering event to whomever would listen. I wrote a poem while we were there titled, **'Beneath the Kintai Moon'**. These were only a few words that I was able to group together that expressed some of my feelings for Iwakuni, the castle, the bridge and its people's history that I discovered there.

The Kintai Bridge and Castle in
Iwakuni, Japan Spring 2013

Beneath the Kintai Moon

High above the earth's under and
just below the majestic clouds,
Towers a castle of the ages with its
face hidden in a mystic shroud.
And at its bedrock lies a wavy bridge
of wood with endless stories due tell,
Yet no secrets does it whisper;
in fear of the hauntings from hell

Still beneath its mount shape arches,
rushes a tarnished blood stained stream,
While carrying memories to ocean's deep,
it flows beneath the bridge's beams.
For none knows all its secrets,
others dare not to reveal the untold.
About truths of ancient tyrants
and remembered warriors with fearless souls

Tales are shyly betrayed here,
so eloquently yet incomplete,
Of recorded hero victories,
while protecting their cowardly defeats.

More countless unspeakable stories awaits
of bravery and of lost misguided souls
And of undaunted hearts of battle-men
that once lived forever bold.

Great men are remembered and praised,
as their gravestone reflects a silent plea
Perhaps prayers for those gone before;
Or for whom now mourn at their feet

Royal Blood once mixed within these streams,
as it woefully trickled out to the sea,
For no one can rescue banished souls,
none, but for the love of Thee

At last Advent Winter deeply bows out,
bearing Cherry Blossom Buds upon its crisp cool wings
As the bamboo forest adorns its lush spring colors,
while the birds of harmony sings
Yet in their songs that are seldom sung,
are stories gathered by the winds
Of ancient times and of long ago
when all of thee where kin

Yet another heroic night-sun unfolds
to recite the untold tales of doom
While spectators on the Castle's bridge gaze
and where others will gather soon
To listen to the Wiseman poet's secrets reveal,
imbedded within an ancient tune,
And to visit the ageless artifacts and bathe
once more; Beneath the Kintai Moon

Many who listen are suddenly spellbound;
yet recover, as they slowly drift away.
While others are captured in that darker place,
And are consumed for more than a day

Unaware of the bridge's amulet powers,
yet drawn by its spirit to live on
Prayers are whispered to false gods,
while they listen to the poet's song

Anon the night-sun cloaks his shrewd face
and abandon all allusions of Eve before

For the morning light chases him away,
while the timeless songs are sung no more.

A new dawn has come, sad hearts are healed,
as invalid peace floods their minds
Yet darkness awaits at another days end,
to lay claim to its borrowed time.

The moon once more summons heavy hearts,
as they huddle at the Castle Bridge's feet
For his time in the night sky is lonely and brief,
as the entitled stars take their appointed seats.

Still each night distant souls appear,
believing that his sad farewell will be too soon
For a single glimpse into the Castle's enchanted
face, Beneath the Kintai Moon

The two weeks passed very quickly and Alex and I were both exhausted when we finally took our seats aboard the return flight home. Some of the fatigue was mostly due to our nonstop schedule to see everyone and to spend as much time as we could taking in the view of the countryside, while creating memories that would possibly have to last a lifetime. The parties, the food, the entertainment, the social hour events all packed into a two-week span of time. Waving good-bye from the plane as we took our seats was almost unbearable, as our chests tightened and burned with a painful sadness, as we tried to suppress our silent heart-retching tears, which were now flooding our faces, as we somehow managed to fabricate a pleasant smile. Speaking was totally out of the question for Alex or I and for them that we were leaving behind, as well. The symbolic frogs in our throats were too incapacitating to verbalize our good-byes, so we continued to smile and wave franticly.

Some of the relationships that we had forged, over that short period of time, were like adding on members to the family tree. Now we had to say good-bye while not knowing if we would ever see each other again. If we had been a little younger at the time, perhaps the departure wouldn't have been so painful. Yet we all know how cruel and unpredictable father-time can be. Therefore, the most we could hope and pray for was to set a date in which we could all come together, just once more without offending God by seeming ungrateful for the time that He had already granted us to share and enjoy, with our extended family in Japan, Amen.

The End

For All the Test of Time
(Old Lang Syne Tune)

May all acquaintances be renewed and
low spirits taught to climb
May all the anger be defused and
repaired hearts healed with time.

** Chorus

For all the test of time, our love
For all the test of time
We'll take sip of wine and dine
For all the test of time

May all the truth replace all lies and
tempers depart thou minds
Shall we seek mercy, grace and peace,
from Our Father Thee Divine

**

May this wide circle embrace our new
and love them all the same
Let's close our eyes, for a prayer of
hope, and give thanks that they all came.

**

Let precious memory start right now,
and never review the past
Let all of us now take a vow that these
bonds shall forever last

**

Must miles of distance keep us apart,
for long waiting is unkind
Should promises within our hearts be
united at Christmas time

**

When love-ones' journey is no more and
Night mourning becomes a new day
Memories will pass the test of time
In our hearts they will forever stay

**

And when the pain is much too bare, let
us all remember this day
For who are we to question Him, just
surrender; to His way
**

About The Book

This is the fifth and final book in this series. During the writing of the manuscripts the author was moving periodically and found it very rewarding to weave in some of the places and people into the story. A large percent of the story and characters are fictional. The story was written to entertain the author's coworkers at various locations, partly while completely her obligation of active military service. The first manuscript rough draft began in 1988. The author had no aspiration of ever publishing. Twenty-one years later her coworkers persuaded her to publish her work

This book "Beneath The Kintai Moon, the journey of Life" was completed and published 2015, which is approximately 27 years later after the original rough draft of the first book in this series. We applaud O.F. Willisomhouse for the published works and twenty years of military service.

Printed in the United States
By Bookmasters